THE BLACK SPRING CRIME SERIES – CURATED BY EDITOR LUCA VESTE

Praised and endorsed by some of the biggest names in Crime Fiction . . .

'Time to strap yourself in.' — **Ian Rankin**

'I love, love, love great new crime fiction. How do I find it? Usually I ask my friend Luca Veste. I owe him hundreds of hours of great reading. Now he's doing it for real, not just for me — he's working with Black Spring Press, which means they're going to have a crime list that everyone will get excited about — and everyone will buy. Luca Veste is our genre's best talent spotter — Black Spring Press will be one to watch.' — **Lee Child**

'Crime fiction is going through a new Golden Age, finding readers looking for strong stories that explore the world around us and the problems we face. An independent publisher like Black Spring is the perfect fit for these fresh new voices and ways of seeing — and in Luca Veste they have a crime editor who knows the terrain like a skilled tracker. A great writer himself, he has an eye for the brightest and best. It's going to be an exciting and enriching journey for readers. Time to strap yourself in.' — **Ian Rankin**

'I know nobody with their finger more acutely on the pulse of crime fiction. I value his recommendations; they show a great eye for what's worth my reading time.' — **Val McDermid**

'Nobody knows more about the world of crime fiction than Luca Veste. He knows the business inside out and he knows all the movers and shakers. Most importantly of all, he knows a great crime novel when he sees one.' — **Mark Billingham**

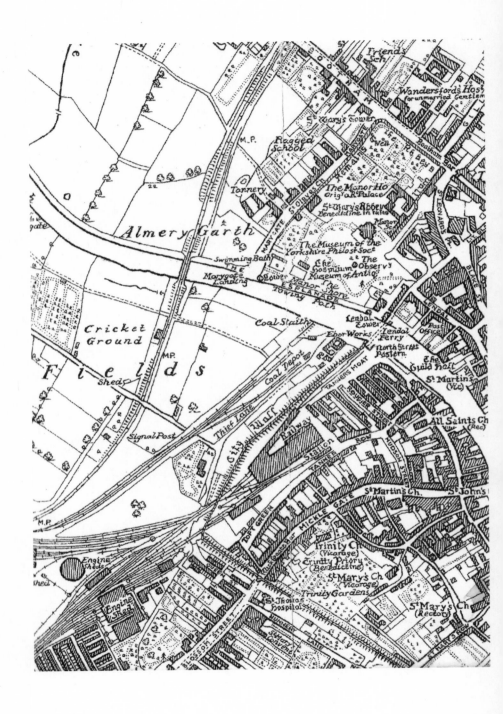

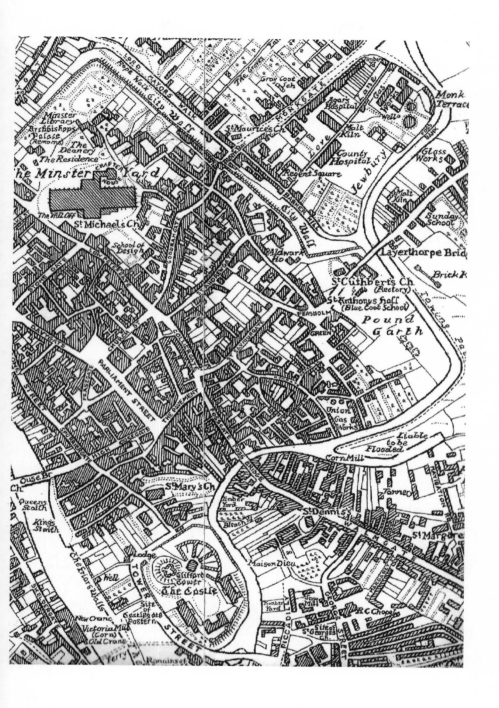

Winter of Shadows

Winter of Shadows

Clare Grant

This edition published in 2024
By The Black Spring Crime Series
An imprint of Eyewear Publishing Ltd.
The Black Spring Press Group
London, United Kingdom

Cover design by Juan Padron
Typeset by Subash Raghu
Author photograph by Emma Cattell

ISBN 978-1-915406-36-1

Black Spring Crime Series Curated by Luca Veste

www.blackspringpressgroup.com

To my children Ella, Harry and Bonnie, with love

YORK, JULY, 1862

◊

You slipped up, trusted someone you shouldn't have, believed the serpent smile, the treacherous touch instead. And it is too late.

They warned you – never think, never feel – but you did and you fell for a stranger's duplicitous kindness, craved it so badly that you forgot what you are.

You forgot you are a whore and no one is ever kind to whores.

In the darkness, the young woman whispers the words to herself, scratching at the scab of her mistake. She didn't see this coming, but she should have. It was always going to end badly for her, one way or another, and, as she waits, she knows that is the truth of it. And another certainty, no one will care.

Her end must be close. She can't go on much longer now. Her thin body burns with pain from the inside out. She lies on the bed, too weak to move. Her anger is still strong though – so raw she can feel it pulse though her blood. How could she have been so gullible?

She draws her arms around her knees and curls into herself. She is as helpless, as powerless, as a lamb to the slaughter.

Noises, a rush of air, a flickering light and behind it a body in the gloom, coming closer.

Her chest heaves to take in breath.

God help her. Never any chances, never any choices. Even her moment of dying will be someone else's decision.

1

A hand gently strokes her dark hair, caresses her pale cheek, smoothes her covering. She looks up at the face in the shadows.

She wants to scream.

She sees the moment is now . . .

CHAPTER ONE

◊

River Ouse, York, August 1862

'Ferryman! Ferryman!'

Under a damp tarpaulin in his boat, asleep like the dead, John Goodricke finally heard the shouts above the sounds of the deep, shifting river.

'Ferryman!'

Awake now, cursing softly, he fumbled his arthritic fingers around stiff wet rope. A sharp push with his boot heel and the ferry floated free of its moorings into the late summer mist rising from the water. John Goodricke picked up the oars and steadily began to row.

The full moon still shone high above the Minster and the slumbering city. Morning was some hours away, as was his mug of hot sweet tea. He wasn't rushing for anyone. The silly sod can wait, he thought. And so, he settled his strokes, his mind following the slow rhythmic sounds of the oars, his thoughts drifting backwards and forwards, for his time on this dark river was nearly done.

He passed his eyes over the giant skeleton of a half-built bridge to his right; it spanned the Ouse, dwarfing his boat. A way of life was changing; he would be redundant in the New Year.

This fantastical feat of engineering – the third such attempt – would end his job forever. Its two forerunners lay deep in river mud, lumps of rotting wood, the unlucky builders, poor souls, washed downstream, out to the sea. But this bridge, with its cast-iron carcass, would, he was told, last for centuries to come.

Now, the boat knocked against the bank and John Goodricke turned to see his passenger. Slumped in the shadows of Barker Tower, a young drunkard, hat askew and coat un-buttoned, registered the ferry's guiding lantern and hauled himself upright. He staggered towards the boat. Goodricke saw the dribbles of vomit caught in the man's dark beard. If he had a ha'penny for every inebriated customer he'd rowed across this river, he'd be a rich man.

'Chuck us the rope, mister,' another, younger voice called out. The lad was one of the dozens of homeless guttersnipes who slept along the bank, at least until the autumn chill drove them deeper into the city's narrow ginnels. They all looked the same: starving, skinny, squalid.

Goodricke threw the boat line. The boy caught it, and the small coin that followed. He scurried off into the darkness.

Then a deeper, slurred voice. 'The bitch! She's robbed me!'

His passenger was feeling for his wallet with one hand, clinging to the rocking boat with the other. The ferryman shook his head, taking in the tweed coat and cap. He could have put money on it, an idiot from the countryside. Not the first to be caught out. One of many who waited here for him with sore heads, missing wallets, and for some, though they didn't yet know it, a dose of the clap. Always the worse for their kneet-remblers in the narrow passages along the river's edge. The oldest trade, as old as this walled cathedral city, thrived here still. Women for sale; prices tumbling with age, sickness, desperation – a woman, whatever your budget. It brought men to York in their droves.

'Leave off your blubbering and get in,' Goodricke relented.

The current was strong. Each heave made his muscles work harder against the deep undertow. The passenger put out his hands and clutched the rough grain of the timbers. The water pulled fast downstream, escaping finally to the fresh salty seas, the clean vast oceans. But here the river was a confluence; animal and human ordure thrown in, drinking water, washing water drawn out. All manner of uses. And if the wind was in the wrong direction, the ripe stench of the slums barbed the nose and throat. He was glad the light breeze was blowing eastwards tonight.

Sinewy arms burning, Goodricke was relieved to bring the ferry alongside the staithe. He braced himself, half standing, rope in hand. A sudden thud against the underside of the boat nearly unbalanced him. Teetering, he hastily sat down while the violent rocking steadied.

'What's that?' his passenger mumbled.

'It'll be debris floating about from that storm the other day. Tis likely a branch washed down the river.'

'There's something big down here.' The young man was looking into the water.

'Come on. We're here now. I'll tie us up, then you can be on your way.' Goodricke balanced his leather boot on the boat edge and jumped, just as the ferry tipped again. A stab of panic as he missed the landing. He slid down, feet first, into the river between his boat and the mooring, gasping as the water splashed up to his groin.

He opened his mouth, but his curse was stopped. Something heavy slammed into the back of his knees. He was felled and crashed forward. He grasped for the shifting boat, arms flailing, as he pitched towards the deep shifting water. His chest absorbed the impact first, his hands reaching for the riverbed, and, thank God, he touched sharp stones and thick sludge: he had never learnt how to swim.

Getting up again wasn't easy. He struggled for his footing. A movement, something solid bumped his right leg. For a second, he thought his passenger was in the filthy water with him.

'What are you doing, man?' He turned his head, to speak again, and then froze.

Pale fingers found his thigh through the water.

'Jesus.'

A body came floating up; face down, dark hair spread, undulating in the current.

Goodricke pulled away, stumbled backwards, splashing a wave of water up his nostrils and into his open mouth. It tasted foul. Spluttering and spitting, he regained his balance. Instinct made him look to his drifting boat first. He hauled on the rope and tied the ferry to the mooring. Only then did he speak to his passenger, doubled over the boat's side, choking up his stomach. 'Help me then.'

A loud groan.

Again, more sharply. 'Shift yourself lad. We must get the body out.'

'Nay, I cannot move.'

'Come on, son.' Goodricke looked at his passenger heaving up again and shook his head. 'I'll do it on my own then.'

John Goodricke grasped the slippery corpse under the arms. He took in a breath and inhaled the stench of dirty water. Steeling himself, he pulled. The body resisted, caught in ropes perhaps. Another pull and it came free. He half-carried, half-dragged the corpse through the water. One hefty tug and the river released the dead weight. Goodricke lost his footing and catapulted backwards. The wet body went flying with him and slithered onto his chest like a new-birthed animal.

A girl.

He sighed. She wasn't the first. He'd found many bodies in the Ouse over the years. The river had long been a quick and convenient grave for tortured souls, unwanted babies and unlucky fools. But nevertheless, young women and children, they always touched his old heart.

He rolled her over and studied her pale, smooth face. Blank eyes looked back at him. Heaving himself to his feet, he unhooked the boat lantern and held it high.

'What happened then, lass?' He took in the simple silver cross round her slender neck, the torn white linen gown, entwined round her half-naked body. 'By God.' He stared at her stomach. The cuts sliced into the skin were deep and straight. The raw edges of flesh were white and bloodless. 'Some mischief you've been up to, missy.'

Still Goodricke felt a twinge of compassion. He must be getting soft in his old age. He turned to the passenger. 'Get up the street and find the Peelers. There'll be one up near the Minster.'

The other man stared at the corpse.

'Get on, lad,' he urged. 'Tell the police we've pulled a dead strumpet from the river.'

'What will they do?' The young man stammered. 'Will they find out what happened to her?'

'Nay, they won't even bother to find out her name.'

'What will become of her then?'

'She'll be mouldy in a pauper's grave by the end of the week, at the expense of this parish, along with the other dead waifs and strays.' Goodricke nodded. 'Go on, boy. There's nothing more to be done. Her sins caught up with her.'

The passenger turned and went on his way, wiping his mouth with his handkerchief. His boots clattered briskly on the steep cobbled path leading towards the old city.

Above the Minster, a few ice-white stars glittered brightly. Goodricke breathed in the smells of the night air. How silent it was by the river. He would miss this. Mindless of his sopping clothes, he shut his eyes and settled down by the dead girl to wait for the police. They wouldn't rush; plenty more whores where she came from.

Four months later:

WEEK ONE

13 – 20 DECEMBER 1862

*'Photography was destined to
be involved with death.'
- Nobuyoshi Araki*

CHAPTER TWO

◊

Saturday morning

S o much blood.
Warm, viscous, red.
And that wasn't the worst of it. The sweet, iron stench hit the back of her throat, its instinctive reflux making her gag. It had been a while, but the stench was as bad as ever and Ada Fawkes found herself back at another slaughter, eighteen months ago. She willed the memory to stop.

Ada's eyes locked onto the flesh scraps splattering the narrow-cobbled alley, the steaming innards slithering into the open stone gulley in the middle of the paved street. Guts, gristle, gore, all tossed together for the dogs. Unwise of her to enter the Shambles, always carnage at the start of a butchering day.

She wrapped her heavy cloak tighter, keeping close to the stone wall. Above her, overhanging eaves shaded the street from the early morning sun, as they had done for hundreds of years. Buildings so close you could lean across the upper storeys to hand your neighbour a pound of minced meat. The eaves kept the Shambles chill enough to stop flesh rotting.

Inside small dark shops, huge butchers' cleavers bashed through bones, sharp knives sliced through stomachs, car-

13

casses dangled and spun on straining hooks, well-scrubbed wooden shelves displayed slabs of meat. 'Watch tha sen, love.' A door had banged open and the warning came from a blood-sprayed, skinny man with a bulbous nose. He mimed a movement with his pail, this courtesy giving her time to move out of the way before a sliver of milky-blue intestines landed close-by. She smiled stiffly and walked swiftly on.

Ada Fawkes emerged into the wintry sunshine at the Pavement end of the Shambles, to find an ill-tempered brawl underway. Today's pig market crowds were already inebriated and raucous – fighting was inevitable. It had always been the same: execution days, market days, any day. This is how it is in York, she thought. Roman, Viking, Medieval, Tudor, whatever the century, the city and the people settling differences with brutality.

She found her way through the cheering spectators and hurried her step. Yards ahead of her was Coney Street and her new photographic studio.

A fresh start.

Ada had acquired the old building for its prominent position on York's main shopping street, not its half-timbered frame leaning over as though collapsing with age and exhaustion. At the wooden door she paused, catching her reflection in the shop window. No longer so young either, she thought. She knew she had never been conventionally beautiful – striking at best. At least her long curling hair, Viking-red someone had once called it, softened her face. Her scars were not visible, hidden under her winter layers, but she had always felt conscious of the lines. The intricate pattern branded on her skin. These days Ada spent little time on her appearance; though her clothes were elegant

– a forest green mohair dress and matching cloak, clearly not purchased in York – they were casually worn.

She turned the key in the lock and pushed open the door, bending slightly as she stepped under the low lintel. The air in the studio felt warm from the coals she had banked up the night before. She had lain in bed last night unable to sleep, thoughts roaming, convinced that this studio was a mistake and that here, in York, few would want her modern photographs, her stylish portraits. Now she made up her mind: time to push aside those memories that would never be forgotten, at least in her waking hours. Ada took off her cloak, picked up the poker and stoked the fire into flames.

The novelty of the new studio worked on her spirits as she made ready for tomorrow's opening and any lingering doubts receded. Photography was a sensation. This marriage of art and cutting-edge science entranced everyone. The Queen was so obsessed that she could not move a muscle without requesting a photograph of herself, her many children, even her poor husband on his deathbed. Victoria had sparked a craze and, in London, photographic portraits were all the rage. Pictures printed onto little cards to share with family, friends and strangers, collected and displayed in albums and scrapbooks. The shadows of bodies captured forever.

Carefully Ada took her camera out of its case and touched the smooth solidness of the walnut wood. It had travelled around many continents with her and now it would bring the world to York and send York to the world. Her photographs would immortalise its people and places. She would create the portraits beloved by the Royals and the aristocracy, but make them cheap enough for everyone to buy. She would democratize photography. Ordinary women, men and children would become visible.

True, there were already a few photography studios in Coney Street, but their melancholic portraits of stern-faced men holding thick biographies were drab and old-fashioned. Occasionally a wife would be allowed to perch on a low chair beside them, subservient, modest, lesser. These stalwarts of Yorkshire's committees and societies dulled the windows of Ada's competitors.

Ada Fawkes wanted her studio to be different: a beacon of colour and light.

She moved swiftly now, pulling out straw from wooden crates, unpacking her purchases, sent up this week from London. A golden birdcage, iridescent peacock feathers, an emerald-green parrot and more. She carried each object up the stairs to her large bright first-floor studio, until she had to stop and catch her breath.

She continued on, her boot heels clattering swiftly to and fro over the floorboards as she moved her belongings from one side to the other, placing, rearranging, adjusting all manner of things. She passed her eyes over the room again for this had to be right, she needed this studio to succeed.

It was all a gamble, yes, but Ada was convinced these cartes-de-visite – as these small portraits were known – would become as popular here as they were in London and Paris. She pictured the images: young women as they yearned to see themselves, half-smiling, half-pouting into the camera, sucked-in cheeks, necks flatteringly stretched, hair tucked teasingly behind ears. What young woman, or indeed any woman of a certain age, could resist such perfection? And men? Oh, just as obsessed.

Ada Fawkes was staking her future on this venture. She had to make this work.

She needed the money.

By the time the wooden clock on the mantelpiece downstairs struck four o'clock, Ada's back ached with bending over and her hands were roughened with cleaning. Leaning on a brush, the last specks of dust swept away, she smelled the fresh paint with satisfaction. Even in the winter dusk the pale walls glowed with light. In front of her, a photographic backdrop as bright and colourful as any London theatre scene. Her treasured camera, waiting on its stand for her first client. Richly coloured costumes hung from a rail; Ada knew well enough what fantasies her clients held: a rustic shepherdess, a Greek goddess, a woodland nymph. She touched the soft, delicate clothes of their dreams. And there, of course, was the grinning skull on an oak table: the essential prop for melancholy young men with tortured yearnings to be Prince Hamlet. She patted the old head. God knew who it belonged to. Certainly not a Viking king as the antiquities dealer had claimed. She imagined the photographs she would take and smiled to herself. Being here, it revived her passion for work, gave her a sense of hope she had not expected.

***

A little later, Ada was satisfied she could do no more; everything that could be was in order and in its place. Besides, she longed for her warm fireside and a glass of red wine. She'd surely earned that comfort today.

Outside her studio, she breathed in the sharp air. It had the feel of snow and she pulled her cloak tight. York's evening atmosphere was already lively as she began to carefully thread her way through the street traffic – a flux of people, horses, carts. Shrill voices shouting out their wares to passing figures, and drunken men, whistling, singing and shoving one another with ale-induced affection. Ada crossed the narrow-cobbled street and passed under the clock of St Martin le Grand. One of the beggar-children who clung like limpets to the city's nooks and corners, called out to her, 'If you please, miss, give a poor girl a halfpenny.' Ada looked at the pinch-faced child, maybe less than ten, holding a lucifer match in one gloveless hand, a stay-lace in the other.

Ada took out a coin from the purse of threepenny-bits she always had ready. 'Here you are, please buy yourself something warm to eat. And take my gloves.' She pulled them off and pushed them into the girl's basket. At the same moment, a sturdy gentleman, his arm draped heavily around the shoulders of a younger woman, the worse for a drink or two, lurched heavily into her left arm. She gasped at the jabbing pain that spread down into her fingers.

'Sorry, madam. Are you hurt?' the man asked.

'Not at all. Nothing broken,' Ada said. 'Good evening to you both.' And she brushed off further slurred apologies, hurrying on.

The smell of roasting chestnuts and charcoal drifted through St Helen's Square and clouds of smoke plumed into the frosty air. Burning braziers sparked fiery orange in the dusk, their light catching the gold boxes of the nearby confectioner's window, enticing Ada to stop and look at the chocolates arranged to perfection on glass stands. Behind her, she heard voices rising, a sense of excitement brewing. She turned and saw a crowd jostling around a newsstand, people grasping for the final edition of the day. A young man in an ink-stained apron was pushing through, nearly tripping himself up with two bundles tied with brown string. These were straight off the press, rushed from *The Herald* offices around the corner.

Two policemen shouldered their way through. 'About your business,' the bigger one was shouting. A few jeered in reply. 'Haven't you got better things to do, Gage?' someone shouted.

'It's Constable Gage to you,' the policeman snarled, raising his ham-like fists in a threatening gesture.

More jeering.

'Cock.'

Assuming this taunt was not a reference to his new issue cockscomb helmet, the man-mountain grabbed the nearest lad. 'Right, son. You're for a night in the lock-up.'

The crowd bickered and shoved as newspapers passed from hand to hand. The voices grew louder. In the crush, Ada stumbled nearer to the billboard. She looked up and read the large ink-black headlines:

Has the Butcher of York claimed his 3rd victim?
Another woman savagely mutilated.
York City Police fail to investigate grisly crime.

She had no warning. A wave of nausea, a dizzying flash inside her head, a void of darkness and the stone pavement slammed into her. The noise around her receded and fell silent. She had the strangest sensation of being alone in the cacophony of the city. She lay head down, and drew deep breaths in slow inhalations, a method she had been taught to keep terrors at bay. These attacks had plagued her ever since Paris.

And then voices buzzing, arms lifting her, hands brushing down her clothes.

'I'm absolutely fine,' she lied to kind enquiries. She was shocked, bruised, nothing worse. Keen to be home now, she straightened up. 'Thank you, I'm perfectly well. No harm done.'

'Here, have this one,' said a man.

She walked away and, when she looked down, she was holding a newspaper in her hand. She hastened along Stonegate and reached the Minster as the first promised snowflakes of winter began to fall, dusting her cloak and hat, melting softly on her cheeks. Feeling cold to the bone now, she turned into Minster Yard where jewelled light glowed through the cathedral's vast stained-glass windows and lit the path around the east end to Chapter House Street.

She followed the line of the cathedral walls until she was on the other side of the Minster and turned right by a solitary gas lamp into a cobbled side street. Within moments she was standing on a worn stone step to a tall house of red bricks. Her key turned easily in the lock and at last Ada Fawkes was on the other side. She closed the door firmly behind her, leaned her back against it and exhaled deeply. Home. Candles in shining brass holders had already been lit, a blue-patterned bowl of early hyacinths on the polished hall table scented the air. She felt warmth on her skin.

Ada heard heeled shoes tapping on the wooden floor and a softly accented woman's voice.

'You're in good time. Supper's in an hour or so. Has the day gone well?' said Camille Defoe, Ada's housekeeper, sweeping towards her along the wide hallway, smiling. She could have been upwards of fifty-five, perhaps older, but the tilt of her chin, the set of her shoulders and her fine clothes marked her as a woman who did not care a bit for those who expected ladies past their youth to fade into matronly appearance. Now, watching her approach, Ada saw the older woman's expression change.

'Ada, what has happened?'

She held out the newspaper. 'Three women are dead. They're saying they were murdered, that there's a killer, here, in York.'

As Camille read, Ada struggled out of her cloak and pulled off her soaked hat, untidy hair falling over her shoulders. She pushed it back roughly. 'Camille, what if . . .'

Camille let the newspaper drop and took Ada's hands in a firm grip. 'Stop Ada. Terrible though it is these poor women's deaths have nothing to do with you. That life is behind you. C'est finis.'

'But if this is murder,' said Ada quietly, 'and if they ask for my help, if they need me again, how can I refuse?'

CHAPTER THREE

◊

Ada sank into a chair and held her cold hands close to the coals of her bedroom fire. Her unbuttoned boots lay on the floor beside the crimson pile of her damp stockings.

Usually, she felt a sense of comfort in her room: her books piled next to her large brass bed, polished wooden floorboards softened with oriental rugs, a French landscape painting above the fireplace chosen for its striking play of light on water. But, she couldn't help it; fears were taking shape around her tonight. She stared at the fire, massaging the scars on her hand and collar bone, as if the wounds were still itchy and raw. The damaged flesh had cicatrised and her healing skin appeared like veinlets on a sweet chestnut leaf. This rubbing was a habit now whenever she was tired or angry. It was a relief when she heard a voice calling her to supper.

Ada breathed in the robust scent of herbs and garlic as she pushed open the door into the large kitchen. Thomas Bell was taking glasses out of a corner cupboard to put on the table, already set with the plain white weekday china. He smiled at her, his laughter lines deepening. Fifty-odd years had streaked his hair silver-grey, but his demeanour was as alert as ever, remarkably untouched by his experiences. Nearly two years ago, the former cavalryman had sailed into Whitby, done with fighting foreign wars. When the cold, the heat, the disease, the drink hadn't killed him, Thomas Bell had vowed to return home and never leave. It was fate, Ada liked to tell herself, that he was back in England when she sought his help.

Now Thomas was studying her face quizzically. 'Are you feeling better, my girl? For I thought we might have a glass of wine to mark the occasion. It's not every day you start a new venture like this. Come on, sit down, you must be tired.' He pulled a chair closer to the warmth of the black range.

Ada nodded and there was nothing more to be said now for the scullery door banged open. Ada sat a little straighter as Camille entered. 'Et voila! Here we are.' Camille presented a platter of toasted bread and cheese and placed it on the table before them. With a folded white tea towel over her arm, like the professional chef she once was, she went back to the scullery and returned carrying a tureen of soup. 'French onion.'

Ada and Thomas exchanged looks; it was a mutual relief that tonight's meal wasn't too French. Occasionally, Camille had a yearning to recreate her glory days and the outcome was generally unpalatable; cervelles au beurre noir, escargots a la Bourguignonne and God knows what else. The brains and snails lived especially long in their memories and digestive systems. It made the beginning of every meal slightly tense.

'Very nice,' said Thomas pouring from a bottle of Claret, a French custom they had happily embraced. He passed a glass to Camille and another to Ada who took it gratefully.

'Cheers,' said Thomas, raising his glass. 'Well done Ada, it's been a lot of hard work getting the studio ready but the worst is behind you. Now you can enjoy your photography again. Here's to new beginnings.'

'Thank you.' Ada smiled at him and took a sip. Outside the small-paned window, snow drifted into the walled garden beyond, giving her a feeling of being cocooned. Inside candles in silver sticks cast a warming glow over the table. She felt herself relaxing a little as bowls of hot soup were passed round and the three of them talked companionably over the day.

Thomas finished his meal and poured more wine, glancing at Ada. He judged the moment was right. 'This Butcher of York story in *The Herald* tonight, love,' he said setting down the bottle on the table. 'You are not to worry. We don't know if it's true. And if it is, it's not your business; the York Police are there for that.'

Ada sighed. 'I know. It's just . . . well, anyway, I'm sure I'm over-reacting. But, in that moment, it was as if I were back in Paris. I couldn't stop the images coming into my mind, like dreaming while I was still awake. A bad dream.'

'We understand, Ada,' said Thomas gently, looking over the table at Camille opposite. 'But everything will work out, you'll see. That's all in the past. It's behind you now. Everything will be fine.'

Ada nodded, dismissing her uneasiness, wanting to believe his words. 'I'm feeling better now, really, just a little tired and a bit bruised and sore from falling. I'll be absolutely fine after a good night's sleep.'

'That's the spirit.' He held a match to his briar-wood pipe. Smoke curled above his head, scenting the air. 'This is the right decision. York, your studio, it's a fresh start. You can keep busy with work, get taking those photographs again. Camille and

I, we can take care of everything else. In time, you will grow accustomed to being here.' He smiled reassuringly. 'This is a new life for us all. Look how well we rub along. Yes,' he said, catching her sceptical look and smiling. 'Even Camille and I, virago though she is.'

'I understood that, my English is better than yours. And someone needs to keep you in order,' smiled Camille getting up. She took another bottle of wine from the large oak dresser where the best blue and white crockery was displayed and handed it to Thomas. 'Open that, you big goose. Make yourself useful for once.'

Ada knew how much they wanted this to work for her. And they had invested their own savings in her new business. 'Yes, let's have another glass and toast our fresh start in York.' She forced a cheeriness she did not feel.

***

Through Ada's tall bedroom window, the great towers of the Minster were as silhouettes against the dark night sky. Snow was gently falling on the cobbles and the gardens of the large turreted house opposite. The faint shouting and singing of the market day crowds could still be heard. Those who hadn't stumbled home, or found a bed in one of the city's many brothels, would drink themselves into a stupor and be lying face-down in one alleyway or another come the morning. Ada turned away.

There was a comfort in being in her room tonight. She poured herself a large cognac from a decanter set on a small table and took it to the fireside. She sat back in her armchair, wriggled herself comfortable against the velvet cushions and curled her bare feet under her body. She warmed the glass with her hands, breathing in its heady fumes. The fire burned bright, casting dancing shadows on the ceiling and walls. She watched them as she sipped, relishing being on her own, peaceful, quiet. She looked around her room with satisfaction. It was simply furnished; there was little of the fussiness and clutter of current trends for decoration. She knew it would seem plain to many but it suited her tastes well. Her bed, a writing table, quill pens, ink, and paper, by the window and a carved wooden bookcase with her well-thumbed books were all she needed.

Yet Ada found her thoughts drifting and within moments her mind turned inevitably to that turbulent moment in the square earlier when she had first read those bold, black headlines in the newspaper. A little knot of fear settled in her stomach. What if one person had murdered all three women? What if the Butcher was real? What if he went on killing?

No, it was rumours and gossip, that was all, she told herself. If it was really true, it was the city police who must catch such a dangerous criminal. She should try not to have these dark thoughts. This was her life now, drama-free and calm. And it was the right decision to be here for where could she have come if not to York? After Paris she could certainly never have gone back to her family's home. Nothing had been more necessary to her than leaving there. Whatever happened now or in the future, she reassured herself she would never go back to that rigid, suffocating life; she would rather eat snails and brains for the rest of her days.

***

Despite her reluctance, Ada found her tired mind returning again to her childhood years.

Her family had lived comfortably in an old stone house with a large acreage of dairy, sheep and grouse moorland in North Yorkshire. How lucky she had thought herself then. Her childhood had felt carefree. She and her younger brother Harry had roamed the fields, learned how to milk cows and feed pet lambs. They had their own pony and trap. They danced at harvest, at Christmas, on the first day of May. Her world had been uncomplicated – until the morning of her twelfth birthday.

'Eleanor, the child runs wild like a savage, and that hair, well, she looks about as ugly as a tramp. She's twelve today, old enough. Her behaviour must change or we will never secure her a husband.'

Her father's words to her mother. They were spoken harshly, at the table, in the house passed down through the eldest sons for generations. On the other side of the breakfast-room door, Ada had felt her world change. Everything she thought was fixed, slipped away from her.

Ada recalled her mother's pleas, her soft voice entreating her husband to allow their daughter more time: to go to school, to have an education, to see more of the world than just Yorkshire. She could still feel her younger self, pressing her head to the door so hard it hurt, holding her breath, hoping.

'A man does not want or need a clever woman,' her father had said in that confident dismissive voice of one used to authority and which, all these years later, still made Ada seethe. *'A girl needs only the tools to be a fit wife and mother, nothing more. She shall have a governess to teach her how to be a proper young lady. By God, she needs it. Piano, needlework, religious instruction, housekeeping, French, that should do it.'*

She had learned of her future in a few brutal words. She was to be prepared for marriage, while Harry would go away to be properly educated.

Ada barely spoke to her father again.

Her tired thoughts moved forwards to another vivid and bitter memory, turning sixteen, four years on. It was 1837, the year Princess Victoria became Queen, the year Ada lost any religious faith and the year she knew for certain her mother was dying.

Once such a good-looking woman, her skin had leached to an alabaster-white, her striking auburn hair had turned grey. Occasionally, though even then, her mother's old vitality and energy had returned and then she'd quietly, secretly, encouraged Ada's learning.

Together, in the bright drawing room, they'd read and talked of politics, books, art and new innovations: the bicycle, the photograph, postage stamps. On summer days, they'd walk slowly, breathing in the smells of the hedgerows and moorlands. The fresh air would even briefly bring a bloom to her mother's cheeks. They'd paint the scenes around them: sunlight flickering through shaded woods, vibrant green river pastures, the yellow stone of an ancient abbey.

'You have a talent for art. You have an eye for colour and composition. I wish I was well enough to take you to Paris to see the great masters.'

Ada had watched her mother weaken, though even at her life's end, she'd still engaged with the world outside as Ada had read aloud to her: instalments of *The Old Curiosity Shop* or articles from *The Times* of the British army's progress in Afghanistan. Then in the early wintry months of 1842, soon after reports of the soldiers' desperate final stand at Gandamak, her mother had died.

Two days after the funeral, her father had called her into his presence for the first time in many months, and Ada remembered that conversation, very well:

'With your mother in her grave, your position here has changed. When Harry marries, after our period of mourning, his wife will be mistress of this house. Your place will be to serve as required and make yourself agreeable to her. Your future here and any monies will lie within Harry's discretion. I tell you this for your own good. You have shown great reluctance in the state of matrimony. Quite simply, Ada, you are too passionate, too rude, every suitor I introduce is put off. You must try and make yourself more agreeable to them or you will remain a spinster, living here at the beck and call of your brother and his family.'

Ada had said nothing to these words; they were not a surprise to her. Her father's reproaches were not new. She had long felt the crushing weight of her dependency. So she did try, a little. Over interminable dinners and frustrating chit-chat, she'd endured the attentions of single wealthy gentlemen who, despite their education, had little of interest to say to her.

She'd refused all offers.

Ada thought of her brother. Harry might have stood up for her, but his disposition was to be malleable and he'd always taken the easy way out, obliging their father with a suitable wife, the Honourable Charlotte Humphrey. Their wedding had joined two vast North Yorkshire estates.

The dainty-looking heiress whom Harry had proudly brought into their home, had become its new mistress. And, as her father had predicted, from that first day Charlotte had made it clear that Ada – as the spinster sister-in-law without means of her own – should not come and go as she pleased. Her life was now at the beck and call of Lady Fawkes. And, after Charlotte had dutifully provided two sons, it was made clear that her future was as an unpaid child-minder to her nephews.

Ada shifted in her chair and gripped her glass. She fixed her eyes on the fire and looked into the sparks of burning coal. There had come a moment when she had known how to win.

She'd had to lie, of course. She had not the slightest guilt about that, she knew that there were worse things than lying – accepting defeat was one of them.

***

It was the last Saturday in November 1845, the days were shorter and colder and Charlotte had said they must all go shopping in York for scarves and gloves.

At two o'clock on that frosty afternoon, Ada had slowed her step to glance in a gallery window, for a small crowd was looking at something. She froze. It was hardly too much to call them miraculous. This extraordinary, incredible exactness. Before her, the most perfect pictures. They had stopped time itself. She felt a charge run through her veins. The most magical images she had ever seen; life captured in light, shadows caught and held. She had read of photographs, named for the Greek 'drawing with light'. But here, now, before her were William Henry Fox Talbot's pictures of St Mary's Abbey, the King's Staith, the Minster. Ada couldn't stop looking. This was art, as great as any Turner painting. This was science, as revolutionary as Robert Chambers' *Vestiges of the Natural History of Creation*. That very day she used the last of a small gift from her mother to purchase her first camera.

'It's only a hobby, lots of lady amateurs are taking this up,' she said in response to her family's concerns. 'It's very respectable. It is an amusement like needlework. When I've learnt how to use the camera, I will be able to make splendid portraits of my nephews.'

Thomas Bell, her family's gardener and a friend to her even back then, had suggested an old stone outhouse. It was a dark, cold room smelling of damp earth, its light obscured by thick cobwebs at the windows. Everything was layered with dirt; it looked like it hadn't been used for years. Thomas had helped make it ready. He'd mended a cast-iron stove so she could warm the room. He'd carried over a pot sink from the greenhouses and fixed it under the outside tap. She'd scrubbed walls and floors until her hands were red-raw and the air reeked satisfyingly of carbolic.

It was a place of her own.

The cold of that winter made no difference, nor did the noxious smells and the corrosive poison of the chemicals. With the help of complicated instructions in magazine articles, she'd persevered with teaching herself how to use her camera. Endless failures and mistakes – trying for hours to get one good image only to smudge it before it dried. All the while handling her Jamin glass lens with tenderness, as if it were a baby, as she worked with ruthless perfectionism.

She'd taken to wearing the oldest, patched dresses. The developing chemicals became so ingrained she could not wash the black stains from her clothes or her hands. Her family had tolerated her dabbling, considering it a suitable occupation for a spinster aunt, especially once it became known that the Queen and Prince Albert were passionate advocates of photography. By the following spring, the quality and power of her photographs was much admired.

'A picture of every being dear to me in the world,' Charlotte had gushed when she saw Ada's photographs of her sons, 'and I would rather have such a memorial of my dear boys, than the noblest artist's work ever produced. Imagine, I will see them as they are now for years to come.'

She'd turned to Ada. 'My dear, you must make a portrait of my dog next.'

Her family had been blind to photography's radical potential. Ada had not.

When she'd perfected her skills – enough to make a living – she'd left home.

Ada smiled to herself, stretching her bare feet towards the fire. She would never forget her sister-in law's reproaches, her brother's shouts, their threats to cut her off without a penny. She had not cared then and she did not care now.

She was surviving.

The sound of the midnight bells ringing through the city startled her and dragged her back to the present. The fire was dying. Ada stood up, wincing, for her body had stiffened from lifting heavy boxes earlier. She poured coals from the bucket into the grate and jabbed with the poker to force them into flame. Wrapping herself in her soft paisley shawl, she settled back in her armchair and taking up her half-finished book, was soon immersed in Jane Eyre's flight from Thornfield Hall. Sometime later, the novel fell onto her lap and she slept.

Perhaps it was no surprise, given the day's events, that she dreamt of him again.

CHAPTER FOUR

◊

It was early Monday morning but the atmosphere in the Mansion House, the grandest residence in York, was already tense. Its current incumbent, Lord Mayor George Brass, tightly buttoned into a black suit, seams straining over his prominent belly, slammed his fist down on the breakfast table. He stood up, walked to his window, high above the square, and looked down on the crowds passing below. Christmas shopping always packed them in. He should have been feeling good.

George Brass took his duties as the city's premier citizen seriously. He juggled his own vast wealth with a tight hold on York Corporation's fiscal budget. His time in the service of his city had been satisfactory — until now.

Brass turned and glared at his brother-in-law, Robert Nutt, the city's chief constable. Nutt, who sat at the polished mahogany table in the banqueting room, chewing his breakfast, washing it down with the pint of the Mansion House's finest champagne, felt the force of that look and swallowed his fried black pudding quickly.

'This should have been a good day, Bob.' Brass smoothed his scant hair carefully, so as not to disturb its careful combing and hitched down his waistcoat. 'Aye, it should have been excellent.'

Record crowds over the weekend had swelled his bulging coffers. Most importantly, invitations to his annual Twelfth Night Ball had been sent out by letter carriers. Tomorrow they would be presented by white-gloved butlers, on silver plates, to everyone who mattered.

He wanted this ball to be bigger and better than ever; the social highlight of the year. The great and good would be in York to celebrate his triumph. Lendal Bridge, the realisation of his multi-guinea dream to link his national railway network with the city and its money-spinning attractions: the oversize Minster, that ruin on a hill Clifford's Tower, broken Roman rubbish, Viking God knows what, Dick Turpin's grave. He knew how it worked. Throw in some ghost stories, race days at the Knavesmire, plenty of public houses and the tourists would flock to quaint old York all year round – in their thousands.

But below his window, in his city, was this spreading hysteria about a three-time killer. It was wrecking his grand scheme.

'No. This has got to stop.'

He picked up *The Herald*, waving it at the policeman. 'All this nonsense in the papers about a murderer running amok, even the bloody *Times*. They just love it. Why do people want to read about this bollocks, Bob? It's bad for business, bad for York and bad for me. I want this stopped before my bridge opens, before my Twelfth Night Ball.'

'I'll get my best men on to it,' the police chief answered quickly.

Brass walked over, spreading his fingers on the table and leaned into his brother-in-law's face so close Nutt could smell his tobacco breath.

'I know you will, Bob. But we also both know you might as well set a litter of kittens after a lion. York police have become a laughing stock. No. This needs sorting and fast.'

'What do you want me to do?' Nutt pulled out his white handkerchief and mopped his brow.

'It's already in hand, Bob. I've sent a telegram to the Home Secretary. I've told him to pull his finger out of his backside. I want his best detective up here and prompt. This Butcher of York, he needs to watch out. No one makes a fool of me.'

***

In London, a hastily convened private meeting deep within the corridors of Whitehall was soon to take place. As he waited, Sir Richard Mayne took a moment to look out of his tall first floor window, down on the hustle and bustle heading to and from Trafalgar Square. For a moment he wished he was there on the noisy street. Though his grand office was panelled in English oak and hung with gilt-framed paintings, he would have traded it all and been glad to be one of the top-hatted gentlemen heading for a steady Monday morning in a bank. He felt too old for this. Sir Richard was not often so unfair to himself. Though over sixty years of age, the Metropolitan Police commissioner's razor-sharp mind worked as fast as any younger man's.

He turned sharply as the door opened and a uniformed porter announced the arrival of his colleague, Superintendent Williamson. Despite some thirty years between them the two men shook hands with real affection. Neither of them would have attracted attention in the street – the monastic-looking older man or the younger with undistinguished brown hair and beard

– yet between them they controlled a network of law agents, informants and spies which extended beyond England's borders into Europe and the rest of the world.

'I have had a letter from the Home Secretary,' said Sir Richard as soon as they were sitting in comfortably-worn leather chairs either side of his desk.

Across from him Adolphus Williamson, affectionately known to his colleagues as 'Dolly', eyed him levelly, pausing from lighting his pear-wood pipe. 'Ah. I take it, it's not good news.'

'No Dolly. Frankly it couldn't be worse. It's the last thing we need on top of the embarrassment of Jack Whicher's Road Hill murder investigation. Arresting the sister, I mean the sister for God's sake, for slitting her own brother's throat; we'll never ever hear the last of that.'

As a former barrister, Sir Richard's mind flashed back with an unfortunate recall for the details and the headlines that had besmirched the department he had created twenty years before and nurtured like his own baby through to maturity. They had called his detective system *low and mean* and his police force *a cowardly and clumsy giant who wreaks all the meanness and malignity of his nature on every feeble and helpless creature who comes in his way.* And there was the mockery – *'clueless'* – one journalist had written.

He sighed. All public and parliamentary goodwill was gone. Was it Whicher's fault? Or was the success of the branch too closely associated with one man. Maybe that was his failing, wondered Sir Richard. But when he had given permission for Charles Dickens to interview his detectives for a magazine article, he couldn't have foreseen how their exploits would grip the nation's imagination. His best man Jack Whicher was an instant celebrity. Everyone became obsessed with reading about murder mysteries. The appetite for crime stories was insatiable.

It was all going so well until Whicher accused 16-year-old Constance Kent of lifting her sleeping half-brother from his cot, slitting his throat and dumping him in the privy. No one could believe it. In the next moment, the press turned on them. There was outrage. The case was thrown out of court and all their reputations suffered.

And here he was with another problem. If he didn't sort it, the Home Secretary had threatened to shut down the Detective Branch. He waved the letter towards his superintendent. Williamson, head of Great Scotland's 30 or so detectives, didn't need to read it. He knew all too well what was happening in York.

The news from the North was all over today's newspapers, usually more obsessed with London stories, but the Butcher of York had gripped their readers. Bad enough in itself, if it were true, but the publicity around the brutal deaths of three women risked damaging the personal wealth of George Brass, the city's powerful Lord Mayor and his friends in high places were not going to risk that.

Always a gentle presence, Dolly Williamson, with his habitual sprig of greenery in his buttonhole, remained silent. He sat back in the chair by the fire and let Sir Richard get it off his chest.

'Brass is a megalomaniac. And we all have to jump to because he's one of the richest men in the country and the PM relies on his donations to keep him in power. He's worried that precious tourists will stop swarming into York on his railways. It's all about him getting richer. He doesn't give a damn about those women. He runs York like his personal kingdom, appoints his useless brother-in-law as police chief and then orders the Prime Minister to sort this out.'

'I know we can't have a killer on the loose,' Sir Richard said. 'But I resent his arrogance.'

Dolly nodded, his face registering nothing, letting his boss get to the end.

'And there's another issue Dolly. The Queen. She loves detective stories. She's following this case and has asked to be kept informed of our progress.'

The police chief judged Sir Richard had finished, before finally speaking, 'No pressure then.'

Sir Richard took a breath, sank back and shook his head. They both knew there was a Herculean task ahead. Frequently, the requests for help from the provinces were too late. Sir Richard had sent his men many times when chief constables or magistrates called in Scotland Yard, only to find the local peelers had stomped over every inch of a crime scene in their 12-shilling boots. And they knew it was nigh on impossible to work with local policemen, resentful about outside interference and ignorant of proper evidence or crime analysis. Nothing would surprise the two men sat in London about police practices in York.

The superintendent pursed his lips in thought and leaned forward. 'Well, we could look at it another way. We've moved on a lot since Whicher was in charge. We have all these new methods of analysing crime at our disposal. It's an opportunity to put things right again, move on from the Kent fiasco. Let everyone see what Scotland Yard can really do. We can show them we are at the cutting edge of crime-fighting.'

'Dolly, you're right as always.' Sir Richard regarded his police chief with respect. 'Tell me everything you can then. What the hell is going on up there?'

Williamson considered a moment. 'This is what we know. A young woman's body was found a few days ago by a lamp-lighter, with strange knife cuts on her stomach. The local bobbies didn't take it seriously, assumed the prostitute was killed by an unhappy client and that was it. They did sod all.'

Williamson took a moment to draw on his pipe before continuing. 'But then an old ferryman started mouthing off in the pub after a few, you know how ageing gents love a gossip over a pint, talked of how he'd pulled a young woman from the river, late summer, with strange slashes on her stomach. A boatman chipped in and said he'd found a young woman on the river bank, back in early October, mutilated the same way. Maybe they were showing off, exaggerating in drink, but a journalist from the local newspaper made a connection and suddenly we have headlines screaming that a multiple killer is on the rampage through the streets of York, stalking women. This might all be rubbish, maybe these are three unrelated deaths, sad, but hardly unusual these days. But we don't know the truth of it because two of the bodies are long buried.'

Sir Richard frowned and leaned forward. 'Why didn't we hear about all this before? Why didn't York police ask us to look into it?'

'No one cared. As far as they were concerned these women were getting what they deserved. But now that's changed. The city is convinced a multiple killer is running amok. Womenfolk are terrified. The mayor is furious, says it's salacious nonsense made up by the newspapers. But, of course Brass wants that to be true because he thinks if there really is a murderer prowling York's streets, it's going to cost him money. A lot of money.'

Sir Richard nodded. 'We have got to sort this mess out. Who have we got available?'

'Tanner is on an Atlantic steamship chasing the railway murder suspect, Whicher and Walker are in Warsaw giving the Russians advice on setting up a detective service and the Russkies are worried about the Poles assassinating the Tsar. They've tried a few times. Anyway, that's all very hush, hush. Then there's Browning still in Somerset.'

Sir Richard frowned. He did not want a detailed list of every detective's whereabouts. He only wanted to know about one man. 'Straker, how is he now?'

A fair question, but Williamson had hoped to keep Detective Inspector Straker out of this. He did not believe the officer was ready to return to duty though Straker had sworn he was fully fit.

'He says he's ready for anything sir,' admitted the superintendent reluctantly.

'I know he's only had straightforward assignments after that dreadful case in Paris. But he is the right man for this,' said Sir Richard. 'He has the most up-to-date knowledge on all the new scientific tricks. After all, that's what we sent him across the Channel for. If Straker can sort this York case we can set up some press interviews about our ground-breaking investigative methods and how we use the new science of photography to crack crime. This might turn out well yet.'

'I'll get back to the Yard and brief him.' Williamson hesitated a moment. 'Sir, you just mentioned photography?'

Sir Richard looked faintly surprised as though his remark was an unimportant afterthought which they both knew it was not. 'I did, didn't I? Well it is the future of crime fighting. And Miss Fawkes? She's in York now?'

'Yes Sir Richard. I believe she is.'

The police commissioner was matter of fact. 'That's it then. The public, the Queen even, will be fascinated by her work. She could save our bacon.'

There it was and they both knew it. A tacit admission, a mutual recognition, from those who understood the job inside out, that the police force needed women. Sir Robert Peel himself had raised it publicly years ago and been lambasted for it. Consequently, Ada Fawkes's role in solving the Paris murders was not talked about any more than was the fact that Whicher had employed a police sergeant's wife to help investigate the Road Hill House killing. Not one woman in the force, yet it was beyond the power of the greatest detective to differentiate menstrual blood on garments from those of a fatal stabbing.

Enough said.

'Well, there you go.' Sir Richard stood up. The men shook hands. Dolly Williamson walked to the door. He paused and before leaving turned and asked, 'And who will tell Miss Fawkes?'

Sir Richard was already dipping his pen in his inkwell, thinking of his best reply to the Home Secretary. He looked up. 'Oh leave that to Straker. I think that's best. Don't you?'

Outside in the corridor the porter was back again, waiting patiently, overcoat and felt hat in his hands. Williamson thanked him and followed him, in silence, past many closed doors. He glanced at them with curiosity, catching low voices and wafts of tobacco. They continued along carpeted passageways, down turning stairways until he was out on the street.

After the cloistered atmosphere of Whitehall, the morning bustle made all his senses jangle: the thunderous sound of carriage wheels over stone, the smell of labouring horses, the shrill voices of costermongers and vendors shouting out their wares. He walked towards Trafalgar Square and turned into Great Scotland Yard. Ahead of him, opposite the back entrance of the Metropolitan Police's headquarters, was a red-brick building where the three modest offices of the detective branch took up the ground floor.

Williamson nodded at pairs of uniformed constables as they passed briskly beneath the yard's gateway to begin long shifts on the streets. Westminster, if lucky, the slums of the 'Devil's Acre' if they were not. The large clock on the wall overlooking the paved square was striking eleven and the public house in the corner of Scotland Yard was doing a brisk trade already. A few of his men would be having a lunchtime pint, but Williamson steered towards the office, without a stop, for the man he needed would not be with them.

***

Detective Inspector Samuel Straker was not at his desk either. A smoking Turkish cigarette was half-crushed in the ash tray. A chair was pushed aside. Williamson looked at what lay upon the desktop. Beside a tin box of cartridges, manuscript tied up with red ribbon, and a jack-knife he saw a black circle smudged on a scrap of torn paper: a fingerprint.

'Chief,' a deep voice from behind made him start. Straker strode through the doorway, his long overcoat billowing out behind him. 'I must hurry. I'm on my way to arrest the diamond thief. I can prove it's him. Do you remember me telling you that everyone's fingerprints are different, well . . .'

'Good man Straker,' Williamson interrupted. 'I can wrap up the rest of it. You can give me the details. You need to get to York. You can catch the mail train from King's Cross tonight.'

'York?'

'That's right. Sir Richard's orders.'

'The Butcher?'

'Yes. No problem with that I assume?'

'I'm more than ready for a such a case.' Straker reached inside his jacket for his cigarette case. 'Besides, I want to test some of the new tricks I picked up in Paris.'

Williamson thought again about Straker's final investigation with the French detectives. That manhunt would have done for many officers. Not Straker – determination, guts, independence – that man would never be finished off. Williamson sighed to himself, if only this matter was as straightforward as a difficult murder case.

'Straker, there's one slight issue.'

The detective inspector looked at him sharply, instincts on alert. 'I know it won't be straightforward. It's the North. I don't expect the York police to welcome me with open arms.'

'There's that of course. Look, there's no easy to say this so I'll just tell you straight. Sir Richard wants you to make contact with Miss Ada Fawkes.'

'Ada? She's in York?'

Williamson was taken aback by Straker's reaction. The flash of shock in his eyes. He was reminded how little he knew him.

'Yes. We want you to work with her on this.'

'Work with Miss Fawkes?'

'Yes. Is that such a problem?'

Straker slammed his hands on his desk. 'I will not drag her into another investigation. Never. Is that clear enough?'

Williamson had expected some resistance, but he was not prepared for the ferocity of Straker's response. 'I knew you wouldn't want her to work for us again, not after . . . after, well everything, but I thought . . .'

Straker controlled himself. His face became expressionless, his voice steady. He was always a man in full control of his emotions, logically driven. 'We cannot ask this of her. It is wrong. We agreed, we promised that the Paris murder case would be her last one. I won't break our vow.'

'I'm not happy about it myself Straker. But the future of the detective branch is at stake. If we are shut down how many villains will get away with it? What about the victims? Justice for them? Their families. This is for the greater good. This is the only reason I would break a promise Straker. You must solve this York case. You need Miss Fawkes.'

Straker sighed. 'I understand what you are saying. But there's more to this matter. I do not know if she is finished for this life now.'

'It's one last job. You must convince her Straker. I am not exaggerating when I say the future of Scotland Yard depends on you both.'

'I can do it on my own. Leave her be.'

'Straker. You are a good man, a man of integrity,' Williamson gripped his detective's broad shoulder. 'But Ada Fawkes is our one and only crime scene photographer. We need her.'

Chapter Five

◊

The Minster bells ringing seven woke Ada the following morning. She felt so tired after a restless night that she might as well not have gone to bed. Stumbling to her washstand, she lifted a jug and poured water into a bowl. She winced at its coldness, breathing in the scent of lavender as she began to lather soap between her fingers and down her arms. It cost more than a joint of good beef, but never could clean the dark stains from her palms.

She rubbed her skin dry with a towel, scooped a handful of pale yellow ointment from a jar and massaged it into her flesh, the thick grease soothing, softening the whitened ribs of her scars. It smelt vile: chamomile overlying goose fat but it relieved the tautness of her skin, at least for a while.

Downstairs Ada found a more pleasing aroma of ground coffee beans filling the kitchen. She was glad the others were absent, preferring to gather her thoughts in silence. She helped herself to coffee from the enamel pot on the range. It was helpfully strong. In between sips and a few bites of buttered toast, Ada laced her boots tightly over violet cashmere stockings. She left the room, calling down the stone-flagged passageway which led to the garden and to where Camille was sat on a stool at the open back door. She was plucking a brace of pheasant in an apron but still managed to look elegant, Ada noticed, feeling herself dishevelled after her bad night.

Camille looked round and smiled, 'Au revoir, ma chérie. Bonne chance.' In the hallway Ada took her cloak from a row of hooks, swung it around her shoulders and picked up her work bag of soft Italian leather. She'd paid far too much for it in Florence, but she loved it. She was pleased her first appointment was with Jane Auden, an old school friend and her elder brother William, a doctor. It made her day easier somehow. They were coming for a portrait that afternoon. It was a birthday gift for Jane and Ada had been invited to dine with them later. She opened the front door onto Chapter House Street and walked out into the sharpness of the December air.

Snow had fallen in the night and lay thick on the cobbles. It struck her as beautiful, and she wished she had time to photograph the wintry Minster ahead of her. By God though it was cold and despite her silk lined cloak and warmest merino dress, Ada shivered, feeling the morning's bitterness deep in her bones. She crunched through the snow and turned to make her way around the exposed east corner of the Minster. Fresh flurries of snowflakes, caught by the northerly gusts, whipped into her face. Winding her crimson scarf tighter over her mouth and nose, she walked on, head down, turning gratefully into Minstergates, its narrow street and high stone walls giving welcome protection. Hearing the city bells strike eight, she hurried on past her favourite bookshop, for once not lingering to peer in the window or so much as glance at the statue of the goddess Minerva above the shop door, guarding its entrance.

As she moved through the streets Ada thought how different the sights and sounds of the city were with its covering of snow. People were emerging from shops, houses, hurrying to work as usual but the tread of their shoes was muffled and their voices carried further. The clatter of horse and carts was muted. Vagrants and homeless burrowed further into the shadows. Small huddles of children warmed their fingers around the braziers in St Helen's Square.

The city felt too still. There was an air of something about to happen, expectancy. But wasn't that a feeling everyone had when the sky was dark and heavy with snow yet to fall? She shook her head; it was simply a freezing winter's day.

***

Along the road in Silver Street, Police Constable Gage pushed chipped bowls of lumpy porridge through the iron bars. Cold hands; rough, chill-blained, filthy reached out to him, as he worked his way from cell to cell along the stone-flagged corridor on the first floor of the police station. Constable Gage was moving as fast as his broad bulk would allow, ladling the watery slop from pail to bowl, but the clamour, the noise from the cramped lock-ups was worse than usual. 'Help us Bevers,' he bellowed down to his colleague filling in charge sheets at the scuffed front desk. 'There's too many of 'em.' Pale, hungry faces stared out at him. Culprits, waiting to be sent to gaol – or the gallows.

'Nay, I can't. Chief wants summat done. I've to get t' doctor's right away. Ask him if he can do a post-mortem on that dead whore t'auld lamplighter found last week.' Bevers came to the bottom of the stone stairs. The young policeman was the same age as his giant colleague, but at least eight inches shorter in his polished boots. His too-large second hand coat and his slenderness, made him seem smaller still.

Gage shouted back, turning his great head and pushing away the carrot-orange hair which fell in his eyes. 'Who cares? Less of 'em on the streets, the better.'

'Dunno, but I reckon there's summat 'appening,' Bevers said, turning back to the enquiry office, a small liver-coloured room as plain and shabby as the cells.

'As long as it doesn't spoil our Christmas drinks on Friday eh?' yelled Gage, rattling iron bars as he hastily pushed through more porridge.

'Aye, strange though,' said Bevers talking to himself as he put on his greatcoat. 'A dead street walker getting all this attention? York Police spending money? I can't fathom it.'

'Are you still here Bevers? Or is that an old biddy I can hear nattering away?' Chief Constable Nutt, florid-faced, breathing heavily, came into the station. 'Get on with the job.'

Without stopping Nutt carried on past the desk into the short corridor by the stairs leading up to the cells. 'I'll be in my office.'

'Right you are, I'm on my way sir.' Bevers tucked his police-issue rattle carefully into his breast pocket, positioning it to protect his heart from a blade, and pulled his helmet firmly over his hair, straightening the rim.

'Get on with it constable,' Nutt snapped, looking back. The stench of the unwashed above him reached his nostrils. He belched, feeling queasiness in his large stomach. He groped for the knob, opened the door and slammed it shut behind him. Thank God, he thought surveying the comfortable room, satisfyingly warmed by the coal fire. Above the fireplace hung a wooden-framed portrait of the Queen, on another wall, a tattered Ordinance Survey map of the city. Nutt prodded the coals with a poker, settled his body in his arm chair, loosened his waistband, and took a cigar from a box on the table to the right of him. He leaned forward and pulled a spill out of a tin on the hearth, lighting it from the coals. He took a breath, drawing until the tobacco leaves were glowing. The smoke filled the air, masking any lingering odour of over-crowded cells. He took in a mouthful of smoke and shut his eyes.

Three loud knocks disturbed his champagne-induced sleepiness. Nutt jerked, heaved himself up, buttoned his waistband and tugged down his waistcoat. 'Who is it? What do you want?' He moved swiftly to his desk, picked up a pen, dipped it in ink and opened the police ledger.

A brusque voice said. 'It's me. I need to talk to you.'

'For God's sake, Jack, come in then and get it off your chest.'

As the door opened Nutt leaned over his desk and made a show of studying the lines of immaculate entries in the charge book. Oh yes, he was always busy with his impressive statistics. Nutt brought hundreds of cases before the magistrates; disorderly conduct, cluttering the streets, drunkenness, unruly Sabbath behaviour, vagrancy. So what that *The Herald* had nicknamed his men the Petty Crime Police, he didn't care. The city corporation was delighted with his efficiency. His impeccable crime-cracking record had been enough to see off Government attempts to centralise his police force. York could run its own affairs without any interference from London.

'What do you want Jack?'

The sour-faced sergeant smirked as he watched his boss pretending to work. 'They keeping you busy then, Robert?'

Nutt looked up and scowled. 'Just get on with it.'

Stone went across to the fire. He was a thin man of fifty or so with a hardened face, and the cold eyes of a snake. He stretched his arm along the mantelpiece with an air of entitlement. 'Oh you'll want to hear this alright, Robert.'

'Well?' said Nutt, his voice sharp, as he sat heavily in his chair.

'The editor from *The Herald* has been here this morning,' Stone said quietly.

Nutt breathed deeply. 'What the hell does that nosy bastard want?'

'He wants to know about those dead bints – or 'victims' as he calls 'em,' sneered Stone. 'Victims! Are we supposed to feel sorry for 'em or summat? I sent the bastard packing. Silly bugger, says his readers have the right to know what's going on and he needs to print the facts.'

Nutt gripped the arms of his chair. Newspapers, freedom, information: words he preferred not to link together. Nutt had long considered hindering reporters an essential duty of York Police. He had stopped journalists looking at their charge sheets when *The Herald* had begun to highlight, in many articles, the plethora of petty arrests in the city at the expense of serious crime investigation. He had ended daily briefings when editorials began openly criticising his policing methods.

'I doubt we'll be able to hold them off for long,' Stone continued. 'They're persistent buggers. Of course, we'll do what we can, deny everything, refuse access to the crime sheets, we've enough to do without caring what happens to the likes of those women.' Stone looked over to his boss. 'Our old friends at *The Herald* won't find out anything from us.'

Nutt frowned. 'That would be our usual fallback I know, but this is different. We've got to be careful. We need to be seen to be doing something and quickly. It's likely some bloody know-it-all detective will be coming up from London who thinks he's better than us.'

'You want me to handle this?'

'Yes,' Nutt nodded, dropping the end of his cigar into a half-full tea cup.

Stone walked across to the door. He turned and asked quietly. 'What shall I do? How far do you want to go?'

'We need to look like we've got our fingers out for starters. Go and make some arrests. Take Gage. Doesn't matter who, anyone drunk or hanging about the streets. Visible action that's what we need. Let's get some more bodies in the cells.'

'Anything else?' Stone waited.

Nutt pushed his large body up from the chair and walked over to the fire. He stared into the coals for a moment, gathering his thoughts. He spat a globule of phlegm into the fire. For a brief moment the sizzle of frying spit was the only sound. Then Nutt turned and spoke. 'We need to make this go away. We need to get this Butcher nonsense stopped and stopped quickly. End it. Find me someone, anyone. Make it convincing. We need a man to hang.'

Stone, nodded.

A sudden knock on the office door startled them both.

'Who is it?' Nutt snapped.

'It's PC Gage sir.' The policeman bowed his head to step under the doorway and came into the smoky room.

'What is it Gage?' said Nutt drawing himself up.

'Telegram just arrived sir,' the younger man held out a white envelope, tiny in his fist and passed it to Nutt.

51

Nutt waved a hand in dismissal. 'You can go Gage.' He pursed his thin lips as he pulled out the telegram and read the words, frowning.

'What does it say?' Stone asked.

Nutt shook his head.

'What's happened?' asked Stone.

'My dear brother-in-law, the mayor, he's called in favours alright. I thought we had a bit of time but it seems not. This telegram's from Scotland Yard. A detective will be on the night train, getting in tomorrow morning. We're to hold off a post-mortem until he arrives.'

'Why on earth . . .' Stone began.

'I have no idea. But this isn't good.'

A London detective, here, in York, shoving his snout in the trough. Chief Constable Robert Nutt would stop anyone poking into his patch, especially bloody southerners.

CHAPTER SIX

◊

Ada Fawkes looked out of a paned window, at the front of her portrait studio, onto Coney Street. Snow was falling steadily now and swirling flakes settled onto the passers-by, turning overcoats, hats and scarves white. Ada cradled a warm drink in her hands as she watched; bitter, rich cocoa, more popular in York than coffee, and as satisfyingly fortifying.

Her thoughts turned to Jane, who would be arriving soon and she speculated about her friend's birthday supper. She felt ambivalent about the evening ahead. It was her first social event since she had returned to Yorkshire. Part of her was looking forward to the distraction but another dreaded making polite conversation with a group of curious strangers. Men, especially, she reflected, were always perplexed that a woman could work a camera. They wanted to know so much technical detail. And if she mentioned she had lived in Paris, some backed away, slightly shocked, as though she was tempting them personally to sin. Or they pressed her for more titillating detail,

'Do ballet dancers at the Opera really have naked legs?'

She told half-truths about her job and brushed aside delicate enquiries about how she came to have scars on her arm, for she could not hide them even with long evening gloves. She was well-practised in conversation, pleasant and light. She hid her past well.

Ada jumped as the door from the street into her studio creaked open. A blast of chill air swept in with the robust frame of Henry Gowland, the cheesemonger from next door. His red capillary veins like skinny worms crawling over his cheeks, stood out even more in the cold. He rubbed his gloved hands together trying to warm them.

'By heck 'tis a bit nippy today, Miss Fawkes. T'aint kept them from going out gossiping though. Whole city's blethering on about this Butcher of York.'

He blustered on, not ever needing a reply. 'I heard it from the coalman who heard it from a maid up at the Mansion House that the mayor is livid. If the police chief weren't his brother-in-law he'd have him strung up.'

Only the jangle of his shop bell stopped him. Eager not to miss a customer, he moved his bulk surprisingly quickly, calling back through the open doorway, 'Aye, tell Madame Defoe that stinking foreign cheese she likes is here now, bugger knows why, nowt wrong with a nice bit of Wensleydale. Anyway, tell her she'll get a good discount from me.'

Ada drained her cup and turned back to her work. She looked around at what still had to be done. Very little – the panelled room was freshly painted, the waxed oak floor mopped clean, oriental rugs brushed and her cherry-wood desk polished to a gleam. On either side of the large stone fireplace hung the oil paintings purchased for a song from young artists she had known in Paris. There was just time to finish her Yule-themed decorations in the two windows. Ada picked up a basket of holly, cut from her walled garden, cleared her pens and inkwell to one side of her desk and set it down. She gathered handfuls of stems together, snipping the ends with scissors. Her decorated windows were already catching the eyes of shoppers. She had used wire to cluster together rosemary, bay laurel, ivy, yew. To these arrangements she had strung pinecones, dampened with starch-water and dusted with flour to look like a pretty sprinkling of snow. For the finishing touches she entwined the trimmed, red-berried holly through the evergreens and added scarlet ribbons to finish. It was customary for shops to shut at midday, but Ada wanted to check everything was ready in her first-floor studio. Besides Jane and her brother could only come in the lunch hour when the doctor took a break from the practice he ran from their home. She tidied her desk and threw the bits of holly leaves and fallen berries she gathered into the fire, where they spat and crackled. She crossed the room to the wooden stairs at the back. At the top, she walked through open double doors into her long, high-ceilinged photography studio. It was different from the elegantly styled room below; plainer, brighter, more utilitarian. Four, tall, small-paned windows flooded the space with light, even on such a December day. On the far wall hung a huge painted backdrop; a winter landscape scene. So dramatic that it might have been painted for a London theatre stage.

The camera standing before the backdrop was ready, but Ada tightened her tripod stand again, double-checking it was secure. Satisfied she straightened up just as the small carriage clock on the downstairs mantelpiece chimed one, and at the same time she heard the studio door creak as it was thrown open.

'Hello, Ada, it's us,' a woman's voice called out.

Jane.

Ada hurried quickly to the stairs, smoothing her untidy hair. She was not prepared for the striking-looking man who was standing by the fire, watching her descent. Jane's brother William was not quite as she remembered him. She met his direct gaze and he smiled the same warm smile as his sister. She noticed his eyes were the same grey-blue and though his hair was fairer, you would have known them for siblings. Jane was looking curiously around the room as she untied the ribbon of her plain dark hat.

'Ada my dear! What a change. You've been so busy. No wonder we haven't had time to meet properly yet.'

'Many happy returns Jane,' said Ada reaching the bottom of the stairs and holding out her hands to her friend. She kissed Jane on her cold cheek. 'I hope you've had a lovely day so far.'

Jane nodded at her brother. 'I've been quite spoilt. William bought me the most exquisite shawl.'

Ada turned to him. 'It's good to see you after all this time Dr Auden.'

'You too Miss Fawkes. But please call me William. We have known each other for so long, even if it has been years since we met. I would have recognised you anywhere though. You've hardly changed at all.'

'It has been a long time,' Ada agreed.

'And do you find me much changed?' He smiled again, his eyes crinkling at the corners.

She scrutinized him. He was a little older than her and the years had been kind to him. If anything the lines on his forehead added distinction to his pleasing looks. His fair hair was well-cut and his teeth, she noticed, were white and even. She did not say any of this. 'Not at all, I would have recognised you too.'

'Your studio is beautiful. I love your decorations,' said Jane looking at the window displays.

'It's splendid,' agreed William, 'and I was very much admiring those paintings by the fire.'

Ada smiled. 'I'm pleased you like them. I was fortunate enough to be introduced to the artist. He painted my friend Camille while he was a pupil at the studio of Couture and she took me to meet him. I very much admired his work and so I bought several of his paintings. He was relatively unknown then. He has become quite famous in France now but very controversial.'

'What's his name?' William peered at the black initials.

'Manet. Édouard Manet,' said Ada taking their overcoats and hats.

'I wish I had more time to study art,' said Jane. 'But we are so busy with the medical practice and research.'

'You've always been dedicated to your work, and I admire you for it.' Ada carried the coats over to a small closet at the back of the room, reflecting as she did so that she had known Jane Auden nearly twenty-five years. Back then, Jane's father had been the new village doctor and the young women had been drawn together as they'd endured village fêtes at the parish church, afternoons of serving tea and scones, made bearable by their mutual love of reading. They'd discussed books endlessly. Jane had devoured Dickens as keenly as Ada. William had been studying at Cambridge then and had gone on to train at St Guy's Hospital in London, so she had not known him very well. Later the Auden family had moved to York, their father's hometown and where he thought he could do much good among the poor. Tragically he had died from the cholera that was so common in his patients.

The women had written over the ensuing years, and by the time Ada moved to York earlier in the year, William had returned to the North too and set up a medical practice with Jane at their home in Marygate. William, like many doctors, also worked voluntarily at the York Lunatic Asylum. Jane, Ada knew, once longed to be a doctor herself, but the law forbade women qualifying and so she helped her brother, mixing medicines, researching cures. It was one of the few blessings of them all being back, Ada thought, for now she and Jane could renew their long-standing friendship.

'Come up to the studio, everything is ready.' Ada led them up the stairs. She looked at their curious faces as they entered the room and could read their surprise at its bright, modern aspect; translucent muslin drapes, white-painted walls, the palest limed floor. Jane laughed out loud when she saw the backdrop Ada had painted. A perfect winter scene; crimson-breasted robins, a red bushy-tailed squirrel and yellow-beaked blackbirds perched on a picket fence, a red-berried holly bush and fir tree branches layered with snow, in the distance a black timber-framed house.

'It's lovely, Ada,' said Jane. 'You are clever. You're going to do so well. This is so different for York.'

'Come on then. I've got your costume ready,' said Ada.

'Oh no. I couldn't,' said Jane, looking down at her sober black dress.

'Go on, Jane,' urged William. 'You should. I want you to feel special.'

Ada thought how kind and thoughtful he was, rather different to her own brother Harry. 'Yes, come on Jane. Please, William, take a seat and make yourself comfortable.' She gestured to a tawny-brown leather chair by the fire.

There was a closed door on the back wall in the far corner of the room to which Ada led Jane. 'You can change in there. It's the old store cupboard which I've made into a dressing area.' Ada turned the handle and ushered her protesting friend through. 'You can hang your clothes on the hook there and there's a brush on the table and powder.' Glowing lamps, reflected in the full-length mirror, made the room bright.

'Would you like me to help you?' asked Ada.

'No thank you. Go and talk to William. He was so looking forward to meeting you again.'

Ada shut the door behind her and turned round. William was on his feet, looking at her camera with interest. 'I'm delighted to have the chance to watch you work Miss Fawkes.'

'Ada, please.'

'Ada it is then. I'm curious. How do you produce your photographs? They are so different.'

Ada began to explain how she experimented with light to achieve an intimacy in her portraits and avoid them looking one-dimensional when Jane opened the door and stepped into the studio wearing a cloak trimmed with white fur and holding a matching muff.

'I feel ridiculous,' she said.

'You look very well, Jane,' William smiled at his sister.

'Stand over here Jane. Like this.' Ada took up a pose in front of the backdrop, turning her body to the side, lifting her chin and looking slightly over her shoulder towards the camera.'

Jane tried to copy her.

'Hold your head higher Jane. Look straight at the camera.'

'I feel foolish,' said Jane.

Ada moved behind her camera.

'Do not speak, do not move and do not complain,' Ada warned. She was a tyrant to her clients, forcing them to pose completely still, until their muscles screamed in agony. She pressed the button.

Seven minutes went by.

'That's it,' she said at last. Jane's slender body sagged, and she rubbed her aching arms. Her brother laughed. For Ada, this was the beginning of a long process. As soon as they had left, with a stern reminder not to be late that evening, she locked the studio door.

The image must be developed immediately.

Her dark room was the old coal shed in the small backyard. She hurried there and shut the door behind her, moving carefully around her table of trays and chemicals, in the dim light of a single half-shuttered oil lamp. Ada took the glass plate from her camera and slid it out of its case. With steady hands, she poured potassium cyanide evenly over the exposure, grimacing as she caught the strong smell of bitter almonds. After the negative had been fixed with sodium thiosulphate, she went outside and ran ice-cold water over the plate from the yard tap, rinsing and rinsing until her hands were red and numb. Back inside she held the glass to dry in front of a small cast iron stove, until it was as hot as her skin could bear. With practised ease, she poured over varnish for protection. Now she could print the proofs. The process was slow work. More than once Ada had to stop and plunge her hands into a bucket of water as the chemicals stung her skin. Her steady stream of cursing was surprisingly Anglo-Saxon in its coarseness.

When she finally finished it had grown dark. Soaked to her undergarments now, she was glad to leave the darkroom and return to her studio. Wrapping up the photographs ready to give to Jane later, she was surprised to realise that she was looking forward to the evening. Dr Auden, she admitted to herself, added an unexpected dash of interest.

Ada closed the studio door, locked it and turned to walk down the dark street. Suddenly she felt very cold, her damp clothes were clingy and uncomfortable, the walk home seemed too long. She was struck by how quiet the city sounded, the familiar evening bustle was subdued and there was an unaccustomed emptiness to the streets. It spooked her. Now, thoughts of a killer, of the three dead women, came to her mind. As she reached St Helen's Square, she saw the shop girls were not lingering over the pink and white sugar mice in the chocolate shop window and housemaids, on last-minute shopping errands, had not stayed to gossip on the corner. The homeless were still there, of course, huddled in the darkened doorways and street walkers were emerging like shadows from the ginnels. As she turned down Stonegate Ada caught her breath. Through the gloom, deepened by the overhanging eaves of the old black-timbered buildings, she saw a shadow come closer. It sharpened into a silhouette and then into an outline of a human figure. A broad-shouldered man was coming swiftly towards her. She glanced round, but no one was near. He stepped into her path and now his features were clear.

A familiar voice spoke softly, 'I thought I would walk you home.'

'Thank you,' she said to Thomas Bell, more relieved than she cared to admit.

CHAPTER SEVEN

◊

It was a mistake to have lain down. Her bed felt too soft, too warm, too comfortable. The longing to stay, to pull the covers high and shut out the world, was deep. The last thing Ada wanted was to go out into the raw-cold night again.

But the firm knock at the bedroom door came. Ada forced herself up as Camille pushed open the door, a misted long-stemmed glass in her hand, for she believed there was no problem that wine would not ease. Ada took the drink and was glad of it.

'Let's begin,' said Camille.

At her dressing table, Ada began pulling the pins out of her hair, its weight tumbling heavily onto her bare shoulders. She did not gaze long at herself in the cheval glass for she was wearing an open-necked, loose silk robe, and though she had grown accepting of the smooth, pale scars which marked her left collar bone and shoulder as well as her hands, she did not always want to dwell on them. Ada looked instead to Camille's reflection as she gathered up a comb and brush from the table-top and stood behind her.

'Keep still now,' Camille ordered, frowning at the thick mass of auburn-gold hair that she must tame into respectable neatness.

Ada braced herself. Within seconds her scalp felt like it was on fire as her hair was scraped, pulled and dragged into order.

'Are you looking forward to this evening?' Camille asked, deftly beginning to twist and twine a length of hair with her hands as though she was curling rope. 'Monsieur Auden is very charming. Non?'

Ada smiled. He was, she thought to herself, intelligent, and yes, attractive, but at her age and with her past, all that was impossible.

'He was always very nice,' she replied choosing her words carefully for Camille's shrewd eyes were watching her own.

But she could see the reflection of her viridian green silk dress. It hung from the wardrobe door, shimmering in the lamplight. It was cut low, closely fitting and suited her well. She was pleased with her choice.

***

Thomas was already waiting as Ada opened the front door a few minutes past seven o'clock. In the street, there was a small open carriage drawn by a black horse, blowing pearly breath into the frosty night air. Thomas was bundled up in his heavy overcoat and his gloved hands loosely held the reins. With a warm greeting he held out a hand to Ada, now wrapped warmly in a wine-red velvet cloak, and pulled her up beside him.

'You look very fine indeed,' smiled Thomas, tucking a heavy plaid blanket over her knees.

'Thank you. I've not dressed up for such a long time it feels strange,' she said and touched the emerald necklace, all that she had left of her mother's jewellery, glinting at her slender white throat.

The city went by. The carriage soon covered the short distance around the cathedral, along High Petergate and under the archway of Bootham Bar, the time long gone, thankfully, when the spiked heads of traitors dripped blood on people passing below. Minutes later, they were following the course of the ancient stone wall of St Mary's Abbey. Ada loved this part of the old city, all the more, because Dickens wrote of the abbey in *Nicholas Nickleby* which she and her mother had enjoyed reading so much.

They were close to the river now and on a quiet road of fine houses; some tall, some wide, red-bricked or white-painted, Thomas reined in the horse outside the grandest of them all. At the sound of the jingling bridle, the imposing double-front door swiftly opened, and a shaft of bright light spilled out, illuminating the front path swept immaculately clean of snow.

Ada climbed the steps leading up to the four-story house and was shown indoors by a shy young maid in a neat dark dress and spotless apron. Silently she took Ada's cloak and showed her, through the lofty hallway, into a softly lit pretty drawing room. Within seconds Jane was at her side, smiling, embracing her.

'Jane, you look lovely,' said Ada, stepping back to look at her friend. Jane wore a dress of silver-grey silk and her hair, usually severe and pulled close to her head, hung in soft, loose curls.

'Thank you. I feel a little ostentatious, you know me, but William insisted I have a gown that wasn't black. Now come and meet everyone.' Jane took her arm and led her further into the large, high-ceilinged room. The other guests, a dozen or so, were sat on comfortable sofas and ottomans or stood gathered around an ornate marble fireplace, basking in the heat of a blazing fire and talking in low voices. William excused himself from the young, sandy-haired vicar, who was stood at his side and approached them. He gave a half bow, taking Ada's crimson silk-gloved hand.

'You look delightful, Miss Fawkes if you will permit me to say so.'

'Good evening, William and thank you,' said Ada with a warm smile.

'Oh, William would you mind introducing Ada to everyone. I must see all is ready in the dining room.' Jane looked at her friend. 'Please excuse me a moment.'

William tucked her hand through his arm. 'Come and say hello to my aunt and uncle. They have been looking forward to seeing you again.'

They made their way across the room to where a white-haired couple, older than the other guests, sat in comfortable easy chairs at the fireside, with small glasses of sweet sherry.

'You remember my aunt and uncle Mr and Mrs Auden,' said William.

'Yes, of course,' she smiled warmly at the couple who must have been seventy or so. 'You came to tea with my mother once during a visit to stay with William's father I recall.'

Mrs Auden, matronly and stout, dressed in a dark silk of another age asked after Ada's brother Harry and his wife Charlotte, who they had last met, 'oh so many years ago now'. Mr Auden, a shrunken bespectacled man, who disliked dining out, especially so late, sipped his drink and let his wife talk. Ada replied politely to the many questions, responding that her family was in good health, living contently in the country with their two children. She chose her words carefully: 'No I haven't seen them for a while. My sister-in-law is always so busy, I don't like to add to her burdens with a visit.'

As they talked of the old days, Ada caught Mrs Auden looking up and shooting a speculative glance at her and her nephew.

'William! Mr and Mrs Auden! What a pleasure to see you all.' A tall, distinguished figure costumed in black was approaching them with the confident air of one who is used to being well-received.

'Good evening, Reverend,' said Mrs Auden, fluttering a feathered fan that had been fashionable in her younger days.

'Allow me to introduce the Reverend Charles Lindley,' said William turning to Ada. 'Miss Ada Fawkes. Miss Fawkes has just today opened a very fashionable new portrait studio on Coney Street.'

Almost a beat too late, Reverend Lindley gestured briefly to his wife, a round-faced, portly woman, who was stood two paces behind him. 'Mrs Lindley.' He turned round again to Ada leaving his wife to begin a rather stilted conversation with the elderly Audens.

'It's my pleasure to make your acquaintance Miss Fawkes. What a coincidence. Can you guess who was baptised at my church, St Michael le Belfrey?' teased Reverend Lindley, his pale eyes riveted on Ada's face as she shook her head. 'Your namesake! Fawkes, Guy Fawkes. April 16th, 1570. You see we have so many tourists asking, that I know the date by heart. You must allow me to show you the register personally. I would be honoured.'

Ada smiled and was thinking of a polite reply, so it came as a relief to her to see a girl of about sixteen approach with a silver tray of coupe glasses. William thanked the maid and served the drinks.

'So what brings you to York, Miss Fawkes?' asked Mrs Lindley with curiosity as they sipped champagne of fine quality.

Ada briefly explained and then they all had so many questions. Ada talked lightly and amusingly about her travels and photography. Some years before she had decided to tour Europe she began. Ada let her eyes twinkle and a smile flit across her mouth to highlight her frivolity for she was well-practised in this whitewashing of her life. She mentioned famous people she had photographed in Paris and spoke of Queen Victoria and Albert and their fascination with photography which made it so much the thing. Bitter experience had taught her that as long as her career appeared as a respectable amateur hobby, she was no threat. Only a few people knew what she really did.

Jane now returned bringing with her a pleasant-looking younger couple. 'Ada, have you met Edward Atkinson, the architect and his wife?' She indicated an elegantly dressed man, quite dashing and on his arm, a pretty, pink-cheeked woman, clearly expecting.

Ada smiled at them. 'Why yes. Mr Atkinson has requested that I take some photographs of his work. I'm pleased to see you again Mr Atkinson.' Even before she reached out to shake hands Ada could smell his strong cologne.

'I'm delighted to see you again, Miss Fawkes. Allow me to introduce Lydia my wife,' said Edward. Ada noticed how courteous he seemed to his dark-haired wife as his arm encircled her wide waist protectively.

'I've heard much about you, Miss Fawkes, you must be so very clever,' said Lydia smiling warmly.

They only had time to exchange the briefest of pleasantries when Jane and William's widowed neighbour Richard Fox, a soldierly-looking man with long whiskers, joined them, 'Perhaps you would be interested in a commission, to photograph our racehorses, Miss Fawkes? I'm clerk at the Knavesmire. It would be special indeed to have our winning horses immortalised. What a fascinating science? Or should I call it an art?'

'That is a big question,' she laughed.

Reverend Lindley, used to being listened to, was soon in full flow again about his church visitors. 'They will be very important to all of us in York for some time to come. Think of it, Mr Fox, so many people coming to your horse races, so many people visiting our ancient buildings, Miss Fawkes. And they will want photographs of the attractions. I believe tourists could provide many jobs for the poor in the years ahead.'

'I hope so,' agreed William, 'for we do not have the industries of Halifax, Bradford or Leeds. There are no great mills or factories. York has been left behind in the industrial revolution. There is no work. I see the results every day, the sick and the poor perishing miserably in hospitals and workhouses. We do what we can with our philanthropy and societies. But it would be a godsend if there were more jobs.'

A gong sounded loudly and the guests, led by William, began to flow out to the black and white tiled hallway and through into the dining room, lit with shining splendour. Blazing wax candles cast a lustre on the magnificent silver, glass and china covering the long, polished mahogany table; a well-tended fire burning in the grate added its golden glow.

They flocked in, admiring the room. Worsted sage green damask curtains shut out the raw, wintry night. Sweet-scented white lilies perfumed the air, mingling with a pleasant earthy wood smoke from the roaring fire. There was no food on the table yet, unless one counted bowls of medjool dates, russet apples and brown cobnuts. In the doorway, on her husband's arm, the elder Mrs Auden looked at the table and paused, a trace of disapproval, creating deep lines around her down-turned small mouth.

Ada, seeing the look, made a point of complimenting Jane, who was hovering, waiting for all her guests to assemble.

'It is pretty, isn't it? William and I much prefer dining like this. I'm not sure everyone approves though,' whispered Jane glancing over at her unsmiling relatives. 'Most of York still prefers to dine à la française of course, but we like this new way.'

Ada agreed, she thought serving meals course by course, rather than having every dish laid out at once on the table at once, much easier on the digestion.

'I think our aunt and uncle believe we are getting above our-selves since we lived in London but fashions change.'

'Well it is very daring for Yorkshire,' laughed Ada.

Guests were ushered gently into their velvet-padded chairs and Ada was shown to her seat on William's left at one end of the oval table. The Reverend Lindley's eyes gleamed with satis-faction as he sat down on her other side.

Two white-gloved servants with decanters began pouring white wine into sparkling crystal glasses. Around the table talk grew louder for drink was now loosening tongues and laugh-ter. Ada surveyed the guests. Opposite her was Dr Henry Scull whom she been introduced to earlier. He was a colleague and friend of Dr Auden's from the Lunatic Asylum and they were of a similar age. She thought he'd seemed pleasant enough, but a coolness in his manner, the set of his chin, his full lips gave him an air of arrogance. Ada didn't know yet whether she liked him though he was clearly an intelligent man.

Beside her William tapped on his glass with his knife and the room fell silent. He rose to his feet.

'Thank you all for coming tonight to help us celebrate this special occasion. I would like to take this chance to say I am lucky to have such a sister, so loyal and dedicated to our work. May I offer a toast, to Jane? Many happy returns, Jane.' William raised his wine towards his sister at the opposite end of the table. The guests stood too and lifted their glasses.

'May this year bring you all the success that you wish for and that you deserve.' He smiled and looked at her over the rim of his glass as he sipped.

'Thank you, William. Here's to dreams coming true.' Jane replied.

'Happy Birthday,' echoed everyone as two maids, curls of stiff white ribbon in their neat hair, swept into the room bearing two silver bowlfuls of caviar. There were murmurs of pleasure up and down the table.

'Shall I say grace?' Reverend Lindley bowed his head in brief prayer, followed by murmurs of 'amen' from the guests before they sat down again and began to help themselves to spoonfuls of the black, shiny caviar in the middle of the table and crisp, toasted triangles of bread.

'How do you find the caviar aunt?' enquired Jane, casting a glance at her emptied plate.

'I have to admit it's very nice,' she replied grudgingly.

'Yes, we are very lucky here to have things so well ordered. It has surprised me to see so much poverty in York.'

Mrs Auden allowed a servant to fill her drained glass with sauternes. 'Of course the main cause of poverty is drink,' she said without irony. 'Some people don't want to work, they are in the dramshops all day long, drinking, all of them, men, women, children alike.'

Her husband nodded vigorously. 'It's not safe to walk some streets for one gets accosted by one dishevelled lady or another. It's disgraceful.'

Dr Scull leaned over the table to disagree. 'Some in this city argue that it is the pestilent conditions here in streets like Water Lanes, the Bedern as well as high unemployment that cause the poor to seek comfort in drink, not the other way round. Quakers like Mr Rowntree, Mr Tuke are sharing these ideas and seeking to change the overcrowded squalor the poor live in as well as persuading them to drink their cocoa instead of liquor.' Ada's opinion of Dr Scull improved.

'No, it's a vice, a choice that these women make. They prefer slovenliness, dirt and ease to labour. A bar of soap doesn't cost that much, does it?' asked Mrs Auden righteously. 'They want gin more than anything. What think you, Reverend Turner?'

'Any woman can become awakened to her sinful state; a brand plucked from burning. Even when there seems no return for those unfortunates fallen so far from grace,' as he spoke his thin, clean-shaven face became animated.

'Quite so, Reverend Turner,' Mrs Auden nodded vigorously. She was about to reply when Jane discreetly indicated for the next course to be laid on the table; a large fillet of wild salmon.

'The fact is we all must do what we can. Jane and I have had the time to become involved in many charities since we moved back,' said William when everyone had been served.

'Yes, indeed we have much interest in helping the poor and sick and in the rescue and reform of fallen women,' said Jane. 'We are on the committees of the Refuge and the Ragged School.'

Ada said nothing, as far as she could tell, charity work was like putting a small rag on a great, gaping wound of desperation.

'There's much poverty here, but at least we haven't the troubles of Liverpool and the Lancashire cities, the cotton famines are causing much suffering,' another guest said. 'The American Civil War is bankrupting the industry with its blockades. The government's doing nothing, sitting on the fence.'

'As far as I'm concerned the Americans can do what they like in their own country, it's not for us to interfere,' said the elder Mr Auden.

'The states of the North have got a point though and some of our mill workers and owners support freedom for Southern slaves, even as they starve,' said William.

'I remember we had one of those Othello chaps here some years ago,' said Mrs Auden. 'A very rousing speaker, he was. An escaped slave, most entertaining and he packed the Assembly Rooms.'

The topics moved on through the courses; leg of lamb, braised celery, wild duck, watercress and pineapple ice cream.

Jane and William have been so generous, Ada thought, she felt fortunate that they were living in York now.

'Do you know much of York's past?' Reverend Lindley interrupted her musings.

'I hope to learn more. It's fascinating to think of the layers of history in these streets,' Ada replied.

Turning from a work conversation with Dr Scull, William caught her remarks.

'I agree with you,' said the doctor, his blue eyes looking straight into hers. 'And every building has many stories. Take the abbey over the wall, for instance. Did you know that Henry VIII's sister, Margaret Tudor, stayed there twice on her way from Scotland to see her brother in London? Then he destroyed it. Maybe she told him how uncommonly wealthy it was.'

Ada laughed, enjoying their common interest. 'I plan to take many photographs of historical sites around Yorkshire, starting in the Spring when the weather improves. I have always taken photographs of the places I have lived. Actually, you may be interested to know that the Yorkshire Philosophical Society has engaged me to give a talk at the museum this week. The secretary is my neighbour and he approached me. I will be showing my photographs from my travels.'

'That sounds most interesting. Don't you agree gentlemen?' said William

'Yes indeed I do, and once our Lord Mayor hears of you, no doubt you will be asked to the Mansion House,' said Dr Scull. 'I don't think George Brass will be able to resist a chance to immortalise himself in black and white. And no doubt he will pay for the pleasure with corporation money.'

'Aye his fancy Twelfth Night Ball and that new bridge by the ferry crossing is costing a pretty penny. He's one of the richest men in England, but I don't imagine he's paying for that himself. He says it's all about making York wealthy again, but I reckon it's all about his knighthood,' someone said wryly.

'You can't say that,' laughed Dr Scull. 'You'll be locked up in the Castle.'

'Say what you like, York Corporation may be wanting, but at least our Lord Mayor speaks up for us right-minded folk.

George Brass wants this city to do well. He won't put up with any outside meddling,' said old Mr Auden.

Ever the charming hostess, Jane headed off this topic and changed to a more neutral subject. 'Is everyone going to the Minster carol service on Christmas Eve?'

'Of course,' murmurs of agreement from around the table.

'I do love proper occasions,' said Mrs Auden. 'It's such a pleasure to be on the decorating committee. We are arranging the fresh greenery tomorrow. It always looks so beautiful.' She turned to Ada. 'Did you know, Miss Fawkes, that we are the only church in the country to allow pagan mistletoe inside our walls? I gather much greenery from my niece's garden. She is a very keen gardener, many unusual plants.'

'I am looking forward to seeing the decorations,' replied Ada.

The guests moved to the drawing room for coffee, madeira and cognac. Cosy with a crackling log fire, over-full guests settled into comfortable armchairs and sofas. Closer together, the ladies could now whisper, deliciously scaring themselves as though hearing a ghost story read out loud from a weekly magazine while safe by the fire. Was the Butcher of York a bogeyman or real flesh and blood? Was any respectable woman safe? Was this a vengeance wreaked on the immoral?

Jane, who had been pouring coffee, brought over the tray of cups and saucers.

'Enough of that horrible talk on my birthday,' she said, overhearing them. 'I'm certain nothing will happen to us. We are not in danger.'

***

At midnight, goodbyes and thank yous said, Ada Fawkes stepped out into the frosty night air, enjoying its cold bite after the rich meal and stuffy warmth of the crowded drawing room. Thomas had returned and climbed down from the carriage and was rubbing the smooth head of the black horse. He smiled when he saw her and put out his strong, steady hand to help her climb up. 'Come on lass, be quick, it's starting to snow again.' He swung himself up on the seat beside her and took up the reins.

At the flick of leather, the horse trotted forwards. The snow was building implacably so that the horseshoes and carriage wheels made deep fresh tracks down Marygate. Layers of snow muted hooves to a soft pleasing crunch and they rode quietly by St Mary's Tower, turning right to pass back under the medieval gateway in the walls. As they did so, the small swaying carriage lantern cast strange flickering beams of light onto the dark stone arch around and above them and lit their entry into the hushed narrow street of Low Petergate. As they approached the heart of the city, the clouds that had masked the full moon shifted and a cold light shone over the Minster, towering over them, ghostly in the winter shadows.

CHAPTER EIGHT

◊

Swirls of steam, smells of coke and sounds of screeching brakes filled the station as the heavy locomotive rumbled alongside platform three. 'York. This is York,' shouted the guard. Detective Inspector Samuel Straker looked out of the small dirty window over the scurrying porters and waiting crowds, rubbing one hand over his jaw. It was quarter past nine in the morning, he badly needed a shave and a hot bath, but there was no chance of either. Instead he combed his fingers through curling, black hair, smoothing it down. His jacket, which fitted tightly over his broad shoulders, was given a cursory straightening. It was the best he could do.

The night train from London had barely stopped when he leant out, grasped the brass handle and opened the door of the first class compartment. Turning up the collar of his heavy overcoat, he stepped down and strode swiftly, carrying his leather hinged bag with ease through the iron and glass train shed and outside. He briefly stood under the shelter of the station's Italianate facade, gathering his bearings. He took a deep breath, glad of fresh air, and inhaled the bitter northern cold. Facing him was Tanner Row busy with carriages and travellers picking their way through falling snow. He looked about him and saw what he needed, a line of waiting Hansom cabs, horses stamping impatiently, bridles jangling. He approached the first one. 'St Leonard's Place quick as you can please.'

The heavily-muffled driver, red-rimmed eyes visible through a slit between his muffler and cloth cap nodded once.

Straker swung his bag in the cab, climbed up quickly and pulled the folded wooden doors across.

'Bit parky today,' the driver said.

Straker hardly needed that spelling out, it seemed at least twenty degrees colder up in the North. More than ever, he wanted to sort this job as quickly as possible and get back to London. But, clattering along Hudson Street and onto Micklegate, Straker looked out at the streets with curiosity, for he'd had little chance to travel to northern cities. He was whirled along a narrow street, following the course of the wide, grey river, past dingy warehouses and entrances to dreary red brick terraces. Between lanes running down to the water's edge, he caught glimpses of tall masts of sailing barges. The road opened out and the driver whipped the horse over Ouse Bridge. He caught the fetid smell of the river, around which the city had grown, as the cab pulled around over-loaded carts of turnips, wagons of squealing pigs, honking baskets of grey geese piled into handcarts, heading for the city's markets. On past half-timbered irregular houses, all small or tall and impossibly narrow. Between buildings, he glimpsed passages leading to God knows what or where, warrens of filthy stews. Ideal for criminals, he mused. This, he imagined, was how England in the Middle Ages might have looked, downright awful.

'Stranger here then?' shouted the cabbie through the trap door in the roof. 'Tha's from London then?'

The detective muttered something non-committal.

'Aye York's a grand city,' the driver went on from his perch. 'We've got everything we want. Mind you I've never been ta London, never been further than Tadcaster. Never seen the point missen.'

Straker sighed for he had thought London cabbies took the prize for being know-it-alls.

'Aye, ah've lived ere all my life and I'm going to tell tha summat, we've seen off Romans, Vikings, Lancastrians and no one gets one t'ower us, especially southerners. God's own country this is.'

Straker chose not to reply. His misgivings were rising again though he had to admit, as they rattled past, the sight of the famous Gothic Minster was even more impressive than he had expected.

'Ere we are then,' said the cabbie, tugging on the reins of his old brown horse. 'Woah girl. Aye the corporation knocked down a stretch of the old city walls to build these big houses. Tis alright for some.'

St Leonard's Place, a crescent row of neo-classical splendour, was certainly out of the budget of most policemen Straker reflected as he climbed from the cab and looked along the elegant curving terrace. He paid the driver the requested coins, grateful to cut off his blabbering. He could see a flicker of interest in the driver's rheumy eyes, no doubt wondering what a Londoner was doing, this hour, at number three, the home of York's chief constable.

Straker turned, lifted the brass knocker on the door of the grandest of them all and banged heavily – three times.

***

The black door opened and a small housemaid looked out at him timidly. He could see her mouth drop open a little at the sight of him. It wasn't the first time he had noticed such a reaction, he was taller, broader, and he suspected sterner-faced, than many men.

'Good morning, miss. The chief constable is expecting me,' Straker said, smiling to ease her shyness.

She flushed a little, grinned back and led him through the generously proportioned hallway into a book-lined study with a very welcoming fire. She closed the door quietly behind her and Straker walked to the shelves to look at the volumes while he waited. They looked immaculate, as if they had never been read. Footsteps came hurrying through the hallway and he could hear a woman's shrill voice, then a door slamming. Moments later Chief Constable Nutt came in, wiping toast crumbs from his mouth, with a handkerchief.

'Good, you're on time Straker,' he said curtly, pushing the cotton kerchief into his trouser pocket. 'This is a matter of urgency, so I needed to have this meeting as soon as you arrived, here, in private.'

Nutt waved the larger man to a low, hard wooden seat and sat himself in his great carver chair behind his vast desk.

'How do you intend to sort this mess?' demanded Nutt with no further pleasantries.

'All I know so far, from my briefing in London, is that a young woman's body was found a few days ago down by the river with peculiar slash marks across her stomach. And that she may be the third victim of a killer who has possibly murdered before in October and August. It looks . . .'

A sharp knock at the study door made Straker pause. He did not want the young housemaid to overhear this conversation.

'What do you want?' called out Nutt.

She opened the door slightly.

'What is it now, Ellen?'

'Mistress has taken ill again. She's asking for the doctor.'

'The usual complaint?' sighed Nutt.

'Yes sir.'

The police chief fluttered a podgy hand to dismiss her. 'Later, I'll sort it out later. Best she keeps to her room, resting.'

The maid shut the door quietly, but not before both men heard cries from somewhere deep in the house. Straker watched Nutt's face flush with anger.

'Now then, Straker let's get to it,' Nutt continued quickly. 'You being here is a waste of all our time. You've been sent up on a fool's errand. So understand this. We are a respectable town and a comfortable town, if you get my drift. There's no unpleasantness here and no trouble-makers, well apart from the Irish immigrants. Law and order, that's what we do well here. We keep a tight lid on trouble. It might not be how you do it down there, but it's our way. I've been chief constable here for more than fifteen years and I know this place inside out and let me tell you straight, there's no three-fold murderer in our midst.'

Straker's expression revealed nothing of his thoughts.

'So a few dead women turn up, that's no mystery. Grubby prostitutes, dirty whores and good riddance to 'em. You're a man of experience Straker, been in Paris I hear, so you understand how it is,' Nutt smirked. 'And it's obvious what's happened here; a fellow has too much drink, bitch tries to steal his wallet, he loses his temper and wallop. Who can blame him? But those leeches, who call themselves reporters, are whipping up rumours that a killer's running amok and every woman is in danger. Butcher of York? It's bloody nonsense! But that hasn't stopped every penny rag up and down the country making merry with wild rumours. And all because daft lonely old buggers like that ferryman want some attention.'

From across the desk Straker watched Nutt pull out his hankie again and dab spittle from the corners of his mouth.

Nutt's face reddened further. 'And what do you think has happened now? Folks are starting to stay away from York that's what and let me tell you we need the tourists; they're our bread and butter. The mayor's furious. He's threatening to shut *The Herald* down, but the damage is done. People don't want to come here. He's had cancellations for his Twelfth Night Ball, left, right and centre. Those dead whores are going to cost us thousands of guineas.'

Nutt paused for breath.

Straker said with a level tone. 'It's all the same to me, sir, whether the victims are street walkers, shop girls or society ladies. Or indeed, whether the mayor's ball goes ahead or not. My job is to look at the facts and get to the truth.'

The police chief's face hardened. 'I believe in plain speaking Straker. I'm not afraid to say this; I don't want you in my city. But I'll tell you this for nowt too. You're here now so you better sort it. This needs to go away.'

Straker raised his dark eyebrows, but said nothing.

Discomforted the police chief cleared his throat. 'Anyway there it is. So let's just get this charade over with. I've been told you want to see the body the lamplighter found by the river last week and attend the post-mortem. That's a waste of time for a start. And if you're asking me, it's not police business anyhow.'

The detective felt his fists clench in frustration and firmly spread his fingers over his thighs. 'Still, I shall be there. And, what of the other two women? Were there post-mortems for them?'

'Good God man, no. Way too expensive. They were buried in the usual way. Each parish buries its paupers once a week and has to pay for the privilege so it's a cheap funeral. They keep any bodies that turn up until Tuesdays and then cart the lot to the cemetery.'

'Did you see them though? Did you examine the remains?'

'No. It wasn't worth the bother. Like I said before, whores, strong drink, bit of a fight; it's a regular occurrence here. The old men who found those corpses might have had a good gawp, but the bodies would have been dealt with, wrapped up in shrouds, taken away and that's that . . . usually.'

'So to be clear, the police didn't examine the bodies and didn't talk to any witnesses, no one interviewed the ferryman who found the body in the river in August or the boatman who found a second body on the river bank in October?'

'That's my point about this whole bloody hysteria, Straker. If no one person has seen all three bodies how can anyone know if they have the same mutilations and if it's the same killer? It's all rumours. Tavern gossip. Addled buggers will say anything in drink.'

The detective looked directly at the police chief. Nutt glared back. Then he leaned forward.

'Sort this out for the best Straker and we'll see you right, if you get my drift,' he nodded conspiratorially.

DI Straker rose abruptly and looked down at the police chief. 'Where is the body sir? The doctor has been told to expect me at the post-mortem today.'

Nutt sighed. 'In the morgue at the York Lunatic Hospital. The old madhouse, as was, except they call it a hospital now. It's still full of loonies, like there's a cure for madness,' he scoffed. 'If you ask me they should all be . . .'

'I'll see myself out.' Straker turned and strode to the door. He grasped the knob and as he opened it, he heard the same harsh crying from upstairs. He didn't look round. 'Please let the doctor know that I will be at the morgue at two o'clock.'

'Anything else, Mr Scotland Yard Detective?' Nutt sneered.

'And I want an exhumation order.'

***

Late morning at Harker's Hotel, and a white-capped maid entered room number five balancing a coffee pot and cup and saucer on a silver tray.

'Leave it on the table over there. Thank you,' Straker smiled and handed her a coin. As soon as she had closed the door, he poured hot liquid to the rim and swallowed a mouthful. He took the cup to the window and looked out over the snow-covered square below, thinking about the person he must yet see.

Straker felt more awake now, he had washed and changed into a fresh white cotton shirt. His eyes gave him away though, rimmed with blue-grey circles of tiredness. There had been no time to find a barber, get a proper shave and trim before he left London so his dark hair was slightly too long and he kept having to move it away from his eyes. All that would have to wait, including the pile of clothes and books he had strewn over the goose feather eiderdown on his bed, as he had scrabbled through his bag.

Cup emptied, Straker put on his frock coat and smoothed it over his shoulders. He carefully adjusted the dark necktie around his starched shirt collar, took a last appraising look at himself in the chevalier mirror, and straightened his fitted waistcoat. It would have to do. Straker checked his pocket watch and walked briskly down the wide curving staircase, through the busy lobby and outside. There was no putting off his next visit and he was confident this one would not go well either.

CHAPTER NINE

◊

'Cab, mister?'

Straker raised his eyes, snowflakes catching on his lashes, hair and overcoat. He shook his head at the waiting Hansom driver, perched high behind his cab, blowing onto freezing fingers. Straker barely noticed the perishing cold for his mind was elsewhere.

'No thank you, I prefer to walk,' he said. The journey he must make was all too short and Straker needed time. Time to think about what he might say though he knew all the time in the world would not be long enough.

As he strode away from the front of the hotel, he put on his top hat which accentuated his height further and set off briskly along Blake Street. Halfway along, he stopped and pulled a badly-folded Ordnance Survey street map from his inside overcoat pocket. He had borrowed it earlier from Harker's reception, but he saw that, unhelpfully, only the main street names were listed. He walked along to the end of Blake Street and turned right towards the Minster, knowing only that he must get to the north side. Ramming the creased map in his pocket, he approached a road sweeper of about twelve or so, puffing on a clay pipe with one hand and half-heartedly pushing a brush with the other.

'Can you direct me to Chapter House Street please, lad?'

'Aye, keep on this path mister, through those gates and bear right through the park beyond, tek first road on the left and tis opposite a big old house with lots of chimneys, reckon tis only a few minutes walk.' Straker handed a coin to the scrawny boy, who nodded and shoved it into one of his patched boots.

Straker made his way past the vast west entrance of the Minster and into the small park. He still didn't quite feel ready so he stopped and felt inside his coat for his cigarettes. He drew in deeply, breathing out a white cloud of smoke and leaned his back against a tree. He rehearsed words in his head. Only when the burning tobacco scorched his fingers did he gather himself, flick away the glowing butt and straighten his shoulders.

He walked on, his poker-face giving away nothing, but inside the pit of his stomach was churning.

***

The shock struck Ada with the force of a blow. Straker watched the colour drain from her cheeks and his heart twisted in his chest.

'Ada . . .' His voice broke. Every word he had prepared fell away. 'Ada . . . I . . .'

She retreated back a few paces. She moved to slam the door, but his large hand quicker than hers, had hold of it and gripped it so hard his knuckles whitened.

'I have nothing to say to you,' she said.

'I would not have come, but I must speak with you.'

She tried, she was breathing hard, but couldn't wrest the door from his grip. She spoke through clenched teeth.

'Let go. You promised, for God's sake.'

'Ada, please listen to me.' He looked down at her and gently touched her arm. She shook him off.

Now she faced him down, anger flaring. 'Listen to you? You have no business with me.'

'I'm sorry, I have no choice,' he said. 'Please hear what I have to say.'

She shook her head in disbelief and stepped back from the doorway, leaving him to come in or not. Then she could not help it, she looked at him, properly. He held her gaze. For a long moment neither could look away.

'How are you?' he asked softly.

'Well enough,' she said. To his eyes she looked gaunter, paler. There were fine lines around her mouth that he didn't remember but her untameable hair still flamed around her face and her hazel-green eyes were as clear and bright as ever.

He reached out his hands for hers, across the twelve months that had passed. To her mind he looked older, wearier maybe, his black hair had a few streaks of silver, but she saw his strong demeanour was undiminished, the startling blue irises of his eyes had the same piercing intensity.

A tread of boots on flagstones made them both start and look away from each other. Thomas Bell, carrying a basket of chopped logs, was coming along the passage from the garden. He looked at Straker with curiosity.

'This is Detective Sergeant Samuel Straker of Great Scotland Yard,' said Ada recovering herself. 'This is Mr Thomas Bell, an old friend, who lives with us here.'

'How do you do Mr Bell,' he glanced at Ada with a brief look of embarrassment. 'I'm a Detective Inspector now, I was promoted after Paris.'

Swiftly Thomas Bell put down the basket and held out his hand to Straker. As they shook, Thomas looked at him appraisingly. He had heard much of this man and conscious of how difficult this must be for Ada, he gently steered Straker to the drawing room and suggested Ada go to find Camille to organise some refreshment. It would give them a moment, he thought.

Camille was busy cooking, sprinkling sugar over sliced apple layered in a dish. 'Tarte Tatin tonight. Are you going back to the studio this afternoon or are you working here?' she asked as Ada came into the kitchen.

Camille glanced up and stopped still when she saw her white face. 'Ada! What's happened?'

'Straker. He's here, now.' Ada spoke in a whisper.

'Straker! Here? Why?' Camille started to wipe her hands with a linen cloth.

'I don't know.' Ada looked at her helplessly.

'I'll make a pot of coffee.'

***

Straker's first impression was of the drawing room's warmth and brightness. The dark floorboards underfoot were covered in thick Turkish rugs, the shutters and the walls were painted in a silvery blue-green hue. As he looked around the room, he could see why Ada had chosen to live here. He knew she must love the light from the huge panes of glass and the large room's pleasing proportions. But this was a life he had no part of; there would never be a place here for him. He walked across the room and took up position by one of the full-height windows looking out over the bleak wintry walled garden. He grasped the frame with both hands and leaned forward, pressing his forehead hard against cold glass. What in God's name am I doing here? he thought. Memories surged into his head; her red-gold hair falling loosely around his shoulders, her mouth pressed against his, her soft skin under his hand. He shook his head. I can't do this, he thought. He heard a noise in the hall, the tread of quiet footsteps coming closer. He straightened and turned, his face a rigid mask, as the door slowly opened.

He looked at her ashen face and was almost lost. He longed to pull her to him, to take her in his arms. But that could never happen again. There was no future for them in this life.

A silence pressed the air, palpable in the few feet between them. He watched her cross to the marble fireplace where the mended fire blazed fiercely. She turned abruptly to look at him. 'Why are you here, Straker?'

For a moment he said nothing, crushing the tumult of emotions raging inside him. He breathed deeply. 'We need your help.'

Four simple words, but their effect was physical, like a punch and she recoiled. 'I don't understand. What for? We agreed, Paris was the end of it all.'

'I know . . . I'm sorry.'

'Then why?'

'I have orders from the Prime Minister.'

She shook her head bewildered, questions forming in her mind. How was this possible? How could he, how could they ask anything more of her? She grasped the edge of the mantel, her head spinning. So it was true, she had hoped for too much. Her new life, the world she was building here, it was an illusion. She should have known.

Straker sat down on the edge of an easy chair, at the other side of the fireplace. He looked up at her knowing the anguish he would see on her face. He felt shame. But he had no choice, whatever the consequences. He needed her. 'There's no one else but you who can help,' he said softly.

She watched the flames licking around a fresh log. After a moment she spoke, 'They agreed that Paris was my last case. That life is finished for me. I cannot go back. I cannot do it again.'

He got up and moved closer to her, wanting to make her understand.

She took a step backwards. 'I cannot go back to that life. I cannot do it again.'

He stopped. 'I know you don't want to. I know you feel you cannot. I would not ask but there is no one else but you.'

'I'm not letting you do this to me.'

He looked steadily at her. 'Hear me out at least?'

'Explain then.' She sat down on the ottoman opposite him.

Straker leaned forwards. 'I have been sent to investigate the death of a young woman whose body was found by the river last week. I assume you've heard stories of the Butcher of York?'

She felt a chill run through her. 'Of course, but surely it's just speculation to stoke public fear. The press have linked this with two other deaths and come up with this sensational story and nickname, but I think the police here do not believe there is a connection.'

'Ada, whatever the local police think everything suggests this poor woman may be the third victim of one killer. You see it is claimed that two women found dead earlier this year bear the same unusual lines on their stomachs. The flesh is cut deep with precision. It is a strong mark like an upside-down V.'

She looked at him. 'You're not saying it's true.'

'Ada, I think it is possible there is a multiple killer stalking the streets of York. There is no certainty yet but I have orders to find out if the Butcher is a bogeyman or a real murderer. If he exists he may be selecting his fourth victim even as we speak.'

She was silent.

'Ada?'

'But why do you need me? You are a detective inspector. What of your colleagues at Scotland Yard?'

'Sir Richard Mayne is under pressure from the Prime Minister to resolve this mystery swiftly. The Detective Branch faces closure after the scandal of the Jonathan Whicher case and needs a good result. But most importantly three women have died and I want to know what has happened to them and I need your expertise.'

She stared at him. 'No . . . I can't do this again . . . You should not . . .'

'You have a skill – you see things in your photographs that others can't. You see the truth in your images. You've proved that so many times. You believe in modern, scientific methods of crime-fighting just as I do. We need you to come back to work. I need you to come back to work. Ada I know Paris was difficult . . .'

She dropped her head so that he would not see her grief.

Straker continued quietly. 'I want to be honest. You should know everything. For those in Whitehall it's not really about justice for these tragic young women. That is the truth of it. This is about power, politics and money. The Lord Mayor of York is the richest man in the country. He thinks these deaths are bad for his business and he's threatening the Prime Minister. George Brass bankrolled the Liberals into power and the

Government needs his money to keep rolling in. Scotland Yard has been ordered to deal with it. And if we don't resolve this case quickly, before that old sod's ball, he will stop the supply flowing. And that could mean the end of the Detective Branch. Every criminal in the land would be celebrating.'

She sensed a bitterness in him that was new.

'It's dirty, sleazy, corrupt and we are caught up in the mess.' Straker looked at her directly. 'I'm not asking you because of that. I'm asking you to undertake one last case because you care. You care about the victims whoever or whatever they are. And I care too. Whatever the politics, we can do the right thing for those who have no voice, for those no one is kind to, as we always have.'

She looked down at her hands clasped in her lap, her wrists where the sleeve of her white cotton blouse had ridden up, at the whitened ridges of scar tissue on skin. True, she thought she had been proud to blaze a trail in forensic photography. Her life had been different to that of many other women. She had proved that she had the talent, skill and stomach, as much if not more so than male colleagues, to solve crimes. But she had paid the highest price.

Straker said something else, quickly, quietly.

'I beg your pardon?'

He leaned across. 'Please look at me. Ada.' He reached for her hands. 'Can we maybe . . .'

She stood up abruptly, pulling hers away. She needed to think, needed to put some space between them. She moved to the window.

He got up and went over to her, resting his hands on her shoulders. He bent forward, he could smell her hair, her skin. 'There is a great deal to speak of if you will let me.'

'Well?' she said.

'You ran away from me. It was a difficult time. You were . . . I didn't know how to reach out to you . . . I . . .'

To her ears his words sounded like excuses. He could have found her if he'd tried hard enough. She shrugged away from his hands and said angrily. 'There's nothing to discuss. I don't want to speak of it, it's done and it's gone. I would thank you never to bring it up again.'

Straker's voice grew harder now, his pride stiffening with her coldness. 'So be it. I will respect your wishes. But we have no choice in the other matter. So I am asking you again, will you work with me on this one last case? Then, I promise, I will leave York and we will part forever.'

Ada did not speak for a long moment.

'Will you work with me?'

She turned to him, 'In truth I don't know if I am capable, it's been a while . . .'

'You told me once that photographs are the most powerful weapons in the world. Who else can use them to fight for justice like you can?' From his inside jacket pocket, Straker pulled out a white sealed note. 'Sir Richard thought you would have doubts and asked me to give you this.'

She took the letter and, with her back to him, read the black scrawled lines. She read them again, then closed her fingers around the note and threw it into the flames of the fire. It flared and crackled. Ada turned round.

'Very well Straker. I will help you one last time. One set of photographs. Then, I never want to see you again.'

His face was expressionless. 'After this is over we will go our separate ways. That will be the end of it.'

'I agree.'

Straker nodded briefly and walked to the door. He paused and looked back.

'Meet me at the morgue, two o'clock this afternoon.'

CHAPTER TEN

◊

Thomas had been at work; there was a lively fire burning in the pot-bellied stove in Ada's garden studio. The oil lamps had been lit and cast a good working light around the whitewashed room. She unlocked a cupboard and took out her camera, letting her fingers caress the wood as she carefully placed it in its bag. Each piece of equipment, the lens, the glass plates, had its own velvety cocoon, encased like beans in a pod, protected from the rigours of many journeys. Firmly she fastened the clasps.

She stood a moment, looking through the small-paned window into her walled garden; its lawn, its borders, its late season vegetables, covered deep with freshly fallen snow. It was so silent. She wanted to stay here, in the warmth of her studio, looking out at this wintry perfection. As she breathed the cold glass misted, obscuring her view.

She turned back to her studio. Looking around she remembered how hard she had struggled for all this; her career, the respect of her peers, the means to earn her own living. She had left everything behind, her family, her childhood home to make her own way in life, but now her hard won independence felt as fragile, as brittle as the film of ice on the water butt outside.

***

When Ada had sailed from England all those years ago, against her family's wishes, she'd believed the worst of their anger was over. It was not. The letter had caught up with her in Heidelberg – an official communiqué from the family solicitor; a warning from her brother. Her annual allowance, already a pittance, was to be suspended. A particular course of action was recommended. Return. Give up her ridiculous nonsense. Her charitable brother, who had inherited all the family estate, would then be prepared to reinstate a modest fund and offer her a loving home.

To hell with that she'd thought. She'd travelled south and kept moving.

Intoxicated with the sights of vineyards, the smells of pine carried in warm winds, the tastes of sun-ripened fruits, she'd worked her way around the continent; Florence, Rome, Athens, Lausanne. The sun and the light had inspired her and she'd taken many photographs for sculptors, artists, tourists. Sometimes she'd stayed days, sometimes she'd lingered for weeks, finding lodgings with other like-minded women on their own voyages.

When she'd finally arrived in Paris it was the fine spring of 1859. She'd read of the city in novels, a place of revolution and romance, a home of artists and artisans. It turned out to be a giant, dusty building site. Huge swathes of the rambling medieval city were in ruins. A man called Baron Haussmann was stamping his vision of wide, grand, straight boulevards on the squalid slums and stinking stew pots. Ada had found it noisy, dirty, chaotic, but there was a blood-stirring atmosphere no writer, even Dickens, could adequately describe. She loved it.

She'd soon found lodgings on the Left Bank, in the Saint-Germain-des-Prés quarter. The most she could afford was a fifth-floor studio of a Rue du Bac town house. Its flights of curving stone stairs winding so high, she'd got out of breath climbing to her two small rooms at the top. Despite its simplicity, she'd revelled in her attic. A swirling oil painting of white French houses along a riverside hung above the small fireplace, a vase of bright red flowers from the flower stall on the street corner was set upon a narrow wooden table. There she could sit by a tall window facing onto the street and see Paris coming and going. Her carved wooden bed, in a smaller room still, was covered with a crocheted ivory bedspread. It was tucked under the eaves, and through the glass panes of a roof light above, she could lie in bed and see the rooftops and chimneys. The other window in her living area faced an internal courtyard, and when it was open, she had smelt the pungent fragrance of garlic and herbs drifting upwards from her neighbours' kitchens and heard the clattering of pans. Ada had found it exhilarating.

'Dine with me tonight mademoiselle,' the concierge had ordered one morning, soon after Ada's arrival.

'Thank you. I would be very pleased.'

'Eight o'clock,' Madame Camille Defoe had said as she passed through the tiled hallway of the ground floor, carrying a wicker shopping basket. Her appearance was far from how English women of a certain age presented themselves. Camille was striking, even on her way to the market. Her styled, tight-fitting striped dress, her glossy black coiled hair, her kholed brown eyes had made Ada feel a little unkempt. What had surprised Ada even more was to learn that she had once been a celebrated chef at the famous Café Riche. That supper had been the first of lots of joyous evenings of food and wine. Ada was introduced to Camille's many interesting friends and revelled in their lively debates; women talking equally with men.

Everywhere Ada went she had sensed an excitement. The city had seemed full of possibilities. Ada had sought work on the Rue d'Anjou, with one of the principal photographic establishments. In the great studios of Paris, Vienna, Berlin, talented assistants of all nationalities could command high wages, as much as 600 francs per month. The best of them were technically brilliant photographers with the eyes of artists. Ada had been hired straightaway.

Now evenings were spent in the lively cafes of the Boulevard des Italiens where white-aproned waiters served white wine spritzers and fresh peach ice cream. Ada had talked into the small hours with photographers, artists and writers. Her work was pioneering, modern and fascinating to all. 'Is photography a science or an art?' one writer had wondered. The debates went on long into the night.

Men especially had many questions about her camera and the process of developing.

'It's tedious. No one asks artists what brushes they use,' she complained later to Camille as they had drunk cognac together around her kitchen table. 'It's the image that matters.'

Ada met people like herself and for the first time she'd felt accepted, like she belonged. In Paris she could work and be respected for that. It had been no one's assumption that her goal in life was marriage.

One autumn morning six months or so later, Ada had been instructed to undertake an appointment. The studio proprietor had been asked to send his best photographer.

If Detective Sergeant Samuel Straker had felt surprised when he saw Ada Fawkes at the riverside offices of La Sûreté, he had not revealed it. This was Paris, he'd reminded himself and women were permitted to have careers.

Her initial impression of him that day in October was of reserved aloofness. His stern face gave away nothing. 'Bonjour mademoiselle,' he'd said politely, his voice deep, his French accent good, but not that good.

'Good day. I understand you need the use of an experienced photographer. How can I be of help?' she'd replied in his own tongue. A pause as he'd realised she was a countrywoman.

'You're English,' he'd said with surprise and, she'd thought, a touch of relief. 'I'm Detective Sergeant Straker from the London Detective Branch at Great Scotland Yard.'

He'd explained he was on secondment with La Sûreté – a legend of a bureau, founded by one of the most ingenious crooks in France. Such was its reputation in crime-fighting, that police forces from around the world sent their officers to acquire its skills.

Straker had requested to work in Paris. He had long been an enthusiastic advocate of the French police's new methods. As he'd talked her through how detectives were beginning to use photography to help solve crimes and had explained that photographs had been used as evidence to convict a murderer in an American law court, she'd watched his serious face become animated. He was not a young man, some years older than her, but he was broad, imposing and full of vigour. He'd told her their usual photographer had been taken ill and they needed to photograph evidence from a murder scene. He'd admitted he hadn't expected a woman, but he was grateful she was English, as his French was only adequate. It would make their working together easier.

Ada had revealed nothing of her thoughts but to her this was destiny.

The meeting had been business-like. He had been polite and it quickly became clear to her, that he had a passion for his work that matched her own. His thick black hair fell forward as he bent over her, he'd brushed it back and his intense blue eyes sought hers as he talked, asking many questions about her work.

'So what is it you want me to do exactly?' Ada had asked finally.

He'd hesitated. 'I need you to take a picture of a body.'

She had nodded her agreement for his request seemed rational to her. She had always recognised that photography would change the world.

'Miss Fawkes, are you sure? Is it too strange a request? Too repulsive?'

'No,' she had replied. 'A photograph captures a moment in time and holds that history within the image. That moment will be given up when it is needed. It's clear to me that photography is destined to be involved with death.'

That was when it had begun. That was when she had become a photographer of the dead.

A loud knock on the door brought her back to the present and she heard Thomas's voice calling out to hurry. Ada looked at her camera packed and ready. Her old life had caught up with her and there was no way of knowing how it would end this time. Badly she suspected. She picked up her bag and stepped outside.

***

So many scandals about this old place, Ada thought standing before the entrance of the York Lunatic Hospital. She craned her head to look up at its grand Tuscan columns, its fine Venetian windows, its elegant facade. Everyone in Yorkshire grew up hearing tales of pauper lunatics manacled in secret cells, inmates kept like animals in their own filth, cells strewn with urine-soaked straw. It had been a living, stinking tomb.

She walked up the wide stone steps and was surprised to walk into an ornate wood-panelled entrance hall crowded with tall parlour palms in silver bowls and small side tables, and hung with gilt-framed paintings on dark cream walls. It had been recently redesigned to reflect new ideas in treatment. And she was impressed. There had been some resistance to progress. The flog 'em and hang 'em brigade had written regularly to *The Herald* with outraged 'Dear Sir' letters describing it as a 'hotel for lunatics'. York was full of these concerned citizens. Presumably they believed those declared insane should still be locked in filthy cages.

Ada looked around the cavernous geometric-tiled foyer, brightly lit by an impressive roof lantern as she waited for Thomas. He was bringing the portable dark room round from the stables at the back of the hospital. Two passing nurses in frilled white caps and aprons glanced over to her, evidently curious. It may have been because she was a striking sight. A woman with unruly red-gold hair wearing a close-fitting damson velvet overcoat matched with a pheasant feather trimmed hat. Or maybe it was the tall, glowering dark-haired man swiftly crossing the hall towards her that caught their attention.

'Good day again Miss Fawkes. Thank you for coming. Let me help you with that?' Without waiting for an answer Straker took Ada's leather bag, avoiding eye contact.

'Careful, my camera's in there. Don't . . .' she said, breaking off as a bow-legged man came towards them, as wide as he was tall, dressed in a worsted frock coat with a snow-white cravat wound round his neck. Bowing to the waist, he said, 'Martin Bray, hospital bailiff, at your service. What is your business here, sir, madam?'

'I'm Detective Inspector Straker of Great Scotland Yard. This is Miss Fawkes. We have an appointment. I was instructed to ask for the medical superintendent.'

'But yes of course, Dr Scull is expecting you. He begs you to forgive him but he is meeting with the visiting committee. It's inspection day. He will join you later and in the meantime he asked me to show you to the morgue. The doctor is already there.'

'I have to wait for the rest of my bags,' said Ada.

'I'll make sure they follow on, Miss Fawkes. If you would follow me?'

Mr Bray was keen-eyed and as talkative as any village gossip. He rattled off a list of building works brought about by Dr Scull, which seemed to justify the impression that Ada had formed at Jane Auden's birthday dinner party, the improvements amounted to a grand new-build house for Dr Scull himself.

At the open door of the female day room, Bray directed them to observe around seventy patients sitting on chairs around the edge of a square room. In the middle was a long table covered with a cheery red and white striped cloth. The women were sewing, drinking tea, or staring vacantly as if lost in memories. It could have been any ladies' society meeting, except she was struck by the silence, there was no sound of laughter. Ada saw that many were wearing loose white dresses like nightgowns and there were so many mirrors on every wall. In answer to her unspoken question, Bray told them in a low voice that the mirrors enabled the nurses to spot any deviant behaviour by the insane.

Yards further on, a smell of carbolic suggested they were getting close to the morgue. Ada felt her breathing grow shallower. She had never thought that she would do this again. She swallowed as she saw closed doors ahead. She had always been able to detach herself, but it had been so long. Did she still have it in her?

As she walked on, she reminded herself of the private letter that the Police Commissioner Sir Richard Mayne had written to her: 'To bear witness to murder is a heavy burden for anyone. I understand why you have chosen a different path. But I beg you to assist us one last time. You are our only photographer of the dead.'

It was only one job, one set of photographs. She just had to get through this ordeal and then she was finished for good. She inhaled deeply, pushed back her shoulders and lifted her chin.

She had one final duty to the dead.

***

The sound of hurrying footsteps behind them, loud on the tiled floor, made the three of them turn. Thomas Bell was approaching, breathing hard with the weight of the bags.

'I'll help Thomas,' Ada said, seeking a few minutes delay before she must begin. 'You go on please. Keep going to the end there and through those doors,' said Mr Bray waving down the passage. 'I'll leave you here. I must re-join the inspection committee. Good day.' He turned to leave.

Straker walked ahead and pushed open the wide door. He noticed the cold first, then the peculiar sweet smell of carbolic acid. In the wood-panelled room he saw a tall, flax-haired man bent over a long scrubbed table lifting a mallet from a brass-bound mahogany case. The man looked up as he entered.

'Ah you must be Detective Inspector Straker,' he said, placing the instrument next to a spine wrench set upon the table and held out his smooth hand. 'I'm Dr William Auden, I'm performing the post-mortem today. I was only informed this morning that you wished to see the body before I did so. A London detective no less. Dead street-walkers are not usually regarded as police business here.'

Straker shook the hand firmly. 'Yes, so I have realised. And thank you doctor, I appreciate your waiting. My colleague will be here in a moment or so. We need photographs of the body.'

'I'm impressed you are taking the trouble. It's so interesting. I'm all for progress. The two of you come up from London then? We are honoured.'

'No. My colleague lives here in York.' Straker hesitated a moment, bracing himself for a reaction, a woman working with the police was a novelty to most. 'The photographer is a Miss Fawkes.'

Dr Auden's voice was incredulous. 'Miss Fawkes? Miss Ada Fawkes?'

Straker looked at the younger man, curiously. 'Are you acquainted with her?'

'I've known her many years. She is a friend to my sister Jane. She was a guest at her birthday dinner last night. Goodness me the world is growing smaller.' The doctor smiled. 'But of course. It makes sense now I think about it. My sister and I have discussed with her the new sciences used in criminal investigations, her ground-breaking work in Paris. But Miss Fawkes prefers that her involvement in all that is not known or talked of here in York, it's a very old-fashioned place. I thought she had given up her police work since her return?'

Straker made a point of not elaborating. 'There is an urgent need to discover the truth of these deaths. Miss Fawkes was asked to help.'

'Indeed. Her forensic photography is of much interest to us,' the doctor said enthusiastically. 'My sister and I lived in London until recently and I worked at St Guy's Hospital. And as you will know St Guy's is at the forefront of developing forensic science.'

'Then you must have worked with Professor Swaine Taylor and his team, gathering medical evidence for court cases.' Straker looked at him thoughtfully.

'Yes, I did. It was a truly exciting time in my career, some of the best times of my life. Scientific analysis of crime scenes is moving so fast that I hear Professor Taylor soon hopes to be able to distinguish human from animal blood.'

'Goodness. That is quite something,' Straker said.

'Isn't it fascinating? And how interesting that Miss Fawkes is working with the police again. My sister and I are delighted she has moved back to Yorkshire.'

Straker momentarily felt a twinge of something. He wondered just how delighted the doctor was. 'Well, we should get to work,' he said sharply.

'Indeed we should.' William moved back to the table. Straker watched him lean over and straighten a well-sharpened dissecting knife.

Conscious he might be scrutinising the other man too intently, Straker turned away to look around, glass-fronted cupboards of bottles and vials, forceps, clamps, a ceramic phrenology head and the largest amputation saw he had ever seen. It was all most impressive, he thought, rather like the doctor. Auden had such an easy air of confidence, in contrast to his own stiff, reserved nature. In fact, Straker mused, the man was as unlike him as it was possible – his manner was affable, his temperament humorous, he was the kind of man people found easy to talk to. He wondered if he might have preferred the doctor to be less so.

'Have you worked with Miss Fawkes before?' William asked as he pulled a coarse linen apron over his black suit, tying its strings twice around his waist.

'Yes. In Paris. I was working there with the Sûreté. We worked on several cases together.' His voice was guarded.

'La Sûreté! Those detectives are quite the legend. Well thank goodness we are making progress here in England too, even in York.'

'Clearly. You have a very modern facility here,' Straker said.

'Thank you. It was built quite recently and is an important part of our research into insanity. We do post-mortems on everyone who dies here and we examine brain tissue for abnormalities. We do find though that most inmates die of the same condition, general paralysis of the insane.'

Dr Auden picked up an ebony-handled saw and brushed its fine blade with a small bone brush. 'Most of the city's post-mortems are done here now by myself and my colleague Dr Scull as we have the most modern facilities in the county. But would you excuse me for a moment? The body is still on ice in the morgue.'

***

Ada watched two hospital porters hoist the shrouded corpse like an animal carcass in the Shambles. The body seemed no weight at all, judging by the casual ease with which they swung and laid her on the stone dissecting slab in the middle of the tiled room. With little ceremony they unravelled the coarse brown linen and sprinkled the body with disinfectant powder.

Ada swallowed hard. There had been many bodies, but it never got any easier. She fought the rising bile and breathed deeply, reminding herself of why she must do this. Her photographs could provide evidence, proof of a crime. Her pictures had caught killers and freed innocent suspects. The courts must take notice of them. Superstition was at last being replaced by real evidence. Hard to believe that not so long ago people thought if a killer touched their victim, blood would flow from the wounds again.

She walked over to the dissecting table. Her nose and lips tingled with the eucalyptus oil she always used to mask the stench of death. Straker came to her side and nodded silently. They stood a moment as they always did, acknowledging death, heads bowed.

'Tell me something about her,' Ada said quietly.

'All I know is that she was found on the river bank by the lamplighter, wearing a plain white gown and a necklace.'

'Is that all?'

'Yes.'

'Poor girl.'

Straker looked down at Ada's pale face, her dark-circled eyes. 'Can you do this?'

'Yes. I'm ready.'

He stood back to let her begin. Thomas had made ready her camera and already left the room. On the detective's command, the porters bundled up the shroud and went too.

They were alone with the dead.

Silently Ada worked through her preparations: coat the glass plate with collodion, dip the glass in a bath of silver nitrate and create the negative, place this into the slide and push the slide into the camera. The methodical process calmed her.

Over and around the camera she adjusted thick yellow muslin cloth so it surrounded her like a tent, blocking out light. She looked at the dead girl through the lens. Ada adjusted the camera angle and studied the body. The young woman's skin was soaped clean of river dirt, the long brown hair was combed through, spilling over her thin shoulders.

'Move the light down,' Ada's voice was toneless. Straker did so and the lamp shone on the girl's hollow stomach. Ada framed the distinctive cut, deep slashes marked into the flesh, edges white, cleanly sliced. She pressed the shutter.

At least the dead are still, she thought.

'Can you take a photograph of her necklace,' Straker asked. 'It might help us identify her.'

'Of course, can you move her hair?'

He leaned over the body and gently pushed the hair back. He touched the silver cross around her neck and straightened it. He noticed its intricate entwining flower design.

She took the photograph and the minutes ticked by for the exposure.

'You can remove it now.' She would take another later and enlarge the image.

Straker undid the clasp and wrapped the thin chain in his white cotton handkerchief.

'We need to photograph her gown too,' she said.

'I'll ask Dr Auden for it when we are done.'

Ada came out from under the cloth to take up another glass plate. Straker glanced at her face. It was fixed, expressionless. He had seen her look like this before, her mouth shut tight, her eyes dark and it made her look wearier, older. Not surprising, given what she looked upon.

He was relieved when she said finally, 'I am finished. I need the lanterns over here now.'

She must develop, fix and rinse. She worked steadily, asking the porters for more and more pails of water until it was done and the floor looked like a small lake.

Ada looked round. 'Straker quickly. Help me. I must clean off the chemicals.'

He came over to her at the sink. Ada was washing herself vigorously, lathering her skin with red carbolic soap. He lifted a jug and poured icy water over her bare arms and hands. She soaped again. He poured another, trying not to see the landscape of scars on her flesh, but she caught his glance. She looked up at him, a challenge in her eyes.

'Does it still hurt?' he asked her softly.

'I do not wish to speak of it.'

He nodded and turned his back as she dried her skin with a rough towel.

'May I come in?' It was Auden's voice.

On Straker's affirmative, the door opened, daylight spilled into the room and Dr Auden entered.

'Doctor, can you tell us anything about her or the manner of her death?' Straker asked.

'She is not very old – 20 or so. But it is hard to tell when you have led a life like hers.'

'Can you tell us anything more about the cuts? They are unusual wouldn't you say? I have seen knife wounds before, but none like these. The blade of the instrument has been used to cut a distinctive mark, like an upside-down letter V. Is that how she died?'

Auden shook his head. 'I cannot say for certain. You must wait until I have completed the post-mortem.'

'It is unhealed. I'd say it is recently done, what think you doctor?'

'Yes I believe that may be so, but again I cannot say until after the post-mortem.'

'I would be grateful if you let me have the results as soon as possible.'

Dr Auden bowed slightly. 'Of course detective inspector. I will be in touch when I have something to report.'

***

Outside Ada gratefully inhaled the cold air wanting to expunge the clinging stench of carbolic. She noticed Straker did the same. At the welcome sound of trotting hooves approaching, they hurried down the hospital steps as Thomas came round the corner of the hospital and drew alongside them with the carriage.

They rode in silence. Minutes later they were passing under the stone arch of Bootham Bar. From the city came the peal of bells sounding the hour and, ahead, in the gathering shadows the Minster stood outlined against the darkening sky.

'I must get home. I need to print the photographs straightaway. Thomas will take you wherever you need to go,' Ada spoke finally.

'Thank you. May I ask when the photographs will be ready?'

'This evening. I will send a message.' Her mind was elsewhere, racing ahead, thinking how best to develop the images.

'Miss Fawkes . . .' Straker leaned towards her, so close they could touch. Startled from her thoughts, she turned, and saw his face. Something cold went through her.

'Will you, can you continue the investigation?' he spoke hesitantly.

She shook her head puzzled. 'But I have finished, I have taken the photographs you asked for.'

'I'm sorry. I haven't been entirely open with you.'

'What do you mean? What are you talking about? There are no more bodies for me to photograph, thank God.'

'Not in the morgue, that's true.'

She looked at him bewildered.

'Ada, we must examine the other two women for the same wounds.'

'But they're . . .'

'Yes,' Straker nodded, seeing the shock spread over her face. 'I need you to photograph the buried bodies. We must bring up the corpses from their graves.'

Chapter Eleven

◊

It was late afternoon by the time Chief Constable Nutt reached the Blue Bell and the mood was already lively. Standing at the bar, he quickly downed a pint of ale and looked round with satisfaction at the dirty, smoke-filled room. The raucous crowd were all men and in his opinion that was how it should be.

Banging down his empty glass, he pushed his way out into Lady Peckett's Yard. He made his way through pedestrians and horses, down narrow lanes and cut through the fish market, oblivious to the stink and the detritus of guts underfoot. He had needed that stiffener – his meeting with Detective Inspector Straker had not gone as well as he hoped.

Out of breath he walked into the police station, managing to bark an order to Stone, standing behind the front desk, holding a pint mug of tea.

'Jack! My office. Now.'

The chief constable was halfway through his cigar by the time Sergeant Stone had got rid of a man complaining about noisy neighbours. Nutt gestured for his officer to sit down. Then he explained the problem.

Stone listened, arms folded over his chest, with the alert air of a man always looking for trouble.

'We need to be seen to be doing something Jack,' Nutt concluded. 'Anything.'

There was a pause. Nutt noticed his colleague's half-smile. That smirk usually indicated an eagerness to impart bad news. He knew it well.

Back in the day, they had joined the York Constabulary together. Equals then, but over the years, their lives had taken different paths. Nutt had married the elder and according to local tattle, less comely of the two Neville sisters while the younger sister had bagged the up-and-coming George Brass. Hanging onto the coat tails of his brother-in-law for dear life, Nutt had been promoted through the police ranks. By complying with Brass's every demand, over the years, Nutt had feathered his nest nicely. It not turned out as well for Stone. Though the young bride he married was pretty enough and well-endowed she had, according to Stone, turned into a lazy, nagging harridan, who he could only mount when she was too drunk to protest. This disappointment, Nutt thought, is what had made his sergeant bitter, resentful and ready to delight in the other's misfortune.

'Spit it out,' snapped Nutt.

'You haven't heard the rest of it then chief?' He leaned on the desk, enjoying the moment. 'Aye, I assumed you hadn't all right, you arriving at work so late.'

'Get on with it you silly bugger,' said Nutt ignoring the jibe.

Stone took a moment for maximum effect and then finally he related the servants' gossip. Nutt looked at him. 'How do you know this?'

'Mrs Stone's sister in law's brother is an under-secretary at the Mansion House. He overheard the mayor and his secretary, that sneaky piece of work Hugh Blake, talking of it.'

'You're sure?'

Stone nodded.

'A woman! A woman!' Revulsion distorted his face. 'Helping the police?'

'Aye. They are saying she takes photographs of the dead. She's worked with that London detective before.'

Nutt didn't know which part of all this disgusted him more.

'This is going to make us a laughing stock across the Ridings. A Scotland Yard detective lording it over us and now this – petticoat policing. It's unnatural. It might be alright for London, not up here.'

He shifted uneasily. He had already heard of Miss Fawkes. He remembered his wife had talked of her. She'd been nagging on, wanting him to pay for a portrait at this fancy new studio just because her sister was having one. Royal connections, trained in Paris, all the rage in the county blah, blah, blah, she'd mithered on. Paris! It made the woman practically a foreigner too.

Outside the police station, the city bells could be heard tolling four.

Stone stood up. 'Well if that's all, it's knocking off time for me Bob. If you need me, I'm in the usual.'

'There's going to be trouble for us Jack, mark my words.' Nutt took a last draw on his cigar and threw the smouldering stub into the fire.

Stone grunted. 'Look on the bright side Bob. At least those other two slags are underground and rotted by now. So there's no proof of anything and we can make this bollocks about the Butcher of York go away.'

'You're right. But we need to shut that old bastard lamplighter up too, Jack, just to make sure and those other old blethering idiots, let's see to 'em.'

'And what do we do about the detective?'

'A warning I think to put him in his place.' Nutt pushed himself onto his feet. 'I'll come with you Jack, a little livener.'

'First one's on you then Bob.'

Nutt followed Stone out shaking his head incredulously. 'A woman! Can you imagine Jack? A woman helping us? They'll be thinking they can be police officers next.'

***

Ada sat in the kitchen, enjoying the scent of thyme and bay leaves rising from the casserole simmering on the range. Camille was singing softly to herself in the scullery next door. She closed her eyes. She tried to empty her mind and think of pleasanter thoughts – a trick passed on to her by a veteran French detective. Later she told herself, she would have a quiet kitchen supper, a nice glass of red wine and her new library book.

Yet the brown leather bag at her feet, tightly clasped shut, kept interrupting those thoughts. The pictures of the dead woman within, intruded on everything, demanding to be made visible. And try as she might she could not prevent the responsibility of those images filling her head until there seemed little point in putting this off. She picked up her case and walked towards the door.

'What time do you want to eat?' Camille called out. 'There's boeuf bourguignon on the stove so it will keep for hours. I thought that would work best what with your talk tonight.'

Damn, she had forgotten about the lecture. Ada sighed. People were travelling from all over the county to hear her speak, see her work. When her neighbour James Gray, the secretary of the Philosophical Society had invited her to give a talk about photography, she had been pleased, for it would generate business. Unfortunately it was tonight. This day felt like it was going on forever.

Putting on her old tweed coat, she went out the back door and crunched along the cinder-strewn path leading to her darkroom.

Inside it was biting-cold and her breath blew clouds of white into the air. She wound her wool scarf tighter around her neck and pulled a rabbit fur-lined hat down over her ears, that had once belonged to her brother Harry.

As she undid the clasps of her bag, the world beyond her studio receded. Her mind no longer saw the broken body of a woman instead she analysed and measured chemicals and calculated exposure times. One of her professional skills was the ability to detach herself – sometimes she had wondered if she had a shard of ice for a heart – but it was how she managed. This was how she could photograph the dead.

From her case she carefully picked out the glass plates. These wet collodion negatives meant she could print her images quickly, sharply, onto paper even in this makeshift darkroom. Over and over she slopped freezing water down her body until the wool cloth clung and made her thighs raw. On and on she worked, colder and colder, until dripping prints hung from thin rope, like bunting on a feast day, stretched from one end of the room to the other.

Ada picked up a lamp, letting its light fall onto the black and white images. She took one down and put it on the wooden table top. The pale body reminded her of the alabaster-white marble effigy in her family's village church. She stood for a moment just looking.

It was the stillness of a photograph that made it so powerful.

Picking up her magnifying glass, Ada now looked closer and observed the engraved crucifix, the wounds in the stomach. 'Who are you? Why has this been done to you? What do you want to tell me?' she whispered.

Ada felt the back of her neck prickle. Somewhere in York, someone was capable of this.

CHAPTER TWELVE

◊

A da was late. York's many church bells were ringing
seven as she finally reached the gates of the museum
gardens. She had told Thomas there was no point in
him coming with her. It wasn't far. But nonetheless, as she
entered the dark snow-covered grounds of the old Benedictine
abbey, close to the fast-flowing river, she quickened her pace
further.

The four imposing pillars of the Museum of the Yorkshire
Philosophical Society grew visible through the gloom. She continued to the entrance and paused a moment before its gran-
deur. Built only thirty years or so ago, on abbey land gifted by
the Crown, it was impressive, one of the country's first pur-
pose-built museums. Ada was also more than aware that her
invitation to lecture here tonight was quite possibly the first
time a woman had been allowed to do so.

In the foyer men's heads turned to watch as she walked
by. One of them, a black-suited gentleman with a bushy beard
broke away from a small group earnestly conversing, and
approached her.

'Miss Fawkes.' James Gray, the society's secretary and her
neighbour, who had invited her to speak tonight, bowed formally in welcome.

'I hope I'm not late,' Ada smiled in greeting.

'Not at all. We are all looking forward to your talk. Our members are most curious to learn more of your work.'

The Philosophical Society, he'd explained to her when he'd called one afternoon at Chapter House Street, had been founded to promote the study of science and history in the county. Indeed he'd spoken at great length, explaining how the society's name was chosen for the Greek meaning of the word philosophy; that is a systematic enquiry into the nature of the world, or in their case Yorkshire. She was honoured to be asked to speak, Mr Gray had assured her. 'Our members wouldn't normally hold with a talk about a foreign place. But they want to learn more about landscape photography and if you would be so obliging as to prepare a future exhibition and lecture on Yorkshire's many great wonders, that would be even better.'

'Your photographs are already attracting much pleasing attention and comment.' Mr Gray waved a hand over to the room where an exhibition of her Paris photographs was already on display. She had hung the pictures last week so members could see them before her talk. She had agreed to this evening for the publicity it would bring her business, but now though she smiled and nodded politely, she couldn't help feeling a longing to be at home by her warm fireside.

'We do hope you will stay for refreshments afterwards.' Mr Gray continued. He gestured at the plates of food being carried by white-pinnied ladies to serving tables. China platters laden with sandwiches were placed on white tablecloths below the marble head of the Roman Emperor Constantine.

'Thank you Mr Gray. That is very kind.'

'But shall we listen to the speaker before you Miss Fawkes? He is most interesting.'

Mr Gray took her arm and steered her towards the closed wooden double doors at the back of the foyer. She could hear a man's droning voice. Before she had any choice, he'd ushered her through them, whispering, 'Mr J. Ford Esquire gives an excellent presentation.'

He showed her into the back row of dozens of upright chairs, all occupied by gentlemen in evening suits, facing a carved wooden lectern. Behind it a slightly-stooped, wispy-haired elderly speaker, who, much to her dismay, Ada realised was just beginning his talk.

'In the autumn of 1861, whilst on a visit to Huddersfield, walking in the neighbourhood of the cemetery, I observed the flag pavement . . .' intoned Mr J. Ford.

Ada looked behind her, but the door was firmly shut. The voice went on.

'. . . the flag pavement covered with pitted or concave markings alternating with corresponding convex protuberances. Two slabs, with the corresponding concave and convex markings, were found in a quarry at Grimscar, about two miles north-west of Huddersfield.'

Zoning out of observations on the effects of carboniferous rain on stone, Ada let her eyes wander over the room. There were several people she recognised. Reverend Turner, across the aisle, easily identifiable in his dog collar, his fine-boned features, pale in the lamplight. Her eyes lingered longer on the blonde hair of Dr Auden, head and shoulders above the other men in his row. She thought that was Dr Scull next to him. Then, as if William Auden could feel her gaze on his back, he half-turned and saw her. She felt a tiny flutter of pleasure in her stomach at his warm smile.

Finally the chairman stood up, thanked the speaker and said he wished Mr Ford could be induced to continue his research. Taking a slip of paper from his waistcoat pocket, he announced a recent donation to the society. 'A beautiful specimen of the curious and singular bird called the Zic Zac, which has been shot by one of my scholars on the Nile.' The audience clapped with appreciation.

The room fell silent when Ada stood up. Heads turned and eyes followed her as she made her way to the front. She heard them shift, sit up straighter as she came to stand before them. Disapproval registered in some faces as they took in the tight striped bodice and high-waisted silk skirt, fashionably hitched to show a peep of scarlet satin petticoat. More than one lorgnette was lifted to middle-aged eyes. Unhesitatingly and without notes Ada delivered a well-paced speech shot through with humorous anecdotes.

'Any questions?' asked the chairman as she drew to a close. There were many. The gentlemen were fascinated by the mechanism of operating a camera and even more fascinated by a 'lady' photographer. They competed to show off their knowledge. Detailed, pedantic questions about makes, models, techniques and precise exposure times were peppered at her from the floor. She answered them all with ease.

Back in the foyer, the crowd surged forward to the trestle tables loaded with a Yorkshire buffet: cups of strong tea, heaps of well-buttered brawn sandwiches, thick slices of pork pie, homemade chutneys and Colman's mustard. Ada accepted a drink of tea and sipped it as Mr Gray introduced various society members.

Reverend Turner smiled shyly when he saw her and held out his hand. 'Miss Fawkes. How very nice to see you again. What a fascinating talk. I do hope you might be persuaded to take photographs of my church groups. I'm a chaplain to various institutions of good repute. It would inspire the young ladies in their work.'

She smiled back and nodded. Then Dr Auden was pushing his way through the throngs, clutching their over-full plates of supper. He was looking about him as though he was searching for someone. His eyes alighted on her and he grinned. His eyes crinkled at the corners, she noticed. How different he seemed to the efficient, professional hospital doctor of earlier.

'Good evening Ada,' said Dr Auden warmly as he reached her side. 'That was as interesting as I expected. You are an excellent speaker. Reverend Turner, how do you do. It was very good to see you last night.'

'Thank you Dr Auden, it was a splendid evening. I was just telling Miss Fawkes about our many good causes in York.' He caught sight of Dr Scull who was approaching their small group. 'Oh please excuse me. I must speak of a matter to Dr Scull. I will no doubt see you at the next Penitentiary Society committee meeting Dr Auden. Good evening to you both.'

Auden shook his head. 'I thought I would rescue you. He's very well-meaning and kind, but he can be very earnest.'

'Thank you, William, for last night.'

'It was our pleasure and far better for us to talk of that than this afternoon.'

She nodded. 'Yes, I too prefer to keep work separate.'

'Jane longed to come, but she was feeling ill, too much champagne I shouldn't wonder,' he laughed, about to say more when Dr Scull returned and asked for his opinion on some private medical matter. 'Well not everyone agrees with us about keeping work and pleasure separate,' he whispered, turning to leave. He glanced back over his shoulder as though he was reluctant to leave.

Ada thought she might get another cup of tea, her mouth was dry from speaking. She turned and almost bumped into a man standing close behind. He held her shoulders to steady her and then, bending towards her ear so close she could feel his breath and smell his cologne, he whispered, 'You must have had some interesting times in Paris, Miss Fawkes. Perhaps you would like to tell me about them over dinner?'

Ada looked up, speechless with surprise.

His gaze held hers for a moment too long. 'Don't be offended Miss Fawkes. I jest with you. But I would be honoured to interview you for an article in *The Herald*, dinner is optional. I'm Rufus Valentine, the editor.' He gave her an appraising up and down look. 'It would be good publicity for you. Fine speech by the way, Miss Fawkes.' He bowed with a flourish, a sardonic smile and as swiftly as he had appeared, moved away into the crowd.

Ada stood for a moment unable to think of a quick retort, much to her annoyance. She shrugged and walked over to a serving table, looking like a plague of locusts had descended. She picked up a cup, sipping the hot tea and letting her gaze drift around the foyer, everywhere groups of men talking. A nearby voice, low and angry, caught her attention and she couldn't help but listen.

'You'll end up as a road sweeper, boy,' said the elder man, pursing his lips until they whitened. 'You'll never make a living with all that nonsense. Art, photography these are hobbies, not real jobs for men. Forget this idea before you disgrace us all. You will do what I say if I have to drag you to the bank myself.'

Their similarities: the quiff of black hair, the shape of thick arched brows, the firm set of square chins, marked them as father and son. The younger man looked not yet twenty and his clean-shaven face could not quite mask his distress and embarrassment.

The boy stood awkwardly staring at the floor and muttered something.

His father turned away, disgust on his face. 'You are a disgrace.'

Ada felt a stab of pity for the young man, standing alone, in the middle of the foyer, uncertain what to do next, and touched his arm gently. 'Can I help?'

He looked at her gratefully.

'I'm sorry I don't mean to intrude,' she said. 'I just couldn't help overhearing . . .'

He sighed. 'That was my father. He hates me.'

'I'm sure he doesn't hate you,' she said.

'He's so strict, so old-fashioned and has such set ideas.'

'Well tell me then,' Ada persisted.

He continued, his eyes on the ground. 'Father wants me to join the family's banking firm. He says I must face up to my responsibilities, marry, have children, and live a life like his. But I have no interest in banking and I will never find a wife.'

Ada said softly. 'My family was furious, disowned me, cut me off without a penny when I wouldn't do what they wanted, live how they wanted me to live. I ran away abroad to become a photographer. They still have little to do with me.'

'My father doesn't think that photography or anything to do with art is a proper career for a man. He says it's a hobby, only acceptable for amateurs and women.'

Ada thought of the artists and photographers she had known in Paris, dedicated, professional and passionate about their work. She understood all too well the loneliness and frustration of struggling against rigid expectations. She reached out and touched his arm. 'I really do know how difficult it can be, going against your family's wishes. Why don't you come to my studio sometime, you'll easily find it, it's on Coney Street. Come and have a cup of cocoa with me. It might help to talk.'

'I so wish I could, but he watches me like a hawk watches a mouse. I'm not allowed to leave our house without someone with me. Last month my father followed me to Leeds, caught me at the music hall. He had forbidden me to go. I was dressed like . . . Well, he said I was not a man . . . I was abnormal . . . a sickly spectacle . . . he thinks to cure me . . .' He stopped abruptly and reddened as though he hadn't meant to blurt out quite so much.

She felt even sadder for him. 'Try. Try to come and see me. I do understand what it is to be a misfit in this world.'

He raised his head and pushed back his long hair. 'Thank you Miss Fawkes. I'm Benjamin Barclay by the way.'

'Very pleased to meet you, Benjamin.'

'Thank you and likewise Miss Fawkes.' He sighed heavily. 'I'd better go home.'

She nodded. 'I do mean it, you are welcome anytime.'

'I appreciate your kindness Miss Fawkes. By the way, I hope you don't mind me saying, but your outfit is very striking.'

She smiled. 'Oh thank you, it's from Paris.'

He nodded. 'Of course. I thought it must be. I would very much like to go there. One day perhaps.'

Ada watched him disappear into the crowd and turned to the museum entrance, feeling exhausted now. With relief she saw Thomas there. She made her excuses to Mr Gray who was talking animatedly about flint axes to an enthralled group around him.

Outside the damp river mist seeped like tendrils through bare tree branches and dying shrubs. She pulled her cloak tighter. Thomas sensed her fatigue and linked his arms with hers, lending his reliable strength as they made the short walk home.

'I delivered the photographs to Detective Inspector Straker on my way here. We talked. I truly believe he is sorry . . .'

Ada, tired after her too long day, found herself snapping. 'I don't care what he thinks. I don't want you to talk about me with him.'

Thomas gripped her arm tighter. 'You don't have to do this.'

She looked at him. 'I do and you know it.'

'Ada, I'm worried for you though he promised me he would keep you safe.'

'His promises mean nothing, Thomas. If they did, he would not be here at all.'

**

Ada sank backwards onto her bed, wretched. Her body ached with fatigue, and pulling her feather eiderdown up to her chin, she crumpled into herself. She had had enough. She closed her eyes, turned her head to the pillow, but there was no way sleep would come.

Her mind went back and replayed the day, back to that moment this morning when her life had turned again. She was desolate, sick of these men at Scotland Yard and these things she must do.

She turned and stared at the shadows in the corners of her room. She breathed deeply. She did not know if she had the fortitude to withstand this, then she felt shame, this was not about her. Three women were dead. She breathed deeply, she would have the courage. These young women deserved justice no less than any of the other victims she had fought for.

But then there was Straker. What a mess. She put her hands over her face and curled onto her side. Long buried memories came to her and she let them take her back to another lifetime.

***

'I need you to photograph a body,' Straker had said. 'We need to identify her. Can you, will you do that Miss Fawkes?'

She had nodded. She had never been squeamish of death; she had grown-up witnessing the English country set slaughter anything that moved. And Detective Sergeant Samuel Straker of Great Scotland Yard was impressive.

Later the same day on La Rue de Harlay, Straker had helped lift her camera equipment down from the police carriage he had sent to collect her, apologising for the rough and ready temporary offices of the police headquarters. It was hardly necessary for no one could miss the fact that the Île de la Cité, once the hub of royal and ecclesiastical power, had become a muddy demolition site. The labyrinth of slums entangling Notre-Dame had nearly gone and Paris had its first clear view of the Gothic facade in decades.

Thousands of the poorest had been evicted to make room for Haussmann's grand new buildings; the Tribunal de Commerce and the Préfecture de Police. The detective had told her he believed the thirteenth century Sainte-Chapelle and its ancient stained glass might be spared. And, there was talk that the Conciergerie, where Marie Antoinette had been held prisoner before she followed the French king to the guillotine, would remain, perhaps as a reminder of what had happened to those who abused power.

The Sûreté's new home would be at 36 Quai des Orfèvres, on the site of the old poultry market he had explained, but for now the southwest side of the island was still a mass of rambling, wooden shacks choking the filthy streets.

As Straker had walked her under an impressive high stone gateway, a tricolour on a pole above the lintel rippled in the light breeze blowing from the direction of the River Seine at the end of the street. A sentry had waved them through a cobbled square courtyard overlooked by many tall windows with peeling, painted shutters. 'Look after these bags,' Straker had ordered a sharp-moustached young man in uniform, who was standing to attention by a closed door in the far corner. They had walked up steep stone stairs, along empty corridors and past doors closed on muffled conversations which Ada imagined to be about gruesome crimes worthy of an Edgar Allan Poe mystery. They passed open doors in which she glimpsed police officers, in their blue tunics, chattering in fast French, and smelled wafts of smouldering hand-rolled Turkish cigarettes and half-drunk coffee.

One final corridor and near the end of its length, Straker opened double doors into a vast light-filled room where five or so plain-clothed detectives were lounging round a table with a top of torn red leather. Two more men, at a wooden desk, upon which sheaves of paper were stacked, were writing with pens so well-used they might once have been employed to issue an order for imprisonment in the Bastille.

The detectives had looked up as they had entered and as one they had straightened their backs and smoothed their moustaches.

'Welcome to the Préfecture Miss Fawkes.' Straker had introduced her to his colleagues in his passable French. One by one they had stood and bowed, while looking her up and down.

'Ignore them,' he had said, 'they think they are God's gift to women.'

'Oh, but we are,' one detective in perfect English had replied, dark-brown eyes twinkling, 'Jean Petit at your service, mademoiselle.'

'The worst of all,' Straker had laughed, taking her elbow and steering her out. 'Now we must see the chief.'

They had walked along a wider wood-panelled corridor towards imposing double doors. She had felt some apprehension, there could be no one unaware of this man's reputation, his name struck fear into the heart of every criminal in Europe.

'Entrez.' Positioned by a high window looking down on the river and the barges, the short, dark man only turned round when they had fully entered the room. Flint-faced, with a long straight scar down his right cheek like a furrow, he had emanated power like no one she had ever met.

Straker had brought her forwards, 'Mademoiselle Ada Fawkes, Miss Fawkes this is Monsieur Jacques Bernard Verdoux.'

Ada had held out her crimson-gloved hand to the most infamous villain of his time. Verdoux had been recruited for the French detective branch from the criminal underworld.

'Do you know what you are here to do?' he'd said in a guttural working man's accent.

Ada had returned his direct gaze. She had kept her voice steady, determined to hold her own. 'I do and I am more than capable.'

'Excellent Mademoiselle Fawkes,' he had said, his rough square hands gripping the edge of his desk as he had watched her like she was prey. 'We have had some good results with our new methods. Are you aware of our successes mademoiselle?'

'Yes monsieur. I have seen the police portraits of those poor lost children. I believe it enabled you to reunite them with their parents.'

'Yes, that was the beginning. Now we are photographing everything and everyone; the accused, the convicted, the dead, the scenes of felony. It is transforming our fight against crime. Miscreants have no place to hide.'

Ada's interest had quickened as he had outlined his vision and for the first time she had felt a sense of her destiny, as if this was what she had always been meant to do.

'Monsieur Verdoux?' she had asked for she was puzzled. 'You do not mind . . .'

'Mind what Mademoiselle Fawkes?' he had said sharply.

'That I am a woman.'

'I had noticed,' the chief had said, his narrow eyes flicking down her body. 'But us Frenchmen we are forward-thinking. Many times we need the help of women in our police work. Is that not so Straker?'

Straker nodded. 'It is and it makes sense.'

Verdoux gestured with his hands. 'Mais oui, women can access places we men cannot. And some of the most fiendish criminal minds I have known are female. How do you say in English, it takes one to know one. Well Mademoiselle Fawkes, Straker will show you our photographic studio. It is temporary, of course. In our new headquarters, we will have the very best in the world. And we have something no one else has. I paid 7,000 francs for a photographic carriage. It is a portable dark room with sinks and chemicals. Anywhere a crime is committed, a body found, we will be there on the spot within no time. We will be able to take photographs at the scene, before the evidence is disturbed.'

'Oh that is most impressive,' Ada had said.

His voice had softened. 'I need a photographer with an eye for detail, someone who can see things others cannot. An artist. Our man is sick, nothing serious, a little problem after his last case. We are paying for treatment at a sanatorium.'

They had been dismissed. Together they had walked along more corridors and down more stairs to the basement rooms. Straker had showed her the printing and washing areas, well organised and spotless and had indicated where she should set up her camera. When Ada had glanced at him, pushing strands of dark hair away from his face, he had caught and held her gaze. There had been a hesitation in his manner and she had suspected he was holding something back.

Eventually he had sighed. 'Miss Fawkes, we are fortunate to have you help us, but are you certain? These men, the officers are rough, brutal even. There will be no concessions because . . .'

131

'Because I am a woman you mean?'

'Because some of the murders we see are so heinous. You cannot believe what one human being can do to another.'

Ada had thought he was uncertain whether he wanted her to stay to help or run for her sanity. In England, she had been expected to produce pretty landscapes and society portraits. Here, in Paris, these detectives would expose a woman to sights so abhorrent without a second thought, if it got them a result. She hadn't hesitated. She had long ago decided that she must seize every professional opportunity she could.

Straker had walked over to a table, where she had earlier seen a dark linen cloth covering something like an oddly-shaped ball.

He had hesitated. 'I don't know how to say this . . . Miss Fawkes, we don't have the body. Our victim has been decapitated. We only have a head.'

She had looked at the covered shape on the table again. 'Is that what I think it is?'

'Yes. And we need a photograph.'

Ada had not flinched when he had lifted away the cloth. Breathing deeply, she had walked to the table and calmly assessed the job. Gently she had smoothed back the tangled blonde hair obscuring the deathly waxen face, the closed eyes. It had been her suggestion to hide the gaping bruised neck stump with a black silk scarf before she had taken her photographs so it would be more palatable for public display.

Posters of the mystery head had gone up in shops and bars and on lamp posts and walls. The image had caused a sensation. Everyone in Paris had wanted to look at it. Ada's photograph had led to the identification of the woman, the killer had been caught and, in grim irony, had lost his own head by guillotine in the prison courtyard of La Roquette.

If she hadn't known before the full power of her art, she did then.

***

Ada opened her eyes wide. Her heart felt like it was being gripped tight. An ache rose from the pit of her stomach to the base of her throat so powerful in its intensity she trembled.

Straker was here.

This, she acknowledged, was surely the cruellest twist of fate.

CHAPTER THIRTEEN

◊

The grey dawn light found Straker sleeping in a chair by the cold ashes of the fire. He was still fully-dressed. Groaning he pushed tousled hair back from his eyes and rubbed his aching neck. He stretched out his cramped legs and walked over to the window. Not a good start to his second day. He looked down on the street below, the early morning stream of shop keepers, market traders, horses, delivery carts were already turning newly-fallen white snow into a brown, mucky slush.

Swiftly he pulled off yesterday's shirt, lathering his chest, face and hands with soap, avoiding looking in the mirror above the washstand. He splashed himself with cold water, briskly rubbing his skin dry with a towel. Straker pulled on a fresh white shirt and buttoned up his waistcoat and jacket, patting his breast pocket to check for his cigarette case and left the room. He needed coffee. Downstairs, the carpeted dining room was quiet, other guests still slumbering in warm beds. He bid the waitress good morning and sat at a table in the window, next to a tall palm tree. He ordered a strong pot of coffee, lit a cigarette and inhaled deeply.

He considered the body lying on the mortuary slab, the two bodies buried in a paupers' graves. Did the Butcher of York exist?

He could not be certain yet. He needed that exhumation order fast. Taking out another smoke, he tapped its white tip firmly on the hard metal of his case. The Home Office telegram was brought to his table as he was stubbing out his second cigarette. He scanned it quickly and put it deep inside his jacket pocket. Straker tried not to think about what Ada must do tonight.

***

Across the city another telegram arrived. Its recipient had been expecting one too. And he had just as much at stake.

In recent years, the Lord Mayor of York's augmentation of his personal wealth had been ferocious. The large fortune he'd amassed from the new railways made even the Prime Minister's family gold seem a little more than housekeeping money.

Now George Brass was omnipresent; in the boardroom where he coerced investors into pouring money into his get-rich schemes and in the corporation chambers where he influenced every decision to his own commercial advantage. His business mantra, 'Do it big or go home.'

Despite it all, the money, the power, the influence he had a few regrets. He wished he had not had to marry so young, when he was still a fresh-faced draper's apprentice on the make. But his wife's family money had set him up, enough for him to enter local politics. She'd been pretty enough then, but her girth seemed to have grown an inch with every year. And now that he could afford any woman, he was stuck with a spouse who embarrassed him every time she opened her mouth, however many jewels he smothered her in. Whenever he went south, to London, he tried to leave her at home.

He had always known that someone like him, the third son of a lowly tradesman, could only achieve his ambitions with hard currency. His brainwave to fund the construction of Lendal Bridge, to link his railway station with the city centre, would create wealth beyond even his dreams. His Twelfth Night Ball would be a celebration of his schemes, finally come to fruition, the pinnacle of his success. Everyone who's anyone would be in York. It would be the highlight of the Christmas season. Even his guests' overnight journey from London to York in his opulent private train would be magnificent. London society, the Prince of Wales himself, would have seen nothing like it; the luxury bedrooms with private bathrooms, lined with peacock-blue velvet, the carved oak-panelled dining car laid with silver and crystal for a twelve course dinner prepared by the chef of Brown's hotel. For entertainment, there would be soloists from the Royal Opera House singing Brass's favourite arias from *Nabucco* and *The Magic Flute*, performed in the red silk salon. And York would be at its best. In the week before his ball, a cordon would be thrown around the heart of the city. In a cleansing so thorough, the poor would be evicted from the centre, the homeless cleared from the streets and vagabonds arrested. York would be like a winter wonderland hung with garlands of greenery, red ribbons and flaming torches.

It had been a year in the planning.

Then as Christmas approached and the end of 1862 drew near, the death of a whore, of all ridiculous things, was threatening his grand plan. He had pulled in every favour, at the highest levels, to get this Butcher of York nonsense dealt with swiftly.

And now the telegram was in his hands.

136

He was prepared for every outcome. He had not grown rich by ignoring problems. He had grown rich by treating everything as an opportunity.

Downing a mouthful of Jerez sherry, George Brass turned away from the window from where he liked to look down on his people. He set down his glass on the mahogany sideboard, tugged his waistcoat down over his belly and straightened his jacket. Waiting downstairs were three of the city's magistrates. This meeting was a formality; little was expected of them other than to agree to whatever he told them to do.

He looked at his secretary Hugh Blake, 'Send them up.'

The beak-nosed man busily writing in a ledger looked up with narrowed, sharp eyes.

'Go on, get on with it,' snapped Brass.

Blake rose swiftly and with an obsequious half-bow left the room.

The Lord Mayor's brother-in-law came in first.

'Morning George, it's a parky one and it looks like more . . .' Nutt began.

'Stop babbling like a woman and listen,' said the mayor, holding up a piece of white paper. 'These are orders from the Home Office. You and the magistrates must agree to an exhumation. They want progress on this matter of the Butcher of York and so do I. These scurrilous rumours have gone on long enough. We need to resolve this, one way or the other.'

'But we can sort this out between ourselves, George.'

'Shut up Bob and listen. Believe me this is the last thing I want. But whether this Butcher of York is real or a bogeyman we need to act. These stories are scaring people away. I've had cancellations for my ball. I'm being made to look like a weak imbecile who can't control his own city.'

From a mahogany box on his desk, the Lord Mayor selected a Cuban cigar as fat as his thumb. 'And what if it is true?' he went on. 'We must think ahead, embrace the opportunity. The eyes of the country are on us Bob. Even Her Majesty, God bless her, is obsessed with this crime story. This is why I've had the best Scotland Yard detective sent up. We need to know, either way.'

The mayor blew pungent smoke towards his brother-in-law's face. 'Bob, if there's a killer, this detective can catch the bugger while you take the credit and we make money. Folk are mad for grisly murders and they'll come here in their droves if we've got one here. It's a win-win for us. We catch him, execute him, there'll be public tours of the Castle gaol, the condemned cell and a large tombstone. Dick Turpin's infamy will have nothing on it. The tourists will flock in. But, and this is a big but, only if it's all sorted before my ball. If it's not there'll be hell to pay, for everyone. I'll make sure of that.'

Nutt coughed and said, 'There is another way to end this quickly, George. We silence the old gobshites who kicked these rumours off. We can make sure there are witnesses at this exhumation who will say anything we want. The detective will be there, I know, but we can make out he's past his best or whip up rumours about his perversion of gawping at corpses. If there's no murderer, well it's business as usual.'

'I don't disagree. In an ideal world that would have been the best solution. But we have one big problem.'

'What's that?'

'It's a who. A woman. Ada Fawkes.'

'Fawkes you say? She's that fancy new portrait photographer on Coney Street. That detective wouldn't ask a woman to take pictures of rotting stiffs would he?'

'He would and he has. She's the official police photographer. It's perverse. And here's the worst thing, if there's evidence she will have the proof. There will be photographs. We won't be able to cover up anything. If there's a killer everyone will know about it thanks to that bitch and her camera. No, we have to do it this way.'

Brass tugged a bell rope and a liveried servant slipped into the room.

'Tell the magistrates they can come up now.'

The three formally-suited gentlemen walked in and dutifully signed the exhumation order.

***

It was mid-morning and Camille left Chapter House Street to go shopping with her long list of food. Ada watched her go with mixed feelings for she had only wanted a simple affair, a few friends and neighbours for drinks with maybe a plate of shrimp-paste on toast on Christmas Eve next week, not a full-on culinary feast.

'I'm French,' Camille had said when Ada tried earlier to tell her how drained she felt after yesterday. 'I don't do miserable food. If you want me to do this, I'll do it my way.'

'Do what you think then,' Ada had sighed.

Today Camille was in her element. Quickly she had learned the roguish ways of York's shopkeepers. It was not enough to treat them with contempt, she must better them. Armed with large wicker shopping baskets, she and Thomas made their way around the Minster wall and parted at Low Petergate – Thomas needed tobacco – and Camille continued the few yards to Henry Burton's, the city's finest wholesale and retail wine and spirit merchant. Camille critically inspected the window display; dark bottles of Madeira and small casks of port promising winter cheer in a thicket of ivy and red-berried holly. Pushing open the door, setting off the jangling brass bell, Camille stepped from the snowy street down into a wooden-floored room steeped in an aroma of spirits.

'Good morning Madame Defoe. How nice to see you.' The florid-faced wine merchant glanced up from his order book, affecting a nonchalant air but noticing his customer's sharp brown eyes dart over the bottles, the flagons, the casks; sherry from the Jerez vineyards, rum from the West Indies and whisky from the Highlands.

Taking his time he moved quietly round from behind the long counter, brown linen apron strings tied tightly around his portly middle. Camille always shopped here and Burton knew what to expect from the haughty woman in black. First there was a ritual to be observed. Extravagant hand gestures, a toss of the raven-haired head, a dismissive shrug of shoulders. Her accusations: his wine was watered down, how could she trust an English merchant, they knew nothing of a good vintage, how could she be confident his finest claret was not a vin de table in a fancy bottle. He loved it. The same charade, the same out-come. Long enjoyable minutes of haggling, teasing, pleading and then it was done. Burton made a note of her purchases in his ledger, very satisfied.

'Send my order round on Christmas Eve please. And make sure the champagne and pouilly are well chilled,' she commanded.

He watched her outline as she stood in the doorway. These French ladies knew how to look after themselves, he thought, thinking of his own pudding of a wife. 'You will ruin me Madame,' he said, wishing she would.

Outside Camille found Thomas peering in the buttermonger's window. He turned to her. 'Look at that display, now you have to admit that's impressive.'

White swans made of lard floated in real water in front of a rock sculptured from stilton.

'It's nothing. We have much better in Paris. Come on or we will run out of time.' They continued along to the street end, crossed King's Square and reached the top of the Shambles. In front of them bronze turkeys, wild ducks, fattened geese and links of fresh herb-flecked sausage hung on wooden poles. Beef ribs, pork joints, mutton chops lay displayed on the shammels with bunches of brightly-coloured rosettes and ribbons marking their prize-winning quality. A twisted, jumbled meat market, underneath overhanging eaves, where men daily slaughtered and dressed dozens of animals brought from the country into the city markets. Further on, at number ten, Camille stopped – barely glancing at the centuries-old shrine of the butcher's wife and Catholic martyr Margaret Clitherow – eyes only on her next opponent in battle. The butcher cheerily sharpened his knife as he listened and nodded; orders given with precision about plumpness, freshness, and marbling.

'That's everything. Merci monsieur,' she said firmly. But even Camille was no match for a gleaming-eyed Yorkshire butcher selling his wares. Wiping his hands down his blood-stained brown apron, Mr Addyman smiled. 'Now then Madame Defoe, you'll be wanting to try this new line of winter sausage?

I've just made them myself this morning, sage and onion from t'garden. Special offer today. I'll pop a few in for you shall I?'

Before she could say no, he had cut a couple of links.

'Ay, chops are good 'an all, bit of kidney in them. Ginger porkers from Mr Brown's old oak woodland t'ower near Marston Moor. There's only a few come in this morning, saved 'em for my best customers. A few of those for your supper Madame?' Three large ones went into her basket. He always beat her. But she had a grudging respect for the city's butchers and the taste of their meat. She was used to the best in Paris, but Yorkshire was special; lush green river pastures, heather and bilberry moorlands and wild hill tops of the Dales gave flesh a special flavour.

Onwards past Pavement and Whip-Ma-Who-Ma Gate, there was noise and movement everywhere. Small-paned bow windows shone with decorations, street hawkers shouted their wares, Christmas shoppers shoved and pushed. At the long queue for the fishmongers in Fossgate, they waited, hearing, watching the spectacle of the street. Inside the ice-cold shop Camille assessed Whitby shrimp, mussels and oysters for freshness and pressed the Scottish West coast smoked salmon sides for firmness. Bartering over, order placed, they turned back towards the Minster and behind them heard the sounds of carol singing drifting from crowded pubs where the most destitute and wretched sought solace in ale and gin.

***

Thomas had almost finished unpacking the shopping when Ada came into the kitchen, a letter in her hand. 'This came while you were out.'

142

Hearing the hesitation in her voice, Thomas looked up sharply. 'What is it?'

There was a frozen look on her face.

Swiftly Thomas came to her, took the note from her hands and scanned the lines. He sat down heavily.

'What is it?' said Camille, entering the room.

'The exhumation. It's going ahead,' Thomas replied.

'When?'

'Dawn, tomorrow.'

Camille crossed herself.

***

Straker's breath misted the cold glass as he looked out of the window at the lamplighter working his way down Silver Street. The fire in the office was well-stoked but somehow he could not get warm today. It would be worse later, he thought.

He crossed the room and picked up the photographs placed in a pile on the desk. He was studying the images of the body in the morgue when the door opened. Straker watched Nutt saunter into the office, an odour of tap-room ale and cigar smoke clinging to his wool overcoat.

'Right Straker I suppose we are going to have to put up with you now,' said Nutt. 'Well you better get this mess sorted then. Or there'll be trouble.'

Straker held his tongue for there was no point, whatever he thought of this man. Anyway he did not have time for Nutt's pettiness. He passed over the bundle of photographs. 'We need to know who this woman is. We can put out the image of her head and shoulders, without showing the injuries or her body.

I know the exhumation is at first light tomorrow, but there's no point wasting time. We must get going on this, the sooner the better. We can start by knocking on doors: brothels, shops and pubs. It's a small city so someone ought to recognise her. How many men have you got?'

Five,' Nutt replied. 'But Bevers is on the swans so he's not on full time duties.'

'Swans? Did you say swans?'

'Aye, swans. It's one of our duties here.' Nutt smirked, pleased to put an obstacle in Straker's way.

'What in God's name is that about?'

'A police officer is responsible for feeding the swans on the Ouse. He gets to live in the lock keeper's cottage for fifteen weeks, at a peppercorn rent. The men take it in turns, keeps it fair. It's Bevers duty until February. And we are down another lad, injured in a street brawl. So there's Bevers some of the time, Gage and Stone. I have to oversee things here, I can't be spared for the leg work, so that leaves just the three.'

Straker reached in his jacket for his silver case and took out a cigarette, certain now he would run out well before he returned to London. 'Well, let's have the three of them in for a briefing and discuss what we know.'

He inhaled deeply, held the smoke for a long time in his lungs and finally breathed out. Nutt grimaced at the fragrant smell. Cigarettes might be in vogue in London, but in York real men smoked pipes or if they were richer, cigars. Anything else was for foreigners in Nutt's opinion. Grudgingly the police chief opened the door, shouting for his men. Straker walked to the fireplace so he was standing as the police officers came into the room. They saw a broad, intimidating figure, silently watching them as they sat on chairs and the window ledge. Nutt made a point of reclining on the chair behind his desk as though he was still in charge.

Straker waited for them to settle. 'Good afternoon. As you probably all know by now, I'm Detective Inspector Straker. I'm leading the enquiry into the unexplained death of a young woman. You've all heard the rumours about the so-called Butcher of York. My job is to find out if we have a multiple killer on our hands.'

He paused watching their faces. 'We will be undertaking an exhumation at dawn tomorrow.'

There was a low whistle.

'So let's get going now. Let's begin with what we know. The body was found by a lamplighter in the early hours of December 12, about three o'clock. Who went to that crime scene?'

'What's that when it's at home?' asked Stone.

'The place where the body was found.'

'Bloody hell so that's where I was then, "at the crime scene" and I thought I was down by the mucky river,' said Stone in a mocking tone.

Straker fixed him with a look. 'Well?'

'I don't know. The body had been moved by the time I got there.'

'Did you look at the ground where she'd been lying?'

'What the bloody hell for? I just said, the dead whore had been carted off. There was nowt to see.'

'Well you might have seen blood for one thing, evidence as to whether she was killed at the crime scene or taken there after she was dead.'

'What the hell's he going on about,' muttered Gage to Bevers.

'Can't help with that,' Stone shook his head.

'Did you speak to the lamplighter Stone?'

'Nay, he'd got off home for breakfast.'

'Did anyone see anything?' Straker persisted.

'It's always quiet down there, apart from whores selling what they have to sell. And twas a cold night so likely people stuck to banging against t'church walls, it's more sheltered for the job.' Stone smirked.

'Can I ask a question?' Gage looked at Straker. 'Why do you care about this death? It's most likely just another prostitute who tried to rip off a punter and got her neck rung like a Christmas goose, had what was coming to her.'

Stone nodded his agreement. 'That's the truth of it. What does it matter if there are a few less of them on the streets? No one cares. They're trouble, always drinking, thieving or killing. We fished a poor sod out of the river earlier this year. He'd been robbed by a couple of hookers and shoved over Ouse Bridge.'

Stone winked at his colleagues. 'But we soon caught the slags didn't we lads, necking gin in t' King's Arms. Daft sluts had only gone t'pub round the corner and still had his wallet on 'em. We nicked 'em good and proper.'

There was laughter around the room. Straker's eyes narrowed. He leaned over the desk, picked up a photograph and handed it to Gage. The ruddy-faced giant of a policeman paled.

Bevers peered round his colleague's thick arm, trying to see the black and white image in his hand. 'What is it?'

'Modern policing methods, constable. Pass it round Gage,' Straker ordered. 'Now look at her. Closely. I don't believe this woman was killed because of a squabble over a few coins. I saw her body in the mortuary. Her wounds indicate something

146

more systematic. Her stomach was mutilated with a very specific mark, as you can see.'

Bevers looked like he wanted to throw up. Even Stone sat very still.

'No one deserves that,' said Straker. 'And look at that necklace. It's silver and more expensive than you would expect someone as destitute as her to possess.'

Nutt blustered, 'It might just be a present from a punter. We don't know that it isn't. And we don't know whether the other street walkers had slashes in their stomach. It's all speculation.'

'That's the point isn't it? We need to ask questions. Chief Constable Nutt did you send an officer to talk to the lamplighter who found her body?' asked Straker.

'What! That blethering owd cripple! He's not right in the head. Waste of time. It was that idiot who told *The Herald* reporter the stories about the cuts on the other bodies that were found a while since.'

'Did anyone here see those two bodies?'

'No, what was the point?'

'Did one of your men talk to the men who found them, the boatman Jack Hawker or the ferryman John Goodricke?'

Nutt bristled. 'Look here. The thing is Straker we are used to this sort of business. It often gets a bit lively in York. It's the tourists. They come here for a trip out; market days, race days, hangings, hirings. They have a drink or two, visit the stews. Strumpets ready to oblige for a nip of gin. It turns nasty. Happens all the time.'

Straker decided it would be a waste of time discussing the ethics of modern policing or the importance of treating all victims with equal consideration, so he chose to continue with the briefing. 'To be clear then, the situation is that, other than hear-say, we do not know if the other two bodies bore the same cut marks on their stomachs. Who did the post-mortems?'

'Dr Hubert Duff. He's one of York's longest-serving general practitioners. We always use him if we can, he's quick and very cheap,' said Nutt.

'And?'

'He didn't actually examine the bodies. The corporation won't pay out for post-mortems of whores so he recorded that they died of fright.'

Straker could barely keep the contempt from his voice. 'Without observing them?' Despite everything he knew about doctors – and post-mortems were a long-standing joke at Scot-land Yard – he was not prepared for that answer. He'd be telling his colleagues this one when he got back. It was nearly as good as another he'd heard recently, a Dr Cooke who reported that a decapitated 28-year-old woman had committed suicide by cut-ting her own throat.

Bevers coughed, dragging him back to the room. 'If it is the case that a killer roams the streets, surely we could tell by how he looks?'

'Murderers do not announce him or herself to their vic-tims with wild hair, misshapen features and twisted bodies,' said Straker. 'In my experience killers live undetected amongst us. No one wants to believe it but they are husbands, fathers, brothers, uncles or even sisters.'

Straker thought of his colleague Jack Whicher and the out-cry over his certainty that the young woman Constance Kent had slashed the throat of her three-year-old step brother. Truly, the public wanted to believe killers looked like depraved monsters, not their own ordinary kin.

'Right, that's all for today. We will regroup tomorrow after the exhumations.'

Straker turned to Stone. 'Talk to *The Herald* newspaper editor. See if anyone has reported anything. Surely someone is missing her.'

He pointed at Gage and Bevers. 'You lads, go to the shops, inns, banks, market stalls show everyone these.' He handed Bevers two photographs. 'We will be getting illustrated posters printed and pasted around the city, but in the meantime you can show these about.'

Gage and Bevers moved towards the door relieved to leave. 'And another thing lads.' Straker's commanding voice brought them to a standstill. 'These photographs were taken by Miss Ada Fawkes. She will be assisting the police with this investigation. Some of you might know of her.'

'That lady photographer?' asked Gage. 'I thought she took pretty pictures of lasses and makes them look better than they are. They all want one, even my sister, who is so ugly, only a bucket over her head could improve her.'

'She has helped me with other investigations.' Straker had resolved to keep any explanation brief.

'So a woman is working with the police?' Gage looked at him in puzzlement.

'Yes Gage, a woman. The police commissioner of the Metropolitan Police himself believes that we have need of women in the force. They can do things we can't.'

'We all know that,' sniggered Stone.

Straker looked directly at the policemen. 'It's common practice these days. The London Detectives, the Metropolitan Police, the French police use their wives and fiancées to help them with enquiries.'

'She's not your wife or fiancée though is she Straker? Unless there's something we should know about the two of you?' Stone again.

Straker made no attempt to hide his annoyance. 'Miss Fawkes is highly respected by the Police Commissioner Sir Richard Mayne. We are just fortunate she lives here in York, so she is available to assist us on this investigation. We should all try and move with the times. The world is changing.' Or at least the rest of the world, he thought.

'Just one thing, sir.'

'Well Bevers?'

'It's feeding time.'

Straker looked at him confused.

'The swans. They need feeding afore it's much darker. Gage can help me.'

Straker, who unlike his Scotland Yard colleagues never swore, found it difficult to hold his tongue. He turned away for a moment to summon up his patience, catching Nutt and Stone making no attempt to hide their amusement.

When they had gone and he was alone, Straker took out his cigarettes and lit another, without a doubt he had not enough boxes with him to last him through this case. He crossed the room and took up a position with a clear view out of the window. The day was fading fast. When all this was over, he'd like to return and order Nutt onto night watch duties, permanently.

He pulled out his timepiece. Not long now.

Chapter Fourteen

◊

A low throaty growl warned of the graveyard. On the other side of the high iron railings a snarling dog rattled its restraining link of chain, impatient to be loosed. The harsh noise disturbed the silence of the cemetery, but this security was a necessary precaution against body snatchers.

The horse and carriage passed through the open entrance gates towards and into the dark yard in front of the graves and the chapel.

Thomas reined the black mare to a halt. Ada looked round wondering if they were the earliest to arrive but then she noticed a shadow, and she saw a lone figure emerge out of the darkness. The figure walked purposefully towards them.

Without speaking Straker came to her side of the carriage and held out a leather-gloved hand. Ada looked at him, perhaps there was a flicker of a question in her eyes for he held her gaze as if to affirm his knowledge of her capability. She gripped his hand firmly and stepped down. Her boots sank into the snow and she nearly lost her footing. A strong arm went swiftly round her waist. Straker steadied her.

'Thank you detective inspector,' Ada said moving away from him and reaching for her work bag.

Straker turned to Thomas. 'Thank you for coming too, Mr Bell.'

A door opened in one of the buildings. Light spilled out of the doorway of the cemetery lodge and two men, bundled in grey greatcoats, stepped into the frosty air. They introduced themselves as the chaplain and the superintendent. The small group exchanged brief courtesies, but the strained atmosphere, the knowledge of what they were about to do, made any further small talk unwelcome. There was no time to waste. Thomas settled the horse and slipped a hessian nose bag over its head, briefly rubbing the white blaze on the mare's forehead. He went to the back of the carriage, lifting out Ada's field camera equipment for the men to carry. As she looked round her Ada caught sight of a stooped man, with an old fashioned broad-brimmed beaver hat pulled low on his head. He was holding a candle lantern and moving towards them along a path that led from deeper into the cemetery.

'Ah, Mr Scruton there you are. Lock the gates please,' ordered the superintendent and then turned to the waiting party. 'We can't be too careful. It's the Jerry Crunchers, we've had lots of them here. They come down from Edinburgh. Those Scots are so tight they won't even steal their own corpses. Well we're not having it. What's ours is ours.'

The old gravedigger turned the key in the solid iron rim lock, gestured with his lantern and started off back down the dark path, his limp making his gait slow and uneven. They kept close to each other as they followed him, past the chapel barely visible through a line of lime trees. Their wintry branches hung heavy and low over the path, tipping snow on hats and coats as they passed by. On they went to the end of the graveyard, to where the carved marble tombstones became rough wooden crosses.

Ada walked in silence behind the young chaplain, who was glancing side to side at the darkness either side of the path. Ahead the older superintendent had begun a stream of nervous chatter. She heard him tell Straker that he kept an alphabetical register of burials in a fireproof closet in the lodge and he could locate every corpse in the cemetery, even these two unidentified young women, whom no one had claimed as kin.

'I marked them under U for unknown,' he said to Straker with pride.

But he too fell silent at the sound of a rasping cough. Ahead of them they saw a bow-legged figure, pressing a brown handkerchief to his nose and mouth. As they came closer they realised the man was standing at the edge of a cavernous slash of black and on the surrounding ground two simple wooden caskets had been placed side by side. A single lantern hanging from a pole thrust deep into the earth illuminated the grim tableau of death.

This deep shaft was a pauper's grave, twenty-four bodies might be buried here, paid for by one of the many parishes. Corpses were dropped off every Tuesday and Friday by contracted delivery men and as soon as the hole was full, the grave was closed with a few words of prayer from the chaplain and rarely any mourners.

A second grave digger, shorter than the other, a pickaxe in his bare left fist, rose from his knees as they approached. He held up his other hand by way of warning.

'Stay there,' he said sharply.

Ada caught the unmistakeable sweet odour of earthy decay mingled with something astringent, sharp, that stung her nostrils and the back of her throat.

'Ah've thrown in some lime chlorate and ah've got a lighted candle down now, if it stays alight, we're dandy,' he informed them. 'I've known men suffocate in fumes from these deep graves. Aye, just dropped down dead when they reached the bottom. Then them that's climbed down to help, dropped dead too. And tis a bad un, this un. I emptied a cess pool t'other week and the smell of that was rose water compared to this.'

'It's graveyard miasma,' the superintendent explained through his large cotton handkerchief. 'The cadaverous vapours can indeed cause suffocation. It can't be helped. It's better than it used to be, before this cemetery opened.'

He was referring to nearly thirty years ago when this cemetery had become the solution to the city's overcrowded medieval parish churchyards. The local newspapers told of bodies disturbed, dismembered and sliced up to make room for more. Older people spoke of foul stenches and a peculiar taste in the mouth during morning service – grave odour seeping from putrefying bodies, inches under the surface. They had piled up the earth so York's burial grounds were higher than the pavements, but still bones and coffin edges stuck out, catching the ankles of the unwary.

'Yes, this is a massive improvement, a morally improving place,' continued the superintendent through the cloth. 'Our chapel is based on the temple of Erectheus in Athens. It's quite the fashionable promenade now. We even have catacombs. Our inhabitants like to be buried in proper company. Of course our hospitality is abused by some. People will steal the plants out of the ground and pinch the flowers.'

Snowflakes began to fall dusting the exposed coffins with white but nothing in the world could make this picturesque, not even virgin snow. Silently they waited. Minutes ticked by. Straker had moved to stand by Ada and she was grateful for his solid presence next to her.

'It's clear,' said the second gravedigger. 'Don't know what state them'll be in. It's right cold for this time of year though, keeps 'em fresher.'

The chaplain stepped forward, his black muffler wrapped around the lower half of his pale face. He pulled it down, clasped his hands and bowed his head over the caskets. He briefly offered up a prayer and made the sign of the cross in the air. Swiftly he moved back, pulling the wool over his mouth and nose again, coughing.

On a nod from the chaplain, the two gravediggers, with folded kerchiefs tied to cover all but their eyes, took up a crow-bar and a spade. The thin wood creaked, then splintered as they levered the lid off the first box. The cheap four panel casket was barely held together with a nail.

Thomas set up the tripod on one side of the coffin. Straker took up the lantern and opened the shutters fully, holding it high so the light spread out. The first gravedigger pushed the lid fully away with the edge of his spade. It fell with a soft thud that made them all jump. The escaping stench made skin shrink.

Ada shut her eyes, allowing herself a brief moment to gather herself, then she focused. She raised her chin, squared her shoulders and curtly nodded her readiness to Straker. On her command the detective lifted the lamp higher still so its light fell onto the shadows of the open coffin and Ada looked down on the remains. She saw a small, malnourished body. The tiny hands, almost bone now, were clasped over a thin chest. Of the young woman who once was, only her dark brown hair was still pretty. It fell in long tresses over a decaying shroud.

For several moments no one spoke.

Straker took charge. 'I must remove the cloth. I have to see her body. I wouldn't ask such a thing if it wasn't absolutely necessary.'

The superintendent nodded. 'Do what you have to.'

'First, what can you tell me of them?' Straker asked.

The superintendent thought a moment. 'Well, both women were buried in this public grave though their deaths were two months or so apart. After the holes are dug, we keep 'em open until they are full, unless a death is caused by typhoid or such like. Aye, but it's hard graft to dig 'em out even though the soil's quite sandy, so we keep 'em open as long as possible. We filled in this one with eighteen corpses and closed it mid-October.'

Straker nodded. 'And before they were buried, did you see the bodies?'

'Nay sir. The parishes provided the coffins and they arrived already boxed, in the covered hearse.'

'Thank you.' Straker turned away and passed the lantern to Ada. From his overcoat pocket he pulled out a small parcel of white cotton cloth which he unwrapped and tied over his mouth and nose. Next he pulled out his jackknife and walked towards the coffin.

Ada held the light as high as she could.

Straker knelt over the body, reached down and taking the thin cotton shroud in one hand he held the material taut at the breastbone. In one swift movement he slit the linen from top to bottom. The ripping sound was ghastly to everyone's ears.

'Good God man,' the chaplain burst out in a tone of horror. 'What are you doing? This is a sin.'

The superintendent, his hand clasped to his face in shock, was breathing heavily.

Ada swiftly rubbed eucalyptus oil over and under her nose, wound her black silk scarf round her mouth, moved the lantern closer and drew the slide so the concentrated light fell on the length of the waxen corpse.

'Straker,' she whispered. 'Look for a necklace? I fear the body's too far gone.'

He parted the edges of the cloth lain over breastbone and Ada held the light closer still and they saw it glinting, a small engraved silver cross hung around her neck. She heard herself gasp slightly.

'We must inspect the other body,' commanded Straker.

Again the chaplain protested. 'This is the devil's work.'

The detective held up one hand. 'No sir. It is not. This is a police investigation.'

He moved to the second coffin and Ada came to stand by his side. In the light the body was startlingly luminous. Ada's hand trembled, making the lantern's beam flicker eerily over the corpse. Straker seized her arm and gripped it, holding it steady. Here too, the light revealed an engraved silver crucifix. Ada looked at Straker with large eyes, processing the implications. He stared back at her, seeing his emotions mirrored; a resolve, a determination, a doggedness to see this case to the end.

The sound of bells tolling four made them start.

'We need to hurry,' urged Straker.

Thomas moved swiftly to secure the camera on its tripod and Ada took up her position behind the lens.

'Now!' urged Ada to Thomas. First the soft yellow glow of a match, then a flash of bright white light. The magnesium burned with such searing intensity, everyone turned their heads to avoid its flame. It was as impossible to look at as the sun.

The gravediggers gawped. Scruton couldn't contain himself. 'It's witchcraft. Look at that! That ain't natural.'

The other man crossed himself. 'And that's no woman. That's a devil's helper.'

Ada's eyes did not flicker from her task, though it didn't stop her mouth moving. 'This is a camera not a cauldron,' she said angrily. 'This is science not witchery and this devil's helper might just hunt down the monster who is doing this.'

The men all stared at her. Ada shook her head exasperated.

'Next.' She called to Thomas. 'Ready.'

Burning white light flooded the second coffin. Ada let the process take over her mind and looked out through the lens into another world.

Finally it was done. The release of concentration and tensed muscles made her reel slightly as she stepped back.

'Alright love?' Thomas asked.

'Yes, fine thank you.'

On a nod from Straker, the waiting gravediggers closed the coffins. Now holding ropes, they lowered the first back into the grave. They lifted the next one, it slipped slightly and as they jerked the ropes to steady it, the lid slid away and clattered down into the pit. Quickly the chaplain moved to the grave, intoned a very short prayer over the grave and crossed himself. Ada had turned away and was walking alone back towards the cemetery entrance by the time frozen clods of earth thumped down onto the exposed body in the open casket. The others fell into step behind her leaving the gravediggers to their task. No one spoke.

Three young women murdered by the hands of one.

Ada Fawkes had the proof.

The Butcher of York was a living beast.

CHAPTER FIFTEEN

◊

That morning's letters lay unopened, stacked in a neat pile amongst the barely-eaten breakfast plates. Ada and Thomas trying to warm their chilled bones, sat silently in chairs pulled as close to the range as possible. Ada had toyed with a half slice of buttered toast and finally pushed it away in favour of strong coffee. Thomas barely managed one boiled egg before he took up his pipe and tobacco.

It was only after he had drawn smoke that Thomas spoke. 'I'd not have had you do that for anything.'

Ada looked at him, eyes shadowed with grey-blue circles. 'We had to know.'

Camille, looking fresher than the other two, came out of the scullery. Her impeccably tailored silk blue day dress rustling as she moved. 'Well thank goodness what had to be done is done.'

'Yes I'm glad that's over. And we are certain now there is one killer. The women were wearing the same necklace,' Ada said.

'The Lord Mayor and his sidekick Nutt must believe it now,' Thomas drew deeply on his pipe. 'They have to. The photographs are proof.'

'And you have finished your part now Ada, I hope?' Camille asked.

Ada shook her head wearily. 'I cannot stop. Other women may be in danger. The Butcher might kill again. I have to help. I must do what I can.'

'You must get some sleep and you may feel differently.' Camille touched her shoulder.

'I won't feel differently. I have thought long and hard and I know I have a duty.'

'Ada I have been here for you while you recovered your health. I have helped you set up your new home and business. I would gladly do it all again. But I did not do so for you to be dragged into another murder case and end up nearly dead again and back in that sanatorium.' Camille's dark eyes flashed anger.

'Camille, I know what you are sacrificing to be here with me. But I saw those poor young women buried in a paupers' pit and no one caring what has happened, I can't bear it,' said Ada. 'We have to catch this killer.'

Ada looked at Camille, seeing the emotions flit across her face, and waited.

Finally Camille shrugged theatrically and held up her hands. 'D'accord.'

'Thank you,' Ada smiled at her. 'Now let's talk, share our thoughts. At least clarify what we know, it might shed some light.'

'So the two women in their graves, God rest their souls, were killed by whoever murdered that poor girl found on the river bank last week?' Camille asked.

'Yes we believe so. In truth the bodies are decomposing so we have only the crucifix and the eyewitness accounts of the men that found them that they were disfigured, the same cuts to the stomach . . . so it points to one killer.'

'But why would this murderer slice their bellies like a butcher cutting meat?' asked Camille.

'I don't know. It's baffling. I just hope the post-mortem that we are waiting for from Dr Auden will tell us more. We don't know if she died from these cuts, or if they were inflicted afterwards for another reason.'

In Paris Ada had photographed many bodies of people who had died violently at the hands of others. She had learned murder came down to the same motives; money, passion, revenge. But this felt different. Three young women with nothing and no one to care what had become of them. What had anyone to gain from their deaths?

If she was any judge, and she had seen soft flesh cut before, nothing she had witnessed before was comparable to this careful precise mutilation. It did not make sense to her. This killer was surely not a violent client or a jealous lover. These were not frenzied attacks, carried out in a fit of rage.

'Would you know what I think?' Thomas's voice broke into her thoughts. 'These killings remind me of the old battle stories I've heard tell; triumphant warriors who mutilate as an act of revenge on an enemy or take a scalp as a trophy.'

Ada looked at him thoughtfully. 'So it might be an act of revenge on these women. Or another possibility, perhaps he wants to let us know he's the killer and show off how clever he is at getting away with this, so he leaves a trademark like a stonecutter or a goldsmith.'

'But why? It is beyond my understanding,' said Camille.

'He had created fear and therefore he has power,' said Ada. 'But I don't know why someone would have this need. I have a feeling we will have to understand his mind to find out why he does what he does.'

'Of course we are assuming it is a man, but then in my experience women kill with poison, easier to slip something in a dish of sautéed mushrooms or sweetened cocoa,' said Camille. 'But I don't wish to understand such a monster. He should be sent to the guillotine.'

'That's the French for you,' said Thomas. 'Behead anything that moves. You'd have been watching those heads drop in the basket, cheering them on Madame Defoe, front seat, with your knitting.'

'And I would have cheered louder still if you were in the tumbrel, Monsieur Bell.'

Their bickering brought Ada back to the present and the work she must do. Draining her cup, she stood up. 'I must develop the photographs and then we have somewhere to start.'

Ada headed out of the house to her studio. The stove was already banked up with coal so the room felt warm, but not for long. The tin pails of ice cold water from the garden pump were waiting to soak her to the skin. Thomas had, with his usual efficiency, prepared all she needed.

She shut the door, locked it and stood for a few seconds in the dark studio looking round. Her camera was on the bench and she moved to touch its smooth wood case briefly like someone might a charm. She breathed deeply and began to work, quickly losing herself in the process so the world receded.

The work took longer than usual for she had needed to use prepared waxed negative papers outdoors in the cemetery rather than glass plates and it was hours later that the photographs were finally laid on the table in front of her.

When she looked at them she was filled with a sadness so consuming she thought her heart would break.

***

Straker sank back in the armchair, stretched his damp leather boots closer to the warm fire of his hotel bedroom and lit his first cigarette of the morning. He put his head back and exhaled, watching the smoke swirl thickly above his head and disappear into nothingness. He wished his visions from last night would go the same way. Instead they burned in his mind.

He drained the dregs of coffee from his cup. He must finish his report. He was due to meet the mayor in an hour to update him on the exhumations. His body still felt chilled and he leaned forward to feel more heat in his bones. As he watched the glowing coals, his mind drifted into the past to another bedroom fireside, another life; a green-eyed woman sat opposite, laughing joyfully, hair tumbling loose. He pictured that woman as he had seen her in the early hours of today; skin ash-grey with fatigue, forehead furrowed with concentration, red-gold hair drawn back tightly, pupils enlarged with concentration as she photographed the dead.

Damn it. He hadn't wanted to come to York. He hadn't wanted to involve her. He hadn't wanted her to suffer again. But he had his orders and he had no choice.

Wrenching his mind back to his report and the notes that he had begun, he moved to the small writing desk under the window. His mind was straighter now. The sooner this case was solved the quicker he could get back to London and leave her in peace.

It was scant comfort. The day he left York would be the last time he ever saw her. Ada Fawkes.

***

Dusk was falling by the time Straker walked into Silver Street police station to find interest in apprehending a killer was negligible. The detective's frustrations had stacked up; a murderer rampaging through York, a difficult and fraught meeting with an angry mayor, his London bosses demanding ludicrously fast results. But none of that mattered, oh no, for this was the Friday before Christmas, the day of that much-loved police tradition, the Christmas piss-up. No crime was getting in the way of a Yorkshire policeman and his pint.

'It's not going to bring that bloody stiff back to life lad,' was the most explanation he could get when he tried to explain the urgency of identifying the dead woman in the morgue.

Wages in pockets, silver shillings jingling, the forces of law and order set off out of the station door. The ensuing evening already planned out: ale, a roast beef supper, more ale.

Silver Street was lively with that day's traders in various states of inebriation shouting and laughing. A few jeered at the policemen as they turned left, walking the few yards past St Sampson's Church, into the market square and their first stop. The low black door of the Three Cranes was blocked by two earnest-looking women in temperance sashes. They were guarding the entrance as if this were no longer a hostelry, but an arena in which good and evil struggled for mastery over an immortal soul.

The policemen tried to push past. 'Working men, think of your children,' called out the younger one, her rosy-cheeked face lit with piety. 'You should know better officers,' added the elder, frowning through her gold-rimmed pinch nose spectacles.

'You lot, you bloody cocoa-munchers, you bloody spoil everything,' Nutt growled, pushing his way past into the crowded tap-room, followed by his loyal team.

Straker, hovering behind, had two choices; join them or not join them. He opted for joining them, a few pints to bond with his team and an opportunity to hand round the photograph of their mystery woman. Then he would bail out before the evening turned nasty. The Three Cranes had already grown riotous and the heady reek of spilt ale mingled with cheap tobacco. Raucous market traders and laughing women, flushed with ruby port, streamed in and soon the bar was rammed.

'I'll get them in men. Pints all round?' asked Straker, heading for the narrow bar, knowing what was required of him.

'Aye lad,' replied Stone on everyone's behalf, formality overlooked at this time of year. Beer slopping on bare wooden floorboards, dirty glasses passed over macassar-oiled heads and Straker was supping warm, watery, flat ale with York's finest. He would rather have had a strong cool French pilsner, but he might as well have announced himself a raving lunatic as admit that in here, in this company.

'Your round again sir,' shouted Stone.

Then one after the other, a straight pub crawl from Church Street to Monk Bar; the Golden Lion, the Old White Swan, Cross Keys, Golden Slipper, Royal Oak. Straker's photograph of the body in the morgue was shown everywhere. It elicited mixed reactions, fascination, humour – 'she looks a bit frigid, that your lass?' – and a lot of hostility.

Then in the mahogany-panelled parlour of the Oak, he had a result. A young man, no more than twenty or so, with dirt engrained fingernails, a shiny face and a clay pipe clamped to his brown teeth.

'Aye, I think I know her, she's from the Refuge though tis a bit hard to tell in this light. I deliver coal there every Tuesday. So she's that girl found a few days ago, down by the river?'

'Can you look again. Make sure?' Straker urged, standing over the long wooden table of drinkers. 'Hold it to the light.'

The young man shifted on the bench leaning towards the stone fireplace so the photograph caught the glow from the fire. 'Yes, I'm certain it's her. She was kind to me when I jammed my fingers between our coal wagon and a wall. Bled like buggery. She took me into the scullery and bandaged up my hand.'

'She's a housemaid there then?'

'Aye, pretty girl, brown hair, cleans out the fires and suchlike. She waits for us with the empty coal scuttles. Always looks a bit sad. Not surprised that God awful place.'

'Do you know her name?'

'Mebbe Rose or summat.' He squinted again at the photograph in his hand. 'They're something these. Fancy that. I am seeing a real person really dead. I can't get my 'ead round it.'

'Where is this Refuge?'

'Everyone knows that. It's up Bishophill. Someone really took a photograph of a stiff?'

'That's bloody sorcery,' said an older man with hunched shoulders, looking down at the photograph as he arrived at the table with two ales. Thank God, they didn't know the photographer was a woman Straker thought, or Ada would be burned as a witch.

Straker made his excuses and left his colleagues. York's constabulary were on their way out of the Royal Oak onto the street, steadying each other for balance. Working back along to the Golden Slipper, Cross Keys, the Old White Swan, Golden Lion, the Three Cranes. He watched them go, bellowing 'Good King Wenceslas' into the night. They howled as Nutt sang the page boy's lines in a high falsetto.

Straker walked the other way. He had a name. The chase had begun.

***

Across the city in Chapter House Street, Ada woke, hearing the sound of her name softly called.

'Ada. Ada. It's late, you've had a long day.' Camille was leaning over her as she lay on the drawing room sofa. 'Why don't you go to bed?'

'I wanted my head clear of the day before I went up,' she said, struggling to sit upright. 'I thought reading would help, but I must have nodded off. It's so warm by the fire.'

'You need to get some proper sleep.' Camille smoothed a velvet cushion and picked up Ada's fallen book from the rug. She took the empty brandy glass from the small polished oak table next to the sofa and saw a pile of envelopes from that morning's post. 'You haven't opened your letters yet.'

'I meant to. I'll do it now.' Ada, seeing a black-edged white envelope took that first. 'Oh God, who's died now?' She scrutinised the writing. 'It's Isabella Fox's hand. Do you remember?

I met her while I stayed at the Hydro sanatorium. The Queen's lady-in-waiting?'

'Yes I remember she was a good friend to you there.'

'Indeed she was. And that explains the stationary, thank goodness. Prince Albert's been dead for, well two years I think, but the Queen grieves on. Isabella told me once she clings to her mourning like a comforter and all her staff must stay in mourning too.'

Camille turned to leave. 'I'll make you a hot water bottle while you read it.'

Ada slit the envelope with a silver paper knife, pulled out a sheet of black-edged white paper, unfolded it and began to read the tiny black handwriting.

She had known Isabella Fox for little more than a year though Ada felt they had been friends for longer. They had supported each other during their difficult early time at the Hydro in Malvern, when each hour, each day, each week had seemed an eternity.

It had been her first afternoon there, Ada remembered, that they had been introduced by the clinic's director Dr Gully, a man described as the most gifted physician of the age. It had certainly seemed to Ada that treatment at his clinic was modern and progressive. His therapy had showed her that she could find a way back to the light from the darkness she fell into after her last case in Paris. Dr Gully's patients had been encouraged to meet, to listen, to talk to each other about their lives and problems. It was a radical approach and one that had worked well for them both.

Over many walks in the beautiful Hydro grounds the two women had talked. Ada had learned that Isabella was in Malvern to take the waters as part of a recovery after a long bout of pneumonia, but felt a deep sadness and loneliness in her life at court. Isabella had listened in pity when Ada had spoken of her recurring nightmares and attacks of panic after her final case in Paris. She had been awed by Ada's job as a forensic photographer. And when, in due course, she finally learned of the full extent of Ada's loss, she had wept with her.

As soon as Ada had felt well enough she had picked up her camera again and taken photographs at the Hydro. Isabella had been astonished by the skill of her photography and had sat for portraits with her daughter Lucy whenever the young woman visited. When Isabella had returned to her Royal duties in London, she had showed Ada's portraits to the Queen who had much admired them.

This friendship had helped Ada's recovery as much as Dr Gully's treatment. She had met Isabella afterwards at Windsor, but they not seen each other since Ada had come north to York.

Ada had looked up from finishing the letter as Camille returned with a stone bottle wrapped in a square of soft red cotton.

'Thank you, just what I need tonight.' Ada smiled.

'How is your friend?'

'I don't know. It's quite strange. She writes that she is travelling up to Balmoral for New Year. She told me once she hates it there, all that flinging and reeling, but I suppose she has no choice, she's at the Queen's beck and call. She asks me to meet her train when it stops in York at noon on December 29. She says she has an urgent request and no one who can help, but me.'

'That is intriguing. Maybe it's an important photographic commission.'

'That would be rather nice. Anyway we shall see.'

'Now it's getting late. I'll put your bottle on the table here. Don't be long or it will go cold.'

Ada, still holding the letter in her hand, stared into the fire. Her friend must really need her help. Questions swirled around in her mind. Nothing to be done now, she set down the letter on the table, rose and stretched.

In her bedroom she sat at her dressing table to take out the pins from her hair. It fell heavily framing her wan face. She looked at her image reflected in the mirror and thought of her day. She knew that there was little chance of sleeping tonight; she wondered if she would ever sleep properly again.

WEEK TWO

20 – 27 DECEMBER 1862

*'In the days when men were burned at the stake
for practising "black magic", the photographer
would have been an undoubted victim.'*
- Alvin Langdon Coburn

CHAPTER SIXTEEN

◊

Saturday morning, York City centre

O vernight the damp mist from the river had seeped into every nook and cranny of the city and those outside on this bitter morning hurried to reach their destination. Straker, the collar of his dark wool overcoat turned up against the biting cold, walked the short distance from the police station to Coney Street and pushed open a shop door. Stooping slightly as he passed under, he stepped into the room, removed his hat, bowed slightly and addressed Ada with a politeness as freezing as the December air.

'Miss Fawkes.' His tone was detached but his eyes took in the shadows under her eyes. Clearly she had slept as little as him.

'I have the photographs ready for you. I've laid them out in the studio upstairs. The light's best there,' Ada said, pushing back her untidy hair. She started to walk towards the stairs.

'Miss Fawkes.'

Hearing the sharpness in his voice, she stopped and turned to look at him.

'I have news,' he said. 'I believe, thanks to your photograph, the young woman in the morgue has been identified. She may be a housemaid called Rose who lived at a house called the Refuge.'

'I know of it. Bishophill Refuge, it's a home for fallen women. There are five or six such places in York but it's the principal one. These places are charities and rely on voluntary subscriptions and donations. It's grim by all accounts. But how do you know?'

He explained how the young coalman from the Royal Oak tavern last night thought he recognised her from the photograph, but he'd had a few pints and wasn't absolutely sure.

'I need to show them your photograph to confirm it's her and find out what I can. Will you come with me? They might speak more easily to a woman than a detective from London.'

'When?'

'Now if it's convenient Miss Fawkes.'

'I just need to get my things.' She returned from the cloakroom at the back of the studio, pulling on her cloak and glancing around the room.

'Are you looking for this?' Straker asked.

Turning, she saw him holding up a long, mulberry cashmere scarf. 'It was on the floor, just by the table.'

'Thank you.' She took it and started to wrap it around her shoulders. Fumbling, she dropped the length down her back and as she twisted to catch the end, Straker bent and picked it up. Instinctively, maybe out of habit, he wrapped it gently around her neck. The tips of his fingers grazed her neck. She turned to him, surprised and he stepped away abruptly, his face inscrutable.

'I'll hail a cab,' he said quickly. Out in the raw morning air, he whistled and a white horse and Hansom drew up.

'Cold enough for thee?' said the muffled cabbie leaning over. 'Where's tha going?'

'Bishophill Refuge please,' said Straker. He held out his hand to Ada. She clasped it as she climbed in, not looking at him. He stepped up and sat next to her, avoiding touching. They did not speak.

They went over Ouse Bridge, and left onto Skeldergate, past narrow lanes of red brick houses running parallel to the river and the dingy warehouses of Queen's Staith. People were huddled for warmth around street braziers or leaning against the walls of Fetter Lane. It was probably warmer outdoors than inside their dank, bare overcrowded rooms. The narrow streets sloping down to the side of the river were even more notorious than the Water Lanes slums on the opposite bank.

They rounded the curve past Baile Hill and Bishophill. At the turn of the century, it was a fashionable street overlooking fields and gardens, but the rich had long since abandoned this area and now it was crowded with public houses, beer shops and brothels. The congested rookeries, yards and terraces of dilapidated artisans' cottages stretched up to the city wall.

'That's us,' the cabbie said. Ada saw, as they pulled up outside number forty three. Bishophill Home had once been a smart, private residence – large enough for a middle-class family and servants. But even today's sprinkling of white powdery snow could not prettify its despondent aspect.

'Wait for us please,' ordered Straker.

'That'll be extra,' replied the cabbie.

Straker nodded and turned to look at the Refuge. This was where the desperate, the starving and the homeless sought shelter, York's solution for fallen women. And you had to be very despairing to voluntarily submit to its religious doctrine, harsh discipline and brutal laundry work. It was similar to prison, but with a drabber uniform. The penitentiaries in York, like those in other parts of the country, operated specifically for the purpose of reforming their inmates and to secure them paid jobs as wash-house drudges, so they could continue their penance of cleansing stains out of the dirty. In truth there was little chance of these girls entering respectable society, even if they could endure months of Christian charity. Most had suffered neglect, abuse and had little education. Some had learning difficulties and all had been brutalised during their time as prostitutes. These women were outcasts; destitute or diseased or drinkers. Mostly all three.

Straker knocked on the front door. It opened slowly and from a brown-ochre panelled hallway, a shortish, plumpish woman about fifty or so, dressed in an old-fashioned black and white taffeta plaided morning dress stared out at them. A metal hoop of keys hooked to a girdle around her wide waist suggested this was who they needed to talk to.

'Yes? How may I help?' she asked curtly.

'We would like to speak to the matron, please. May we come in and explain our business. It's of great importance,' Straker said.

'I am the matron, Miss Brockett.'

'How do you do madam. I'm Detective Inspector Straker of Great Scotland Yard, I'm hoping you can be of service to me.'

Her face expressed surprise, then interest. 'Oh do come in detective inspector.' Her voice changed to the politer clipped one she kept for her well-to-do visitors. 'The girls are doing their chores.'

Miss Brockett's cold blue eyes sharply assessed her two visitors as she showed them through a door to her left, into the large front drawing room. Her private parlour, she explained.

Ada couldn't help judging its gilt mirrors, rose-patterned carpet, jardinières of ferns, curvaceous padded chairs and enormous carved wooden sideboard as she found a small space to stand, squeezed next to an over-large round mahogany table crowding the bay window.

'Miss Brockett I am in York at the request of The Home Secretary and the Lord Mayor to investigate . . .' Straker began.

She interrupted. 'Oh goodness me. I read about you in this morning's *Herald*. The story says you are up here to investigate these terrible murders. Fancy that. A famous detective, in my parlour.'

Matron went on. 'Does he exist then the Butcher? Oh it's a terrible affair. It makes you frightened to leave the house, Detective Inspector Straker. But I am sure you will keep us safe.'

Ada blamed Charles Dickens. He had glamorised detectives in his best-selling weekly *Household Words*, so much so that people believed these men had mystical powers to sum up a character or a crime scene in one glance.

'Our business is urgent, madam,' Straker said. 'Indeed we are investigating the death of a young woman and we think she may have lived here.'

'Here!' She clasped her podgy hand to her mouth.

'If you would be so kind as to look at this photograph, Miss Brockett, and tell me if you recognise her.' Straker took the tissue-wrapped photograph carefully from his leather bag and unwrapped it. The waxen black and white face of their mystery brunette looked as peaceful as a sleeping child and Straker felt protective of her as Miss Brockett grabbed it eagerly from his outstretched hand.

She paused and then looked up in a horror that she was clearly enjoying. 'Is she . . . Is she . . .?'

'Yes.'

'You have a picture of such a thing. It is ungodly.' She crossed herself.

'So is murder, Miss Brockett. Now do you know who she is?'

'It's Rose,' the matron confirmed and crossed herself again. 'God rest her soul. I will pray that her mind became awakened to her sinful state in her final moments.'

She shook her head and folded her hands together as if in devout prayer.

'This will be a terrible shock for everyone and you particularly as her matron,' said Ada. 'As it's nearly Christmas and it's nearly lunchtime, shall I pour us all a little sherry, and you can tell us all about it.'

'Oh thank you,' said Miss Brockett fluttering her smooth hands. 'It has been such a shock.'

Ada went to the mahogany sideboard and picking up a decanter from a round brass tray, poured three cream sherries. She handed them round.

'Your good health Miss Brockett,' Ada watched as the matron took a large gulp.

Then she asked her to start at the beginning with the story of poor Rose. Matron sank back in a padded easy chair, her voluminous dress billowing around her and took another mouthful.

'I became the matron here, ten years ago, I think, about seven years after the home opened. We have a very strict policy, for good reasons as we are sheltering troubled young women. Our girls are carefully selected, no older than twenty-five, not in the family way and not diseased. Our mission is to reform them and help them to re-enter society in a respectable position.'

Ada and Straker nodded.

Miss Brocket went on. 'Rose Fisher was troublesome, as I knew she would be from the moment she arrived here, uncouth, disruptive and with an unruly temper. Mrs Milner is the laundress and her main task is to instruct the girls in washing, starching and ironing, she complained often of Rose's laziness and bad attitude to her work. After two years, we found her employment with a suitably strict Chapel woman, Mrs Barker who takes in washing. But within a week the ungrateful girl had run away to her old life of sin. Oh but she turned up again, like a bad penny, practically starving, and I was told to take her in. She duped those committee ladies, said she had repented. I did my Christian duty, but I'm certain she never renounced sin.'

'What made you so certain?' asked Straker, his face unreadable.

Miss Brockett's voice hardened. 'One of the girls saw her in the garden, close to the river. Rose was hanging out washing, but was stood close to the wall talking to someone. It's a problem with having such a garden. Men from Skeldergate get on the wall and talk to the girls when they are hanging out the washing, exercising or sitting under that old pear tree. Harriet asked her who she was speaking to she said no one she was just singing.'

'Well perhaps she was,' Ada said.

'There's more. A few weeks later Harriet saw her at the same place by the wall. This time she thought she saw Rose pick up something and hide it in her apron.'

'Did Harriet see anything of it again?' Straker asked leaning forward.

'No, but the laundress mentioned that Rose had a necklace which swung from under her dress as she was in the wash house, scrubbing. She didn't think Rose had it when she came to us and was curious.'

'Did anyone mention any of this at the time?'

'No detective inspector. No one thought anything of it. The girls and men, well it's a never-ending struggle. We try and keep the girls protected. We paint the glass of their bedroom windows and fix the sashes so they can only open half a pane at the top.'

Straker nodded. 'Tell me what happened the day she disappeared. When did you realise she had gone?'

The matron shrugged and shook her head. 'That morning, well she had just vanished. Her bed was empty, not slept in. She's not the first girl to run away from here, we've had a few go this year, gone back to their old sinful ways no doubt.'

'Did you mention it to anyone?'

'No, she has no family.'

'Did you report her missing to the police?'

Miss Brockett laughed. 'No, of course not. We thought she'd run away. We presumed Rose had gone back to her old life. Many girls are too full of sin and this is a Godly place. She . . .'

Straker cut her off. 'So you told no one. Did no one go looking for her?'

'Of course we had to report it to the committee.'

'What does the committee do here Miss Brockett? And did they do anything?'

'The Penitentiary Society is responsible for overseeing this home, ladies and gentlemen, well-to-do types, who run lots of charities in York. The committee meets here every month and I report to the ladies every week, tell them what's going on, any problems and suchlike. Well as far as anyone was concerned that was the end of the matter. Sometimes our girls run away, we had one escape out the window, another over the wall just last month. We never look for them.'

'What do the girls do here, what's their routine?' he asked.

She thought a moment, taking another sip of sherry. 'Well we have worship twice daily and the chaplain Reverend Turner comes in once a week to give Bible classes. They carry out their duties; plain needlework, laundry, scrub floors. The ladies visit and teach them how to read and write a bit. They are not allowed out of the house and may not receive or send letters without being vetted by me. They are up at six, bed at ten and no heating or lighting after that, except in my private rooms of course. They wear a plain grey dress and are given the Bible. No lying, swearing or insubordination.'

Ada was certain she too would have climbed out of the highest attic window to escape from here. She asked, 'How was Rose in herself?'

'She had become rude and disruptive. She was always talking of her elder sister. She died and Rose blamed us. It wasn't our fault, she couldn't come here. We have to have rules. If girls are found to be in a delicate state of health, they are not permitted to come here. They are sent to the Union Hospital.'

Ada winced, Straker catching her expression raised an enquiring eyebrow.

'The workhouse hospital,' Ada explained to him. 'Girls, women with diseases go there. And never come out.'

Miss Brockett looked indignant. 'Well what of it? That's the right place for the likes of them. Rose and her sister arrived here homeless orphans, threadbare clothes barely covering their modesty. It was obvious to me straight away that the elder girl shouldn't be here, she was in a terrible state of sin, she could scarcely walk or talk.'

'How old were they?'

'Rose was barely fifteen then, so I think her sister, I can't recall her name, was sixteen.'

'What happened to her sister?' Straker asked.

Miss Brockett turned her flushed face to him. 'We had to turn her away detective inspector, we had no choice. She was taken to the Union, became sicker and died. In my opinion her health gave way when her mind became awakened to her sinful state. I'm told she was paralysed by the end but, thank the Lord, she died in a peaceful state, expressing a simple trust in Christ. I'm told she had a deep sense of her wrongdoing. There was no return to the sin from which she had fallen thankfully. A brand plucked from the burning.' Miss Brockett looked piously at the oil painting of Jesus as a boy in a carpenter's shop, hung above the marble fireplace.

Ada persisted. 'What about Rose?'

'Well for a time all was well. The ladies were very pleased with how she settled in but it didn't last. She became abusive, talked back to me, refused to do her needlework, that sort of thing. Rose seemed distracted, always wanting permission to leave the house to visit a friend. Well, of course we didn't allow it.'

'Did she make any friends here?' Ada said.

'A girl called Elizabeth Rooke, but the Ladies Committee made her leave. We heard soon after that she was locked up in the Castle gaol for indecency.'

'Do you know where she is now?' Straker asked sharply.

'Oh Elizabeth died in prison. Her death was attributed to a visitation of God according to the inquest report in *The Herald*. Another poor soul saved from the flames. But there's Esther's still here. She's confined to bed with rheumatism. She shared a room with Rose.'

Straker leaned forward and looked directly at Miss Brockett. 'May we speak to her?'

'She doesn't know anything. I questioned her of course, but she says she didn't hear or see anything.'

Straker said softly, 'Still we would like to speak to Esther Miss Brockett. In fact since Miss Fawkes is here, she could have a word, a young girl might prefer to talk to a woman rather than a grisled old detective like me.'

Miss Brockett hesitated. 'I'm not sure that would be right.'

'Miss Fawkes is helping the investigation. She knows what she is doing, she will be very considerate.'

'That's strange work for a woman.'

'Madam, the police commissioner himself believes there is a need for female police officers. Perhaps, while you and I wait, I may talk to you further about our high profile criminal investigations. You are no doubt aware of the infamous Road House Murder two years ago. I could tell you all about Mr Whicher's detective methods while Miss Fawkes talks to Esther.' Straker, leaning forward slightly, smiled at the matron.

Miss Brockett immediately heaved herself onto her wide feet and led Ada up the carpeted staircase to the first floor and gestured to another narrower flight of wooden stairs. With a heavy tread, she returned to her parlour, smoothing her hair as she went.

Ada made her way up the wooden stairs and to the second floor and up again. At a crooked door at the top, she knocked quietly, opened it slightly and put her head round. As her eyes adjusted to the gloom, she made out bed frames pushed into awkward spaces under the eaves of a tiny garret room. It smelled of mildew and damp. She heard a small whimper and turning to the sound, made out a small shape under a darned woollen blanket.

'Esther?'

Over-large eyes stared back at her.

'Esther?'

A soft moan and a small nod confirmed it, but the effort started her coughing. Esther's tiny body was wracked with the struggle until the bed itself shook.

Ada bent forward and gently introduced herself. She explained that she had questions about Rose's disappearance. She found she hadn't the heart to tell her Rose was dead. Esther struggled to sit up, lank hair falling over her face. Ada smoothed it out of the girl's eyes and gently supporting her shoulders, helped Esther prop herself up on the pillow. She was fifteen or sixteen, perhaps. Hard to tell, she was so emaciated.

'I miss her, she was kind,' said Esther finally.

Ada sat closer to her on the bed and took the small hands lying on the blanket in hers, stroking them tenderly.

'She had a friend. A kind gentleman she said.'

'Who was he?'

Esther coughed again, covering her mouth with the blanket trying to silence the noise. 'I don't want to make trouble, miss. I want to stay here. If I'm a nuisance they will send me to the workhouse.'

'They won't do that.'

'They do. Bad girls like me. I have sinned. I am shameful. Our dear mother matron has made me realise how unworthy I am of forgiveness. I hope she will come up and see me some-time like she does the other girls. I would like to see her face again.'

Ada thought of her own mother who had loved her uncondi-tionally and could have wept. Girls like Esther had no chance. Ada could only imagine the life that had brought her to this moment, where waiting to die so young in a pitiful attic room was better than any other part of her short life.

'Rose asked me to keep a secret,' whispered Esther.

'She would want you to tell me now so I can help her.'

'I can't. She made me swear.'

'Please Esther, I care about what has happened to her,' said Ada, certain she would only get this one chance with the dying girl.

'I wish I could see matron,' said Esther. 'I would so like to ask her forgiveness.'

Ada moved closer, stroking the girl's little arms, feeling tears prickle in her eyes. 'Esther please if you know something about why Rose left, tell me. I promise matron will come and see you.'

Oh dear God she thought that a girl had been made to feel so ashamed of herself that seeking absolution from a sancti-monious old bitch like Miss Brockett was to Esther as though her mother had wrapped her in her reassuring arms and made everything right.

Esther began speaking so quietly Ada had to bring her head nearer still. 'Rose was kind to me. She said she missed her sister so she would love me instead. She stole a blanket from the laundry so I had could have another. It's so cold up here.'

'And what happened?'

'Sometimes she would leave her bed and creep into mine. We both used to share with our own sisters, it's so much warmer. She would talk to me when the pain in my chest stopped me sleeping. One night Rose said she had a secret. She would tell me, but I wasn't to tell anyone else because secrets aren't allowed here.'

'What was it Esther?'

'A man had been very kind to her. He said he could help her have a better life.'

'Who was he?'

'She wouldn't tell me. But she told me he talked to her, listened to her. She showed me a necklace, a silver cross, he gave her. He said it was a token of his friendship. He really cared for her. Do you think she is with him?'

Ada sighed to herself. 'Where did she meet him?'

'I don't know. We only see the men who visit here. We are not allowed out except to go to church.' Another coughing fit shook her small body, leaving her gasping for air.

'Esther?'

She looked up and there were flecks of red blood at the corners of her white lips.

'Esther, is there anything I can do. Is there something you would like?'

'I had a doll, my ma made her for me. She was made from all our bits of clothes . . .' Esther's voice faded as though she was drifting into her past. She closed her eyes.

Ada carefully took her hands away and stood up. She looked down at the little bed and its pitiful occupant and turned away. She marched swiftly down the flights of stairs and pushed open the drawing room door.

'Miss Brockett, Esther asks to see you now,' she said, standing squarely in front of the matron's chair.

Straker looked up at her sharply, sensing her tension.

'Oh no Miss Fawkes, the fallen girls must be given time to fully repent their sins. That is best in solitary contemplation.'

'Esther does not have time. Have you called a doctor?'

'The Good Lord will take care of those who choose to be saved from the flames,' said Miss Brockett, folding her hands piously in her lap.

'Miss Brockett be aware I am acquainted with many of the ladies and gentlemen who form the Penitentiary Committee. Many of those ladies are in the Temperance movement, in fact I think that is a requirement of your position here.'

Miss Brockett stuttered. 'I. I. keep an offering for visitors, Miss Fawkes.'

'We both know it's a bit more than that.'

'You can't prove it.'

Ada remained silent, her face stony.

Miss Brockett dropped her polite visitor's voice. 'Alright what do you want?'

Straker sat back in his chair, keeping quiet, leaving this to the expert.

'The truth, Miss Brockett. Could any of the girls meet a gentleman?' Ada asked.

'They can't. We do not allow them to have gentlemen friends. What did that girl tell you? It's most likely lies.'

'Esther said Rose had a gentlemen friend, I'm asking again Miss Brockett who visits here?'

'The committee inspects every month, there are the errand boys, delivery men and the vicars visit of course; Reverend Turner and Reverend Lindley. The girls do leave the house to attend church twice a week, but always under supervision.'

Straker interrupted now, adding the officialdom. 'We will need a list of everyone who comes here Miss Brockett.'

'I am very busy, what with Christmas.'

'I think you could manage that by tomorrow and call the doctor, today,' Ada said.

'Well, yes I suppose so. I will inform Dr Auden later.'

Straker stood, his broadness making the room seem even more cluttered and moved towards the door. 'I look forward to receiving the names.'

Ada said, 'One last thing. I want to send a gift for Esther. I would like you to give it to her as though it came from you. And I would like to know that you have done so.'

Outside in the street, the cold fresh air was as welcome to Ada as the waiting Hansom, the black horse feeding contentedly from a nose bag while the driver, up on his seat, sucked on a clay pipe.

'Coney Street please,' said Straker, holding out his gloved hand to Ada. She held his grip, stepped up into the cab and sank back onto the hard leather seat.

'Blackmail!' Straker tried not to sound amused as he climbed beside her, turning his long legs to squeeze them in.

'You should have seen her Straker. Poor Esther.'

He shook his head. 'What did she tell you?'

'Rose had a secret. She had a gentleman friend and he gave her a necklace, a silver cross. Apparently he was kind and said he would take care of her. No wonder she went to him.'

They were silent.

The cab rattled over Ouse Bridge. Ada had a thought as they approached the turning onto Spurriergate. 'Do you mind if we stop here a moment. I need to get something.'

Straker called up through the hatch to the driver, who grumbling to himself reined in his horse. Straker swung his legs out of the cab, turned and offered his hand to Ada. She climbed down, looked briefly through a paned bow window and went into a brightly-lit shop close to St Michael's Church.

'There'll be waiting time,' shouted down the cabbie.

Minutes later Ada handed up a brown package tied with green ribbon to Straker. He held out his hand to help her climb back in. As she took the parcel from him, he raised his dark eyebrows.

'It's a doll for Esther. It's nearly Christmas. Or have you forgotten?'

He shook his head. 'I know all too well how time is pressing.'

CHAPTER SEVENTEEN

◊

Outside snow whirled around the old narrow streets, paupers, vagrants, skeleton children huddled in doorways and those who had homes hurried to seek shelter. Straker strode along Davygate and down Church Street, pausing to buy copies of *The Herald*, *The Times* and to hand out coins to those desperate enough to be out in the cold.

He reached Silver Street station reflecting on how much he wanted this case solved quickly so he could leave York and never come back. Glad to be inside, he passed by the front desk, along the corridor and opened the door to Chief Constable Nutt's office to find it empty. No doubt the man was in the pub or having a cosy chat with his brother-in-law. He lit a cigarette, and sat in a chair for a while, inhaling deeply.

Footsteps on the flagged corridor outside and a rap on the door dragged him from his thoughts. 'Yes, come in.'

'I'm the day officer today,' said Bevers stepping into the office and turning to show the duty band on his left cuff. 'Just brewing up. Would you like a tea sir?'

'Thank you, that would be very nice. Where is everyone? We are supposed to be having a briefing now.'

'I'm sure they'll be here soon sir.'

He raised an eyebrow and drew on his cigarette.

While Bevers disappeared off to light the spirit lamp and get the kettle on, Straker considered the case. Basically it amounted to bugger all. He scanned the newspapers. Little news so close to Christmas, no wonder they had whipped readers into a frenzy with speculation about the Butcher of York.

Bevers returned with a tin cup and a cracked china bowl of sugar. 'Here we go sir, nothing a mug of tea can't sort, my mother always says.'

'Thank you Bevers and why don't you join me while we wait for the others?'

'Cigarette?' Straker held out his silver case.

'No thanks sir. I don't smoke.'

'Have a chair Bevers.' Straker looked at the keen-eyed constable thoughtfully. 'Can you remember what enquiries were made when the two bodies were found in August and October?'

'None at all as far as I know,' replied Bevers. 'Shall I get the Occurrence Book?'

The constable was up and out of the room. A few minutes later he returned with a large black leather-bound notebook. Straker made space, pushing the half-drunk mug of tea, plate of biscuits and ashtray to one side.

'Here you go,' said Bevers opening up the book and turning over pages of sloppy handwriting. He pointed. 'There, half-way down.'

Straker's eyes scanned the scrawling black ink.

August 28

Unidentified woman found at the ferry staithe close to Lendal Tower by John Goodricke, ferryman of this city. Body removed for parish burial. No further investigation.

Straker flicked forwards.

October 6

Unidentified corpse of prostitute found on River Ouse bank at King's Staith by Jack Hawker, boatman of this city. Body discovered at quarter past four. Parish burial. No further investigation.

Straker frowned. 'Was there an appeal for witnesses or identifications? Did *The Herald* run any stories about the deaths at the time?'

'No sir. Chief Inspector Nutt stopped the press reading the charge books after *The Herald* mocked him off – something about there being so many robberies in the city every day and surprisingly few arrests. He went mad, refused to talk to 'em anymore,' said the constable. 'I remember he weren't interested in those dead girls. The chief likes to keep our books clean, he don't want unsolved cases recorded. It's the police fund, you see, the chief insisted on one being set up a few years back and the Watch Committee pays us extra for clean record sheets and plenty of convictions. He was hoping to get us a few extra shillings for our New Year's Day dinner so he didn't want any unsolved crimes in this record book, just plenty of convictions.'

Straker nodded. Nutt lived up to his expectations. 'So how does he keep up the department's tally over the year?'

'We only apprehend easy targets like vagrants, street walkers, children and drunks. And if we enter the charge and make ourselves the complainant, we serve the warrants, prosecute and get a renumeration so everyone gains . . .'

Straker sighed and reached for a cigarette. 'Can you show me the entry where Nutt recorded the discovery of Rose's body?'

'Yes, it was December 12 . . .'

A sound of guffawing from the front office caused Bevers to glance towards the closed door. Straker nodded and held up his hand. Bevers closed the Occurrence Book. Straker got up swiftly and strode to the door. He pulled it open. 'My office now Sergeant Stone, Constable Gage.'

'Good night out sir?' said Gage cheerily as he came in.

'Aye, you look paler than a dead girl's arse.' Stone added.

The men cracked up at their own wit. Chuckling they made themselves comfortable in the empty chairs.

Straker sat down at the desk across from them and spoke very deliberately. 'We are starting from the beginning and doing this properly from now on. There has been enough time wasted.'

He leaned closer and handed over the photographs Ada had taken in the cemetery.

'She's better looking than that lass you got friendly with on Friday, Gage,' smirked Stone, glancing down at the first one.

Straker's hands clenched. 'We need posters of the silver cross and we need billboards appealing for help to identify the bodies. We can describe hair colour, height and the dates they were found.'

'Who wants to think about these birds, dug up from the ground like rotting spuds?' asked Gage a look of disgust on his face.

'A descriptive recreation of the scene, the date, might help someone remember something. We have to know who all these young women are,' snapped Straker.

Stone had taken another photograph and was looking at it closely, lingeringly, his eyes strangely bright. Then he said quickly. 'So that woman, the one who has the fancy studio on

Coney Street, she made these. Bloody calling cards for corpses now. She won't be able to charge them her fancy prices.'

Gage said suddenly. 'These pictures, it's sorcery if you ask me. Tis like black magic to call up evil spirits.'

'Aye, are you sure that lady photographer doesn't dance around a fire at midnight with a broomstick,' Stone sneered.

'That's enough both of you,' Straker snapped.

'It's not right, she's a woman,' muttered Gage.

'Well top marks for detection constable and what's your problem?' Straker's expression darkened even further.

'Women need a husband. They need menfolk to look after.'

'Aye, cooking, cleaning and lying flat on their backs,' Stone made a gesture with his hips.

Gage nodded. 'It's well known wedlock keeps lasses out of trouble. My mother says women like this Miss Fawkes are no better than they should be – bluestockings.'

Shaking his head, Straker, stood up to and walked to the fire-place. He turned and stared at them a moment, until he could see them flinch a little. Then he spoke briskly. 'Let's get started. What do we know so far? Well a little more now. We know that the latest victim is Rose Fisher, an orphan who disappeared from the Refuge and turned up dead on a river bank a week later on Friday December 12, her stomach cut. Rose must have been somewhere in that week. So was she held somewhere against her will or was she already dead? And we have another clue, the engraved silver cross. We have established that all three women were wearing one. So there's a connection. We must show the photograph around all the jewellers. Maybe someone will rec-ognise it. I'm hoping we know more about how and when Rose died when the post-mortem results come back.'

Straker looked at their blank expressions and wondered what he had done in a past life to deserve this team. 'Sergeant Stone instruct the printers we urgently need posters appealing for information. Get them to start the lay out. The photographs are coming later today. Any questions so far?'

'Clear as muck,' said Stone.

Straker ignored him, 'We need the help of *The Herald*. I want to give the newspaper a statement. I want to talk to the reporters and ask for their help in finding witnesses. We can make an appeal.'

'Chief Constable Nutt used to have his press briefings at the Blue Bell, before he stopped talking to the papers that is,' said Bevers.

'I'm sure that was a mutually convenient arrangement. I want them here at the station,' Straker replied.

'They'll be half cut by now in t'George Inn, sir. It's half past three.'

'Get a message to them Constable Bevers, they'll want this story. From my experience it's best to have journalists on your side. It can prove very useful in investigations. Oh by the way, how do you think all these rumours started about the Butcher, the stories in the paper?'

Stone said scornfully, 'That's an easy one. T'owd Lucifer.'

'Lucifer?'

'Aye, the lamp lighter John Peck. He's the one who started all this talk. He's paid by the local press for tip-offs about any-thing unusual he sees or people getting up to summat tha' shouldn't in the night. He found the latest body by t'river bank. He found Rose. He'll have been in the pub talking, hears gossip about t'other bodies, puts the stories together, and gets a few bob for his trouble. It's a small city, people like a gossip here. Everyone reads *The Herald*.'

'Find him and get him here fast.'

'He won't know owt.'

'Just do it. Get on with it lads. Quick as you can.'

Straker watched the door close, sat down in the chair and ran his hand through his dark hair.

Bluestocking indeed! He happened to know Ada Fawkes's lace-tops were a different colour entirely.

Chapter Eighteen

◊

It was Tuesday morning before they found t'owd Lucifer sober enough to be interviewed. The lamplighter had been hauled from his usual corner of the taproom in the Three Cranes as he was settling down to his first pint of the day. How he managed to climb ladders or balance a long torch to light street lamps, God only knew thought Straker looking at him slumped, half-cut and hardly able to stay upright on a chair.

After a few questions, Straker gave up and asked Bevers to interpret his mumbled speech.

Bevers bent his head closer to the old man's toothless mouth, wincing at the odour of bad breath. 'He wants a penny for his trouble.'

Straker pulled out a coin. John Peck took it and shoved it deep, with fumbling hands, into his grimy brown trouser pocket.

'Now tell me what happened,' said Straker.

The lamplighter shook his head. 'Aye twas a bad business.'

'Go on,' urged Straker.

'Ah'm on the New Walk, having a pipe, tekkin the weight off me feet and ah sees her in t' moonlight lying on the river bank.'

'Had she been in the water?' Straker asked.

'She was dry as a bone when I clapped eyes on her.'

'Was there blood on the ground around or under her?'

'Nay lad. Twas like she was asleep in her nightgown, hands crossed, peaceful as owt. Twas later, moving t'body into the cart, well it was awkward like getting her in, that we saw them strange cuts on her stomach.' He shook his head again. 'Twas wrong and I was reminded of summat. Came to me later.'

He paused. Straker gritted his teeth.

'I'd heard it from t'owd ferryman you see. Those slashes on her belly, he'd seen 'em, the same, on the stiff he found. Well she found him, jumped out on him in the water.' John Peck grinned toothlessly at the thought of Goodricke getting a fright.

Straker sent him on his way, back to the Three Cranes with a coin for his trouble.

Nothing was clear. So many unanswered questions, he felt he was no closer to knowing anything.

***

Later, after Miss Brockett had finally sent the names of the visitors to the Refuge that she had promised, Straker walked out in the York evening, glad of the cold air. He made his way to Chapter House Street. The names meant nothing to him but perhaps Ada could help.

Camille, who had been rolling out pastry for that evening's supper of game pie made a good job of not seeming too pleased to see Straker when she opened the front door. 'She's in her studio, go on out,' she said tartly, barely glancing at him as she returned to the kitchen.

Lamps had already been lit against the early dark of mid-winter and light shone out through the window panes. Straker saw her standing still, hair tumbling below some peculiar fur-lined hat, looking closely at a photograph pinned to a wooden board through a large magnifying glass. About her head black and white images, pegged from strings, ran across the beams. Catching her like this, her unaware of his presence, made his heart race. She seemed so vulnerable. He took a deep breath and knocking brusquely on the door, he pushed it open. She turned, surprise on her face.

'Detective inspector. You made me jump. Have you news?'

'Miss Brockett sent the names of the Refuge visitors this afternoon. I needed some fresh air so I thought I would drop it off for you on my way back to my lodgings. And I've interviewed the lamplighter John Peck for what that was worth.'

She nodded. 'I was looking at the pictures of all three women again. See this one of Rose, the clean cut into the stomach, deep V-shaped incisions across her abdomen, right through the flesh into the cavity. He must have taken his time and these marks must have some meaning.'

She passed him the magnifying glass. Their shoulders brushed as he looked through the lens.

'It must have been a very sharp, fine blade to slice through flesh with that precision. The edges of the skin are clean-cut not sawn or hacked,' he said. 'And Peck said there was no blood at the scene. These cuts must have been inflicted at a different location.'

Ada nodded. 'I think so too. And something else.' She held the image to a lamp on the table for closer inspection. 'We saw Rose soon after she had died. Even if the killer had cleaned her up, the edges of the skin look too neat and there was no blood.'

He leaned over to study the photograph in her hand. 'Jesus. So you think they were made after death? What killed her then? And why cut her stomach?'

Ada shook her head. 'The first body was in the river. Rose and the second body were found on the river bank? Is the river significant somehow or the months of their deaths?'

'The one fact we are sure of is they all wore a crucifix. The girls did not have a farthing to their name so were they given to them by the killer? Did he lure them somewhere by pretending to be a friend, a sweetheart?'

Ada put down the magnifying glass. 'Too many unknowns. Let me see the letter from Miss Brockett.'

He pulled a folded sheet of paper out of his jacket pocket. Ada took it, opened it and scanned the lines.

Bishophill Refuge, York
December 23, 1862

Dear Detective Inspector Straker,

I am so sensible of the importance of your detective work and I have compiled the list of names you requested. I imagine you are engaged in much thought and calculation in your dogged pursuit of the criminal. I am humbled to help such a mind in what little way I can.

Our main visitors to our modest home are our dear Penitentiary Society members who take such a keen interest in the physical and moral wellbeing of our young women. The gentlemen members who visit are trusted advisors and are much concerned with the reform of public women. They are the Rev Charles Lindley, Dr William Auden, Dr Henry Scull and Mr Edward Atkinson. They have all been members of the committee and, may I say, our oldest friends for some time, apart from Dr Auden, of course, who joined us last year when he returned from London.

To help the girls in their spiritual conduct, our chaplain the Rev Jacob Turner, visits twice weekly for Bible classes and prayers. He joined our little flock at the beginning of the year. The girls attend St Martin-cum-Gregory's Church on Sundays under my strict supervision.

We have been shaken by the events at our simple penitentiary. We pray for our lost soul, for our Rose, with all our hearts. She is in a better place. I wish to inform you also that I prayed with poor Esther and it brought her much comfort before her death. She beseeched me to remember her kindly in my prayers and asked for my forgiveness for her sins. Please be so kind as to inform Miss Fawkes, her request was met.

Be assured I attach a very great importance to your work.

Yours most sincerely
Miss Anne Brockett

Straker saw Ada's expression darken, he had seen that look of anger before.

'Sanctimonious bitch.'

Straker spoke with more measure. 'One of these men must know more, we must talk to them all.'

'We know the girls talk to whomever they like on the other side of that garden wall and what about all the tradesmen who call at the Refuge? Miss Brockett has forgotten to add them.' She shook her head. 'It could be anyone?'

'Well I shall start by questioning these men who are directly connected to the Refuge. They must all have known Rose Fisher.'

'And Christmas is nearly upon us. That makes it harder, you may well be interrogating the vicars between church services,' said Ada.

Impatient now, Straker had already turned to leave. He looked back.

'Between hymns if I have to. We have so little time. Nothing will get in the way of this investigation. No one is above the law of the land, not even in York.'

CHAPTER NINETEEN

◊

It was a new custom in England to send greetings cards at Christmas. The next morning, Ada received two. She slit open an envelope, wondering if she could make cards with her own photographs next year.

'Isn't this pretty?' said Ada pulling out a seaside picture. 'All the stationers are selling them this year. Oh, it's from my God-mother Susan in Whitby. She wishes us all a Merry Christmas and suggests I visit in the New Year.'

'You should,' said Thomas, looking at her over the rim of his mug of tea, noting the tiredness in her face. 'Do you good to get a bit of sea air. I wouldn't mind a run over the moor tops myself. We should go early spring, up through Farndale, catch the daffodils.'

'If this ever ends, that would be very welcome,' Ada agreed, cutting open the other envelope and holding up a picture of four fluffy kittens with ribbons round their necks. 'This one's from my brother Harry and Charlotte. Charlotte must have chosen this one, it's awful.'

Camille looked up from the letter she was reading. 'Pierre has written and sends his love to you.'

'How is he?' Ada thought fondly of Pierre, Camille's grown-up son working in Paris at the Élysée Palace for the French Government.

'He's very well. I'll read it properly later. I've so much to do.' Camille stood, smoothing her cashmere day dress over her slim hips.

'Do you really think we should go ahead with this evening?' asked Ada.

'Ada it's Christmas Eve. Can we not put everything to one side just for a few hours?'

'If only I hadn't invited people round, but it seemed like a good idea a few weeks ago. I thought it would be good for my new business. Now I'm dreading it.'

'It will be very pleasant. It's only a neighbourly drink before we go to church.'

'Hardly. You don't do simple drinks.'

'You will enjoy it once everyone is here.'

'I don't think I will,' Ada said.

'Not even the handsome Dr Auden?' enquired Camille, raising a curved eyebrow.

'No, you know I'm not interested,' Ada laughed. 'I can't see what a man would add to my life. If I marry, he gets my house, my business, my money and what do I get in return? Nothing.'

Camille looked at her out of the corner of her eye. 'Marriage is not the only option for women. There are many ways to enjoy the company of men. Plenty appreciate a companion for the theatre, a meal or dancing. And us? We have the fun without the wifely duties.'

Ada laughed, glancing at Thomas now hiding behind that week's newspaper. 'Camille! That's so French. I think the citizens of York are a bit more old-fashioned. Well what do you want me to do to help then?'

Ada didn't expect to be trusted with much. In her day, Madame Defoe had been one of the most celebrated chefs in Paris. It was said, mostly by Camille, that the Emperor of France himself had been in ecstasies over her puff pastry.

***

It did not take long before the aromas of baking and braising drifted out of the hot, steamy kitchen. There came a steady stream of dishes: tiny vol-au-vents stuffed with chicken, ham and mushroom, flavoured liberally with Madeira and thyme; golden, light-as-air choux buns cooling, ready to be filled with a rich, tangy cheese sauce; blinis awaiting cream soured with lemon and slivers of peat-smoked salmon. Each laden tray was given to Thomas to take to the deep chill of the pantry, where, out of sight, one or two were hastily gulped down.

It was not until afternoon, that Ada was free, flush-faced from the stuffy kitchen to escape to her studio and take advantage of the last couple hours of daylight. In addition to everything else, she had to prepare for an exhibition she had planned for the spring.

'On your way out, can you ask Thomas to slice the salmon? I'll say one thing for your backward country, the fish is very good. Oh, and I thought you could wear your red velvet – it's pressed and ready,' called Camille.

'That seems a bit dressy for this evening,' said Ada, pausing at the door.

'You should appear well when you are at public events or hosting. The ladies will be looking at you and your clothes. You are an artist. You can't look like some dowdy old frump and expect them to commission you to create beautiful portraits. I've asked Martha and Grace to come early and help you dress. Make you chic for once. They will be serving the canapés too.'

Ada smiled as she liked the two blonde sisters very much. Their mother ran the haberdashery on Goodramgate. The young women worked there and were convinced they knew everything there was to know about fashion. If she was honest with herself, Ada would be glad of their help. The chance to dress up and look her best was appealing. Jane's brother William was rather good-looking. Death had overlain the last week in York with the murdered young women, and everything else: the poor dying girl at the Refuge, the shock of Straker turning up, the exhumations. She shuddered. Camille was right, it would be nice to put it all to one side for a few hours on Christmas Eve. And Camille was in her element, the joy of planning, preparing food to transform an event from the ordinary to the sublime. Ada knew Camille hid her pleasure with snappy orders and plenty of scolding. The two giggling blonde sisters who would help her later in the kitchen would obey her commands while smirking behind her back at her foreign mispronunciations. Ada would not spoil it for any of them.

'There's something else,' Camille mentioned casually as Ada was turning to leave.

'I've invited Detective Inspector Straker. I asked him as he was leaving here last night. I took pity on him. He looked lonely.'

'I'm surprised he agreed to it.'

'It's Christmas Ada, the man is in a hotel. He knows no one here.'

She had little choice but to accept it with good grace. Anyway, truth to tell, she had thought about it herself, but was wary of giving him the wrong impression. They could never be anything more to each other again.

The unmistakeable smell of burning bread wafted through from the kitchen.

'Le pain!' Camille shrieked.

***

It was dark and there was much Straker still needed to do, but little he could achieve this late on Christmas Eve. He left the police station and walked to his hotel. The day had been long and frustrating. There had been small successes: posters printed, the ferryman John Goodricke interviewed again. His statement confirmed that he had seen the same stomach wound on the body he had found, but the long list of people of interest nagged at him and there was no sign of the boatman who had discovered the second body.

There was possibly a breakthrough as pub gossip and posters appealing for information had turned up names for the two unknown victims. It was a small city after all. He needed to be certain though.

And though he longed to have a bottle of malt whisky sent up and settle in for the evening, he had agreed to Christmas Eve drinks and in truth he longed to see Ada and could no more stop himself going than taking his next breath. He sent for a jug of hot water and stripped down to his bare chest. After a wash, he dressed to go out, putting on a fresh shirt and winding a black cravat round his neck. He adjusted his jacket, put on his coat, left the hotel, now lively with festive diners eating beef dinners, and headed out. Walking past the heaving public houses on Stonegate, he skirted the crowds spilling out from narrow passageways onto the street. Ahead, the vast height of the cathedral soared into the sky, the stone walls of the Minster Gates framing the ancient window of roses, the colours glowing as dozens of flickering candles played on the white and red rose petals of the glass. The centuries old window had been created as a celebration of the union of the Houses of York and Lancaster when Henry VII was king, though it had not healed the ancient rivalry which still ran deep in the veins of every Yorkshire man and woman.

Straker walked on, following the shadowy path past the imperious statue of Emperor Constantine, around the walls.

Tonight, of all nights, on Christmas Eve, the Minster should have lifted his heart and soul, but Straker's thoughts were dark.

***

In her bedroom Ada was at the mercy of the blonde sisters, who at sixteen and fourteen thought that they knew everything there was to know about hair styling.

'I don't want to look like mutton dressed as lamb,' Ada protested. Armed with stiff brushes and long, sharp hairpins, the sisters worked on an elaborate up-do of curls and coils.

Camille, who thought, because she was Parisian, that she knew everything about fashion, had agreed with them that this was the perfect style to compliment Ada's low-cut crimson velvet. When Ada suggested a ribbon trimming to cover a little more of her décolletage, it was met with derision. 'How old do you want to look? Fifty?' asked the eldest sister scornfully. 'Yes, do you want to look like every old matron?' said the younger.

The dress fitted like a second skin over her tightly-laced corset and black silk stockings. She stepped carefully into matching kid shoes. Finally she pulled long, red-laced gloves over the scarring on her hands and arms. Ada stood up to face Camille.

'Regarde-toi,' Camille said, taking her shoulders and turning her to the mirror. 'So elegant, ma chérie.'

The sisters looked at each other and giggled. 'You'll do, Miss Fawkes,' which she knew was a compliment in Yorkshire.

Ada's opinion of the figure reflected back at her was that she did indeed look like mutton dressed as lamb, but too late, the guests were about to arrive. Anyway what did she care? She was not in the market for a husband or a gentleman friend.

'It's very nice girls,' she said, wishing her hair was in its usual loose and comfortable style and her movements unrestricted by such tight lacing. Pins stabbed her scalp like bee stings and she felt she could hardly breathe. Camille placed the emerald necklace that had been her mother's around her neck and fastened the gold clasp.

'You look beautiful. Believe it,' said Camille smiling.

Downstairs, Thomas, looking distinguished in his evening suit, placed champagne, well-chilled from a few days in the cold outhouse, into the silver ice bowl and looked round with a critical eye. Red-berried holly, variegated ivy, fir branches sent over from Stag Hall decorated the top of the drawing room mantle. He was particularly pleased with his table centrepiece of Christmas roses and sweetly-scented white narcissi grown in his greenhouse.

'Oh love, you look a picture,' he said when Ada came in.

'Thank you and so does the drawing room.' She felt embarrassed to have so many compliments.

The household was tense in those few moments of limbo that always occur before the first guests arrive. Ada, nervous for the evening's success, once again wished she was having a quiet night in on her own with Jane Eyre and Mr Rochester.

'Why did I let you talk me into this?' she murmured to Camille. 'What if people don't enjoy themselves?'

'They will. And it's only neighbours and friends for a chat and a Christmas drink. It's not a society ball.'

Suddenly from the hallway Thomas could be heard greeting guests and dealing with mufflers, cloaks, hats and gloves from those who had walked through the snow from their nearby homes. Laughing and chattering they hailed those they knew well and politely reintroduced themselves to acquaintances.

They were all welcome; the music professor, the drawing master, the race course clerk, the dressmaker, the headmistress, the bootmaker, the solicitor, the banker, the doctor and the rector. How much less socially rigid York was than other English cities. It was too small, too countrified for such pretensions. Ladies lived next to dance teachers, Honourables alongside plumbers and glaziers.

Ada welcomed each one and they returned her greetings with friendliness and interest. Ada knew she attracted some attention as a working woman, although here women ran businesses from dressmakers, to schools to shops. It was her trade that heightened curiosity in York's eyes, as well as her Parisian couture clothes and Royal connections.

In the softly lit green-blue drawing room, everyone gathered, talking politely, holding glasses of champagne. The ladies in particular looked round admiringly. The fire in the grate warmed and welcomed on a winter's night. A glass chandelier caught the shining candlelight and threw down sparkles onto wine glasses, brooches, watch chains and Ada's emerald.

When the hot vol-au-vents were handed round, any last Yorkshire reserve melted away and the chat began to flow, loud and lively.

The blonde sisters, now smartly clad in crisp white aprons and caps, their long hair twisted into immaculate plaits, circulated with more platters; oysters, blinis and morsels of light-as-air choux. The wine merchant's apprentice, roped in for the evening, served glass after glass. Camille, who knew the neighbours well, talked animatedly to all. Thomas happily discussed horse form with the race course clerk. Time flew.

'Miss Fawkes, Ada. You look charming,' a deep voice behind her and a light touch on her arm. She turned. William Auden bowed and taking her hand, brought her gloved fingers to his lips as he smiled up at her through his lashes.

Laughing, she welcomed him with a slight mocking curtsy and turned to hug his sister. 'Dear friend. I am so pleased you could come tonight.'

'We were delighted to be asked,' said Jane.

'I feared it might be too low key for you, or you would be having some grand dinner party yourself.'

'Not us, we don't go in for too much formality these days. Not since mother died. You remember how she loved big occasions?' Jane smiled.

'Oh yes I do. I remember my mother leaving for one of her balls, she came to my room to show off the most beautiful silk dove-grey dress . . . It seems like a lifetime ago.'

'It does,' William agreed. 'These days we don't have time or the inclination for that lifestyle. We live very quietly. Our medical research is everything to us. And there is much we can do here to help alleviate the suffering of the poor.'

Jane nodded, about to speak and then saw Camille beckoning her over. 'Excuse me Ada, I will catch up with you later.'

Ada smiled at her departing friend and turning back to the doctor, glimpsing Camille shooting them an appraising look. I see what you are up to Madame, Ada thought.

'Your work is fascinating,' William was saying. 'I was engrossed by your talk, but it is your forensic work that is so pioneering, I would like very much to hear more about that. Maybe you could show me around your studio and let me see how you create and develop a photograph? Photography would be of much use to me in my work, as you can imagine.'

Though she had known him for many years as the brother of an old friend, Ada realised that she had never really talked to him in depth before. As at supper the other evening, she found him to be attentive, charming and amusing.

'I should warn you, any encouragement to talk about photography and you will not get a word in edgeways.'

He laughed, 'I assure you I am very interested to hear more, especially about your time with the French detectives. I am thinking of purchasing a camera. Maybe you could give me some advice on that too.'

'Of course, I would be delighted. I have . . .'

Ada turned her head. Her voice faltered a moment. There, standing in the doorway was Straker. Unsmiling, head and shoulders above everyone else, looking about him.

She saw Thomas move to shake his hand. He asked him something. Thomas pointed in her direction. Straker began to cross the room towards them. He looked grey-faced, tired and he did not take his eyes from hers. He reached them in seconds, bowed slightly and took Ada's hand formally, though barely touching her fingers. 'Miss Fawkes.'

She acknowledged his greeting. 'Detective Inspector Straker, I am glad you could come. Camille, Thomas and I did not want you to spend Christmas Eve alone.'

He nodded and turned to William. They shook hands firmly. 'Doctor Auden, I'm pleased to see you again.'

'Detective inspector, good to see you again too and in a pleasanter setting this time.'

As they talked the eldest blonde sister passed by with a platter of devilled eggs and offered the plate.

'Do you have any of that delicious smoked salmon left?' asked Dr Auden.

'Yes sir, in the kitchen. I'll fetch it now.'

'Excellent. Why don't I come with you and help,' he laughed, turning to Ada. 'It's my favourite. I'll be back in a minute.'

Straker seized the moment of their being alone.

'Miss Fawkes. I must . . .'

His sentence was interrupted by the sound of a gong. Camille instructed the wine merchant's apprentice, who was getting rather enthusiastic in his task, to stop serving. Holding glasses, their guests fell silent.

'We,' said Camille, gesturing to Ada and Thomas, 'we are so pleased to welcome you to our first Christmas Eve in York, to gather together and eat and drink. So a toast to friends old and new. Merry Christmas everyone.'

Their neighbours raised their glasses calling back. 'Merry Christmas'. More drinks. More food. Smoked salmon, country pâté topped with pickles, spicy devilled eggs, were passed round on piled-high platters. Straker tried to speak again, but before he could, Ada was called away, claimed by one guest, then another. Gentlemen were asking questions about cameras and developing techniques, the female neighbours interested in her fashionable Parisian pointed-waist bodice.

From the other side of the room Ada noticed the detective standing aloof from the merriment. He did not come near her again and did not look at her. Unexpectedly, she felt very conscious of his presence. He had a way of drawing attention even as he stood still. Ada listened attentively to her guests, trying to be interested, wondering why Straker had come if he wasn't going to make an effort.

She watched Thomas, carrying two glasses of whisky, move to Straker's side and saw the detective's stern face relax a little as the pair of them talked quietly. Then Jane was next to Ada again in her customary plain black silk gown. Smiling she took her friend's arm and pulled her towards a far corner of the drawing room.

'We haven't had a chance to talk.'

'It's impossible isn't it? But actually I would like to come and see you,' said Ada. She hesitated. 'Jane, there's something I want to talk to you about, a personal matter.'

'Of course. Anytime . . .' Jane looked over at her brother, standing in the doorway talking to a blonde young woman. She frowned slightly, a quizzical look on her face then touching her friend's arm said with concern, 'Ada, is there . . .'

'Good evening Miss Auden, Miss Fawkes.' A pleasant-looking man interrupted them. 'This is very good. You have captured the atmosphere of the romantic ruins of Fountains Abbey Miss Fawkes. Is that not so Miss Auden?' He gestured to a framed landscape photograph on the wall.

Ada and Jane turned to talk to Edward Atkinson the architect, who had dined with them at Jane's birthday supper.

'Good evening Mr Atkinson,' said Jane. 'Yes, she has captured the great cloister beautifully. Our friend here is very talented.'

'She is indeed. Thank you so much for inviting us tonight
Miss Fawkes.'

'I am so pleased you could come Mr Atkinson. Is Mrs Atkinson here this evening? I do not see her.'

'She is nearing her confinement and did not feel well enough
to attend,' he replied.

'Mr Atkinson,' said Jane. 'Have you spoken with my brother
this evening? He is anxious to talk to you about the new plans
for Bootham County Lunatic Asylum.'

All the while Straker was watching, waiting for his chance
to talk to Ada. He found he could not enter into the mood of
the evening or make small talk. His mind was in another place.
His instinct told him the connection, the link between the three
victims was the Refuge. The other two young women, if they
were who he thought, had also lived there. The trouble was
that many of its visitors were well-known men, stalwarts of
York society. No one would believe they could be suspects. As
Ada had said when she read the names on Miss Brockett's list
yesterday, this was tricky ground. And at least some of those
names were here tonight.

His thoughts were interrupted by the gong sounding again.

'It's nearly time for Midnight Mass. We must hurry,' Camille
called out. Laughing and joking, the friends and neighbours
bundled back up in hats, scarves and mufflers, and stepped
out into the street. All seemed as usual as they walked, ladies

shrieking as they stepped into thick powdery snow, footsteps crunching, vocal cords readying for a good sing-song, as they hurried along Minster Yard, past the Treasurer's house and into Dean's Park. Ahead of them a stream of red-faced men, chatting women and excited children was flowing towards the west front of the towering cathedral.

As the guests passed the Chapter House, Straker caught up with Ada. Taking a firm hold of her arm, he pulled her with him into the shadows of the Minster walls. Removing his hat so he could draw closer to her, he spoke softly. He was so close his hair brushed her cheek, his breath warmed her skin and she shivered involuntarily.

'I know their names.'

Startled she looked up at him. Before he could speak further, a group of church-goers called over to them, wishing them season's greetings and they were caught up in the flow. Straker took her arm and let them be propelled through the great wooden door and into the candle-lit glow of the vast, medieval vaulted nave. He steered her towards a stone pillar on the south aisle and held her arm tighter as the congregation pushed past them to get to the seats. Over his shoulder she glimpsed Thomas and Camille look round for her, but she was hidden from view by his broad back. Shielding her from the moving crowd, he quickly told her what he had discovered.

'We need to confirm it's them as soon as possible. Tomorrow. I know it's Christmas Day, but we can't wait.'

'How did you find out?'

'It was the posters illustrated with engravings of your photographs of the necklace, the appeal for information on the young women going missing in August and October. Some people came forward. Most of them were timewasters, but two names are possibles.'

'Who are they?'

'Annie Wren and Emily Eden. Both worked in laundries in York, and we know that's the line of work they were trained in at the Refuge. The young woman found dead in August may be Annie Wren. She was employed in the laundry at the Ragged School. I'd like us to visit the school tomorrow. Bring your original photograph of the necklace.'

Ada's voice was soft and low so only he could hear. 'I will meet you here by the Minster at the park gates at ten. It's not far to walk.'

Straker nodded and stepped aside. 'Keep it quiet for the moment.'

'Of course,' she said. 'Are you joining us?'

'No. I struggle with all this now. I've seen too much evil.' He bowed slightly then walked towards the door. She watched his departing back for a moment then moved down the aisle to where she could see Camille beckoning to her. She passed along the crowded row and sat on the empty seat between Camille and Jane whose head was bowed in prayer.

'I thought we had lost you,' whispered Camille.

'Detective Inspector Straker had to go, police business. He was apologising.'

'Oh, what's happened?' asked Jane.

'I think he just wants to call in on the duty inspector or something,' she said vaguely.

'My brother's had to leave as well,' whispered Jane. 'A message arrived as we left your home. A lady has gone into her confinement. Another Christmas Day baby perhaps.'

They fell into silence as organ music rose and expanded, filling the vast space of the Minster, the heart of York, built from ancient oak and stone and bound solid with centuries of worship.

Ada breathed in, absorbing the solemn atmosphere, feeling the link with generations gone before who had stood as she did in this place. The altar was ablaze with candles, adorned with holly and mistletoe. Above her head, the soaring height of the great gothic arches, seemed to reach up to the heavens themselves. Then, hidden from view behind a four-hundred-year-old screen, guarded by the stone carvings of fifteen English kings, the choir began to sing. Ascending voices lifted above the strains of the organ. She felt the hair on her skin prickle.

Ada thought of the souls she carried with her – those she had loved in life and those she had cared for in death – she absorbed the power of this night and let her own soul remember them. Here, in the solace of ritual, she briefly suspended the past, the present and the future. She bowed her head to hide her emotions.

At the eagle lectern, the Archbishop wished them all peace on earth and good will to all men.

***

Outside in the raw air of Christmas, the congregation full of beer and cheer, wished each and everyone tidings of comfort and joy as they made their way home. Ada lingered on the steps with Camille and Thomas, greeting acquaintances and friends, bidding farewell to their guests.

'Merry Christmas,' said Ada.

'And Merry Christmas to you too,' replied the killer before disappearing into the cold night as the church bells rang out for Christmas Day.

CHAPTER TWENTY

◊

Christmas morning and in the wintry streets church-goers dressed in their Sunday best were returning home to warm firesides and roasting meats. The bells of the Minster started to toll the hour of ten as Ada and Straker passed underneath the thick stone arch of Bootham Bar, centuries now since the gateway had been built in the city walls, a replacement for the old Roman entrance and even now, it stood strong and sturdy. Out on the other side though, away from its protection the falling snow whipped into their faces, layering their hats and overcoats with white.

Their footsteps crunched as they passed the White Horse Public House, already lively with regulars in various states of merriment. They soon gained Marygate Tower, where the abbey wall turned down towards the river.

Head down, her thoughts far away, Ada stumbled on an icy patch. Straker caught her wrist and held out his elbow. Ada slipped her hand through his arm, gripping his solid bulk. She did not seek this intimacy but her leather boots had little traction on a day like this.

Straker finally broke the silence between them. 'Thank you for coming with me. It will be it easier for the women who knew Annie Wren to talk to you rather than me.'

'I agree,' said Ada stiffly. 'And we are here. This is Marygate.'

He looked left down the street, one side formed of the medieval walls of St Mary's Abbey, the other a row of houses of different heights and widths. 'That didn't take us long.'

'Nowhere is very far away in York.'

They made their way past windows aglow with lamps and candles, looking warm and festive. They soon encountered the Ragged School, where no bright light welcomed home comers. They observed the unloved red brick building that until recently had been the old Workhouse – that institution had moved to bigger premises to meet growing demand. This miserable-looking place, according to the witness information, had been the home of Annie Wren, before she went missing.

A boy in too-large patched boots, was sweeping snow from the steps and coughing hoarsely with the effort. Straker expressed surprise that the thin child wore no coat. 'I had always thought of York as a well-to-do place, not like the streets of London.'

'It's no better here than any other city,' Ada said in a low voice. 'York looks after its poor children, but only because it wants them off the street, out of the way of the tourists. This school's funded by public subscription, charity trustees, they make themselves feel better by feeding and clothing children badly while training them for a life of more labour and more poverty.'

Straker handed the little boy a coin. 'There you go lad, you're doing a fine job there.' They walked up the front steps. Straker knocked firmly on the door. After a short while, it opened a crack and brown eyes peered out at them.

'Can we come in please?' said Ada.

The eyes turned away and a girl's voice shouted, 'Mrs Grubbe, Mrs Grubbe . . .'

The door swung open and a grey-haired woman wiping her hands on a grubby apron stepped into view. The brown eyes peeped out from behind her bulk. Before she could speak, Straker introduced them.

'I'm Detective Inspector Straker and this is Miss Fawkes, we are here on police business. We need to ask some questions Mrs . . . ?'

'Grubbe. Mrs Grubbe. I'm the cook here.'

They entered the hall which was only slightly warmer than the outside street. Mrs Grubbe waved with her hand beckoning them further in. Ada looked around the high ceilinged hallway. The walls were painted a serviceable sludge brown and decorated with, at least to her eyes, a very amateur oil painting of Jesus the Shepherd, surrounded by scabby-looking lambs. An odour of boiled cabbage lingered in the air.

'The master and matron aren't back from church yet. They've been invited for sherry after the service. There's just me and the housemaids.'

'Can we speak to you then? It's urgent,' said Straker.

'Well I suppose, but you better be quick. You'll have to come down to the kitchen, I've dinner to get ready and I'm short. One of my girls ran off and she's never been replaced. It's not the first time and won't be the last. I do my best, but bad breeding always outs,' she rambled on.

'Get along and finish your sewing,' she shouted to the brown-eyed girl, who scurried away through a door at the far end of a passageway off the hall.

Straker glanced at Ada as they followed the cook's wide girth down steep stone stairs to the basement. Down here it smelled of mould and mildew, overlaid with burning meat.

Ada looked round at the stained walls, wet with the steam of cooking pots, the dirty red-tiled floor scattered with crumbs and peelings. Stood over the large, pine table in the middle of the room, a pale girl, thirteen or so in a simple grey cotton dress, was peeling muddy carrots. Another, in the same style of dress, was stirring a bubbling pan on the black iron range. Through the scullery door, she could see a pig-tailed girl, apron sleeves rolled up to the red-raw elbow, scouring pans. A turkey turned in the rotating jack, fixed to the mantlepiece, a tray catching the sizzling fat and dripping juices.

They were not asked to sit and so stood by the dresser, trying not to get in the way of the preparations. Straker, in his bulky outdoor coat, seemed too large for the cramped space and the kitchen girls were openly gawping at him.

'Get to work,' snapped Mrs Grubbe. 'Dinner's not going to make itself.'

'Mrs Grubbe, we've been told that one of your staff went missing in August and it may well be she has been the victim of a crime.'

'Aye. We wondered. I recognised that necklace from a poster in a shop window. I didn't want to get into any trouble, but the supervisor said 'appen he'd better mention it at the station.'

'Is he here?'

'Aye, he'll be in the dining room.'

Straker was already heading for the door. 'Mrs Grubbe, I will just go up and talk to him. Miss Fawkes has some questions for you.'

Ada could sense Mrs Grubbe's puzzlement. 'I'm a photographer Mrs Grubbe and occasionally I work for the detective branch. For instance I have some photographs to show you.'

The cook flapped a hand and sent the curious girls back to their tasks.

'So the children must be looking forward to lunch,' said Ada to break the ice as Mrs Grubbe began chopping peeled potatoes with a sharp-bladed knife and a heavy hand. 'It smells delicious Mrs Grubbe.'

'Oh aye,' she started. ''Tis best meal of the year ere. We've got some of the trustees for the lunch, them that pays for this charity and the Master likes to put on a good show. The children live on bread and broth mainly tis too rich for them this proper food. Anyway what's your business Miss. Better spit it out.'

'I'm trying to find out more about Annie Wren,' Ada said. 'What happened to her?'

'It's some months since she was gone. Haven't seen nor heard of her since late summer. I wouldn't be surprised if she has come to a bad end. Slattern didn't come back from her hours off. It was Race Day and that was that. There's hoards of 'em at the races and mebbit some young men from out of town, splashing out coins, were too tempting for the likes of 'er.'

'What do you mean?' Ada asked.

'You know her type. She came to us from that Refuge. The committee ladies sorted out for her to do laundry work here, get a proper training like. Those ladies, they are angels, the job they have, trying to save the fallen.'

'What do you know of Annie's life?'

'Her parents were York-born, but they both died of cholera. A lot did back then. She had no one, taken into care, fell into bad ways. You know how it is.' She scooped up potatoes with her broad hands and slopped them into a bowl of water.

'Go, on Mrs Grubbe,' urged Ada.

'I don't want to say what happened to her next. It's ungodly. Anyway I didn't want no girls like that in my kitchen, but I had no choice, I was told I had to. But fair dos, the lass was a hard worker and she learnt quickly. She seemed quite willing. I thought she must have mended 'er ways.'

'How long was she here?'

'Nearly a year. She was about sixteen when she came to me. Not many at the Refuge find salvation, but with her being so young like, I supposed she wasn't hardened like some of them. And she didn't have the pox neither, there was still a chance for her.'

'Did she live in?'

'Aye. A small room up in the attic. The ladies arranged it as she had nowhere else to live. And it was handy because she could clean out the grates and light the fires early in the morning before she did the laundry.'

'Mrs Grubbe?' The pale girl chopping carrots interrupted nervously. 'Ave I done enough now?'

'A couple more lass. Then get on t'sprouts. They need a good long boiling. Where was I?'

'You were telling us Annie Wren was useful.'

'Oh aye she was that. Pretty thing she was too, shiny dark hair and neat, comely figure. The Master always liked her to serve when they had visitors or he was working in his study. Wouldn't have anyone else waiting on him.'

'So did anyone try to find her after she disappeared?

'I know the Master asked around, put a notice in *The Herald*, sent a message to the Refuge and so on. He was bothered alright. But turns out she was still a wrong 'un deep down and had run off.'

'What did you make of it, Mrs Grubbe? What did you think had happened to the girl?'

She gave Ada a shrewd look. 'Well, I'm sure you know Miss Fawkes. When that happens to a young girl it usually means one thing only. I thought she'd run off with a fella.'

'Were there any indications? Did she seem any different before she disappeared?'

'Well now I think of it, she seemed happier. In a quiet way though, I caught her staring into nothing a few times, like she had a nice secret inside her.'

'What do you mean?'

'Well she didn't say anything but I could see she was a bit distracted like, little smile on her face. A glow about her, I had to tell her a few times to hurry up with filling the coal buckets and get the copper boiling.'

'Did she ever mention anyone's name, or did you notice anyone hanging about here?'

'No.'

'When did you first notice her like this?'

'Well beginning of August I suppose.'

'What happened when she disappeared?'

'Well nowt. It was her afternoon off. She had a few hours every two weeks, but she didn't come back. Twas a proper nuisance, I had to do her jobs as well as my own. To be honest I wasn't that surprised. Girls like 'er. In the end she was no better than she was.'

Ada nodded encouragingly.

'I waited until the next morning then I told the matron. I said it was most likely a man. They are good Christians here and they agreed with me that Annie was too far fallen to save. She's not the first. She won't be the last.'

'So no one looked for her.'

'Like I said, the Master asked about. He liked Little Jenny Wren, as he called her.'

'And did anyone tell the police?'

Mrs Grubbe shrugged. 'No point.'

'Why not?'

'They'd have laughed us out of the station. Girls like 'er, not worth looking for. No one cares.'

'Did the master or matron report her missing to anyone?'

'Well they told the Ladies Committee from the Refuge of course, for the records. They like to keep their records up to date do the Ladies. Miss Auden, she's the secretary, took an interest on account of placing her here with us. She lives up the road. No doubt the ladies were disappointed in how Annie turned out.'

'Mrs Grubbe, will you look at this please?' Ada opened her leather bag, took out a photograph of Annie's silver cross and held it under the cook's nose.

She looked at it, picked up a towel and wiped her hands. She took the picture. 'Well I never. That's one of them photographs then. It's as real as you and me. It's like I could pick up that necklace and put it on.' She waved her other hand again to stop the kitchen girls edging forward to look. 'Aye but that looks like Annie's cross.'

'This is very important Mrs Grubbe, but your memory is clearly as sharp as a tack. Did she say where she got the necklace?'

'It's true, I've always had a good memory. Well Annie said she was given it at the Refuge. I didn't think anything of it, being a crucifix like, they have a lot of Bible teachings there, very Christian home.'

'Mrs Grubbe what do you think might have happened to Annie?'

Her small eyes narrowed in her pudgy face, 'I think she got what was coming to her.'

Ada nodded and said blandly. 'Thank you for your time Mrs Grubbe. I'll see my own way out, leave you to your preparations.'

'It was in her, she was a bad 'un.'

'Maybe she was just desperate . . .' Ada couldn't help herself saying.

'We're all that at times, we don't do what she did. No, it's an evil soul, that's what.'

'Thank you again.'

Ada, relieved to leave the kitchen, swiftly climbed the stairs back to the hall. She heard two men talking and as she stepped into the hallway saw Straker with a young clergyman. Glancing over to her, his eyes widened in surprise. 'Miss Fawkes!'

'Reverend Turner. How are you?' Ada asked.

'Seasons Greetings, Miss Fawkes and I am well thank you. I'm here to deliver the children's Christmas Bible reading and prayers. Well, I wasn't expecting to see you involved in this enquiry.'

'Miss Fawkes's photographic skills mean she is called on by Scotland Yard on occasions to assist in investigations,' Straker said before Ada could reply.

'Oh I had no idea.' Reverend Turner clearly taken aback stammered slightly. 'I . . . I was fortunate to hear your talk at the museum M . . . Miss Fawkes. I . . . I was just explaining to the detective inspector that I'm the chaplain and one of the trustees here. I like to think of myself as a friend these poor children can turn to.'

'You are chaplain at the Refuge too, I understand?' said Straker sharply.

'Yes, I do a lot of work in the parish. My duty is spiritual guidance to those who are most in need.'

'We are investigating the missing laundry maid, did you know her?' Straker asked.

'Annie Wren,' added Ada.

Turner hesitated a moment. 'Oh, I thought that had been settled long ago. The Master informed the trustees that Annie had fallen by the wayside, some time back now I can't quite recall.'

'We believe Annie to be dead, sir,' said Straker.

Turner shook his head. 'May God have mercy on her soul.'

'Did you first meet her here or at the Refuge?'

'I ... I'm not sure. I can't quite recall her,' he blinked quickly.

He's lying, thought Straker. 'Pretty girl, maybe sixteen or so, dark hair. We are told she worked in the laundry here but was sometimes asked to wait on visitors. Before that she lived at the Refuge so may well have been at one of your Bible readings.'

'Oh yes, now I come to think of it. I vaguely recollect the girl, nice manners, very neat and tidy in her black dress.'

'And did you ever talk to her?'

'Only in my duty as a vicar, no more than that. I can't quite remember.'

'Did you know her at the Refuge?'

'Y ... Y ... Yes, yes maybe,' Turner's knuckles whitened as he clutched his Bible tighter.

'But you are the chaplain there,' Ada said. 'Don't you remember her at all?'

'I started last year and I think Annie left soon after. I can't really remember. There are quite a few girls in my Bible lessons. The young women are found employment as soon as they are thought to be suitable, but the Ladies Committee deals with that. I can't really help any further.'

Straker nodded. 'Thank you Reverend Turner.'

'Do you give the girls' silver crosses as prizes in Bible class or as confirmation gifts?' Ada asked as though an afterthought.

Turner had turned to leave and he spoke without looking round. 'No, no I don't. Perhaps Reverend Lindley might do so. Excuse me. I must make haste.'

He quickly opened a door into a plain white-painted room. Ada saw rows of backs of heads bent forwards, children on low hard benches, huddled close together, hands clutched in prayer, quiet as corpses.

Reverend Turner walked to the front, stood before the orphans and looked towards them in the open doorway. 'Perhaps you would care to join myself and my young charges in Christmas prayers?'

'Thank you, but our duty calls too,' Straker said. Pinched faces turned round as he spoke and just as quickly looked back, palms pressed harder, heads bowed further – terrified of not being deserving enough of one good meal a year.

***

They left the Ragged School and didn't speak until they reached the road's end.

'It's Annie Wren for certain,' Ada said. 'Mrs Grubbe confirmed the necklace as hers, the dates fit and she came from the Refuge.'

'The supervisor knew nothing more than that. He came forward because he was asked to and he thought there might be a reward. As for Reverend Turner, I think he knows something,' said Straker.

Struggling to keep up with his pace in the deep snow, Ada felt a weariness deep in her bones. She tilted her head up, so she could see him from under her hat brim and saw his face looked exhausted too. Suddenly she found herself inviting him back. 'Come home with me. It's Christmas Day. We could both do with a drink. Stay for lunch. We could talk over what we know.'

Even for Straker, used to being alone, a hotel room seemed a grim proposition today and he agreed. They walked on, their boots sinking into the fresh layer of snow, passing no one this time. Most folks had hurried home after church and were most likely piling logs on their fires and inhaling the meaty smells of roasting beef and goose.

Neither spoke until they reached Chapter House Street. Inside they gratefully allowed Camille to usher them into the drawing room where the fire was blazing and the lamps provided a soft welcoming glow.

'Oh thank God,' Ada sank into a chair with relief.

Straker looked at her pale face and even from across the room could tell she was shivering.

'Miss Fawkes, Ada, are you well?' he said coming over to her.

'Yes, yes, I will be fine. I'm cold that's all. I need a hot drink.'

233

Straker walked to the fireside and jabbed the poker to stoke the logs into greater flames. 'I'm sorry, I'm sorry for this, I'm sorry for everything,' his back turned away from her so she could not see his face. 'And it's Christmas. Can you . . .'

The door opened. The moment was gone.

Camille came in carrying a tray, with a coffee pot, cups, glasses and a green bottle. 'I'll leave you to it. I've a bird to baste.'

The detective splashed cognac into two coffees and handed one to Ada. They sipped the scalding liquid in silence, cradling frozen hands around the thin china.

Finally Straker spoke. 'This is like nothing we have seen before. Somewhere out there is a devil in human clothing. Three bodies and three silver crosses. That's it. There's nothing to grasp hold of. No solid clue. No motive.'

'But we have the thread of something,' she said. 'We know Rose was given her cross while she was at the Refuge and Mrs Grubbe told us that Annie was also given a similar necklace while she lived there. So who is this mystery person? It brings us back to Miss Brockett's list of names. Which visitor did the girls trust, who did they talk to?'

She went on, 'We need to find out more about Emily Eden. And then there are the silver necklaces. This person must have bought them somewhere. The problem is they are so common. Every jewellery shop in York sells them. The engravings might help narrow it down. Thomas and I can take my photographs to show the jewellers.'

'There are so many strands to this investigation.' Straker rose and paced the room, stopping to look out at the bleak wintry garden.

'Did you receive the post-mortem results?'

He looked at her. 'No, I haven't yet. Why, what are you thinking?'

'I'm puzzled by the upside-down V-shaped cut on Rose's stomach.' Ada frowned. 'I don't know, it's strange, but I don't think this is about anger or passion. This killer's motive; it feels cold, calculated, purposeful.'

'I sense that too.' Straker turned and walked to the door. 'I'm wasting time.'

'Where are you going? What about Christmas lunch?'

'I must see Miss Brockett now, today. She's our main witness. I need to talk to her again, try and find out more about Annie Wren. We need to know if Emily Eden lived there. If all the girls are connected to the Refuge, that's where we start, the men on the committee.'

'I'll come with you.'

'I think this time I will handle Miss Brockett better on my own.'

***

The atmosphere over the dining table was pleasant enough, Thomas and Camille were talking and bickering for which Ada was grateful. Occasionally she joined in, but most of the time she was silent, letting the conversation distract her.

Ada felt she had little appetite, but changed her mind at the smell of roast goose and sage and onion stuffing, accepting the plate Thomas passed her. There were many dishes: a puree of buttery apples, Agen prunes soaked in Armagnac, a bowl of golden roasted potatoes, a platter of salted, braised leeks, with a boat of wine gravy on the side.

They picked up their silverware and fell silent for some minutes as they ate, in full appreciation for the skill of the chef.

'It's delicious Camille, the best ever,' said Thomas after a while. 'Apart from one time that is – did I ever tell you about our Christmas dinner before the Battle of Sebastopol?'

'Yes, but don't let that stop you,' smiled Ada.

Thomas didn't, any excuse to retell his old war stories. 'Well, morale being a bit low among the troops, myself and a few others jumped the goods train in the dead of night as it was coming up from the harbour. Boxes and boxes stuffed with champagne, ham, plum puddings, all destined for the officers' mess. We pinched the lot, loaded into carts and took it back for the lads. We spread some Christmas cheer I can tell you. They never did find out who stole their dinner.'

They laughed and enjoyed the moment. Sipping wine, sitting together in the warmth and light, talking of old times. It gave them some peace for a few hours.

***

Out in the dark city, Christmas night was well underway, good cheer was spilling out of every crowded tavern onto the snowy cobbles. Straker side-stepped jostling drunks clutching ladies in feathers, buskers singing carols, street sellers hawking hot meat pies and stopped to give as many coins as he could spare to a frozen-looking little girl on Church Street corner, selling lucifer matches. He walked swiftly towards his hotel. God knows, Straker thought, there was little chance of any sleep tonight.

'Good evening detective inspector and Merry Christmas,' said the bow-legged night porter opening the door.

'Good evening Flaxman and same to you,' Straker replied. 'May I have coffee sent up please, strong, and some bread and cheese or anything.'

'Of course, sir.' The porter took the coin handed to him.

Once in his room, Straker lit a cigarette. He paced the floor, thinking of his talk, over a Christmas sherry, with Miss Brockett. Annie Wren had gone missing soon after Reverend Turner had arrived in York. Not only that Miss Brockett confirmed the other probable victim, Emily Eden, had lived at the Refuge too.

Straker tried to put himself in the mind of a lonely young woman without money or family, living the most desperate life imaginable. He pictured the killer visiting the Refuge, choosing his victim. Luring her with all a woman craves most: kindness, tenderness, love. He stood at the window and stared out into the darkness. His eyes caught the bright North Star and took his gaze up to the heavens. Then he looked down on the square below, the medieval streets, the narrow twisting alleyways – swallowed by the shadows.

CHAPTER TWENTY-ONE

◊

Steady persistent pounding roused one body in Chapter House Street in the early hours of Boxing Day morning. Thomas, who had dozed off by the kitchen range, the wrong side of a few whisky nightcaps, heaved himself out of his chair. Rubbing his eyes, he hurried along the hallway, turned the key and threw open the door.

The young man, stamping his cold feet on the doorstep struggled to speak.

'What's this about constable? Christmas Day's barely over.'

'I need Miss Fawkes. She's got to come. The detective sent me. He needs Miss Fawkes, right now, at the Minster.'

'What's happened?'

'There's a dead 'un.'

'What!'

'A body at the Minster, right by the west door.'

Thomas Bell felt a jolt of shock clear his head and quicken his wits.

'Come in officer, out of the cold, while you wait.'

'I'm to get straight back sir. Detective Inspector Straker says I'm needed to help keep people away. He said he doesn't want anyone messing up the crime scene.'

'Tell him we'll be there at the double. What's your name?'

'Constable Bevers.'

'Right Constable Bevers. Away with you. I'll get us organised here.' Thomas turned and took the stairs two at a time.

Ada heard words in her sleep and rolled over.

'Ada. Ada.' Thomas's voice cut through her dreaming state.

She opened her eyes. Thomas was still talking, his voice urgent. 'A body has been found at the Minster. Straker needs you.'

Ada momentarily closed her eyes again. 'Oh, God.' Then, quickly, ignoring the lurch in her stomach, she got out of bed. Wrapping herself in her shawl, she walked to the door and opened it. Thomas's hands reached for her shoulders as if to steady her.

'Straker needs you, now,' he said looking directly into her eyes. 'Ada?'

'I'm fine. I'll get ready. I'll be down as soon as I can.'

She splashed her face with cold water from the pitcher on her washstand and was drying herself as Camille came into the room. 'It will be easier if I help,' she said.

Minutes ticked by as the two hastily pulled, hooked and tucked layers of clothing. 'What hope have we women got of doing anything quickly when we have to wear all this damn nonsense?' Ada sighed, finally laced into a dark bodice with her skirt hitched up above black-stockinged ankles. She pushed her feet into sturdy leather ankle boots. Camille knelt and buttoned them as Ada pulled her long hair into a loose chignon, shoved in the loose strands as best she could and jabbed in a handful of pins.

Downstairs she took a lamp and went out to her studio to check her bag contained everything she needed. She always kept it ready but she added more waxed paper, just in case. She was closing the clasps as Thomas came into get the equipment. They hurried back to the house.

'Ada, have this,' called Camille from the kitchen, hearing their steps on the flagstones. She handed Ada a cup of sweet, strong coffee.

Ada took it gratefully and swallowed, hoping it would sharpen her thoughts. 'Thank you. I needed that.'

They walked silently up the narrow street from home, past the Chapter House of the Minster and through Dean's Park. Ahead they saw lights and in the gloom, the shape of a police-man silhouetted against the large gates of the park, blowing white clouds of breath which hung in the frosty air. People were already gathering on Duncombe Place: drunks, servant girls on their way to work, street sweepers, kept back by a long rope held by two police constables. This was, as Ada had expected, a well organised and secured crime scene. Only as she took a step further and turned to face the Minster, having a moment of doubt, what if she had forgotten how to do this?

The vast twin towers of the west front rose up before her. Ada took a deep breath. She saw on the top of the cathedral steps what looked to be a tiny bundle of rags that a man crouched near. She watched Straker rise to his feet, and almost before she had chance to exhale, he was at her side. She looked up into his face. His stony expression gave away nothing, yet told her everything.

He leaned closer, 'Miss Fawkes. Are you ready?'

She nodded.

'Then let's go.'

A voice like thunder bellowed from behind. 'Why haven't you moved this whore yet? I want this body gone. Now!'

240

Chief Constable Nutt barged his way through the crowd, pushed past Straker and strode up the Minster steps, his large boots adding to the muddle of footsteps already disturbing the snow.

Ada heard Straker curse under his breath.

'You and you,' the police chief had turned from the body and was pointing at two of his men below. 'Get this corpse put in the cart, get it to the morgue.'

'Detective inspector! What are you thinking of man?' Nutt now turned and glared at Straker who had not moved from the bottom of the steps.

Straker spoke very deliberately. 'Superintendent Nutt would you mind if I briefed you on events?' He motioned to the police chief to join him. To his relief Nutt tramped back down and followed him, well away from the crime scene.

'Well?' Nutt said. 'I presume this is another slag who had it coming?'

Straker winced. He kept his response professional. 'The victim is unknown. A Minster warden arrived early this morning to prepare for the first service. He found the young woman's body. He sent a boy to the police station. I got the call at half past five and I have briefly examined the scene.'

'That's as may be but what I want to know is why haven't you got the body moved? All this bloody fuss for a whore. Get that stiff to the morgue. You can do what you want with it there. But not here, not in front of the Minster.'

Straker's fingers curled into fists. He wanted Nutt away from here.

'And so much for your so-called Scotland Yard expertise. It's not stopped the killings has it? Or are you just interested in making a name for yourself Mr Detective, posing for the penny rags? I know your sort, it's all about glory. Now get this slut moved.'

Straker waited until Nutt paused for a lungful of air before he said firmly. 'With respect Superintendent Nutt, I need to examine the crime scene and document the evidence. And that is what I am going to do.'

'What do you mean? Why would you do that?'

Straker explained. 'If this is the work of the Butcher, this is my first chance to look at a body at the scene where the killer has struck. The dead may be silent but there are other things that can tell us what has happened. I must examine the body and what is around it and that will reveal evidence. There are footprints in the snow for instance.'

Nutt gave him a sceptical look.

Straker went on in a slow, emphatic voice, 'So they must be the killer's prints unless he flew over here and dropped the body. But they will disappear when more snow falls. I need to gather the evidence now and we have to get a move on. Miss Fawkes is here to photograph the crime scene so we have visual records to help us with the investigation and to use as evidence in any trial. They may be proof. We can also use photographs to reconstruct how the body was placed at the scene.'

'Hang on, what's this you are telling me?' asked Nutt, his eyes boggling. 'Have I got it right? You are still allowing that woman to take part in this abhorrence?'

In the periphery of his vision, Straker saw a flash of anger cross Ada's face. He was in no mood for this. 'Superintendent Nutt, this is not a brawl with a pen knife over a few coins or a drunk husband who picked up a hammer. This pattern of murder is something I have never seen before. We have to take this chance. Photographs will capture what is before us now before it's too late. This is vital and I need Miss Fawkes's help. There is no one else.'

Nutt seldom showed self-control but the hardness in Straker's eyes and the set of his face stopped any further protest. He gave a cursory nod and turned away without another word, stomping off through the snow towards a waiting Hansom cab.

***

Straker and Ada were alone, Straker pulled down the top of the covering and revealed the face beneath. Ada, holding a lantern, came closer. The young woman looked peaceful as though she had lain down to sleep, seeking protection from the Minster against the bitter night and had slipped into death quietly.

Ada took in the simple white gown, the young face, the pale lips and sighed. She gave herself a moment. In the presence of death, old memories were stirred.

After a while Ada spoke softly, without moving her eyes from the girl. 'Show me the rest of her.'

Straker lifted the cloth, holding it like a screen against the crowd below. Ada allowed herself time to study the body, then slid the gown upwards over the thighs and higher. The sight was such that she knew right away this was no accidental death.

'The stomach wounds. They are the same.'

She looked up at Straker and he nodded.

The sight of the dead girl was as bad as any in their recollection for its pitifulness. The thin figure, skin smooth with youth, had been lain out like a body readied for burial, her hands clasped together, long straight dark hair smoothed down her narrow shoulders.

Ada gently pulled the gown back down, straightening the material. Straker laid a blanket over the body and reached to take the lantern from Ada.

'Now see this.' Straker turned and pointed. 'Look down there to the right. Careful where you step. It looks to me like the killer kneeled there.'

He indicated a flattened hollow in the snow.

Ada nodded in assent.

'And there are footprints. The local police were all over the scene, but their boots are all hob-nailed like those. But see, these ones stand out. They are smooth-soled, not a working man's boot and they are deeply imprinted as though the person was carrying something heavy, see he stumbles here on the step. I tried to follow them but they soon get lost in the street amongst the muddle of horses' hooves and cart wheels.'

Straker held the lantern higher for her and Ada saw gently falling snowflakes melt as they touched upon its heat.

Ada looked at him. 'I need to act fast, before the snow covers everything up.'

'Is there light enough?'

'There is beginning to be, dawn is breaking but if you can organise some more lamps that would help us.'

He had already turned to leave. Ada looked for Thomas as she made her way down the steps. He was by her side as she reached the bottom.

'Let's get set up, so that we will be done before the snow gets much worse.'

Thomas gathered Ada's field equipment and carried it to the crime scene. With practised ease, he prepared her camera.

'Thomas, I need my ruler for the footprints. Is it there?' she asked.

He nodded.

It was Ada's time to begin. She bent over the lens, but her covered fingers felt too clumsy and she pulled her leather gloves off, tucking them in her coat pocket. Straker looked at her outstretched hand as the sleeve of her coat pulled back. For a brief moment he was unable to remove his gaze from Ada's wounds. Her scarred flesh looked bluer in the cold and it made him catch his breath.

'Straker! Take the ruler from Thomas and place it by the footprint,' Ada urged. 'It will be evidence of its size. I will photograph that first, before we lose it under the snow.'

Straker mentally shook himself and swiftly placed the wooden ruler alongside the footprint. It was Ada's turn to position the camera. She did so, bent over the lens and took the picture. She exhaled.

'Can you remove the blanket first, then the gown. I will need photographs of the scene as it is and then of her wounds.'

Straker carefully removed the covering. Folding the wool blanket and tucking it under his arm, he picked up a lantern in the other. Ada moved her camera and tripod closer to the body. Through the lens she looked down into the young lifeless face and framed her shot. The snap of a shutter and the girl's shadow was caught, in her cold bed of snow.

Ada methodically worked on, oblivious to the growing crowd gawping up at her from behind a rope, mouths like tunnel entrances. For them this was as curious a scene as they had ever seen.

'You can move her arms now,' said Ada.

'They are not yet stiff,' observed Straker, lifting them from her chest and placing them by her side. 'She can't have been dead many hours, though in this cold it's hard to be sure.'

Straker smoothed her hair away from the base of her slender throat and pushed back the folds of her gown to expose milk-white skin and something else, a silver crucifix.

'A necklace! I'm sure it's the same as the others.' He took the small engraved cross in his finger and thumb, turning it slowly.

'Well?' said Ada.

'The exact same marking as the others. It's our killer alright,' he replied grimly.

Finally Ada was satisfied that she had captured every image she needed. Thomas took over, starting to pack up the equipment. Ada was shaking with cold now, blowing warm breath on her numb fingers.

At a signal from Straker, two brown-coated hospital orderlies standing by with a stretcher, hurried up the steps, bending down to pick up the body which had been recovered with the blanket.'

'Steady lads,' ordered Straker as they clumsily manhandled the corpse onto boards. Even as he spoke the words, the older morgue assistant slipped in the trodden snow and lost his footing. A sudden lurch and one alabaster-white arm dropped to the side, catching and dragging the covering. The watching crowd gasped in unison.

'For God's sake. Get her covered up. Show some respect,' snapped Straker.

'Sorry, sir,' the younger one muttered.

As the body was placed in a waiting dog cart, Straker turned to Ada. 'I must go. I have much to do at the station and you need time to develop the photographs. Will you let me have them as soon as they are ready?'

'Yes, of course.'

'Keep the footprint to yourself. We shall see if the Butcher's shoes walk him into a gaol cell.'

CHAPTER TWENTY-TWO

◊

Much of Straker's day had been spent tracing the young woman's identity, without success. This being such a cold Boxing Day, people were still hunkered down at home. He had nothing to go on; no officers to make enquiries, no photographs yet and no report of a missing girl.

He sighed thinking of his Great Scotland Yard colleagues. He couldn't ignore the fact that their future rested on him and the outcome of this case, and now there had been another murder, on his watch. Maybe he was too old, too weary, too jaded.

It was mid-afternoon already and Straker's thoughts were running this way and that as he waited in a chair by the coal fire for his visitor. His long legs were thrust towards the hearth with the hope that the heat would dry his damp leather boots. As the mantel clock chimed three, he heard talking and laughing at the front desk. He was throwing his cigarette stub into the fire as Rufus Valentine, the editor of *The Herald*, knocked once and strolled in.

Straker took in the man's genial air of confidence as he held out his hand to greet his visitor. Valentine shook it firmly, looking into Straker's eyes directly. There was an air of arrogance about his manner. Straker hoped he was doing the right thing.

Valentine smiled. 'Good afternoon detective inspector. Well at least it is for me, rather less so for you. Four murders now?

So what have you got for me? An interview about your detective methods? Our readers would love that; inside the mind of a Scotland Yard sleuth.' Valentine's sharp eyes raked over the drawn face and black eyes of the man before him. 'Or perhaps inside your bedroom is the better place, by the look of you.'

A knock at the door interrupted them.

'Sir, are you staying here for a bit?' asked Bevers, a sheepish look on his face.

'For a while yes. What is it?'

'The swans sir. I haven't had chance to slip home and feed them yet. They'll be hungry what with ground frozen and all the snow.'

Straker sighed. 'You've got half an hour.'

'Thank you, sir.'

The editor laughed.

'Well I don't want dead birds on my conscience along with the rest of it,' said Straker, smiling too.

'The readers will love that detail,' teased Valentine.

'Please sit down. Would you like a cigarette?' He proffered his silver case.

'Thank you,' said Valentine, taking one. The ritual of lighting up gave Straker a few seconds to make up his mind.

'Alright Valentine, I will give you a story. I'll give you some quotes, but in return I want you to do everything you can to help find out who this girl is. That is my offer.'

Valentine nodded. 'But I'm curious. Most policemen would have met me in the tavern, are you a Temperance man?'

Straker laughed. 'Good God, no. But I try to keep a clear head. I have to be able to think straight. I make it my rule not to drink in daytime working hours. My colleagues think it a massive joke. I get lots of ribbing.'

'Well you must allow me to buy you a drink one evening after work, while you are in York.'

'Thank you. That would be welcome.'

'So,' Rufus Valentine tapped his pencil against his lips. 'Is Miss Fawkes working on this with you?'

'She's taken photographs, yes.'

'What wouldn't I do for an interview with that woman.'

'Well it's not up to me obviously. I can't speak for her.'

'Well I shall ask her. It would be a sensation. I saw her give a talk about photography and Paris at the museum. Quite a woman: intelligent, independent and attractive. I'm surprised she's chosen to live in York.' His eyes narrowed speculatively. 'Not that I'm complaining.'

A flit of anger flashed across Straker's face. Then it was gone. 'Help me get a name,' he said changing the subject. 'It will be a great service you do me. But correct me if I'm wrong Valentine, it will be mutually beneficial?'

The journalist exhaled a cloud of smoke slowly. 'We are both not as young as we were, or as young as those snapping at our heels, but I am still ambitious to break the big stories. And it is clear to me that you have strong convictions, whatever personal price you pay. Neither of us will compromise. This is a crime of a magnitude and horror we have not witnessed before and if we solve this, it is will take our careers to new levels.'

Or finish them, thought Straker. He looked hard at the journalist. 'We have different motives Valentine, but we want the same outcome. What do you need to know?'

'The Butcher has killed four times. How does he select his victims?'

'Look I can't tell you anything for certain, I have a hunch but nothing I can prove,' said Straker leaning forward in his chair. 'But help me now and I can promise your paper will be the first to have the story.'

'A deal,' said Valentine nodding. 'So let's appeal for help to the public to identify the victim. Tell me what you know. What can I quote you on?'

'Ask me and I'll answer what I can.'

The journalist took out his notebook from his jacket pocket. He had many questions and wrote the answers quickly in what looked to Straker like Pitman's shorthand. He had studied phonography himself when he was still a police constable. He commented on it and the men talked briefly about their early careers and training. Straker was impressed. The man was clever, enthusiastic and outward looking. He found he liked him. But he didn't trust him.

'Do you have any leads as to the killer's identity?' Valentine asked.

'Early stages,' Straker said. The journalist didn't need to know that there were so many contenders, he saw the murderer everywhere he turned.

'Just one more. Then we're done.'

Straker had expected it. The question he didn't want to answer.

'Are the women of York in danger?'

Straker was grave. 'Valentine just help me get a name before he kills again.'

WEEK THREE

27 DECEMBER 1862 – 2 JANUARY 1863

'I do not profess to have perfected an art,
but to have commenced one; the limits of which
it is not possible at present exactly to ascertain.'
- William Henry Fox Talbot

CHAPTER TWENTY-THREE

◊

The Mansion House, Saturday morning

George Brass hated most things about his wife, the sound of her breathing, the way she crunched toast like a shire horse walking on gravel, but particularly her banal prattle over the breakfast table. It was the Lady Mayoress's practice to read extracts from the local newspaper and share with her husband startling pieces of intelligence. Today she was engrossed in the report of the Local Board of Health Committee on Public Lighting.

'Listen to this Georgie,' she said, her brow furrowing in concentration.

'This is what you said; "In these day of garrotting we can have no difficulty in adopting the resolutions which have been proposed, the lighting of the city is a perfect disgrace and with a complete system of lighting we might do with fewer policeman and hence it will prove a saving to the city." You are so clever Georgie.'

Brass lifted his newspaper higher to block his view of her.

The Lady Mayoress cleared her throat in a way that had come to grate on Brass's nerves and read the news that Colonel Bales and his 10th Royal Hussars had issued invitations for a ball at the Great Assembly Rooms. 'Georgie it says here that, "The city of York is expected to be very gay and full of company". Oh I must have a new dress my dear.' She looked down at her figure so short and stumpy that Queen Victoria looked tall and slender by comparison. 'Perhaps, yellow satin with frills. What do you think Georgie?'

Agnes Brass was some six years older than her husband and back in the day had been considered a catch, mainly for the wealth of her father's steady bakery business. The young ambitious George Brass had turned her small dowry into one of the largest fortunes in the country. Knowing he owed her everything, he put up with the gaffes, the awkwardness and the malapropisms which blighted their social engagements. There were many incidents he tried to forget, but occasionally they drifted into his thoughts like reoccurring nightmares. Who could expunge the Buckingham Palace incident when a butler had asked if she wanted sherry or port and she had replied, 'A little of both please.' True this was acceptable in Yorkshire – like having three puddings on one plate – but not in London and how it had been sneered at in the gossip columns.

He was a saint, he thought. He steadfastly had never showed any embarrassment at her stupidity, not even when she ordered two globes for their library, one terrestrial and one celestial, and then sent them back because they didn't match.

And as their fortune grew so had the Lady Mayoress's girth and somewhat extravagant and outrageous dress sense. He put up with it all, quietly wishing she would not exactly die, so much as disappear into thin air. But they had endured a lot in their thirty-one-year marriage and those bonds counted for something, he calculated. Publicly he paid her the respect due as his wife. Privately there were rumours of fast lady friends and illegitimate children. Mrs Brass was never troubled by them.

'That sounds lovely dear,' he replied, not looking at her.

Her small eyes continued to roam over the black and white pages of that morning's *Herald*. 'Can you believe the prisoners at the House of Correction had roast beef and beer on Christmas Day? I hope that didn't come out of the public purse. Oh and they are saying the pantomime at the Theatre Royal was an immense success, it's going to be repeated every evening. Do let's go.'

The Lord Mayor now tackling his full English, tuned out as he chewed on fatty bacon.

'But this is nice, "Christmas Rejoicings at the Workhouse" and, that is down to your generosity my dear, "On Christmas Day upwards of 100 children connected with the Ragged School were regaled with roast turkey and plum pudding at the premises in Marygate. The children expressed their thanks by several cheers."' She nodded her head with satisfaction at the thought of the grateful inmates, little faces lit with joy at her husband's benevolence.

'What!' Brass wrenched himself up, leaned over the long table and snatched the newspaper from his startled wife.

'What's the fuss, Georgie dear? It's a very nice report of your giving a Christmas dinner to the Ragged School children.'

He scowled at *The Herald*, clutching its inky pages in his stubby fingers.

'Not that,' he said. 'This!' He shoved the article in front of her. 'I'll have their bloody jobs.'

She read out loud with a gasp of excitement, '"Shocking Murders. Butcher of York claims fourth victim. The Truth about the Killer. Exclusive interview with Scotland Yard Detective.'''

'I told Straker not to speak to the press,' he banged down his knife and fork on the table cloth. 'No, he will find out that I don't like this at all . . .'

He stopped at the sound of a loud voice on the other side of the double doors.

Brass slammed his hands down. 'What now?'

'I will find out,' said Mrs Brass, heaving herself up from her carver chair in which she was wedged. As she was doing so, they heard a knock.

'Come in,' snapped Brass.

'Good morning Lady Mayoress, Lord Mayor,' Hugh Blake bowed. 'Apologies for disturbing you at such an early hour, but I didn't think this could wait, especially in view of the fact that Detective Inspector Straker will be calling on you in an hour.'

Hugh Blake was tall and thin; nearing forty years of age. His hair was combed and oiled into an immaculate centre parting; likewise his drooping moustache was fixed into symmetrical points. His obsequious expression hid an alertness that missed nothing.

'What is it Blake?' Brass looked at him sharply.

'I've brought you today's edition of *The Times* sir and I think you will want to see it right away.' His voice was soft, disguising the snake in his tongue.

The secretary held out a newspaper, neatly folded over to an inside page. As he did so, the Lady Mayoress for once acted prudently and bustled her voluminous magenta skirt out of the panelled room.

'Here it is sir,' he said.

Brass took it without a word. Blake walked deferentially backwards as though in the presence of royalty and took up a position by the window, smooth hands clasped together.

Brass looked down, his eyes darting over the page, a flush of red creeping over his face. "Another Terrible Murder In The City of York. Dreadful Mutilation of a Fourth Woman". His mouth fell open. "No one is Safe. Killer could be husband, father, son". The editorial even had the temerity to boast of its speed in publishing. "We, yesterday by extraordinary exertion, published the full account of the crime which happened in the early hours of Boxing Day while all good folk were asleep, or, in other words reported a murder which took place at a distance of more than 200 miles from London and which was not made public till eight o'clock in the morning." And went on to apologise for its glut of copy explaining that, "certain examples" of crime took a "stronger hold than others," creating a "more continuous interest."

'Bastards!' Brass stood, gripping the edge of the table. 'Now the whole county's reading this muck. I'm a laughing stock. Can't even keep order in my own city. Who will want to visit York now? They'll think they are going to be murdered in their beds. The opening of Lendal Bridge, my Twelfth Night Ball, all ruined. This is going to cost me a fortune.'

'Well those are all valid points to put to Detective Inspector Straker, a timely visit if I may say so sir,' suggested Blake.

'Yes, I want to know exactly what he's got to say for himself.' Brass pressed his thin lips into a white line, almost hissing with venom.

'Well, that's what he's here for and at great expense to the corporation purse,' supplied Blake. He paused. He knew his boss inside out – rich as a king, tight as any true-born York-shireman – and Brass loved someone to blame.

'Get him here. Now.'

Blake hurried towards the door.

'And get Superintendent Nutt here too,' Blake almost shuddered at the menacing tone of the voice. It was true what they said, he reflected, running swiftly down the curving staircase, taking two treads at a time, George Brass – half genius, half madman.

***

'And here he is. Scotland Yard's finest, the great Detective Inspector Straker.'

Robert Nutt, standing below a huge Joshua Reynolds portrait, as he waited in the entrance hall of the Mansion House, looked to Straker both fatter and diminished by the elegant setting.

'I don't know why I've been summonsed,' Nutt went on. 'Your failure is nothing to do with me.'

'I suppose it's because you are York's police chief and a killer has murdered four young women on your streets,' said Straker, removing his hat.

'But it's your problem, not mine. You are the big London know-it-all called in to sort us bumpkins out. I didn't want help from you, but I had no choice. So, as far as I am concerned, you can bloody get on with it. You can strut round here like you own the place with that bloody woman as much as you like. Help from you? I'd sooner have Burke and Hare bury my grandmother.'

'We can work together Superintendent Nutt.'

'You can f . . .' He stopped mid-sentence as Blake glided silently into his sight, all ears.

'Ah Mr Blake, good morning,' said Chief Constable Nutt with a smile. 'I hope I can be of help to my brother-in-law, our Lord Mayor.'

Straker smiled to himself. He had the measure of Nutt and it wasn't positive. Together they walked up the red carpeted stairs and followed Blake along a corridor and into the mayor's office.

'Refreshment sirs?' asked Blake.

'There's no time for that,' snapped Brass, now sat behind his desk, below another of the Mansion House's over-sized and flattering oil portraits, this one of himself. Brass leaned back and scrutinized Straker. An imposing aloof fellow, a man of honour, highly thought of in Whitehall, could have gone to the very top if he wasn't so principled. Then he looked at his brother-in-law, greedy, corrupt, easily manipulated, the right man in the right job.

'How's your investigation going?' Brass said after a moment. 'I want you to update me and Superintendent Nutt here. We would like to know your progress.'

Straker nodded and succinctly summarised the main points of the investigation so far, emphasising their fortune in having a forensic photographer working alongside them.

'Ah, so all you've got is a few pictures of dead whores. Not so good then,' said Brass when the detective had finished. Nutt, sat on his chair, arms folded, was smirking.

'Not good at all Straker. In fact if you ask me this investigation is a joke. So let me speak very plainly. If you haven't got this sorted before the Twelfth Night Ball, I will personally see to it that your career is finished. As for Miss Fawkes, I will hound her out of the city myself.'

Straker kept his face expressionless. 'Is that all?'

'For now.' Nutt didn't look up from lighting a cigar.

Straker rose and walked out of the room without a word, not trusting himself to speak.

Brass drew deeply on his cigar as the door shut. As he exhaled, he looked directly at his brother-in-law, blowing smoke across the table. 'Don't worry Bob. If he catches this killer, and he bloody better, I'll make sure you get the credit. If he doesn't, well that's the end of him and the Detective Branch. I'll make sure of that too.'

Not always the sharpest, Nutt finally understood what was going on in his brother-in-law's mind. There was no threat to him. He took the credit or Straker took the blame. He didn't like a London detective meddling in his kingdom, but now the benefit was penetrating his slow brain. It was a win, win. It suited Brass to keep him as police chief, they were both doing nicely out of it. 'You're a sly one George.'

Brass tapped the side of his wide nostril. 'Time for a sherry I think Bob?'

They moved to the comfortable wingback chairs by the fire-side with well-filled glasses.

Nutt took a large sip. 'There's one thing still bothering me George.'

'Spit it out.'

'What if Straker gets a bit too close to our private business? He's poking around, finding things out, and well, there might be trouble.'

'Don't you worry, I've thought of that. Leave that to me.'

They exchanged looks and then their conversation roamed on; the latest gossip from the corporation chambers to the costly Christmas shopping sprees of their spouses.

'Now on that subject of the good ladies, Agnes is desperate for a gossip with her sister and she has given me strict instructions to ask if you would care to join us for supper this evening. Perhaps a little turn in the Assembly Rooms afterwards? We have to keep our lasses happy eh Bob?' he winked at his brother-in-law. 'We don't want them getting ideas above their places or daft notions of suffrage.'

'Too bloody right we don't. It's bad enough at home now Lizzie's joined the bloody Temperance Society. She's drinking health tonics instead of port and wine, much good it's doing her, she's skinnier than ever. And she's mithering on at me because I like a tipple of something to relax after a hard day's graft.'

'Don't you worry Bob. I'll see your glass is kept topped up tonight.'

CHAPTER TWENTY-FOUR

◊

Straker, waiting outside the police station, looked up and saw Ada coming towards him around the corner of St Sampson's Church. Without thinking he smiled, his dark expression lifted, his eyes crinkled and his exhaled breath came out like white clouds in the afternoon air.

That smile. Ada felt her heart stolen from her own power. She took a breath. For a moment she could not look away from him.

'Have you got her name yet?' She covered up with brusqueness.

'Yes possibly.' Straker had checked himself and replied with the same tone. 'A few people have come forward after reading today's *Herald*.'

'Well?'

He hesitated. 'I wanted to tell you before you saw him. There's a man here, you know him. His laundry maid has gone missing and the description fits. It's Edward Atkinson, the architect who was at your Christmas Eve party.'

She looked up at him in surprise. 'Edward Atkinson?'

'Yes, he's come to look at your photographs. You've got them with you?'

She nodded and touched her bag. 'In here, I've just had time to develop the images of her face and the necklace. Camille and

264

Thomas will show the photographs around the jewellers to see if they recognise the cross.'

'You know I would have sent one of the constables, but there's hardly anyone on duty.'

'It's better this way, who do you trust to do the job properly?'

Straker nodded. 'Let's get this done. Then we'll talk. I need to tell you what Miss Brockett told me.'

Straker turned and led the way through the station door, past the front desk, along the flagged corridor and opened the door into the office. Edward Atkinson was standing, waiting by the fire, his hands clasped behind his back. He took a few steps forward as they came in.

'Miss Fawkes, Detective Inspector Straker this is a most unexpected turn up.'

'Mr Atkinson.' She greeted him.

'Please sit-down Mr Atkinson,' Straker nodded at a chair.

Atkinson took the seat, crossing his legs comfortably. 'I got in touch as soon as we read the description in *The Herald* this morning. My wife thinks it might be Amy, our laundry girl. She went missing the week before Christmas, on market day. My wife thought she had run away, found the job too much hard work, girls like her do come and go so we didn't think it was worth reporting. Assumed she'd gone back to her home village. But my wife insisted I came today, as you know she's expecting and a little sensitive at the moment. I said it would be nothing, and a waste of time, but I didn't want to upset her, so here I am and Detective Inspector Straker here seems to think it may actually be Amy. I can't believe it.'

'Miss Fawkes, can you show Mr Atkinson the photograph.'

Ada pulled a folder out of her bag and untied the black ribbon knot. She laid out the photographs on the table.

'Here,' said Straker. He pushed over a photograph showing the young woman lying on the snow and watched his reaction closely.

Atkinson looked at the image, not touching it. 'Oh God, that's her! Poor girl. That's Amy. She looks like she's sleeping.'

Straker looked at him sharply, wondering if he was imagining it that Atkinson's response sounded like forced surprise. 'What's her full name?'

'Amy Ward.'

'What do you know about her Mr Atkinson?' Straker asked.

Atkinson sat back further. 'Oh very little. She came to us from the Refuge to help with our laundry work. We have three young daughters and a fourth child on the way. The Ladies Committee asked if we had a position for her, to help her get back into respectable society. I had indicated we needed another servant. My wife believes in helping those who have fallen by the wayside. She's a virtuous woman . . .'

'Does Amy have family?'

'Her parents are from the country. I think they died and that is when Amy came looking for work in York. She fell on hard times.'

'When did she come to you?'

'I think it must have been October time. Again my wife will remember more exactly. She deals with all the domestic arrangements.'

'Thank you, Mr Atkinson, we will need to speak to her. At home would be more suitable I am sure.'

'She feels poorly in a morning, but Monday afternoon at two o'clock I'm sure would be agreeable. I will tell her to expect you.'

'Thank you, Mr Atkinson. You're an architect, that must be interesting,' said Straker.

'Yes, I am designing the new home on the grounds of Bootham County Lunatic Asylum for the director Dr Scull.'

'Dr Scull, he's something to do with the Refuge too I believe.'

'Indeed, he is involved in lots of good work. His passion is transforming the hospital. Our firm has done a lot of renovation work there. It was the old lunatic asylum, totally different now. It's so modern, very impressive. If that's all, I will leave you to it and get back to the office. My wife will be so sad to hear it is Amy.'

Atkinson stood up quickly as though he was eager to leave. 'I'll see myself out.'

He'd scarcely left the room when Straker said sharply. 'How well do you know him?'

'Not very, mainly in a professional capacity. He's already commissioned some photographs and is interested in me photographing his buildings. That's why I invited him and his wife to my Christmas Eve drinks. I need the work.'

He said nothing.

Ada stared at him. 'What are you thinking?'

'I don't know. He seemed confident, maybe too much so.'

'It's not every day a man is asked to a police station to look at a photograph of a dead body. It might just have been trying to hide his nerves.'

'Perhaps.' He looked out onto the street, the weak afternoon sun was suggesting a warmth that wasn't there. He turned back. 'Miss Fawkes, I would like to talk it through with you as we did our investigations in Paris, it might help us. Not here though, at my hotel. We could sit at a quiet table and have tea. I don't trust anyone here and we need privacy to talk openly.'

***

The arthritic porter smiled toothlessly, greeting Straker like an old friend as he held open the door of Harker's. At nearly two o'clock on a Saturday afternoon, the small palm court was busy with people sitting at round tables laden with silver pots of tea and tiered cake stands.

'Damn, too many people around,' he looked at her. 'I don't know anywhere else.'

'We can go up to your room.'

'Are you sure?'

'We can talk privately. It's a little late for modesty between us.'

He nodded. 'I'll have something sent up. Tea or coffee?'

'Coffee please.'

'Go on up. I'll meet you there. It's room five.'

When she had started up the main staircase, he caught the attention of a passing waitress and ordered strong black coffee for two. He took the stairs two at a time, hurrying to his room. Ada was waiting by the door. He glanced round, then turned the key in the lock.

'I know you think I'm being old-fashioned. I just want to protect you from gossip. York's a far cry from Paris.'

'I'm not sure my reputation has concerned you before.'

He gave her a look she could not read as he pushed open the door.

'After you.'

Inside, he walked to the fireplace and stabbed the dying embers back to life. The smell of the burning coal on this winter's afternoon was welcoming. Looking round the comfortable room, she saw a wooden stand by the door upon which she hung her coat and hat. She sat in an easy chair watching Straker swing coal from the black scuttle into the grate. He came to sit opposite her, stretching out his long legs towards the fire. He reached inside his jacket pocket, removed his silver case and lit a cigarette. It almost felt like old times.

Ada was suddenly conscious of the large bed on the other side of the room, its silk plump eiderdown neatly smoothed over pillows ready for the night. She felt a tightening grip in her stomach and a warmth steal over her neck. She glanced at Straker's face mortified he might have noticed her flush. But his jaw was set firm as though he was worlds away with his thoughts. Ada was surprised to feel a little hurt. Why did he not seem to remember their intimacy? Was she so altered, so aged by events in Paris that she, nor even memories of her, had any appeal to him? She looked down to where the scars on her slender wrist met the cuff of her scarlet silk bodice.

'Miss Fawkes?'

'Sorry. What did you say?'

A knock on the door, he rose in one fluid movement and swiftly walked to the door. She heard his low voice speaking gently and he came back with a silver tray. They were silent for a minute while he poured coffee and he passed her a cup. He took a mouthful and set down his coffee on a small round table beside his chair. 'Let's look at what we know, start from the beginning. We have four names now.'

Ada nodded.

'These are the facts we have,' he said. 'Annie Wren was found in the river by Lendal Tower on August 28. Emily Eden was discovered by the King's Staith on October 6. Their exhumed bodies confirmed both were wearing engraved silver crosses and some kind of white linen dress. We have the photographic evidence. The ferryman John Goodricke and the boatman Jack Hawker both said in their police statements that Annie and Emily had the same unusual cuts on their stomachs. This we can't prove because of the decomposition of the bodies.

'Victim number three is Rose Fisher, her body was found lying on The New Walk by the lamp-lighter John Peck on December 18. We examined and photographed her body in the morgue, the day I arrived in York. We saw the same cross, the same gown, and the same wound on her stomach as fitted the descriptions. There seemed to be a link to the river until Amy.

'Amy Ward's body was found outside the Minster on December 26 by a street sweeper. This was the first crime scene we saw for ourselves. We have photographs of her silver crucifix, a white gown and the same distinct wound to the midriff. We did not find blood in the snow, and so we believe Amy was taken to the Minster from wherever she was killed.

'The obvious connection between all four is the Refuge. But we know they had little or no contact with anyone outside there. Esther spoke of Rose having a special friend, as did Mrs Grubbe of Annie Wren. So who is this man? He must have regular access to the Refuge, a man whose presence no one would question. So what about the gentlemen on the committee? What do we know of them?'

Ada stood to take a piece of headed notepaper from the small writing desk to the side of the fireplace. She dipped a pen in the inkwell and wrote down four names as she said them out loud; Reverend Lindley, Reverend Turner, Mr Atkinson, Dr Scull.

'I think the vicars could have spent more time with the young women than the other men, under the guise of Bible teaching or moral instruction. They could easily gain the trust of a vulnerable girl.'

'You've missed off a name,' Straker said.

'Who?'

'Dr Auden.'

'I've known him nearly all my life.'

'We can't take anything on trust.'

'I suppose not.' She wondered if Straker was a little too insistent that the handsome doctor was a suspect. Hardly, she dismissed any hope he was a little jealous.

Straker laid out the rest of his thoughts. 'Edward Atkinson is interesting. He told us he needed domestic help at home, his wife has connections to the Ladies Committee and he's a friend and business acquaintance of Dr Scull and Dr Auden. There was something I was unsure of when he was talking about Amy Ward, perhaps too forthcoming. We will know more tomorrow hopefully, after we have spoken to Mrs Atkinson.'

'What could possibly motivate any of them?' Ada looked at the five names. 'They all have so much to lose. These are well regarded men who do much good work. Reverend Turner is chaplain to York's most desperate.'

Straker frowned. 'I had hoped to learn more about these men from Miss Brockett, but she's desperate for no blame to fall on her so would not say much other than confirming the victims' connection to the Refuge. She did tell me Emily went to work at the County Lunatic Asylum in the laundry.'

She glanced up at Straker. 'There's another link with Dr Scull then. Do you think Miss Brockett knows more?'

'I don't know,' Straker said. 'I think she's trying to hide her little private expenses from the committee, but that doesn't make her complicit in these crimes.'

He set down his cup and swept his hair back from his eyes. 'We know the girls trained as laundresses and three left to go to jobs arranged for them by the ladies on the committee. Annie went to the Ragged School, Emily worked at the Lunatic Asylum and the Atkinsons took in Amy. Rose was still living at the Refuge.'

'But what would anyone kill for? These girls had nothing.' Ada hadn't smoked since she left Paris, but now she took a cigarette from Straker's silver case lying on the table between them. He raised an eyebrow.

'I know, don't say anything.'

He struck a match and cupping the flickering flame with his hands, leaned towards her, so she smelled his musky cologne mingling with the acrid white phosphorous of the flame. She inhaled deeply and tilting her chin, blew a ring of smoke into the air.

Straker sat back, staring into the fire. 'The motive baffles me. Lust, money, revenge, jealousy none of it makes sense. And I think these deaths are planned; we do know there is a time lag between the girls disappearing and their bodies turning up.'

Straker rose impatiently and paced the length of the room. He stopped by the window and looked down on the street, the last of the Saturday shoppers hurrying home to families and cosy firesides.

As Ada watched him, she could see his muscles tense under the close-fitting tweed of his jacket as he leaned his arms on the cold glass. The cigarette and the coffee were making her mind race. Unanswered questions came into her head. Had the girls gone willingly somewhere with someone they knew and trusted? Was it the gently-spoken Reverend Turner, a man so different to those to whom they had sold their bodies for pennies? He would seem like a gallant knight of King Arthur riding to their rescue. Was that how this killer snared them? With kindness?

'Ada?'

She looked at him watching her. 'I was miles away, thinking of the brutal lives of these poor girls. What if they met someone they thought they could trust? Someone they thought was a friend, someone to rescue them from their misery.'

'But why would he choose such women?'

'It's obvious really when you look at it. They are the girls no one will miss. The easiest targets of all; the unloved, the unvalued, the unwanted.'

His eyes hardened. 'You're right. Even my colleagues don't care about violence towards street women, they believe it to be an occupational hazard. They think as men, not as policemen to whom justice should be a right for all. They choose to believe these are girls with insatiable appetites, different to their wives, daughters, sisters. They believe that prostitution is a choice, not an act of desperation.'

Ada took in his weary face as he spoke. He looked older than he had in Paris, a few flecks of grey in his black hair. But, in other ways, he was not altered, or not for the worse. She acknowledged to herself that his life force was as strong as ever.

Three years and many lifetimes ago his passionate words, his principles had broken through every one of her protective layers. He had taken her heart and soul. They had come a long way since then, she had rebuilt the defences so why did she now feel such a pain clenching the deepest place of her body?

Ada breathed in, stood up and walked away from him. She got a grip of herself and turned briskly. 'What if he is enjoying this? We've turned him into a sensation. Up and down the country, people speak his name. He is famous. Everyone is fascinated with the killings, with you, the great London detective, with the photographs of the dead. Are we fuelling his cravings? Is that important to him? Is that spurring him on for he gets more attention the more risks he takes?'

He looked at her. 'You may have something there. The chief at Scotland Yard has told me even the Queen follows our progress in York. This latest murder could not be more public, a body left on the Minster steps on Christmas Night.'

Ada thought of her photograph of Amy's small body lying in the snow. She had immortalised Amy as a victim of the Butcher of York. She had created a portrait of death and it had rapidly become an iconic image, recognised by the whole country. Was this killer breathing in the notoriety like oxygen? Her skin crawled at the thought. 'I can't bear the idea that he's laughing at us, taunting us.'

Straker walked to a chair. 'I feel the same. And the murders are getting closer together, August, October, two in December . . .'

He picked up his overcoat which he had thrown over its arm and put it on as he spoke. 'We must make enquires at the Asylum about Emily Eden, find out what they know. Also Miss Brockett gave me an address for the brothel where Amy Ward lived before she was taken in at the Refuge. It's in Grape Lane, near the Minster. Interestingly the move was arranged by Reverend Turner. He seems to have quite a passion for helping distressed young working women. Miss Brockett tells me his missionary efforts in the parish of St Mary's and the lowest parts of York are commendable. He must be more knowledgeable about working women than anyone in the city. The house is not far from the police station so I'm going to the brothel now and then I'll go back to read the reports again, see if there is anything I have missed. We must start tomorrow by questioning them all. And the Reverend Turner is top of my list.'

'Do you want me to come with you now?'

'No, I'll go alone. I don't want to worry about you at such a place, it's almost dark,' he said firmly.

'What about the Asylum? I could go there.'

Straker's instinct was to say no, to wait until he could go with her. There was no time. He nodded. 'Let us meet here at the hotel tomorrow morning and discuss anything we find out. Nine o'clock? We could talk over breakfast.'

Ada turned and left Straker's bedroom, her face a mask of composure, her emotions held hard. Soon this would be over and she would never see him again, ever for the rest of her life. She should be relieved. But this thought brought her heart no peace at all.

CHAPTER TWENTY-FIVE

◊

From the swiftly moving Hansom cab Ada could see York Lunatic Asylum drawing nearer, its many lighted windows shining out into the early evening gloom as they approached along the tree-lined drive.

'Wait for me here please,' she said to the pock-marked cabbie. Barely nodding his head, he took out his copy of that day's *Herald* and soon engrossed, paid her no further attention.

Inside the building, a brown-coated attendant informed her Dr Scull was taking a short walk in the grounds, most likely to look at progress of the new governor's house. The offer to wait in the warmth indoors was tempting, but she was curious to see the home Scull was having built for himself, designed by Edward Atkinson.

She was about to set off, following instructions to go round to the rear and bear left, when Dr Scull, holding folded drawings in his hands, walked briskly into the lobby.

He started when he saw her. 'Miss Fawkes, what a surprise. How nice to see you.'

Ada moved towards him. 'Good evening Dr Scull. I'm afraid I'm not here for a social reason, I need to ask some questions about one of the girls who worked here, Emily Eden.'

He shook his head. 'That name means nothing to me. Who is she?'

'She was a laundry maid.'

He looked at her sharply. 'No, I don't know her. A laundry maid you say?'

'Yes, it was arranged through the Refuge, the job was a fresh start for her. I thought you might know of or been part of the arrangement, given you are on the committee there.'

'Well, yes now you mention it, I do remember something about a young woman being given work in our laundry. We have a large washing facility here, as you can imagine. We employ lots of women from all over. I don't know their names or anything about them.' There was a note of dismissal in his confident voice.

'Would you be told if they went missing or left your employment?'

'No, of course not. I'd not expect the housekeeper to trouble me with those trivial sorts of domestic detail, really I have so much to manage here.' He gave a little laugh.

She persisted. 'I have a photograph I would like to show you.'

'Let us go to my study.' He put an ushering arm around her back, touching her shoulders. Ada moved to one side. She let him lead the way past floor to ceiling marble columns into a wood panelled corridor, their feet ringing on the elaborate tiled floor. They walked by a line of closed doors until they reached one at the far end, bearing a brass plaque upon which was engraved *Dr Henry Scull, Director*.

'Go ahead in Miss Fawkes.'

His tidy study smelt of tobacco and polish. It was a big room with windows overlooking the gardens at the front of the house. An ornate, painted fireplace, dark gleaming wooden furniture and shelves of leather-bound books gave it an air of an exclusive gentleman's club rather than the office of an asylum governor. A leather daybed in the corner suggested it was a place where Dr Scull spent much of his time.

Ada reached into her scuffed bag and pulled out a photograph of a silver engraved cross. She placed it before Dr Scull, now sitting behind his orderly desk.

'Do you recognise this?'

'No, should I?'

'We think it belonged to Emily Eden. We think she may be the second victim of the killer amongst us, her body was found on October 6. I hoped someone might remember her wearing it, so we can identify her for certain.'

'Miss Fawkes you are speaking to the wrong person. I will send for my housekeeper.' He stood up and pulled a tasselled cord hanging near the door.

'She will be here shortly.'

Ada would rather have seen the housekeeper in her own space, sat down with her for a cup of tea, easier to talk to someone that way. Here, in this office, the woman would feel she must be on her best behaviour, conscious of the director listening to her replies.

'Now how did you come by this necklace Miss Fawkes?' She looked across at him as they sat in facing armchairs by desk, waiting. His face was in shadow.

It was a strange question perhaps. She might have expected him to express more concern for a dead employee.

'Come in,' said Dr Scull at the sound of a gentle knock on the door. The severity of Hannah Gaitskill's plain black dress or her blonde hair swept up into a neat practical chignon could not disguise her attractiveness.

'Mrs Gaitskill, thank you for coming. Miss Fawkes is making some enquiries about a young woman who may have worked here. Who was it again Miss Fawkes?'

'Emily, Emily Eden.'

'Yes that's right, Emily Eden, did she work in our laundry Mrs Gaitskill? I'm told she may have come here from the Refuge.'

'Yes Dr Scull, she did.'

'What happened to her?'

'She ran off the day of the Michaelmas Fair. I believe she took off with one of the travelling men there.' Ada saw her glance at Dr Scull.

Dr Scull nodded. 'There you are then Miss Fawkes. A perfectly simple explanation.'

'Would you mind looking at something for me Mrs Gaitskill?' Ada asked. 'You may have heard that I'm helping with the investigation. I have taken photographs.'

The housekeeper's head jerked slightly, a look of surprise flitted across her smooth, unblemished face and was gone.

'Here it is. Do you recognise the necklace in this photograph Mrs Gaitskill?'

The housekeeper barely glanced. 'Lots of girls wear a cross like this, it's very common. I have one very similar myself, mine was a Sunday School prize.'

'Did Emily wear one?' Ada pressed.

'She has answered you, Miss Fawkes?' said Dr Scull. 'Mrs Gaitskill said lots of girls are given a crucifix. How would she know one from the other?'

'We must confirm that Emily Eden was one of these victims, this necklace is our only way of knowing it is her. Please look again.'

Ada held the photograph closer. 'Did she wear one like this Mrs Gaitskill?'

Reluctantly she took the picture, holding it by the corner. 'I seem to remember she did perhaps wear a cross. I told you lots do.'

'How did she seem before she disappeared?'

'Why is that important?'

'Was she unhappy or excited or different in any way?'

'What a strange question,' said Mrs Gaitskill.

'It might help us understand why she left the asylum.'

'She was same as usual, grumbling about the work, flirting with the tradesmen. She didn't like the hard work. She had a bit of a mouth on her. Fond of the drink.'

'What colour was her hair?'

'Why?' She looked again at Dr Scull who nodded imperceptibly.

'Please Mrs Gaitskill.'

'Almost black. She was very proud of it, always brushing and fiddling with it.'

It had to be Emily, Ada was certain then. Her long dark hair, the only remaining prettiness of the exhumed body. She asked, 'Is there a possibility that Emily could have had a gentlemen friend? Someone who might have given her this necklace?'

Ada heard Dr Scull shift his position. She kept her eyes on the housekeeper.

'I suppose it's possible,' said Mrs Gaitskill after a pause. 'I watch my staff closely though and any suggestion of impropriety I act quickly.'

'I was thinking more about someone befriending her, being kind to her?'

'No, I didn't notice anything like that. As I said before she most likely went off for a few coins or drams with some travelling gypsy who caught her eye.' The housekeeper pointedly looked at the watch, hung on a chain, round her narrow waist.

'Is that all Miss Fawkes?' Dr Scull interrupted. 'Only I know Mrs Gaitskill has much work to finish before the end of the day and I like to be there to speak to residents at teatime. They like to see me, have a little talk to me, it gives them a sense of routine and wellbeing.'

'Yes of course, I'll see myself out.' Ada gathered up her bag and bid them good evening. Mrs Gaitskill had seemed very aware of Dr Scull, looking for instruction as though she did not want to speak out of turn. Perhaps that was natural because he was her employer. Whatever it was, between them, they had avoided any real or helpful answers to any of her questions. Ada had the sense she had failed.

***

By the time Straker had returned to Silver Street police station, York's Saturday night was in full swing. From the cells upstairs, that evening's rag bag of inmates shouted and sang with gusto. Straker called out over the noise, as he strode into the office. He could hear a clang of bolts, a jangling key and hob-nailed boots on stone. A little while later Bevers appeared before him, looking cheerful.

'It's jumpy tonight, sir,' he said. 'We'll have a good few up before the magistrates on Monday morning. The chief likes his cells full over the weekend; drunks, vagrants, Irish, especially them Irish, easy pickings.'

Straker raised his eyes from the charge book, lying open on the desk. That's the long and short of it, he thought; get high convictions for petty crime and the charge sheet looks good, even as your city resembles the halls of hell.

'Who's in Constable Bevers?' he asked wearily.

'Gage is on with me tonight.'

'Just two? For all of York, on a Saturday night?'

'Truth to tell sir, we get a lot of complaints from t'public that there's not enough police out patrolling, but t'watch committee don't let us have any money. That's why we catch the easy ones, drunk and disorderly, public nuisances that sort of thing. Makes us look good on paper, says the chief.'

God spare me, Straker thought as he dismissed him.

His mood darker still, his mind turned back to the case. He started to write up his notes from that day. It had been as bad as he expected. The brothel-keeper in Grape Lane had no interest in talking to the police. She had refused to say a word.

On his desk in front of him were the names of five men Ada had written down in her distinctive large print. What was he not seeing? He sat back, throwing his pen down with frustration so black ink splattered onto the white page, forcing him to rummage for blotting paper under the papers on the desk.

Five smudged names. A multiple killer. A corrupt police chief. Worse than useless constables. Constant badgering from London. And not least, Ada Fawkes. He was under pressure from every direction. The whole country from the road sweepers to the Queen was scrutinising his every move in the daily press.

He was so deep in his black thoughts that he barely noticed when Bevers gently placed a mug of lukewarm, stewed tea on the table.

***

Not far away, across at the Mansion House, George Brass, dressed in black tie, was smoking a cigar and anticipating a pleasant evening ahead. He was waiting for his wife and her sister, who were putting on their evening furs. He was happily pouring himself a large sherry just as his brother-in-law came through the door. Turning to greet him, he saw Nutt's agitated face.

'Well Bob, what is it? Spit it out, the ladies will be down any minute.'

'That bloody detective's been poking about where he shouldn't George.'

'We're not the only ones with interests here Bob. No bugger is going to talk.'

'I just feel it won't be long before Straker works out how the land lies. I've had word that he's been in the stews today, asking questions at Harriet Pegler's whore house. Something about that dead slut found on the Minster steps. Straker got short shrift, but maybe we should send someone to have a gentle word about where he's not wanted, sooner rather than later?'

The Lord Mayor smiled at Nutt benevolently. Yes, he was a weak fellow, and a useless policeman, but he was right about this. It was important for them to protect their business interests. 'It's fine. I've already decided it's high time we had a gentle word. I'll take care of it now. Give me a minute. Help yourself to a sherry Bob.'

The Lord Mayor sat down at his desk and scribbled a note. He was sealing it as a shrill voice drifted down the staircase. 'If he's having a drink in there . . .'

Nutt rolled his eyes at Brass. 'She's a fine one to talk. She has enough opium and morphia for her so-called health complaints to open a bloody druggery. I pay Dr Scull a fortune, every week.' He downed his drink in one.

'Women, can't live with them, can't live without them,' laughed Brass, coming over to slap his brother-in-law on the back.

'I know which I'd choose,' said Nutt.

The pair went out into the large foyer of the Mansion House to greet the ladies. Mrs Nutt, brittle-thin, glared at her husband while the Lady Mayoress, twice as wide, beamed with pleasure at a night out. Peacock-blue liveried footmen stood to attention as the couples made their way outdoors into the wintry street where the mayor's gilded carriage waited to take them the few minutes round the corner to the Assembly Rooms.

Brass caught the eye of his secretary. A look passed between them. Hugh Blake came forward and made a show of arranging the Lord Mayor's huge civic chain of office, while he discreetly slipped a letter into his secretary's jacket pocket.

Then Brass broke into a smile, stepping forward to push his stout wife's magenta taffeta skirts into the carriage. He was looking forward to that night's entertainment.

Chapter Twenty-Six

◊

'Whatin God's name?' Thomas stared in astonishment. Straker was slumped against the door jamb, holding his left arm to staunch a running wound, blood between his fingers. Red was spreading rapidly through his ripped white shirt and torn jacket. Straker tried to stand straight and staggered like a drunkard. Thomas caught him and half-lifted him to a chair in the hallway.

'What happened to you man?' Thomas kept his arm firmly round Straker's body.

Straker's battered face looked up at him, his eyes were the only part not covered in blood. 'Bastards set upon me, they were waiting for me as I walked back to the hotel, I went down.' The effort of speaking was too much, he half-fainted and only Thomas's strong grip kept him from the floor.

'Oh my God!' Ada saw Straker as she came down the stairs. She would have fallen too if she had not gripped the banister.

Thomas looked up at her. 'Don't fret. He's alive. I need to get him onto the kitchen table. Can you get his other arm?'

They lurched under the weight and half carrying, half dragging got him down to the warm kitchen and into a chair. Straker's eyes rolled back in his head, half unconscious now. He moaned as Thomas touched his arm.

'We need to get him out of his clothes,' said Thomas, rolling up his own sleeves. 'I need to see how bad the wound is.'

He gently shook Straker's shoulder. 'Can you hear me. I need to get you out of this jacket. Ada help me. Get a knife, I'm going to cut the material.'

Swiftly, he pulled the wool taut and sliced through the fibres. The detective was eased out of the material, groaning with the pain. He dropped back down into the chair, clutching his arm. Blood trickled faster between his fingers.

Camille came in, tying the strings of a large clean apron. 'There's plenty of hot water on the stove.'

'Has it boiled well?'

'No.'

'Get it properly boiled now. And fetch brandy and a needle and thread. Now Ada, I need you to pump water for me,' said Thomas, rolling up his sleeves.

The scullery floor was soon wet and slippery, as he scrubbed his hands and arms with soap until they reddened. His skin tingling, Thomas readied his nursing tools: well-boiled water cooling in a bowl, clean towels, a packet of salt and a chunk of green carbolic soap. He pulled up a stool, placed it by Straker's side, produced a bone-handled knife and deftly sliced the detective's shirt from his flesh, exposing the gaping wounds. Ada looked away, suddenly feeling queasy.

Thomas sat down and took Straker's left arm, bending it gently one way then the other.

'We need to be careful in case any of your shirt has become embedded in the wounds. I need to clean it out. This is going to hurt.'

Thomas told the two women to leave the room and turned back to Straker.

'Let's get you onto the table.'

'How do you . . . ?' muttered Straker, he stopped with the effort of speaking.

'How do I know what I am doing? I served as a nurse in the army.'

'Talk to me, take my mind off this.'

Thomas dipped a cloth in salted, soapy water, breathing in the familiar smell of carbolic. He pressed it down onto the flesh. 'Eight years ago, I was wounded, i' was the winter of '54. I made it from the front line to Balaclava harbour strapped to the back of a mangy flea-bitten mule.'

Thomas told him about his journey across the sea, describing for him the rat-infested ship's hold, the stench of men's unwashed sick bodies, the landing in Scutari, on the shores of the Bosporus. He worked deftly as he spoke.

'A week later I was dumped at the door of the Barrack Hospital, where unluckily for us wounded, the doctors had turned away Florence Nightingale and her nurses, thinking they could do better themselves without beds, blankets or medicine. When finally they admitted they needed her help, I was just on the living side of death. Thousands of us, naked on that filthy floor covered in our own shit and only thirty five of us survived. I went on to learn the skills of nursing. I wanted to help others as I had been helped. It's not just saving lives, in battle a lot of the time you can't, for me it's making the ending happier, making death as good as it can be. Along the way I've learned a fair bit about the importance of cleanliness and proper dressings. There. Done.'

Straker spoke with a clenched jaw. 'Is it bad?'

'You'll live. It will heal, as long as I have got all the bits of material out. Anything left in there usually leads to gangrene and death.'

The detective gripped the side of the table hard as his arm was vigorously swabbed with cognac. 'Here have a mouthful.' Thomas held the bottle to his patient's mouth. Then he moved closer to the light, threaded a needle as deftly as any seamstress and began to stitch up the wound.

Half an hour later he handed the sweating, bandaged man a cigarette, a stiff measure of brandy and went to fetch Ada.

Straker sat back in the chair, with a new respect for Thomas. He inhaled deeply and thought back over the evening. His memory was sharp despite his beating.

Ada sat down on the stool to listen.

Two men had jumped him, dragged him backwards into the shadows of a dead-end street, punching, beating, trampling. Two on one. He was strong, but one had pulled a knife, he had seen its blade flashing, slashing at his arms and hands as he tried to defend himself. He remembered a voice had shouted, 'Keep your bloody nose out. And stay away from Ma Pegler's'. Somewhere he had heard another man yelling, footsteps running. The appearance of two young scarlet-coated Hussars on a night out from the barracks had sent the thugs fleeing. He had staggered to his feet, made light of it to his rescuers. Somehow he made it to their door.

The wound was more painful than Straker was letting on and he was grateful when Camille came in to say the spare bed was made up and she had put in a warming pan. He tried to protest, tell them he must go back to his hotel. Thomas would take no argument and helped him up the stairs and into bed.

When Ada looked in later, Straker was sitting up. The soft glow of candlelight made dark shadows of his eyes and cheek-bones.

'How are you feeling?'

'I'll be better after some sleep.'

'Could they have been garrotters trying to steal your wallet?' she asked.

'No. Someone is trying to warn me off. I had been to the brothel in Grape Lane where Amy used to work. The owner Mrs Pegler was laughing, sneering. She refused to tell me anything. She said she didn't have to, she had protection. It was like she felt untouchable.'

'Did they want to kill you?'

'I don't know, maybe just rough me up.'

He lay back on the pillows, exposing the line of his throat. He looked up at her and for a long moment neither could break their gaze.

'We are in danger again aren't we?' she said.

'Yes, I believe we are.'

'You said you would never let me be hurt again. Never, after that last time.' She suddenly looked so vulnerable.

'Ada,' he said softly.

'You need to get some sleep. Goodnight Straker,' she cut him off and left the room, closing the door behind her.

CHAPTER TWENTY-SEVEN

◊

All of Ada's morning had been spent in the garden studio. But it was getting her nowhere. She had studied her photographs in the hope they would reveal something she had not seen. There was little else she could do for this was the Sabbath Day and everything must stop.

It was almost a relief when Thomas came to find her to tell her Straker needed a doctor. A Sunday afternoon call at the Audens also presented Ada with a chance to talk privately to Jane about the Refuge. There was something else too, but she was still not sure yet if she could raise the matter.

An hour later, Ada was being welcomed at Marygate and she was shown into a room lined with book shelves. The atmosphere in Jane's study, overlooking her flower garden, was calm and peaceful. Ada almost sighed with relief as she sank down in an armchair by the coal fire. Her leather boots were wet from the melting snow piled high by the pavement sweepers. She unlaced them and pulled them off at her friend's gentle urging.

Jane passed her a cup of hot cocoa. Ada felt herself relaxing. She leaned back in the chair, wishing she could close her eyes and drift away.

'I'm worried for you,' Jane said quietly, a look of concern on her face.

'Oh don't be,' Ada reassured her as she watched Jane pour a cup for herself. Her gaze wandered about the room, taking in the rows of thick medical books filling the shelves. Upon a polished desk, by the sash window, there was a brass microscope and by its side an opened notebook in which she could see immaculate writing and diagrams.

Jane saw the direction of her friend's eyes. 'I still do as much as I can to keep learning. You of all people know how hard it is.'

Ada nodded. They had known each other as younger women when Jane's late father had been the physician to her mother. They realised they had much in common – defiance. They were well aware of their limited options. There was scant opportunity to use their energy or brains. Seething with frustration as their fathers talked only of marriage they dreamed of running away. Once they had grown to womanhood Ada started her career abroad while Jane pursued her ambition to be a doctor.

Over the years Jane had written in her letters how her brother William believed that women and children should have access to female doctors. He had asked a friend on the board of the Middlesex Hospital to let her work on the wards for six months as a nurse, where Miss Florence Nightingale herself was helping before leaving for the Crimea. Jane had studied hard and did her stint on the wards. But no medical school would admit her to train as a doctor and no examining body, Oxford, Cambridge, Edinburgh, Glasgow or Dundee, would accept her for its qualifying exams. Then she was asked to leave Middlesex Hospital. A petition from male students and lecturers objected to her presence.

'The petition was dressed up as concern for my well-being,' Jane had written in her letter to Ada. 'They said: "the dissecting room is no place for a lady who should never have to encounter such foul scenes.'"

Jane had described how the men used the dissecting room like a gentlemen's club. It was a place for boxing, ratting, betting each other to pose naked on the dissecting table or dressed as Ajax, the hero of Greek mythology. It sounded funny, but these boys' games ended Jane's career in London. Their male way of life was under threat and they protected it. And when her brother returned to York to practice, she moved up North with him to their old family home.

Now they had rekindled their friendship and discovered they had yet more experiences in common: coming back to Yorkshire as grown single women, still fighting for their rights to a career, life not quite turning out as they had planned.

Ada's thoughts returned to the matter in hand. Jane was on the Ladies Committee at the Refuge; she might know something, but it was hard to find the right words to question a friend.

Jane sensed her hesitation. 'Is it this investigation? Have you made any progress?'

Ada shook her head. 'There is something I would ask you. The four young women who have died lived at the Refuge for differing lengths of time. Jane, do you know or have you seen anything happen there? There is talk of the young women having gentlemen friends. Miss Brockett says the only men the girls could meet there are the gentlemen of the committee.'

'That's not strictly true Ada. There are tradesmen who are in and out and we have reports that the girls talk to men over the garden wall at the back.'

'I know, but could they see anyone privately from the committee?'

Jane pursed her lips as she thought. 'No, I don't believe so. Perhaps Reverend Turner who takes Bible and confirmation classes, but I should think the matron's assistant will sit in for those.'

Ada could see Jane considering carefully. She had a retentive memory and an eye for detail. She went on, 'If there was anyone who could see the girls alone, it might be the Reverend Lindley. I read the reports every week on disciplinary matters. If my memory is correct he spoke to the girls individually about the evils of impertinence. One girl in particular was persistently rude to Miss Brockett. He must have spoken to her. Would you like me to check the reports? Find out who the girls are?'

'Jane, that would be so helpful. Thank you.'

'The incident would have been earlier this year, if I recall correctly,' she mused. 'Early summer. We thought the heat and the smell from the river might be affecting the girls' minds.' She lifted the silver pot. 'Now let's talk about something pleasanter and have some more cocoa.'

They chatted over old times, Jane's work with her brother helping the poor and in particular her ongoing studies in new medicines. 'Wouldn't it be incredible if a woman could discover something life-changing? That would make the male establishment take us seriously. That thought keeps me going.' Jane smiled.

Their talk drifted to Paris and Ada made her mind up. She leaned forward, her voice low. 'I would like to know your views on a personal matter.'

'I'm listening, Ada.'

Ada lowered her gaze. 'Did you ever want a child Jane?'

'The truth? It is not considered normal in society, but I have not longed for that life. My work drives me in another direction. What of you Ada?'

'I don't know,' she shook her head. 'Something happened in Paris, I would like to seek your advice.'

Jane looked at her sharply. 'You know I am not qualified as a doctor.'

'Jane, you are as good as qualified. There is no one else I can talk to. These are matters I would choose not to speak of to a male doctor. Yet there are no other ones in the whole of England.'

Jane sighed. It was the truth. 'Why don't you just tell me what happened and we will go from there.'

'I've been in York six months, but I came back to England six months before that . . .'

Jane waited for Ada to find her words.

'I was staying at . . . I admitted myself to the Hydro, the clinic in Malvern.'

'Oh Ada.' Jane's face showed her concern. The sanatorium's reputation was well-known. Everyone had heard of Dr James Gully, he was a celebrity in the medical field. 'Don't be afraid to speak. I know a terrible misfortune happened to you in Paris. You have already told me something of it. You can trust me.'

'Thank you.' Ada ploughed on. 'I knew Straker in Paris. Well you know that. But when I say I knew him, well it was so intense working together, the cases, the danger. And we fell in love. So suddenly it shocked me, so much it took over my mind.'

'I had wondered from your letters.'

'I was attacked.' Ada looked up at her friend. 'Jane, I was with child. Straker's child. I had not told him. I lost the baby. He still does not know.'

'Oh Ada, why . . .'

'Why didn't I tell him? I have wondered that myself all these long months. But I am scarred inside and out. I feel damaged. I didn't want him to be with me out of pity, guilt or obligation. I left him rather than see that look on his face.'

It was nearly the complete truth. Ada could not bring herself to tell anyone, even Jane, the whole of it.

'I needed time alone to grieve. The pains in my body and my mind worsened. I was struggling with dark feelings, reliving the attack. I found help at the Hydro and I stayed and got better. At least my body did. Then, when I felt strong enough, I came here to York for a fresh start.'

'It must have been such a shock when he turned up?'

'I never thought I would see him again. And now we must investigate one last case together. I thought I had learned the skill of detachment. But he, these murders, it has brought everything back. I can barely sleep. My dreams are so vivid I wake up believing I am still in Paris, shaking and gasping for breath.'

'Can you not tell him something of this?' asked Jane.

'No, there seems little use in that. And I don't want him to know I lost our child. He longed for one, you see his . . .' She paused.

Jane gave her a searching look. 'Go on.'

Ada shifted in her chair and looked down at her stained palms. She had been going to blurt out something different, but it was not her secret to reveal. Instead she said, 'This has reawakened all the anxiety. Some moments I feel paralysed, like a rabbit caught in lamplight. Some days I can barely eat. I cannot explain it. And Jane it has made me wonder if, if I am damaged inside, that I can never carry a . . .' She stopped.

Jane spoke gently. 'You will need to come to the surgery so I can examine you, try and give you the answers you seek, I can't promise anything. And I can look at your scars, I can make up some balm for them. But as for the scars in your mind, I do not know, I am no expert of the brain. Give me a few days and I will consult some of my texts before we meet.'

'I don't want William to know.'

'Of course not. But you know he's grown fond of you Ada.'

She sighed. 'And I of him, but my life has been very complicated.'

'He's not a young man Ada. He's seen a lot. He does not judge. You can trust him. He would . . . I'm getting ahead of myself. I mean nothing other than you can count on him as a good friend. Why don't you come New Year's Day at four o'clock. William is away in the afternoon then, on his weekly visit to the Refuge. We will have privacy with no danger of interruption. We could be daring and have a glass of sherry as well, welcome in the New Year.'

They heard voices from the hallway.

'That will be William returned from his visits.'

Ada said. 'Good timing for I must ask him to come to us at Chapter House Street.'

'Nothing serious I hope?'

Ada shook her head as Jane called out to her brother. The door opened wide and William was in the doorway smiling at them, his handsome face red-cheeked from the outdoors. His eyes, bright and searching, found hers. 'Miss Fawkes what a delight! Was your visit a social one? If so I feel left out.'

'Good afternoon Dr Auden. William I mean. Indeed we have had a most pleasant hour catching up. But there is something.'

'How can I help?'

'Detective Inspector Straker has been hurt.'

'You didn't mention that,' said Jane surprised.

'He was accidentally caught up in a street brawl. Thomas has nursing skills from the war and is looking after him at Chapter House Street. He requests that you call round at your convenience to look over the wound. He says it is not urgent, a precaution that's all.' They had agreed between them that it was best to reveal nothing of the attack to anyone.

'That's very unfortunate. Of course, I'll come. Tell Mr Bell I will call in as soon as I can.'

'That is kind and I must bid you good day.'

Ada got up to leave and Dr Auden hastened to fetch her coat. He watched her, the way she walked, carried herself. She had something special. Her skills applied to his medical work would be invaluable.

What a wife she would make.

CHAPTER TWENTY-EIGHT

◊

Thomas was calling her name, knocking persistently. Ada heard him in her dreams first, then woke from her restless sleep. It was still barely daylight. She groaned and curled onto her side.

'It's Straker. He's not well. He's feverish.'

'Oh God, I'm coming.' She was out of bed, grabbing her paisley shawl and wrapping it around her shoulders as she pulled open her door. Thomas looked exhausted, his shirt sleeves were rolled up and over his shoulder was a blood-stained cloth.

'I've just changed his dressings again. He's been feverish through the night. It's not serious yet, but I am concerned. He's got a high temperature. It will probably be from an infection in the wounds. Maybe from the dirt on the knife that stabbed him. Will you sit with him a moment while I wash and get this dirty linen soaking.'

'Of course.'

'He wants to see you anyway. I'm making some tea, would you like a cup?'

'Yes please.'

Straker had a yellowish tinge to his face. He looked at her with dark eyes, pupils dilated. 'This is the last thing we need. We are no nearer solving this and we are running out of time.'

'Don't think about it. You must rest today. I will go to see Edward Atkinson's wife. Dr Auden is calling in later. Thomas can send any of your messages. Then he will visit the jewellers with the photograph of the necklace. We can talk later. Camille will stay with you.'

'She seems to resent my presence here. I know it's because of what happened in Paris. I don't blame her.'

'She will look after you though, she's probably making some chicken broth now or 'poulet au feu' as she calls it.' Ada smiled, trying to make light of it.

Straker leaned forward and gripped her wrist. 'Ada. Please be careful. I'm worried. Damn I feel so weak.' He fell back against his pillows.

'It's daylight now. I'll be fine.'

'Somebody doesn't want us poking around. Somebody is trying to warn us off.'

'You think the killer put those brutes up to this?'

'I don't know. Was I given a battering to warn me off the murder investigation? Or because I went to the brothel and poked around where somebody didn't want me to?'

'What are you saying?'

'Maybe there is someone who has an interest in protecting York's prostitute racket. Someone who is furious about a detective poking around the rookeries and stews. Someone who doesn't want us to know who they are.'

He banged his hands on the bed covers in frustration.

Ada decided there was little point in adding to his stress by mentioning the plea for help that she had received ten days ago from Queen Victoria's lady-in-waiting. Isabella Fox was already on the train from London, bringing another complication to the day.

***

York's railway station stood on the south side of the River Ouse on the site of a Dominican friary, within the city's old walls. Two giant archways sliced through the medieval stone which let the trains running north to Scotland and south to London rumble through into the iron and glass shed and back out.

To get there Ada had to cross the river. She waited on the icy bank for the ferry, stamping her cold feet and blowing on her fingers. In medieval times, a chain hung from this point to Barker Tower on the other side. It stopped ships leaving York without paying their dues. Similarly from next week no one would be able to come into the city over the new Lendal Bridge, without paying an extortionate toll. Yorkshire men, like leopards, don't change their spots.

She watched the white swans, gliding close to the oncoming boat, oblivious to the chill of the water. 'Bit nippy,' the ferryman called out as he pulled up to the staithe. John Goodricke was unusually cheery, only a few days to go now until his retirement. He couldn't wait, the arthritis in his arms grew more painful and £15 and a horse and cart by way of a pension was generous.

On the opposite bank, Ada climbed out and hurried past a few women with wicker shopping baskets, stepping cautiously down the snowy stone steps from Tanner's Moat. She walked along the road and turned into the station, York's majestic temple to the railway age, beauty and functionality combined. But she didn't glance at its towering roof where pigeons sheltered from the cold, on the great iron struts, she hurried on past WH Smith and the passengers milling around the departure board. She sought the ladies' waiting rooms. She had a comb in her bag; she must smarten herself up.

She stopped a young porter wheeling a trolley of precariously-balanced leather portmanteaus. He nodded down the platform. 'Keep going, it's next to the refreshment rooms.'

Her attempts to tame her wild hair, now frizzy from engine steam, were in vain. It will have to do she thought, straightening her olive green hat and pulling her mulberry scarf tighter. York platforms had their own particular icy chill.

Outside the waiting rooms, she found a guard, arms folded, shaking his head. Ada wanted to check the London train's progress. She had an up-to-date *Bradshaw's*, but studying its complicated information required so much mental ability, one could never be sure of any arrival or departure times.

'It's half an hour late,' he said in an indignant voice. 'Them London guards, can't even get t'trains off on time.'

Ada returned to WH Smith to browse through books and delightedly picked up a translated *Les Misérables*, which had been published earlier that year. She was well into chapter one before she remembered to check the time. Five minutes. She joined the swell of passengers starting to gather up their bags, baskets and children.

She felt shaking beneath her feet, the platform throbbed and sent vibrations up through her body. The noise was deafening. The locomotive rumbled slowly through the arch. She stood still to watch. She breathed in the sharpness of that addictive smell. Heat and smoke and steam engulfed them all as the giant engine hissed to a halt. Ada thought it was magnificent.

'York, this is York,' shouted the guard above the din. Smut-faced porters dashed up and down platform two, rushed forwards to open carriage doors. Then, 'This is the Edinburgh train, calling at Durham, Newcastle . . .' On and on, the guard went. Above the noise of shouting, the engine and slamming of doors, Ada heard a familiar voice calling her name.

She turned. A lady emerging from the saloon compartment was smiling and waving. Ada reached Isabella Fox as she stepped down onto the platform. They embraced closely, warmly.

Isabella linked her arm with Ada's. 'Let's walk a moment. It's so nice to stretch my legs.'

The journey from London to Edinburgh took ten and a half hours. The York stop was timed long enough to give passengers time for a meal and a stroll.

'I've sent a porter for tea,' said Isabella. She was immaculately turned out, despite the hours of travelling. Her deep blue skirt and jacket were of the finest wool. Around her slim shoulders she had draped a luxurious jewel-coloured paisley shawl and her chestnut brown hair was smoothed into a chignon, an easy style for travelling. She looked as elegant as ever, but Ada sensed an unfamiliar tension about her and Isabella's face had a pallor beyond that induced by a long train journey. She knew her friend would not want to speak openly until they had privacy. That could wait. Instead they chatted easily about this and that as they strolled along the platform.

'You are on your way to join the Queen?'

'Yes, she is already at Balmoral. You know how she loves it there. She went earlier with her private secretary Earl Grey and her other ladies in waiting.'

They spoke rapidly catching up, Isabella wanting to know how the studio was going and how her venture in York was working out.

'Ada, tell me you have not been dragged into this dreadful murder business here? It's all over the London newspapers, everyone is talking about it. The Queen is following the case. You remember how interested she is in detectives and crime?'

'I am and I had no choice. I had a summons from the Home Secretary himself. Yes, I am the photographer for the investigation.'

'But that means you are working with Detective Inspector Straker again. Goodness, how is that going?' Isabella's blue eyes widened.

'Difficult to say the least.'

A stout porter hurried towards them carrying a hamper. 'Your tea, madam,' he said dryly. They followed him back. After he had laid out teapot and cups on a small table in Isabella's compartment and received his tip, they climbed up the few steps into the small private carpeted drawing room.

'Do sit Ada,' Isabella waved her slender hand at one of the velvet armchairs and sat down in the other and immediately picked up the thread of their conversation. 'Did you tell Straker what happened in Paris?'

'No. I didn't want his pity and there were so many complications. I've put all that behind me. Or at least I thought I had. The Home Secretary ordered my help and I have no choice, I must work with him again. But that is enough of my woes. What is this mystery that you need my help with? It must be serious.'

'I didn't know what you would make of my letter. I am sorry if it alarmed you, but I have no one else who I can trust. I decided since my train was stopping here I must seek your help in person,' said Isabella. A look of pain crossed her face. 'But I see now, it is not fair of me to ask you, you have enough on with this investigation.'

'Isabella tell me what I can do. I will help if I can. You know I will and be glad to.'

Ada recalled how she had come to know Isabella at the Hydro in Malvern. Isabella had been recuperating from a nasty bout of pneumonia. Ada had suspected her illness was down to exhaustion for the duties of being a lady-in-waiting to the Queen were unending. Ada had wondered at her friend's strange life in court at the unpredictable whim of the Queen. Ada, at least, had her independence. Isabella's voice broke through her thoughts

'It's Lucy. She has married!'

This was unexpected. Ada remembered Isabella's gentle daughter Lucy with much affection. But she was too vulnerable and trusting. She was child-like and would always be so. Ada had taken a beautiful photograph of Lucy with her mother when she had visited Malvern. Isabella had been delighted to have a portrait of herself with her precious daughter, something she could touch and look at. She had placed the framed image next to her bed, the child she hardly saw because of the demands of the Queen.

Isabella explained she had not heard from her daughter for months and had great fears for her safety.

'She was targeted by a ruthless fortune-hunter. I found letters from him and I think she may be here in York. I spoke to the Queen and asked if I might stop off for a few days to find her. She refused, she could not spare me.'

I bet she couldn't, thought Ada. The last thing the Queen would want was to have her favourite lady-in-waiting away from her side, not at her beck and call, day and night.

'Will you help me? She has no friend here but you.'

'I will do whatever I can. But I am a photographer, not a detective.'

'That is not entirely true Ada. You have a gift. Your eyes see things others don't.'

Isabella bent down and from her carpet bag, she pulled out the photograph of herself and Lucy that Ada had taken last year.

'Please Ada. Here is your photograph. Take it. It is proof of who she is, if you should need it. I have a letter here from our magistrate, confirming this photograph is Lucy. I have the letters here too, written by this man. There is an address on it. I am travelling through York again a few days after the New Year ball, on January 5. The train gets in at six o'clock. I will be returning to Windsor. Would you meet me again then, let me know if there is any news?'

'Five minutes,' shouted the guard cheerily.

'Ada, when my husband died, Lucy came into some money. I had entrusted a companion Mrs Crabbe with her care at my home, as I would not have her institutionalised. A man known to this Mrs Crabbe began to court her. The parish vicar wrote to warn me. I tried to stop the marriage, and have her declared a ward in chancery, but I could not do so in time and Lucy turned twenty-one, so was of age and was free. She should not have married in this way, Ada, not to someone I have not met. You know how vulnerable she is?'

Ada remembered well the trusting beautiful girl with unusual almond shaped eyes and a sweet, engaging smile.

'The Queen kindly permitted me a whole day and night at home but it was too late. A few weeks later I received a letter from Lucy's husband, it was postmarked York, it severed all relations with me. He wrote that Lucy never wanted to see me again. She would never do that. You know how close we are. We only had each other for so many years. I just want to know she is safe. I am ill with worry.'

Ada reached for her friends' hands. 'Isabella. I promise, I will find her.'

'Stand clear. Edinburgh train departing,' the guard bellowed.

They heard the sound of doors slamming shut up and down the platform.

'Ada. Take these, there's an address. I don't need to tell of the need for discretion.' Isabella thrust a bundle of letters into Ada's hands.

They embraced and Ada stepped down onto the platform.

Isabella pulled down the window. 'I need to know, even if it's the worst news.'

Ada nodded.

'Stand clear.'

Jets of steam, ear-splitting noise, the heavy train began to reverse slowly along the platform. Isabella leaned out, calling as the train picked up speed.

'Help me Ada! There is no one else but you.'

CHAPTER TWENTY-NINE

◊

Back across the river, the ferry bumped against the wooden staithe and Ada was out and onto the cobbled slipway. She walked up the slope, past St Leonard's, once England's largest hospital Thomas had told her, where monks had cared for the sick and poor. The ruins briefly distracted her from her thoughts of Isabella and her imminent call on Mrs Atkinson for it amazed her, these layers of the past visible everywhere in York, and yet this was a city intent on destroying its history. She knew that only a public protest had recently saved the medieval walls from being pulled down. She thought it would be as well to photograph York's ancient beauty before it was annihilated.

But for now she must concentrate on the investigation and her appointment with Mrs Atkinson. She turned into Blake Street and stopped before the Atkinsons' four-story home. She knocked on the front door, quickly straightening her hat and wiping melting snow flakes from her cold cheeks. It opened a little and a pretty, young housemaid stared back out at her with big eyes.

'Mrs Atkinson is expecting me I believe?'

'Aye, miss, come in.'

In the hallway she could hear the sound of children laughing somewhere upstairs. The girl took her coat and hat then showed her into the large front parlour. Lydia Atkinson was sitting in a high back chair by a blazing fire, her hands folded over her swollen stomach, her feet raised high on a padded stool.

'Don't trouble yourself Mrs Atkinson,' said Ada as she started to push herself up.

'Thank you. I must admit I am exhausted. I feel I have been with child forever.' She laughed and looked at Ada warmly. Blue eyes twinkled in a round face flushed from the heat. She had a homely air, like the room, thought Ada taking in the aspidistra in an engraved brass bowl, an embroidery box on a stool, a folded baby gown next to it. On a round table was a stack of illustrated magazines and a volume of the sensational read of the year *Lady Audley's Secret*.

'Tea Miss Fawkes?' Lydia rang a small bell.

'Yes please.'

'I was sorry not to be able to attend your house on Christmas Eve. I am feeling so uncomfortable and, to be honest, I'm not one for social events. I am too stupid and too dull in company. Mr Atkinson loves meeting people. He says I should make more effort, that it would be good for me to have time away from our children.'

Mrs Atkinson fell silent as the little maid returned with a tray and clumsily set out the teacups. 'Careful Kitty,' said Mrs Atkinson. Kitty looked down and bobbed the smallest curtsey before leaving.

'She's so cack-handed, she will keep dropping things, but Mr Atkinson says we must give her a proper chance. He's very kind to our female servants.'

Ada took the flower-patterned teacup from her hostess who was staring at her, openly curious. 'But was Detective Inspector

Straker not supposed to be here with you? My husband said he was coming. He mentioned you but I did not expect you alone.'

'He sends his apologies, but he is detained.'

'I admit, I am relieved. I was nervous about meeting a real detective. I thought he would not want to hear me prattle on about my servants. This is easier, talking to you, another lady.'

'I agree and do you know I think it is so much pleasanter this way, we can talk much more easily about domestic matters, like two friends enjoying a visit.'

Mrs Atkinson nodded. 'I am eager to know how you have come to assist in a police investigation. This is a strange pastime for a lady.'

'I have done so before, I have helped Scotland Yard and the French police on other cases. My photographs have helped solve investigations so I am asked to assist again,' explained Ada.

'Oh my goodness so you are like a lady policeman? Who would believe such a thing?'

'It's not as unusual as you may think. Often policemen ask women they know to help with their investigations. It might be it is easier for a witness to speak to a female or sometimes a woman can be in a place that a man cannot. Do you know *Bleak House*?'

'Of course, I read that years ago, when I was with our first child.'

'Remember how Mrs Bucket helped her husband Inspector Bucket catch the murderess Mademoiselle Hortense, by befriending her and spying on her. A policeman could never investigate like that, become so close to a young woman.'

'Oh of course not, it would be improper and impossible. I never thought of it that way.' Mrs Atkinson took a sip of tea. 'I am far too silly to do anything like that. I cannot imagine what

Mr Atkinson would say if I suggested such a thing.' She laughed and moved onto the weather.

Ada waited until there was a pause. 'Your laundress Amy Ward, can you tell me anything about her?'

'Hardly anything. Poor Amy, a pretty dark-haired thing.'

'She came to you when?' prompted Ada.

'September. She came to us from the Refuge. You know about those girls, but I am a Christian and willing to give a sinner a second chance. My husband is on the committee there. He suggested it because Mrs McGuire needed help and so he made the arrangement with the ladies there. But he chose Amy himself, he's very particular about our staff and said she was the most suitable. I have been so lucky with my life; such a good husband and my children. I wanted to do my bit for those less fortunate.'

'Did it work out?' Ada watched her closely over the rim of her cup.

'She seemed a hard worker, cheerful. There were no complaints,' she replied. 'My husband seemed to appreciate her, he said his shirts had never been so well-ironed.'

Ada let Lydia talk on – sometimes she learned more this way. 'Honestly Miss Fawkes? In truth I was surprised when she went off.'

'Oh how interesting. Tell me what happened that day?'

'Well because of my being with child and not wanting to go out much, I was here the day of the Horse Fair. You know what a big occasion that is, everyone comes to town. That's why I remember exactly. Everyone was out. Amy asked me for an hour off to see the horses. She never came back. Mr Atkinson said she must have run off with a young man.'

'Did you believe that?'

'I don't know now. I did think she was settled here. We couldn't believe it when we saw *The Herald* on Saturday. I made Mr Atkinson go straight to the police station. He thought we should wait and didn't want to trouble them.'

Ada said. 'It's kind of you to arrange the funeral.'

'It's the least we can do to pay for a proper send off. We've asked our parish vicar Reverend Lindley to hold the service at St Michael le Belfrey. Amy attended the church and his Bible classes regularly. I doubt there will be many show up, poor girl was an orphan, but our household will attend.'

'I would love more tea Mrs Atkinson,' she said quickly, seeing the tears well in Lydia's eyes.

'Yes, of course.'

'Please, don't move. I'll pour.' She topped up both tea cups. 'Do you happen to know if Amy wore a silver cross?'

'No, I don't,' she shook her head. 'She became a devout girl though. She attended church and Bible classes. She wanted to be confirmed.'

'Would anyone here know about the necklace?'

'Perhaps. Would you like to speak to our housekeeper? She would be the one most likely to know, seeing as they worked together all day.'

'That would be very kind.'

She rang the bell. Within seconds, the maid came in again.

'Please fetch Mrs McGuire.'

'Ma'am.' She bobbed a curtsey and hurried out.

Lydia leaned forward a little. 'While we are waiting Miss Fawkes, please tell me, is it true?'

'Is what true?' She had an idea what was coming next for it fascinated everyone.

'You've met the Queen? My husband told me so after your party.'

'Yes, I have. I was introduced by one of her ladies-in-waiting, a friend of mine. We talked about photography. The Queen as you know is very interested and has her own dark room.'

'I know, we have many of her cartes-de-visite. We collect them. My daughters love to put them in their albums. It is a great hobby of theirs. We buy them at the stationers. As soon as there is a new one, we buy it. But what is she really like? When did you meet her?'

Ada searched for her words carefully just in case a Royal commission ever came her way, it was not impossible, after all it had happened to another woman. Only recently Frances Sally Day had been lucky enough to get a job taking portraits of the royal family for a series of cartes.

'We met earlier this year at Windsor Castle, just before I came to York. The Queen loves photographs and paintings and we looked at them together. She is still so sad about Prince Albert, but her children are of great comfort to her. She has many photographs of them. I showed her my work and she was kind enough to compliment me.'

Mrs Atkinson's face lit up. A heavy knock stopped their conversation and a short, stout woman with fading ginger hair scraped into a tight top knot, stood stiffly in the open doorway.

'Mrs McGuire come in, Miss Fawkes wishes to speak to you about Amy.'

'I am sorry to disturb your work Mrs McGuire but how did Amy seem before she went missing?'

'Right enough,' she replied with an Irish lilt to her voice. 'She was glad to be working here and not at the Refuge. I can't deny I wasn't pleased about her coming here, but she turned out a nice little thing. Hard worker. She had repented and well, we don't all get a good start in life.'

'Did she have a young man?'

Mrs McGuire paused. 'Perhaps. She went to church twice a week, I had the sense, when she came back, that she was bubbling with something. Might be the power of prayer but in my experience of young girls, it usually happens when they've had their heads turned. I did wonder if there was a boy in the congregation. I'm of the true faith so I don't go to that church.'

'Did you know she wore a silver cross?'

She frowned. 'A crucifix yes. It sometimes slipped out from her bodice when we was working. She had worn it since she arrived here. I assumed it was something she had been given as a Sunday School prize or presentation. It wasn't expensive, quite common. My nieces were given similar ones when they were confirmed.'

Ada looked at her closely. 'Were you surprised when she didn't come home?'

'Truthfully I was. I thought she was happy enough here. I told Mr Atkinson she hadn't come back and well, he suggested she must have run away with a young man. I didn't like to question him. I thought he must be right. I told myself, she must have gone with someone she knew. I felt a shudder run through me when I saw it in *The Herald* that morning. I went straight to the master and mistress and told them I thought Amy fitted the description. Mr Atkinson said he was certain it would not be her, but I was right.' Her voice dropped. 'I couldn't believe it. The Butcher of York got our Amy. It don't bear thinking about. God rest her soul.' She crossed herself.

Mrs Atkinson's upper lip was starting to wobble. Ada, aware of how close to the surface emotions could be in pregnancy said swiftly, 'Thank you Mrs McGuire.'

The housekeeper nodded and left the room.

Lydia clasped her hands. 'I wish . . . Well Mr Atkinson was away all that day on business, if he had been here, I might have insisted he went looking or had gone to the police straightaway. Do you think if he had told the police earlier . . .'

'I am sure it wouldn't have changed anything,' she said reassuringly.

'But he didn't go looking for days, he had so many site visits for his jobs. He works so hard. It seemed like he was out all the time that week even Christmas Night, a flood at one of his properties, he said.'

Ada stared at her.

***

A few minutes later, she was outside. The heavy yellow-grey clouds were threatening more snow. She pulled her coat tighter and stepped across the road. No more than a minute or so's walk round the corner was Reverend Lindley's parish church. It was on her way home and she thought she might as well see if he was there. She turned up the street and entered Minster's Yard. It seemed strange to her that St Michael le Belfrey had been built so close to the Minster, the popular story was that it was a humbler place for the commoners, deemed unworthy to pray in the great Minster.

She reached the portal of the church, lifted the black iron latch and pushed open the heavy door. Inside the air was as cold and damp as outside. The noise of the streets faded and her footsteps sounded too loud on the slab floor, echoing as she walked up the nave towards the chancel, passing tall arches separating the side aisles. This building had stood for three hundred years or so and had barely changed. Maybe that accounted for the sense of being in a different world. Slowly she walked towards the altar. The heavy silence became more overpowering, her own breathing seemed unnaturally loud to her ears.

'Miss Fawkes.' The Reverend Charles Lindley seemed to appear from the shadows.

Ada's heart leapt in her chest. 'Oh, Reverend Lindley.'

'The church has such a calm beauty, don't you agree?' Even as he greeted her so courteously, she sensed he was watching her closely.

She tried to steady her breathing. 'Yes it does. One feels its layers of history. I was on my way home and thought I would look at the baptism register you mentioned at the Auden's dinner party. You aroused my curiosity.'

'I would be pleased to show it to you.' If he was surprised to see her, he showed no sign, talking easily about the church's Tudor history as he led the way to the vestry.

'It's quiet today,' he went on, 'but on a Sunday, well I'm proud to say this is one of the best attended churches in York.'

The vicar walked with a light tread, his black leather shoes barely making a noise on the marble slab floor, surprising in a man so tall. He led Ada down a few wooden steps into a small, cold room that smelt fusty and old. Stacks of books were piled on a wooden bench, robes dangled from a row of wooden hooks, and a watercolour painting of the church hung on the white-washed wall above a small table on which an oil lamp was burning.

From an oak cupboard he lifted down a thick, leather-bound book. He opened it up on a table, smoothing over the yellowing paper. He took the lamp and placed it alongside.

'Here it is. I have the page book-marked. It is very popular with tourists, as you can imagine. There on the left, third from the top.'

She could barely read the faded ink. Guy Fawkes, son of Edward Fawkes. The entry was dated 16th April 1570.

'There you are, your namesake Miss Fawkes. But I'm sure a lady like you will not meet such an unpleasant end.' He smiled at his joke, showing prominent white teeth.

She wondered why she felt uncomfortable. Perhaps it was because she remembered Jane talking of him disciplining the young women at the Refuge. She glanced at his long fingers, his neatly filed pointed nails, touching the ledger. How far did he go?

'A most interesting history,' she said. 'I would very much like to take photographs for my collection, glimpses of bygone York.'

'That would be delightful Miss Fawkes. We must make an appointment, I can tell you so much more, give you a tour of the antiquities.' His lean face had a reserve which made it impossible to read.

'Indeed. I would appreciate that, perhaps in the spring.' Ada looked around the gloomy room, seeing a watercolour of pink roses in a pale green vase. 'That's pretty.'

'My wife painted it, she's very fond of flowers. She grows them in our garden.'

'How nice to have a garden in York, so many houses have yards.'

'Oh no, we have a house in the country. She spends much of her time there, the air does not suit here, it is so damp with the two rivers, it affects her bones.'

'You must miss her companionship when she is away.'

'I am very busy. In some ways it allows me to work without distractions.'

'Of course, your parish duties must be very demanding. You must have a lot to do here with services, Bible classes and so on.' She was thinking on her feet now. 'And there's your charity work at the Refuge. I hear you are taking the funeral for Amy Ward.'

Reverend Lindley looked at her sharply. 'Yes, dreadful business. She was a relatively new parishioner here, she had come to work at the Atkinsons and been there for only a few months.'

His face became watchful. 'You are very interested Miss Fawkes?'

She decided to take the risk. He might tell her what she needed to know even without Straker here to make the enquiries official. But when she asked him if he would be kind enough to help the investigation and look at her photographs, he frowned, 'This seems very irregular.'

'Detective Inspector Straker is following other leads and I am simply collecting information.'

'A lady detective? By God, that is something strange. I do not think I can talk to you about such an unsuitable subject for female ears.'

'The murderer must be caught and fast. He may kill again.' She sensed his body stiffen. Was it because he disapproved or had he something to hide?

Reverend Lindley carefully closed the ledger and replaced it in the cupboard. He turned to her, his voice was wary. 'Well how can these photographs you talk of help?'

Ada set her bag on the table and pulled out a photograph of Amy Ward. He clamped his hand over his mouth.

'Goodness. I never thought.' He shook his head.

'What do you mean?'

'That we would ever take photographs of the dead. It seems ungodly.'

'It's no different really to death masks made of famous people like Oliver Cromwell or Henry VIII or paintings or tomb carvings.'

'But this detail, these images are as real as if they are still alive, merely sleeping. The paintings well it is art, a depiction, an illusion.'

She pressed on. 'Please look at the necklace. Do you give Sunday School or confirmation gifts like these?'

'We do give suitable little prizes. My wife buys them.'

'Do you recognise this?'

He looked again and his eyebrows drew together in a frown. 'I'm not sure, perhaps my wife would know, she's not back in town until the mayor's ball.'

Ada mentally noted that detail. She said. 'Tell me about Amy Ward. She attended church here?'

'Yes she was one of my parishioners. She had been a resident at the Refuge. She had shown great promise and had committed to redeeming herself for her past sins. They don't all, you know. Mr Atkinson and I are on the committee there and we arranged for her to leave the Refuge, have a fresh start. Mr Atkinson was kind enough to give her a position as a laundress in his household and she attended my church. She was pleased to do so, she had been a diligent and receptive pupil in my Bible classes at the Refuge. She had wanted to remain within my flock.'

'Did she confide in you about anything?'

'Miss Fawkes you know I cannot answer that.'

'Did you ever have cause to speak to her or offer guidance about anything while she was at the Refuge?'

'I give moral guidance to all the young women. They are criminals after all.' He handed her back the photograph. 'Well if you don't mind, I must take my leave, I have sick parishioners to visit.'

His voice was firm and dismissive as he held the door open for her to leave.

She walked out, feeling his cold eyes upon her.

CHAPTER THIRTY

◊

'M iss Fawkes. Ada.' Straker's deep voice came from the drawing room. To still the sudden clenching of her heart, Ada took a moment to smooth back her hair and straighten her skirt. She walked into the drawing room, her head held high, hoping she conveyed composure. But she kept her step. Even from the other side of the room, she could see he looked desperate. The light of the blazing fire on his stern features made his skin paler, the shadows under his eyes blacker.

'I thought you were supposed to be resting in bed,' she said.

'I feel much better than I did and I wanted to speak to you as soon as you came in.'

'Has Dr Auden been?'

'Yes, says he can do no more than has been done by Thomas. He's coming by again tomorrow. He told me to rest today. Sit down by the fire, you look frozen. Would you like some spiced wine, Camille has just brought in a jug. It's over there, on the hearth, keeping warm.'

'That would be lovely.' She saw him wince as he shifted his body. 'Don't move, I'll get us some.'

The smell of cloves, oranges and honey mingled with wood smoke as she poured. She passed a glass to Straker and then

320

she sat on the ottoman stool close to the fire, wrapping her hands around her drink, savouring its warmth, the taste of the hot sweet liquid.

'Tell me everything that has happened,' he said after a moment.

She told him about her day. 'Edward Atkinson is not all he seems. He knows more about Amy Ward than he made out. The housekeeper Mrs McGuire said that he was reluctant to report that she was missing. She hinted at him having an attachment to Amy.'

'He would not be the first to favour a pretty servant.'

She looked at him sharply. 'I sense more to it than that. He is a regular visitor to the Refuge, one of the young women comes to work for him and then she disappears from his home. And significantly he was away from the home on Christmas Night. He has also been absent regularly in recent months. He told his wife he was working.'

'Mmm. Perhaps he has a habit of dalliances with other women. What do you know of Atkinson?' he asked.

'He was introduced to me as a client,' she said. 'He commissioned photographs of his work. I've met him a few times socially. He seems well-meaning, progressive, full of ideas, if not a little arrogant. He is well-respected and seems to have many acquaintances and friends. I liked him enough to invite him to our Christmas Eve drinks.'

'We will have to talk to him again.' Straker adjusted his position and a cushion dropped to the floor. He leaned over and grimaced. 'Damn, this arm hurts.'

Ada rose and picked up the cushion to replace it under his head. As she did so he reached out, touched her wrist gently and looked up at her, his eyes almost pleading.

'Thank you. I'm so sorry to have brought this upon you as well. I will leave tomorrow, go back to my hotel. It is too much that you must have me in your house.'

Before Ada could speak, the door opened and Thomas entered carrying a basket of logs.

'Dinner is almost ready or would you prefer a tray Straker?' Thomas said in the cheery manner of a nurse.

'I would prefer to join you at the table, although you may need to cut up my food.' Straker smiled, it briefly lit his tired face.

'I'll lay you a place then and I'll give you a shout when it's time.'

Ada sipped her wine. 'I saw the Reverend Lindley too. Amy Ward was one of his congregation and of course he knew her from the Refuge. He is responsible for the moral wellbeing of the girls. I showed him the photograph of Amy's silver cross to see if he recognised it. He said he could not be certain, It was his wife who bought such things for prizes for his Bible classes, Sunday School pupils and confirmations. She lives mainly at their country house and is not back until after New Year for the mayor's ball.'

'Conveniently absent,' Straker said. 'And he's a regular visitor to the Refuge. He could have grown close to any young woman. There is opportunity there too.'

They looked at each other. It seemed like all the gentlemen of the committee had opportunity.

Supper that night was companionable but subdued and they exchanged news of the day and pleasantries as they ate a warming cassoulet flavoured with thyme and bay. They avoided any discussion of death and suspicion until the meal was done.

'That was delicious, thank you,' said Straker smiling at Camille as he pushed away his plate.

She nodded curtly. 'Je vous en prie.'

No one had any appetite for dessert. Thomas poured more coal on the range, stoked the fire to greater warmth and they sat around the cleared table with glasses of wine.

'And so how did you get on Ada?' asked Thomas.

Ada filled in the details. 'And what about you?'

Thomas pulled out his tobacco tin, and after some false starts, drew on his lit pipe. He recounted how he had taken the photograph of the silver cross to the jewellery shops of York.

'Everyone was fascinated by the picture and wanted to gossip about the murders. And there are so many of them. Jewellers are quite a business here. I had no idea. It goes back to the Vikings, they loved their jewels. And did you know the Medieval silversmiths had shops on Silver Street where the police station is now? It was all very time-consuming and interesting, but no one was able to pin down with any certainty the purchase of such a common necklace. The jewellery is brought up from London these days, no doubt with a hefty mark up, but it's still cheap enough to make it very popular. Then I had a bit of luck. I came to a shop on High Petergate, the jeweller recalled he sold some crosses like this. He remembers because they all had to be engraved. Mostly they are sold plain because it's less costly.'

'Can we find out the purchasers?' asked Straker.

'The merchant assures me all sales are recorded with the requested engravings. He has the master ledger at home as he has been working after hours. He has promised to make it available to us tomorrow. I am returning in the morning.'

Straker pushed his chair back, wincing as he rose and walked over to the window. He looked out through the glass into the dark garden at the snow falling.

He was tempted to go to the jewellers himself, he hated this helplessness. He wanted to check out for himself such a potentially significant thread of the investigation. For once he must rely on others.

Straker turned and nodded, 'Thank you Thomas. Yes, go first thing. It's vital. We need to have those names.'

CHAPTER THIRTY-ONE

◊

The black and white tiled vestibule was as impressive as she had expected. The Mount, a row of imposing white stuccoed houses and one of York's finest streets certainly had the appearance of a fitting home for the daughter of Queen Victoria's lady-in-waiting.

Except Ada now knew Lucy wasn't living here.

And warning bells were sounding in her head.

'You're already up to your neck in problems,' Camille had cautioned over breakfast that morning when Ada told her where she was going. That was true enough but she could not let her friend down. She had planned to go early before Straker was out of his sick bed. He had enough pressure, without knowing she had promised to solve another mystery.

'I must go. I've given Isabella my word,' she had replied. 'I have to do this for her. There's no one else. Besides it's a job for a woman. It needs discretion and emotional intelligence.'

'What are you going to do?' Camille had asked.

'I have looked over the letters Isabella gave me and I have the address of Lucy's husband Alec Lovelace. It all seems in order. They have made no attempt to hide the marriage. If she's there I have a letter from her mother begging her to get in touch. She just wants to know she is well. Then I'll decide.'

Thomas was on his way back to the jewellers. The detective was still sleeping off Dr Auden's night-time draught and Camille had said she would watch for him while baking cakes for New Year's Eve tomorrow. So Ada had set off, taking a Hansom and here she was in front of the gentleman Isabella Fox believed had married her vulnerable daughter for her money. And he was telling her Lucy did not live here.

'Come into the parlour Miss Fawkes. My mother can explain this so much better than I. It is so upsetting for me.' Alec Lovelace smiled, revealing sharp white teeth, looking anything but upset. His oiled hair, his waxed moustache were immaculate and he had the entitled air of one who knew he was handsome. Ada followed him through double doors into a high-ceilinged drawing room, expensively wall-papered in green and gold. Silk Persian rugs covered the rose-patterned carpet. In a curved French-style chair, beside the fire, perched a bony-faced, silver-haired woman, holding a cane between her lace-gloved hands.

'Miss Fawkes is asking after our poor dear girl Lucy. She is acquainted with the family,' Lovelace explained with a drawl.

'And what is your interest in this sad affair Miss Fawkes?' His mother flicked her wrist imperiously at the sofa.

Ada perched with as much gravitas as she could manage. She wouldn't be intimidated.

'Lucy's mother Mrs Fox is very worried. She has not heard from her daughter for eight months or so. By her mother's authority, given to me in writing, I would like to know where Lucy is.'

'It's so very tragic Miss Fawkes. My son did everything he could. He has the patience of a saint, but we could not go on.'

'What do you mean?' Ada was taken aback.

Mrs Lovelace sighed. 'We did everything we could. After she lost the baby, she was virtually an invalid you know, she would not eat. We called the doctor. He diagnosed cerebral disease. It confirmed our fears, she's feeble-minded. We had no choice.'

Ada stared at her. 'My understanding is that your son persuaded a vulnerable young woman with her own fortune to marry him against her widowed mother's wishes. I believe she attempted to have Lucy made a ward in chancery to prevent the marriage. What have you done with her? Where is she?'

'It was done properly,' said Lovelace impassively, smoothing back his fashionably long hair. 'Two doctors certified her admission to Acomb House Asylum, as are the legal requirements. It's a private home run by a surgeon-proprietor, he was a medical superintendent at the county asylum. It's the best there is and it's not cheap, three guineas a week, extra for laundry.'

'When was she taken there?'

'Eastertime.'

'So long ago. Why didn't you let her mother know?'

Again Mrs Lovelace spoke. 'We didn't want to worry her. We thought that with careful treatment she would soon be better and no one would be the wiser. Her mother has a highly-pressured job with our dear Queen and that must come first. Lucy is in good hands.'

'I would like to see her.'

'My dear that would be delightful but sadly not possible at present. Her recovery is proceeding well but she can have no excitement. Thank you very much for your interest. Please pass on our best wishes to Mrs Fox. Please assure her that Lucy is in the best possible hands and we hope with all our hearts she will recover.'

Mrs Lovelace rose, her head tilted imperiously and bid Ada good day.

She had no choice but to leave. Unanswered questions whirled in her head as Alec Lovelace walked towards the door. He held it open and smiled coldly at her.

'Eliza will show you out.'

Back in the entrance, Ada saw the same young housemaid, waiting by the central staircase under an enormous crystal chandelier. She bobbed a curtsey to Ada and her employer, keeping her head down, avoiding eye contact.

Unusually for a servant, she wore a light-coloured, almost white dress, as though her employers sought to draw attention to her dark skin. Ada had often met and talked with black musicians in Paris; artists from America or Africa, but here in York, it was rare to see a person of such colour, other than occasionally on ships anchored down at the staiths. She had heard some rich families maintained black servants as novelties. It was not a surprise to her that such a man as Alec Lovelace might do the same.

He was half-watching the maid walk across the hall, his eyes following her, even as he bid Ada goodbye.

Eliza opened the front door and bobbed another curtsey. 'Good day miss.'

As Ada reached the entrance, the young woman seemed to stumble forward and Ada reached out to grip her arm. She felt an urgent tap on her wrist. The maid flashed her eyes downwards and nodded. The move was over in seconds as a twisted wrap of paper was slipped into Ada's hand. She quickly closed her hand round it.

'Oh dear. Clumsy girl,' drawled Alec Lovelace lounging in the doorway. 'I'll speak to you later in my room. In private.' He smoothed his moustache over his fleshy lips.

Ada saw the maid flinch. There was nothing she could do, for now at least. She walked away and carried on until she stood by Micklegate Bar. Only then did she open her hand.

The note was scrawled in pencil on torn brown sugar paper.

The lady's in danger. Help her.

There was a gloomy mood at Chapter House Street on Ada's return. Thomas had been back to Berriman's the jeweller and it hadn't turned up the answers they had hoped for. Over coffee around the kitchen table, he was recounting his morning to Straker and Camille.

'Somebody bought five silver crosses in early August. The ledger showed a name, but it was smudged and indecipherable. The ink had run, looked like tea had been spilled on it. The necklaces were collected, not delivered, so no address. The engravings were flowers. The jeweller's wife wrote up the order, but she is visiting her sister who lives at the family farm at Byland Abbey. She might remember the full details of the order if we are lucky.'

Straker shook his head. 'It's something, but not much. It is likely the buyer used a false name. The murders appear meditated, planned and precise so this man will be careful enough to disguise his identity. Still, we need to get a photograph of the necklace to Mrs Berriman. She might remember some detail.'

Ada, pouring herself a coffee from the pot on the range suddenly stopped and turned. 'Thomas, you said five necklaces, but there have been four victims so far . . . that means . . .'

'. . . There will be another murder,' finished Straker.

She felt her skin crawl.

329

CHAPTER THIRTY-TWO

◊

Later at her Coney Street studio, Ada tried to concentrate on mounting photographs for framing. There was much work to catch up on. She could not afford to let her business slide. But her thoughts were flitting between the investigation, Lucy, and how lasciviously Alec Lovelace looked at his housemaid. 'When all of this is over, I will get Eliza away from him,' she promised herself.

The shop door opened with a jangle of the bell and Camille walked in. 'I am going to do the shopping, but I wanted to see you. I didn't want to speak where Straker might hear.' She paused. 'You are not sleeping again are you? You look dreadful.'

Ada looked down. 'It's nothing Camille, really. Nothing I can't cope with. The nightmares are back. I have terrors that I can't explain. But I'm not where I was a year ago in that dark place. When this is over I'll take a break, have a few days by the sea.'

'Ada I'm afraid for you. That may be too late.'

'I can't give up. You know I can't.'

'You must tell Straker what happened. He will understand why you must stop.'

'No.'

'He should know.'

'I cannot . . .'

'You should not carry this alone.'

'I'm not alone. I have you.'

'But soon I must return to Paris.'

Ada looked at her, feeling a pain deep in her chest. 'I know it and I dread it. I also know I must see this through whatever it costs.'

It was early evening by the time Ada reached home. She had just taken off her coat when a loud knock sounded through the hallway. Ada opened the door to Dr Auden.

'Doctor. I wasn't expecting you this late. But you are welcome, come in, out of the cold.'

'I said I would look in on Detective Inspector Straker as soon as I could. I would have come earlier but I had to make an urgent visit to an elderly patient on Goodramgate.'

'That's kind of you to come now. He's in pain and tired. He's resting in his room.'

The doctor removed his hat and smiled at her, his eyes twinkling. 'And, of course, it is very nice to see you again. It's very quiet. Are you alone tonight?'

'For now. Camille is at Evensong and Thomas is having a drink at the Cross Keys while he waits, he's going to walk her home.'

'Good man, it's best to be safe. I'm sure there are plenty of folk taking extra care at the moment,' he said. 'I was hoping you would be here and that I might see your studio after I have examined the patient. I would very much like to hear more about your work. It could be so useful in my medical practice.'

Ada found it was very pleasant to see him again. Chatting easily about his day, he took off his overcoat, draping it over a chair. He was so cheery and affable, it occurred to her to seek his help about the problem of Lucy.

'Would you care to have a glass of sherry with me when you come down? We can look at my studio, but there is something I want to ask you about an asylum here in York.'

He looked at her. 'Well, I have some knowledge of them of course. But Dr Scull at York Lunatic Asylum is your man. He knows the system here better than me.'

'I know but it's a private affair and I need to ask your advice as a friend.'

'You can rely on my discretion and a sherry would be nice.' He started up the staircase. 'Jane was saying how she enjoyed seeing you on Sunday. When I complained I had not joined you, she said it was strictly a ladies get together.'

'Yes, it's so pleasant for Jane and I to see more of each other now I am back in York.'

Ada followed him up the stairs to Straker's bedroom. By the light of the fire, she saw he was half-sleeping. He jerked awake and struggled to sit up. She knew he hated anyone to witness his physical weakness.

'I'll wait downstairs,' she said.

Dr Auden smiled across at her as she left. 'How are you feeling today detective?' he asked, opening up the clasps of his dark brown Gladstone bag.

'Much better, thank you. Thomas has been looking after me very well,' said Straker briskly. He had caught the look between the doctor and Ada. It irked him.

'Of course. He learnt from the very best, Miss Nightingale herself,' said Dr Auden. 'It's interesting, don't you think detective. My sister would be an excellent doctor but cannot because she is a woman. She is told she must be a nurse instead. Yet she would be terrible in truth, no patience at all. Yet Thomas is clearly a brilliant nurse and that seems strange to some these days because he is a man. Yet there have been male nurses for centuries, way back in monastic orders, the Crusades. Social norms confine us all. Now hold steady while I unwrap this bandage. I need to look at the wound, check how it's healing.'

Straker winced as his arm was gently prodded. It was still painful. 'Do you miss London, Dr Auden,' he asked to distract himself.

'I am getting used to it. It's no secret I didn't want to come back, but our mother was ill and Jane's attempts to get a licence to become a doctor had stalled. It seemed the right decision for us both at the time.' His face darkened momentarily. 'You know I worked at Guy's Hospital with Professor Swaine Taylor. You will be aware of the scandal. It was in the newspapers at the time.'

He nodded. Great Scotland Yard and Alfred Swaine Taylor were well acquainted. Straker had been many times at Court Number One of the Old Bailey while the professor gave medical evidence. Taylor had studied with Europe's greatest expert on arsenic poisoning, Mathieu Orfila and had gone on to make a breakthrough in forensic science; in particular detecting evidence of poisons. Taylor had become an expert witness in criminal trials. Straker's colleagues had been jubilant. It was all about hard, irrefutable evidence now. Never again would some weasel get off at the jury's whim. This was the future. Taylor was such a cause célèbre, so famous for his work that Charles Dickens took a tour of his laboratory. And then it went wrong. A few bodged testimonies on a couple of poisonings, killers getting away with murder and forensic science was plunged into disrepute. Scientific evidence had gone backwards. And here he was now being treated for a knife wound in York by Taylor's protégé in toxicology. Funny how life turned out he thought.

'Yes,' said the detective. 'It was a bad business for all of us and a good day for the criminal class.'

Straker almost felt sorry for William Auden. Or he would have done if he hadn't felt a worm of jealousy stirring. He had a sudden vision of this good-looking, clever man so obviously interested in Ada, still here in York, when he had gone back to London.

'You're not wrong there. We were working on a test for detecting the presence of plant poisons. It would have been a major breakthrough,' said Dr Auden. 'It was hard for our profession to be taken seriously after the unfortunate court cases. It set us back years. And it wasn't Taylor's fault, just that the scientific proof wasn't there then.'

'Yes, we struggled with evidence too. We got such a pasting in the press after the Kent Road murder case cock up,' said Straker.

'At least you all kept your jobs.'

'For now,' said Straker, thinking of the pressure he was under from Scotland Yard to solve this case.

'It takes some adjusting to, suddenly being the pariahs. We were working on tests for the most undetectable poisons. Our team in London was at the forefront. Just a few years ago we were consulted on hundreds of cases. Our workload was staggering. Not surprising really, we got some wrong, it was early days. There's still so much to discover. We can tell if a stain is blood, but still not what or whose, animal or human. So many poisons we can't detect. Hundreds of murderers are still getting away with it. Orfila has offered a prize this year you know, the Prix D'Orfila, to anyone who can create an infallible test for plant poisons. It will make them world famous.'

Auden's fulfilment in his work, his frustration with his current situation, was understandable to the detective. The doctor was a younger man but they shared a fierce professional pride.

Auden continued, 'Queen Victoria herself is said to be obsessed with poison cases. I met her once. She asked for a private briefing with our team at Guy's. She reads all the murder cases you know. Someone should write a book about it. They would make a fortune. It's amazing how many ladies I meet who are fascinated by my work.'

Despite himself Straker laughed. 'Even I a grizzled old detective, experience something similar myself. Ladies seem to prefer talking with me about crime above anything.'

Downstairs in the drawing room Ada was taking two small glasses from the oak corner cupboard when she heard the front door opening. She felt a tiny bit disappointed. Thomas and Camille, both red-cheeked from the icy wind, were stamping snow from their boots.

'Good evening Madame Defoe and to you too Mr Bell,' Doctor Auden appeared, at the top of the stairs.

'You are doing a good job Mr Bell, the patient is recovering well,' he said as he came down.

'That's good to hear,' Thomas nodded.

'Miss Fawkes, I will leave looking at your studio to another time.' Was there a trace of regret in his voice she wondered? 'I have just realised that time is getting on. Jane will be waiting to have supper with me. She wants to talk about plans for our garden, lots of new plants for the spring. You're a keen gardener aren't you Mr Bell?'

'Vegetables and cutting flowers,' he replied unbuttoning his heavy tweed coat.

'Jane loves flowers too. Well goodnight everyone.'

'Go carefully,' said Ada. He smiled at her, briefly placing his hand on her arm then he turned and walked out into the narrow street and into the deepening shadows around York Minster.

CHAPTER THIRTY-THREE

◊

'**A** man has confessed.'

Straker was sitting on the edge of the bed, bare-chested, struggling to get his shirt over his bandaged arm. He had called out to her through his open door as she was heading swiftly past to go downstairs for breakfast, her Prussian blue silk robe swirling around her yellow-stockinged ankles.

Ada stopped. 'What! To the murders? When?' She came into his room.

'A young man turned up at the station late last night and admitted to killing all four women. He's already in the castle jail. Nutt is obviously delighted. He has made it clear the case is closed and we have our man. He sent me a note first thing.'

'Who is he? Is it true?'

His face darkened. 'I don't know. I think it's unlikely. But Nutt has charged him and he's in front of the magistrates today. I am on my way to the jail now.'

He rose to his feet, tangling a shirt sleeve as he tried to put his arm through. Ada went to help him.

'You can't go. I'll do it. Thomas talk some sense into him,'

Thomas was walking into the room with a breakfast tray. He set it down on a table, took the detective's arm and steered him back to bed.

'You're not fit Straker. You must rest another day. You'll rip your stitches open.'

Straker lay back down defeated, his forehead and hair damp with effort. He was too weak to fight them.

'I'll go and get ready.' Ada left the room.

Straker grabbed Thomas's sleeve and pulled him close.

'Don't let her go anywhere on her own. Do you understand? It's not safe.'

Thomas nodded. 'I know.'

Ada left the house with Thomas, heading past College Green and onto Goodramgate. On the corner, outside the Cross Keys, they hailed a Hansom cab approaching from Monk Bar.

'Wooah girl.' The horse jingled to a stop, snorting plumes of air.

'Castle gaol please,' said Thomas.

'Hope tha's not on a one-way journey,' shouted down the small hunched figure. Ada climbed in first and Thomas handed up the photography equipment. Her leather work bag, she held close to her body, within was the key evidence: the photograph of the footprint in the snow, next to Amy Ward's body.

'Gee up oss.' The ebony mare stepped up her pace, heading down the street, passing bakeries, drug stores, wine merchants, grocers opening up for New Year's Eve trade.

'Does Straker really think this man is innocent?' asked Thomas.

'He is uncertain,' she replied. 'It's strangely convenient to have a man confess. But we have evidence so we may prove it one way or the other.'

'Nearly there,' shouted the driver through the trapdoor in the roof.

Ada said, 'I hope I'm remembering correctly that you once told me that you knew the prison governor from ages ago.'

'I'll get us in.'

'Everything depends on it. We must see this man this morning, before anyone knows what we are doing. I must photograph him. We will know if we have the murderer before us or not'.

'Then this could all be over today.'

She looked at Thomas, 'I pray it's him.'

Perched up on its hill Clifford's Tower, the remains of old York Castle, loomed above the high prison walls where Ada and Thomas waited at the main gateway.

Thomas spoke at some length to the one-legged turnkey at the gatehouse, who after much grumbling about his morning tea break, finally unlocked the outer door. Limping into the castle yard, he waved them past the medieval ruins and the inner wall towards a mock Tudor Gothic round tower. The governor's house.

More waiting in its draughty cold entrance hall for the grizzle-haired porter then, a long walk behind him, along a dimly-lit, brown-tiled corridor to the governor's office.

'Come in,' said a reedy voice from within.

'Leave this to me,' whispered Thomas in Ada's ear.

'A Mr Bell and a Miss Fawkes to see you Mr St Aubrey,' announced the porter as he opened the door and gestured them through into a small untidy office lined with bookshelves.

'How are you Bell, my dear chap? It's been too long,' said the silver-haired man behind a scuffed desk piled with papers and books. He stood and held out a veined hand. 'We were delighted to hear you made it back safely from the battlefields. Apologies for my croaky voice, I have caught a cold in this dreadfully damp place.' He coughed and sucked on his pipe.

'Sorry to hear that and thank you sir, I am well. May I intro-duce Miss Fawkes. Miss Fawkes is assisting the police, at the Home Secretary's command, in this murder investigation,' explained Thomas. Turning to Ada, he went on, 'And this is none other than my old teacher Mr Evelyn St Aubrey.'

Ada was conscious that the governor was looking at her with some interest.

The elderly man bowed his head politely. 'I am very pleased to meet you Miss Fawkes. I am acquainted with your family. My first job was at the village school near your home, a little bit before your time. I briefly taught this man here when he was a mere boy. Happy days.'

His watery eyes had a look of wistfulness. 'I ended up teach-ing young prisoners here, thought I could do some good with a bit of poetry. Somehow that led to me becoming deputy gover-nor and then governor. Over thirty years I've worked here now. Too long.'

Thomas nodded. It was generally known in York and across the Yorkshire Ridings that Evelyn St Aubrey was a good man but a bad prison governor. Inmates ran rings round him. The Debtors' Prison ran its own affairs, even having a strict set of laws to control its lucrative alcohol-smuggling ring. St Aubrey, more from incompetence than corruption, had virtually ceded control of the entire gaol.

Indeed the governor was a gentle soul, far too kind-hearted and Thomas was banking on it. He needed his help.

'But Thomas dear chap, it's so good to see you and look-ing so well,' the governor went on. 'What a shocking mess all that Crimean War business was. We saw those dreadful photo-graphs of the soldiers in *The Times*. No idea it was so bad out there old boy. We tried to do our bit you know. Our debtors did a bit of fund-raising, arm-twisting and so forth for money, food, blankets for you fighting men.'

'Very kind of them,' said Thomas. 'Sir we are here on an urgent matter, Miss Fawkes needs to see the prisoner who has confessed to the murders of the four women.'

'It's a bit irregular, against the rules you know, old chap,' said St Aubrey.

'Miss Fawkes must take his photograph.'

'Do you think I should allow it?'

'Yes, I do. It may be vital evidence.'

'But he's done it, Bell. The boy has told the magistrates everything.'

'We think there's a possibility he may be under pressure, made a false confession.'

'And you have good reason for that?'

'I wouldn't be bringing Miss Fawkes here, now, into the depths of this gaol sir if I felt it wasn't necessary. We must see him.'

'There's no time. He's been fast tracked for execution. The magistrates want this out of the way. The boy's already in the condemned cell. There's nothing I can do. I am sorry but my hands are tied.' He shook his head behind a cloud of smoke.

'This man's life is at stake. He may be innocent.'

'I can't. I am under orders.'

'Mr St Aubrey, do you remember the poems you used to read to us in school and how you loved to quote that young poet Shelley. Does the one about the masters brutally oppressing the working men come to your recall? It was something like . .
. *And many more destructions played, in this ghastly masquerade, all disguised, even to the eyes, like Bishops, lawyers, peers or spies.'*

341

The governor leaned back, half-smiling. 'I do remember the words Bell and the meaning. It was a lifetime ago, but I remember the next verse well.'

His rheumy eyes seemed to look into his past as he quoted, *"Last came Anarchy: he rode, on a white horse, splashed with blood; he was pale even to the lips, like Death in the Apocalypse. And he wore a kingly crown; And in his grasp a sceptre shone; On his brow his mark I saw – I am God, and King, and Law!"*

He sighed. 'Oh Bell, I was a young man then with principles.'

'The system is still as corrupt. Some powerful citizens in York may be riding roughshod over justice to protect their own interests. Miss Fawkes needs to see that prisoner. There may be an innocent man on his way to the gallows. We need to be sure.'

'You are a good fellow Thomas. You always were. If you believe you are doing the right thing, then I must too. I will do what I can.'

Evelyn St Aubrey docked his pipe into a large ashtray and walked to the door. He spoke to the porter waiting outside. Turning to them he said, 'I'll take you down. I will need to instruct the turnkey myself. Come. Follow me.'

He took his greatcoat from the wooden hat stand and pulled open the door. He looked taller as though he had regained some of the spirit of his youth. They followed him outside and through a metal gate into the medieval castle bailey, over the ground they called the Eye of York, the centre of the Yorkshire Ridings, covered with well-trodden, dirty slush. They walked up the wide stone steps, swept clean of snow, into the prison.

Beyond the elegant honey-coloured symmetrical facade, the impressive central bay window and grand entrance the prison became a place of nightmares. Long corridors and twisting stairs led them down and down. Passageways narrowed, painted walls and tiled floors became cold dripping stone. As they walked a stench of unwashed bodies and human waste assaulted their noses. This was the oldest part of the gaol. Ada looking around her in the near darkness, the flickering light cast by torches fixed to the thick walls barely reached the corners, could easily believe that nine prisoners had suffocated one night in a cramped, windowless cell. Claustrophobic at the best of times, Ada struggled to breathe, trying not to focus on the crushing lowness of the underground ceiling of stone.

Their footsteps sounded loud and echoing and the noise sent several large rats running ahead. She had no idea in which direction they walked, but the growing smell of damp and mildew suggested it was towards the river as did the clammy cold shrivelling her skin.

In front of them emerged a solid wooden iron-bound door, gnarled and pitted with age. They stopped before it. There were brief words with a guard whose face was barely visible in the darkness. Ada heard the harsh grating of stiff bolts undrawing. People said Dick Turpin spent his last hours here more than a century ago. She wondered if he had heard the same rasping noise as he was locked in the condemned cell for his last night on earth.

'Visitors,' the guard called out casually.

'Leave me be,' whispered a young man's voice.

'Well you've got them anyway.' He opened the door fully and stepped aside so they could enter.

Ada held her breath as she entered the cell behind Thomas. The door banged behind them. A key turned in the lock. She breathed out loudly and took a step into the tiny room. She pulled back as the astringent stench of fear, urine and faeces caught her nose. She clasped her gloved hand to her face and looked round. A thin strip of daylight beyond a barred window did little to help her eyes hievit to the low light. In the murkiness, Ada made out an iron bed and a small charcoal stove, smouldering; little comfort for those about to drop into eternity.

Thomas held the lantern higher, weak light finally found the fettered, skeletal figure on the straw-covered floor. His back was against the opposite wall, knees pulled under his chin. Rusty manacles chained skinny legs in ragged trousers. A ghastly face looked up at them.

Ada gasped and bent down in front of him. She looked hard at him; his cracked, dried lips, tear-streaked cheeks and eyes like dark pits in a too young face. Ada saw thin wrists sticking out of a torn shirt, dirty bare feet – so much smaller than the footprint in her photograph. This was a destitute boy unable to afford shoes, never mind five silver necklaces.

'You poor boy. Why are you doing this?' Ada touched his arm gently.

Silence.

'I know you are not the killer.'

Silence.

'Tell me what happened. I want to help you.'

The boy wiped his running nose on the back of his hand. 'They told me I could go home if I said I did it.'

'But you didn't do it.'

'I did it. I killed 'em.' He looked down at his feet.

'I know you didn't.' She turned to Thomas, setting up her camera and nodded.

When they had finally finished and come out into the fresh cold air, grateful to be leaving the gaol behind, the sensational news was already out on the streets. Ahead of them, pasted high on a stone wall, was a black and white billboard poster. 'The dreadful life and confession of the Butcher of York.'

Ada looked up at the headline and said:

'They are going to hang this boy.'

CHAPTER THIRTY-FOUR

◊

'Look at this child. Look at his feet,' Ada angrily thrust the photographs towards him. 'This isn't the killer. So why would he say he is?'

Straker pulled himself upright on the sofa and scrutinised a black and white image. A blank-eyed young man stared back at him. He looked at the next one, a bare foot, a wooden ruler laid alongside, testifying to its length. It was much shorter than the footprint in the snow.

'He doesn't know anything,' said Ada, gesticulating at the photographs she had just finished developing. 'The prison governor says he's called Tim Trent. He doesn't know where the boy lives, assumes he's a vagrant.'

'He's looks no more than a child.'

'He is a child in age and mind. They are going to hang an innocent boy.' In frustration Ada turned away, crossed the room, noisily threw a shovel of coal onto the fire and flung herself into the armchair by the hearth.

'Why don't you tell me everything that happened this morning,' said Straker.

She described meeting the prison governor. She told him about Tim Trent, laying out for him the witless young man, the lack of mental capability to lure young women, the inability to afford food never mind jewellery. She pointed out that he had to have access to a site where a young woman could be hidden for days and then unseen, have the means to deposit their bodies in public places around the city.

'When's the execution day?' asked Straker. 'How long have we got?'

'Two days. It's scheduled for Friday, the day before market day so it will attract big crowds wanting to make a long week-end of it. The corporation is expecting record numbers. And conveniently just before *The Herald* goes to press on Saturday so the mayor can boast to everyone that justice has been done. We have to do something.'

Ada looked at Straker's face. She could almost see his thoughts processing. 'I need to see the magistrates and con-vince them this is a false confession. First I need to get a mes-sage to Nutt.'

'I'll fetch pen and paper.' Ada returned with the portable wooden writing desk from the bureau.

Straker scribbled out a note, blotted the black ink and took another sheet of paper. 'Call it insurance, but I'm writing a letter to the Lord Mayor as well. I don't know who to trust, if any-one. I'm asking for a meeting with the magistrates tomorrow at twelve o'clock.'

She caught Thomas, as he was on his way out with Camille, escorting her to meet friends for a New Year's Eve drink. He promised to deliver the letters straightaway, in person.

Ada went up to her bedroom, she needed to change out of her clothes, soaking wet from working in her darkroom. Impa-tiently she stepped into a silk green dress, fumbling with the pearl buttons. She tied her hair back simply in a loose knot and returned to the drawing room. She was especially glad of its warmth and light tonight, the eve of 1863.

'So much is puzzling me,' she said, pouring a sherry from the decanter on the sideboard. She held the glass up to Straker. He shook his head, 'I'm already too fuddled from that damn sleeping draught.'

Of course he would want to keep his mind clear, focused. She watched him as he half-lay on the sofa in his loosened white shirt. His forehead furrowed in concentration, his lined cheeks leaner, his countenance more brooding. Ada remembered when he had been different. She saw them again in her mind's eye walking with arms linked tight, a late night high-spirited supper in Les Halles after his favourite opera — Gluck's *Orfeo et Euridice* — his head back laughing, describing his own dismal attempts to play the 'Dance of The Blessed Spirits' on his childhood flute.

Straker had changed but there was still purpose in his eyes, strength in his form, a vitality of spirit.

She walked over and sat opposite him. 'I've brought the photographs. I thought we could talk things over again, see if we can unravel the threads a bit more.'

'That would be useful, I would appreciate that.' He lit a cigarette. 'I haven't had a chance to say yet, but I have seen the two post-mortem reports carried out by Dr Duff, they are inconclusive so we don't know how Annie and Emily died. Not a surprise really. And we haven't got the results yet for Rose and Amy.'

Ada leaned back and took a sip of dark Jerez sherry. 'So what do we know?'

Straker began, 'Our main focus is still the Refuge. Our young women all lived there at some point and three left to work in laundries connected to the committee gentlemen. These five men knew the young women, had contact with them and have means and space to hide a person or a body.'

He leaned forward to flick his ash In the fire. 'Edward Atkinson, an architect, with access to half-finished, unoccupied buildings, including Dr Scull's new home. Mrs Atkinson said that on Christmas night her husband was absent for some hours because of a flood in a property. That night Amy's body was left at the Minster. The Atkinson's laundress hinted to you that her boss was sexually involved with Amy Ward and he did not want to report her missing, does that point us towards him?'

Ada got up to pour herself another sherry as he talked.

'Meanwhile Reverend Lindley admitted to you that his wife lives for the most part at their country home. Is the Reverend Charles Lindley hiding something more than his collapsing marriage? And I am interested in your friend Jane's remark that Lindley was responsible for discipline at the Refuge. How far did he go? But I think the most interesting of our suspects is Dr Scull at York Lunatic Asylum. He has so much space there and you thought his relationship with his housekeeper Mrs Gaitskill uneasy as if she might be covering up something for him.'

Ada interrupted, 'But Rose's friend Esther at the Refuge said Rose had met a kind gentleman who befriended her. I think the killer deliberately set about nurturing a trusting relationship with his victim that he could exploit. That makes me have doubts about Dr Scull or Reverend Lindley. Neither of my encounters with them made me think I would trust them or warm to them if I was a young woman. I think we need to look at Reverend Turner.'

'Yes, he's much closer in age to the girls, would they not turn to him as a natural confidante?' agreed Straker. 'Your Dr Auden is a regular visitor but maybe too old?'

'Hardly. He's not . . .'

'Ada,' Straker cut in, 'can I see Amy's photograph? I was reminded of something just then, as you spoke of nurturing, it's been niggling me.'

She rummaged in her bag by the side of her chair, pulled out a bundle of photographs and flicked through until she had found the picture. She passed it over.

'Yes, here look. Look at Amy's hair, smoothed down, not messy as you would expect if her body was hastily tumbled onto the ground, the gown straightened like she was cared for, even in death. We didn't see the other bodies at the crime scenes, but what if they were the same? It makes me think you are on the right lines. These women are taken by someone they like, know and trust and the killer in return has some feelings for them. Do you think a crime like that is possible?'

'Yes, I do. He keeps them alive for some days. He might become close to them in an odd way. I wonder if the women knew they were facing their end.' She shivered.

'What about Annie, the first victim, why was she found dumped in the river? That doesn't fit the pattern?'

'Maybe he panicked, heard someone and tossed her body in.'

'I'm thinking why would you risk leaving a body in the city centre at all? Why not throw them all into the river, so they are washed away and hope they end up in the sea? No one would be any the wiser.' Straker lit another cigarette.

'I think we are right about him craving recognition. He's arrogant. He wants us to know this is him, the Butcher. At first no one noticed or cared because his victims were street women. He wasn't getting credit for his cunning, his cleverness so he became more daring, killed more frequently. The last two murders are just days apart. Now he has the whole country transfixed. York lives in fear because of him. He is in control. He is enjoying making us look like fools. He's letting us know he's much smarter than us. We have become part of this madness and he won't stop.'

Straker looked at her.

Ada spoke softly. 'We know our killer that I'm sure of. I am certain he is one of these five men.'

He moved and groaned. 'Damn this injury. Come what may I am not lying here any longer. We must talk to Reverend Turner and we must get to the jeweller's wife Mrs Berriman. Tomorrow we will present the magistrates with our evidence about Tim Trent. Time is slipping away.'

Ada finished her drink and stood, as much as she wanted to stay here, warm by the fire, with this man. She pushed back her red-gold hair, now escaping from its loose clasp. 'It's nearly supper time. They will be back soon, Camille is serving oysters and smoked salmon as they do in France, it's a big celebration over there, well you know that of course. I appreciate there's little to celebrate, but a glass of champagne won't hurt. Will you join us?'

Watching her, he thought she looked weary, vulnerable but still so beautiful. She passed by him and as she did so, he placed his broad hand on her slender waist. 'Stay a moment,' he urged, his voice hoarse.

He met her eyes. Neither could look away.

The sound of voices from outside, the front door opening and closing broke the moment.

351

'They're back.' Ada turned abruptly away and left.

Damn, why had he done that? Straker was furious with himself. He thought of Superintendent Dolly Williamson trusting him to save the Detective Branch, with the Queen and the country following his every move. He must focus each waking second on this investigation. Yet at this moment his heart felt like it was gripped by a tight fist. His thoughts were only of Ada. He longed, he ached with every fibre of his being to keep her with him, to wrap her in his arms forever.

Straker stared into the fire.

Unfortunately he already had a wife – gentle, gracious Clara, who was no more to blame for where they found themselves than he was.

Straker had been shocked by the swiftness of it. And when it had happened, it wasn't calm or gentle as he supposed love to be. It hurt.

In truth his life had changed the day Ada walked into the headquarters of La Sûreté in the Autumn of 1859.

Straker had never known this before, not this longing so painful, he could not sleep or eat. He had never experienced this suddenness of falling – and falling seemed to him like the right word – in love. His friendship with Clara Kellaway, a daughter of a family friend, was different. It had been pleasant and companionable and it had deceived him into believing he was in love. And perhaps it had deceived her.

He had said nothing to Ada of course for he was not a free man. Straker had been tortured by the wrongness of his desire. For weeks he had struggled with his conscience. Perhaps it was Paris, its joie de vivre, its relaxed atmosphere that had finally convinced him his feelings were worthy and without taint. Whatever it was, in the aftermath of a case solved; the release of emotion, Straker gave up any resistance. So did Ada.

But he had not, for Clara's sake, revealed everything he should have done at that moment.

For the next few days he had been almost ill with guilt. It had tormented him until he could bear it no more. He had asked Ada to meet him and on a mild Sunday morning they had walked arm in arm in the Luxembourg Gardens. His throat constricted as he had tried to find the words. Finally he had stopped walking and suggested they sit down on a bench in a quiet corner, under the chestnut trees.

'I must tell you something.'

She had looked at him gravely.

'I am married,' he had said simply. 'The concealment is burning my heart. I cannot bear it any longer.'

Ada had leapt swiftly to her feet and as quickly he had grabbed her hands. He had pulled her back beside him.

'Ada, please listen to me. I have done no wrong in loving you. You have my word on that.'

She had struggled to rise again, but he had his hands on her shoulders.

'Hear me speak Ada. It is not what you are thinking.' He had gripped her shoulders tighter, forcing her to look at him. 'I am no Mr Rochester. I am not living a double-life. I am not seeking to become a bigamist. Nor will I pretend my wife is a mad woman that must be locked away in some attic and thereby justify or excuse my actions, my love for you. For she is neither mad, nor lives in an attic. The truth is both ordinary and extraordinary. She lives comfortably in our marital home in London.'

Ada had struggled to break his grip. 'Spare me the details Straker. I believed you to be that one man I could trust. I was wrong.'

'Ada listen to me. This is different and it's so hard to say.'

'It's always different. You don't need to explain.'

'I do Ada. My wife has a companion, a woman, Kathryn. They share a romantic friendship. Clara and I, well our relationship was insupportable to her, it always has been.'

Ada stopped struggling. Instinctively she touched his cheek. 'Oh, Straker I'm sorry. Did you love her? Do you love her still?'

'I did when we married, but now well I love her like a sister. Can I tell you what happened?'

He had explained how the truth of their union only became obvious when it was too late for them.

'She had no enjoyment or gratification in our embrace. She could not love me like a husband. Distaste, indifference, ignorance I did not know what to make of her reluctance. I do not think she did either. I do not think that her reason for choosing me was to preserve herself from her troublesome feelings in love. I believe she was confused and hoping for the best. Then Kathryn became our housekeeper. They grew close. I was not surprised by the time she told me for I had seen their relationship grow. Clara eventually admitted the friendship and intimacy of women was more to her, that she had never cared very much for men. She said it must seem monstrous to me.'

Straker had shook his head and reached for Ada's hands. 'I am not such a man. I have seen many things and I do not judge. My regret was and still is how much I wanted children. But Clara did not choose this path for herself either and being childless is painful to her too. I could not be angry with her or think of my own misfortune for long. No one was to blame. So we took measures, not unlawful, but unusual measures. We respected each other, we accepted our situation and we found a way of maintaining our different lives. I moved to Paris and she stayed in our London home. There is still a room for me there when I need it. Clara and Kathryn are now like husband and wife and live a happy life in Kensington.'

Suddenly Straker had looked stricken. 'But I cannot divorce her. You know what that would mean Ada? I would have to prove adultery with evidence. Her reputation would be ruined. I could not do that to her. I did not think it would matter because I did not expect to fall in love. My career, being a detective was enough, until I met you.'

Taking her face in his hands, he had said. 'Ada I believe I am morally free to love you, as Clara loves another. She will never want me. But I cannot marry you. God knows I would, this very day, this very moment. Say something Ada, tell me you are not shocked?'

'You underestimate me Straker. I'm not shocked. I met many women living different lives as I travelled on the continent. Like me, they wanted freedom to be who they really are. In Rome especially I had such friends; a sculptress who dressed like a man, an artist who told me, "in the way of male, I like only the bulls I paint." I was not judgemental, nor disapproving then. I am not now. Tell me about Clara.'

'You would actually like her Ada. She is clever, perceptive, principled. She is a member of the London National Society for Women's Suffrage.'

'You are an honourable man Straker and I knew a long time ago marriage was not for me, I . . .'

'Stop.'

Straker, pulling her into his arms, had kissed her for a long time. In the Luxembourg Gardens, Paris, they had barely attracted a glance.

Straker dropped his head in his hands. He must leave this house, go back to his hotel. He must keep a clear head and focus on this investigation. Nothing else mattered. He must keep a professional distance. His beautiful, clever, opinionated Ada could never know how much he still adored her.

CHAPTER THIRTY-FIVE

◊

'T was a good 'un last night lads. What a state I was in, woke up in t'back yard, head down t'drain. Our lass went mad.' Stone's voice was loud above the others. Sounds of laughter drifted from the front desk back to his office.

Silver Street lock-up was a world away from Great Scotland Yard. In his modern London office Straker expected and found efficiency: files in tall drawers, meticulous records, log books, incident books. Straker looked around this room, taking in half-drunk tin mugs of stewed tea on a window ledge, a plate of biscuit crumbs, a crumpled newspaper on a chair. Reaching painfully in his inside pocket for his cigarettes, he looked up as he heard the door creak open.

Constable Bevers put his head round the door, flinching when he saw the flint expression on Straker's face.

'M . . . Mornin' sir,' he stuttered. 'We weren't expecting you today on account of your indisposition.' Gage followed him into the room. 'Bad business, sir. You see, that's what we are up agen here, hievingg', hieving' scum in this city.'

'Is that what you were told about what happened to me?'

'Aye, a robbery gone wrong, t'chief said. He's had us round up the usual vagrants for questioning.'

357

'I bet he has and none of them will have done it.'

'What do you mean sir?' said Bevers.

'Forget it Bevers. Get Stone here, now, I need to talk to you all.'

Straker lit a cigarette. He briefly shut his eyes. God help him.

'Free the prisoner. What the bloody hell for?' Stone banged his hand on the mantlepiece on which he was leaning. 'He's confessed.'

'We have crime scene evidence,' said Straker.

'What the bugger's that when it's at home?' Stone interrupted.

'It means we have proof that the killer cannot be Tim Trent.' He handed them a photograph of the prisoner. The condemned man stared lifelessly at them, as though he was dead already.

'Miss Fawkes been busy again?' said Stone. 'She ought to find herself a husband, being on her back would stop her interfering with police business.'

No one else had laughed, not when they had seen the fury on Straker's face.

Stone threw the photograph down on the desk. 'Well, how does this prove he's not the killer?'

'Look at him Stone, think,' said Straker. 'He's half-starving. How do you think this man affords silver necklaces? Where would he keep a young woman? If you have no money in this city you live with how many others, I don't know, twenty or so in one room? And then there is this.'

He placed the photograph of Tim Trent's ten inch foot alongside the footprint in the snow. 'Different sizes. An inch or so smaller. That, Stone, is crime scene evidence.'

'That's nowt. The bugger could have nicked some shoes,' said Stone.

'He would struggle to wear large shoes, carry a body up steps in snow and carefully arrange a murder scene. But be my guest. Explain your theory to me. I'd be grateful,' said Straker, his eyes like hard pewter.

'It's simple. Slags. He targets slags. He could have stolen those necklaces, given 'em as payment. Up for it with anyone they are, they like it. And t'owd bitches 'll do it for a gin if they have the clap.'

'That's it. That's your theory?'

'Doesn't matter does it. He's rid us of a few whores. It's hard enough keeping the peace and controlling crime at the best of times without those slappers getting drunk and putting themselves about. Oh we've got our man alright. He's confessed. And he'll swing for it. Pity, he's been doing us a favour, less sluts on the street.'

'Sometimes people confess to things they haven't done Stone,' said Straker.

Stone smirked, 'And why would he do that then?'

'I don't know yet, but we are going to find out. Where's Chief Constable Nutt?'

Silence hung in the air like thick tobacco smoke.

'He's having breakfast with the Lord Mayor at the Mansion House,' offered Bevers finally.

Straker sighed. A private meeting before he and the magistrates met at twelve o'clock. He wondered what they were plotting.

'Has anyone spoken to Tim Trent's family or friends? Have we got an address for him?'

'What would we talk to 'em about?' asked Gage, arms folded over his gigantic chest.

'So we can find out something about him.'

'Well that's a bloody waste of time,' said Stone.

'That is how I catch criminals or do you know any better way?' Straker glared at them.

It was going to be a long day.

Three men in front of him, three orders.

'This is what you are going to do. One, I want to know who owns the brothels on Grape Lane. Harriet Pegler is running the girls, but who is really behind the business. Two, I want the arrest report for Tim Trent. Three, I want the boatman Jack Hawker found.'

Stone snickered, 'Grape Lane! T'street's allus been known 'ere as Gropecun . . .'

'Do it. Now.' Straker watched them go. Bevers looked over his shoulder, lingering as the other two left the room.

'What is it Bevers?' He wasn't a bad sort, Straker thought, might even have potential. The constable fidgeted with the buttons on his tunic top. 'Well?'

'They're not there.'

'What aren't?'

'The prisoner's notes. T'weren't written down. I overheard summat or I think I did. It's probably nowt.'

'Go on.'

'Chief Constable Nutt was here in the station office that evening after the lad Tim Trent confessed. I was the duty officer that night and I was upstairs seeing to the prisoners in the cells, giving them tea. We just had a few in and it was quiet, no Irish, so not like the usual madhouse. They musn't have realised I was there because when I came down, the office door was open and I could hear him talking to Sergeant Stone. The boss said he wanted it kept quiet about the prisoner. Stone said he thought that was a good idea, given where he lived, and said something about that being unfortunate.'

'Did they say anything else?' asked Straker.

'Nowt. I said to meself, Bevers that's a bit unusual. I thought the boss would be singing from the rooftops at catching a killer. Well I was curious. But that's the point. I looked. There's no report. There should be something in the book. There's nothing.'

'Thank you constable. You did the right thing telling me.'

Straker watched Bevers leave. He leaned forward, dropping his head in his hands with frustration.

What the hell were Nutt and Stone hiding?

It was a short while later that Gage banged on the door. Straker looked up from the desk.

'Miss Fawkes for you sir, says it's urgent.'

'Well let her in.'

Gage allowed her to pass through, a smirk on his face. Straker pushed back his chair and stood up.

'I wasn't expecting you this early. Our meeting with the magistrates isn't until twelve. What is it? Is everything alright?'

Ada sounded out of breath, her cheeks flushed pink. Too warm from fast walking, she unwound her long scarf as she talked.

'Tim Trent lives at Stonebow Lane.'

'How do you know that?' Straker asked sharply.

'Thomas heard it.'

'What, when? Did no one think to give me this information sooner?'

'He only found out this morning while he was running an errand for Camille at the market. He caught me as I was leaving the house on my way to the studio.'

'Go on.'

'Tim Trent lives with his sister. She looks after him, he's not quite the full shilling or that's what Thomas was told.'

'And the sister, is she?'

'A prostitute?' said Ada. 'Well, yes. I don't think there's a woman who lives in Stonebow Lane who isn't. The sister earned money for them both. She's the only family he's got and he's not able to look after himself. If she didn't take care of him he would be in the workhouse.'

'How did Thomas hear this?'

'Everyone's talking about it he says. It's all over the market. The boy's known a bit, does a few odd jobs there, helps with the livestock. He loves animals apparently.'

Straker walked over to the yellowing city plan of York tacked to the wall. Ada moved next to him, so close she could smell the Turkish tobacco on his jacket, the spicy amber cologne on his skin.

'Where is Stonebow Lane?' he asked peering at street names.

'It's actually very near, but it's such a small street it's not on this map. It's about here.' She pointed to spot between St Crux at the corner of Fossgate and St Saviour's on Hungate. 'It's notorious.'

'I must go there now before we meet the magistrates. There must be something more to learn, something that will help us further prove his innocence.'

'I will come with you.'

'No. It isn't safe.' She was so close to him that he could see the scars criss-crossing the pale skin of her collarbone.

'You can't forbid me.' Ada looked up at him, eyes flashing with anger. 'You came to me and begged for my help. 'There is no one else', you said when you dragged me into this. Don't tell me now what I can and can't do.'

'I'm thinking of you.'

'Well don't think of me. And don't tell me what to do. I'm not your wife.'

Straker froze.

Ada was too furious to check her words. 'I am not bound by law to obey you on this matter or anything else. I answer to no one. I'm a forensic photographer. And you need me. So let me do my job.'

In the long pause that followed, Straker's face changed. His expression grew distant and cold. 'So be it Miss Fawkes and be assured when this is over, I will never trouble you for your services again.'

From the police station the walk to Stonebow Lane was short. They turned right into Parliament Street, into Whip-ma-Whop-ma Gate and were soon onto Fossgate.

Here, besides York's bustling streets of shops and businesses, there existed a parallel workplace. Three narrow stone-flagged alleys. The brothels were stacked on top of each other. Tiny two-story red-brick cottages, built so close the streets were dark even in daytime. Small broken windowpanes covered with dirty, tobacco-stained nets. The front doors scuffed and battered.

In a matter of minutes, clients procured in the public houses in various states of inebriation could be scurried by torturously turning passages to the beds of the cheapest whores in York.

Stonebow Lane was perfectly placed; St Saviour's Church at its top end, where married men could beg for forgiveness before or after, and at the other, the Blue Bell or the Golden Fleece where country punters sought Dutch courage. Straker knocked at the first of a line of eight identical cottages. 'Aye?' A small, wizen-faced woman, maybe her in forties, fifties, hard to tell after decades in her line of work, stood holding the door firmly.

Straker asked for Alice Trent.

'Nay, never heard of her.' Her expression remained blank, the result of years of practice at facing down authority. She made to close the door. Straker stuck his leather boot across the threshold.

'Madam, I would be very grateful for any information.' He dipped his hand into the inside of his black overcoat and pulled out a silver coin.

'What do you expect for that? A frig of your shaft?' she sneered.

'Information. Nothing more.'

She nodded at Ada who was pressing her scarf over the mouth and nose. The lane was clearly used as a public privy.

'Are tha sure? These well-to-do ladies aren't always as prim and proper as they seem.'

'If you can tell us where Alice Trent is, that's all. We want to talk to her.'

'Ah don't care what you want to do with her. She's not one of mine.' Looking up and down the alley, the madam grabbed the coin and rammed it into her grubby, low-cut bodice.

'Try two doors down. If she's young enough, she might be one of Miss Maude's lodgers. She likes 'em to barely have grown 'ere.' She cupped her breasts, laughing.

Straker didn't knock on Mrs Maude's door. Taking Ada's arm firmly he walked straight in. The tiny room had only one item of furniture, a dishevelled bed. The girl perched on it was wearing a flimsy dress, pulled down enough to show the bruises on her thin shoulders and arms. She had clearly just finished her toil on the mattress. There was a stench of human odours.

'Does Alice Trent live here?' Straker asked gently, moving closer to her.

She nodded blankly, this close she smelled of gin.

'Upstairs.'

Ten steep steps brought them into another damp room where mould flowered on the bare walls and the flaking ceiling. A makeshift pallet bed took up most of this room. Under the covers, they saw a shape, a movement and the girl they were searching for, emerged, her face startled. Her long tangled hair fell messily over her neck and shoulders. She could have been fourteen years old.

'Alice.' Ada said.

'Yes.' Her voice was small and timid.

'Alice, I have seen your brother.'

Her voice was stronger. 'Tim?'

'Yes, I have seen him. He's in prison. I have a picture of him, look.'

She handed her the photograph she had pulled from her bag. Alice took it and stared. She touched her brother's face as if he was there before her.

'Tim. How? Is it magic?'

'No it's science. It's called a photograph. You can keep it. But we need to talk to you. You might know something that can help free him.'

Alice nodded.

The girl's looks had remained unremarkably unspoilt – so far. Those like her fell into darker circles of hell with each passing year on their backs. The unending cycle of drink and despair swiftly ravaged youth.

'What happened to you?' Ada asked, perching next to her.

'Our mother died some years ago. I don't know when or how old I was. Father was a labourer, but work was scarce and he drank. We lived in one room with other families, slept on the floor. In the day we begged in the streets. At night, well sometimes father was there with a bit of bread, sometimes he wasn't. Then he didn't come back no more.'

Ada nodded, her answer was no surprise. 'I know it's hard but anything you tell us might help Tim.'

Alice's voice was low and weak. 'We were hungry. Then this lady got talking to me, she said there was work at her house in Hungate. In return I would get food and a bed. I asked her if she would take Tim as well. He's not right, see, he's not all there. I have to look after him. It wasn't our father's fault. He dropped him and Tim fell badly and hurt his head. He talks funny sometimes, can't remember things.'

She dropped her head, scarcely speaking above a whisper. 'At first I served ale to the gentlemen. Miss Maude asked me to watch the other girls in the house, see how they were with the clients. Tim did jobs for her too, made up the fire, got ale from the pubs, fetched from the market. Then the Reverend Turner came to the door. He talked to Miss Maude and soon after we were taken away on account of our ages. That society of well-to-do ladies and gents, those ones who tried to stop the Sunday afternoon band performances at the barracks, the Youthful Depravity Brigade found me a place at the Bishophill

Refuge. Reverend Turner took me. First time I had gone in a carriage.'

Ada looked up at Straker over Alice's head.

'And Tim?' she asked.

'He's harmless but he's daft in the head. He stutters so he doesn't speak a lot. He was too old to go to one of them poor schools. The society fixed up a stable job for him, one of the big houses on Marygate. He's good with animals, used to look after anything injured we found; cats, mice, pigeons. Tim visited me at the Refuge. I wasn't allowed out. We talked over the garden wall sometimes. Everyone did that.'

'What happened there? Why did you leave?'

'Some of the girls were vicious especially if they thought the Reverend Turner was paying another girl more attention. You see he's very kind and all the girls like him. I liked his Bible stories so I listened to him and asked questions. Then I was accused of theft, by one of the girls. Reverend Turner had praised me in class for remembering a parable and she was jealous. She stole a vase from the matron and hid it in my bed. Some other girls pretended they had seen me. The ladies had a meeting with the other vicar, Reverend Lindley. He said I had not repented my sins and I must leave. I had nowhere to go. I came back to Miss Maude's rather than starve.'

Straker, standing looking out of the window, his back to the room, wished he did not have to hear this. He found it harder the older he became.

'What happened to Tim after that?'

'I thought he was still working at Marygate. It wasn't unusual for me not to see him for a few months. I can't read, so I didn't know what had become of him until one of the girls here

367

told me. He wouldn't hurt a fly wouldn't Tim. I don't know why he's done it. Why would he say he's murdered them girls? He doesn't know what he is doing. Is he going to hang?'

Straker turned. 'No Alice, he won't hang. I promise.'

CHAPTER THIRTY-SIX

◊

'We need to talk. Now.' Straker caught Ada's arm.
'We're near the Coffee Yard, Number Three has its own roasting oven. It's good, for York.'

'That will do.'

They walked in silence along Stonegate and nearly halfway along, she led him into the narrowest of alleyways which opened into a small paved courtyard.

Straker looked round, pleasantly surprised. The aroma of roasting beans was rich and pungent. That morning's coffee break was in full swing, the noise of chatter and laughter flowing freely and echoing around the stone walls enclosing the square. York was a city of contrasts; the whirl of normal life existed in close quarters with heart-wrenching depravity.

They stepped inside Number Three. The dark, smoky room was buzzing with conversations flowing from the tables. They found one free and squeezed into the chairs pushed into a tiny corner by the window. It looked out on a very old timber-framed townhouse. Straker caught the eye of a boy who swiftly brought over a pot of coffee and two cups.

Straker poured. For a second or two they didn't speak.

'She's still a child,' said Straker shaking his head.

'We have to save her brother.'

369

'I promised I would, but I admit it's going to be difficult. George Brass is howling for blood. His fiefdom of York rests on hanging the Butcher of York.'

'But we have photographs. We can prove Tim is not the killer.'

'I know but they will wriggle. They want a scapegoat. The mayor's ball must go ahead and if that means executing an innocent man so be it. I fear it will take another murder before they admit Tim is innocent. By then it will be too late for the boy.'

A figure caught his eye, threading his way through the crowded room towards their table. There was no mistaking the elegant man approaching.

'Detective Inspector Straker, good to see you again.' Rufus Valentine was leaning over their table. 'And Miss Fawkes too, what a pleasant surprise. How do you do?'

'You know each other?' Straker asked.

'Oh we've met, haven't we Miss Fawkes?' Valentine smiled at her. She returned his greeting, Straker noticed.

'Mr Valentine. Will you join us?' Straker gestured to the waiter to bring another cup.

Valentine sat down and chatted away easily. 'York's first newspaper was printed here in this yard and we reporters still here come for our breaks. Tradition you might say, but really it's because this is the only decent coffee in the city. And the best place for gossip.'

The editor looked sharply from one to the other. 'How fortuitous to find you both here. A man has confessed and already has an appointment with the drop. Can you tell me any more Straker?'

'Let's just say it's an ongoing investigation,' said Straker momentarily cautious.

'Well this confession does seem a little convenient to me. From what my reporters have found out so far, he's a simple-minded lad without a penny to his name.'

Straker decided to share information with the newspaper editor. In his experience it was likely to be more beneficial. 'It's true I have serious doubts. But we will have a hell of a time convincing the mayor and his magistrates of that. Valentine, meeting you is indeed fortuitous. We have photographic evidence of his innocence and after we have seen the magistrates at noon, we will be happy to share this with you.'

'Excellent. I believe we can be of help to each other then.' Valentine sat forward in his chair. 'Our readers will be fascinated. Imagine the accused man saved by one photograph. It's sensational.'

'That is what we hope Valentine. I will meet you later then. In return, keep us in the loop and let me know if you discover anything else.'

Valentine nodded. 'Miss Fawkes, I would very much like to talk to you about your role in this investigation. A photographer and detective, it would be a terrific story. I could make you as famous as Florence Nightingale. We could discuss it over dinner? Think about it.'

Straker's face was inscrutable. He placed a few coins on the table and rose swiftly. 'We must take our leave. Time is against us. Until later Mr Valentine.'

Valentine nodded his head and leaning back, watched Ada Fawkes's departing rear thoughtfully.

In St Helen's Square, across from the Mansion House, the crowds were milling around shop fronts, chestnut sellers' braziers, hot-soup stalls and as Ada was concentrating on avoiding any collision in the busy street, she felt a tug on her coat.

'Pretend you are looking in the window,' whispered Straker. 'I've just seen the mayor's secretary Hugh Blake talking to two rough-looking thugs on the other side of the square. Those two ruffians look familiar to me.'

Ada glanced across. 'I don't know them. But I would recognise those particular bruisers again.'

'I might be imagining it but they have a look of the men who attacked me. Hard to say, it was so dark and sudden. Let's wait until they've gone.'

Straker took a quick look round, watching as the trio split in different directions. He touched Ada's arm and together they crossed the square to the Mansion House entrance. His senses were on alert for trouble.

York's legal authority had been placed in a row behind a polished mahogany desk. The five magistrates sat in a line, poker-faced. Two empty chairs were before them.

Hugh Blake was leaning back against the windowsill, arms crossed, watching closely. Near him, to one side of the line of chairs, was a sombre-looking clerk sat behind a writing desk, pen and ink ready to take the notes.

Brass looked pointedly at Ada. 'Miss Fawkes we meet at last. I have heard a lot about you.'

The magistrates smirked behind their cigar smoke. They scented a woman's blood, it stirred their own and they shifted in their chairs.

Ada tilted her chin. 'Gentlemen. Indeed you will have heard of me for I have had the pleasure of photographing the Lady Mayoress at my studio. Chief Constable Nutt, your wife also has an appointment. They were most interested in hearing of my recent discussions on photography with Queen Victoria at Windsor. Her Majesty has kindly taken an interest in my upcoming exhibition here in York. You know she used to be a patron of the Photographic Society of London.'

'Aye, I've heard of the Queen's photographic collection. It's vast I believe,' said one magistrate with interest.

'My wife wants her portrait done next,' said another.

'Aye and mine.'

'Well the portraits of the Lady Mayoress and Mrs Nutt will be on display in my show. It may well go to a London exhibition after here which the Queen will most likely visit.'

The magistrates, as one, leaned forward in their chairs, straightening chests, smoothing hair. They had not expected such a striking, confident woman. Miss Fawkes was no shrinking violet. In fact she was rather exciting.

Brass steered the conversation away from this admiration of Miss Fawkes to the matter at hand. He was keen to get this over with. He had much to organise before the execution.

'Now what's all this nonsense about arresting the wrong man. He's confessed. That's good enough for us. The hanging will take place tomorrow morning, usual time.'

He looked down the row, the magistrates nodding in agreement.

'But we can prove his innocence,' Ada said.

Straker held up three photographs. Brass raised an eyebrow and nodded at Blake who swiftly moved across the room. He took them to place on the table in front of the Lord Mayor.

'You can see a photograph of footprints in the snow, taken at the murder scene close to the body of Amy Ward. The next shows the length of one of those footprints. You can clearly observe the ruler marking it as eleven inches, quite a large foot,' Ada explained.

The mayor looked and passed it along the line.

'The next photograph is of the prisoner's foot, measured against the same ruler. You can see it is a good inch smaller.'

Nutt's anger erupted. 'The prisoner's sister is a whore. He's destitute and that makes him a villain in my eyes. He will have pinched these shoes.'

Murmurs of agreement.

'These images show a smooth-sole, the shoes of a wealthier man, not the hob nails of a poor man,' said Straker.

'That does not prove they were not stolen,' Nutt snapped.

'And there is this.' Ada passed over the photograph of the silver cross. 'We can prove all the victims wore this same necklace. This boy is a penniless wretch, starving, how could he afford such jewellery?'

'If he's a thief he could have stolen those too.'

More nodding.

'But no one has reported a theft of four necklaces. We have enquired in every jeweller's shop. Chief Constable Nutt you have nothing in your report books of such a theft do you?' said Straker.

Nutt grudgingly conceded the fact.

'But I do know this. There is one name in the accounts ledger of a jeweller's shop. Earlier this year, this person requested five crosses to be engraved with flowers, paid for them and collected them. That was not a penniless young boy.'

'Who is it then?' demanded Brass.

'We are still investigating.'

'Bloody nonsense!' Nutt pushed back his chair and rose to his feet. 'Trying to pull the wool over our eyes. You have nothing. These photographs prove bugger all. He's bad through and through, right from the cradle. He and his whoring sister.'

'Aye, hang him and be done with it,' one of the magistrates broke in.

'We'll be doing the city a favour,' said another.

'Gentlemen.' Straker stood. 'Then we'll see what the people of York think. I have an appointment with the editor of *The Herald* today. I will be cooperating with an article revealing we have photographs. I will instruct posters to be printed. They can see the evidence for themselves. We will have copies of these photographs at the police station, the library and *The Herald* offices.'

Brass let some time pass before he spoke. He looked at his magistrates, feigning a consideration of their opinion. He gave a barely perceptible nod. 'Well in light of new leads, perhaps we can delay the execution pending further enquiries. I am minded to be benevolent. It Is the Christmas season after all. Provide me with a full account and proper evidence and I will consider the case.'

'Just let him go now. He's innocent.' Ada was on her feet too.

Brass fastened his gaze on her. 'Miss Fawkes we cannot afford to be impulsive. What if you are wrong? What if I have freed a killer? I could not live with the guilt my dear. I must think of others. You have five days to prove his innocence to my satisfaction or he hangs.'

Nutt looked round in surprise. 'That's Twelfth Night, the evening of your ball, are you sure?'

Brass smiled without warmth, 'Bob, nothing could be better for business.'

It was early afternoon. Straker felt restless, tetchy and his arm throbbed. The shouting and singing in the cells upstairs sounded even louder than usual. He lit a cigarette and reflected on the Mansion House meeting.

Damn it, it was barbaric, an execution should be the last resort of a civilised country, or better still, done away with. His mind drifted back. There was a case early in his career which first made him doubt. He was young then, a nervous witness at a murder trial. The accused, a woman of barely eighteen, had stabbed her husband with a kitchen knife. The evidence was given. The dead man, a habitual drunk had struck their two-year-old daughter and the young woman had tried to protect her child. As the judge placed his black cap over his grey wig, the girl had sobbed, clutching the edge of the dock and cried out for her mother.

It still haunted him. Surely we should be better than that?

He was brought back to the moment by a brief knock on the door, followed by Gage and Bevers.

'Have we got the post-mortem results from Dr Scull in yet?' Straker asked.

'Nay sir,' said Gage.

'For God's sake. Why not?'

'No time to pick them up. We had orders to go out on patrol,' said Bevers.

'Orders from whom? We are supposed to be investigating a multiple killer?'

'Chief Constable Nutt sir. Twas New Year's Eve last night or have you forgotten? A big night for trouble here,' Bevers replied.

'Aye, tis the lasses. No stopping 'em. Gangs of 'em necking port and lemon like there's no tomorrow, tipping ower, the streets awash with vomit and worse. All hell breaks loose well before the bells strike midnight.'

'It was bloody dangerous. They turned into hoydens. Gage barely made it back alive, his height's like a challenge to 'em. They swarmed on him, begging him for kisses, tore his tunic, grabbed his bollocks, he was in a right state.'

Gage nodded. 'It's true sir. I'm like a magnet for 'em.'

'We had orders to round 'em up, boost crime figures. Aye, if we hit yon target, we get a bonus, goes towards our staff day out in August, at the races.'

'It's heaving in the cells,' said Gage.

'Damn it, I'll go and see Dr Scull myself now.'

CHAPTER THIRTY-SEVEN

◊

Thursday teatime at York Lunatic Asylum, and the noise of cups and cutlery clattering on china was at a height. Dr Scull was making a round of the busy tables. He spoke kindly to a patient here and there, wishing them a Happy New Year.

'What time is my son collecting me?' asked an old woman with a feather in her hair. 'Soon Lady Edith,' boomed Dr Scull, although she asked the same question every day. 'Enjoy your teacake.'

A white-coated orderly caught Scull's attention and informed him of Straker's presence. He strode off into the entrance hall, surprised to see the detective studying the art on the walls. 'Detective Inspector Straker. I see you appreciate my collection. But you catch me on my rounds. I always like to be seen at mealtimes, it's good for the patients' morale.'

Dr Scull briskly led the way along a corridor. He opened a wide door, waving his visitor through, and gestured to the winged armchairs by the fire. 'Forgive me, if I seem a little hurried. I am pressed for time. I am dining with friends this evening.'

Scull sat back in a chair and crossed his legs. His immaculate black leather shoes gleamed in the firelight. Straker cast his gaze over them and the man opposite.

'Tea? Something stronger perhaps?'

'No thank you.'

'You are no doubt here for Miss Ward's post-mortem results. I have them ready. I sent a message over as soon as I finished writing them up this morning.'

'Everyone at the station was on other duties so it seemed easier to come myself in case I have questions.'

Scull got up, went to his desk, unlocked a small drawer with a brass key taken from his pocket and pulled out a file. 'Here. Let me give you a few moments to digest it. Cigar?'

'No thank you. I prefer cigarettes. I acquired the taste in Paris. Do you mind?'

'Please, go ahead.'

Straker fished out his silver case and lit a cigarette, scanning the document as he smoked. He suddenly stopped.

He looked across at Scull, surprise on his face.

'Amy's stomach was missing! Is that how she died?'

'It's inconclusive. Her killer could have done this after death. But it certainly accounts for the particular shape of the knife wounds.'

'What about Rose Fisher?'

'I have that autopsy here too.' He held up another folder. 'You should know that Rose's stomach was taken out as well.'

'Both girls! What the hell happened to them?'

'I don't know. I could not reach a conclusion as to the cause of death.'

'Why would someone remove the stomach? Have you come across such an act before? What's to be gained?'

'A bizarre trophy, it is not unknown or perhaps it mattered to the killer that our post-mortem analysis could not include the stomach or its contents.'

He stood up. 'I'm sorry. I cannot help you further. Please excuse me, I must compose some urgent letters before I go out.'

Straker strode swiftly back into the city passing under Bootham Bar, still digesting the grotesque detail of the removed stomachs. He could find his way easily around now, York was so small compared to London or Paris. The cold air had helped clear his head, he thought, as he walked into the George Inn. It was time to extract a promise from Rufus Valentine.

Chapter Thirty-Eight

◊

Across the city, Ada Fawkes was back in the hushed atmosphere of the doctor's hallway. A young housemaid took her velvet cloak. A clock chimed four somewhere within the house, and a door to her left opened slowly. A faint smell of coal tar drifted from the surgery.

'Hello Ada my dear,' said Jane in her capable and efficient manner. Ada knew she liked to give off such an impression to patients, a reminder that women had the gravitas to practice medicine.

She had almost not returned for her appointment today. The Lord Mayor's refusal to free Tim Trent was uppermost in her mind. They had five days to save him. Ada had only come because there was a small chance Jane might have some useful information. Her friend had promised Ada she would look at the Refuge records.

And there was another pressing matter. She had brought a letter for Dr Auden. She needed his help. If Eliza's hastily scribbled warning was true, Isabella's daughter was in danger. She hoped William would know how to get Lucy out of the lunatic asylum.

'Come in, I'm just finishing up some work.' Ada followed Jane into the white-painted room, its large window screened with muslin cloth. William's private patients came here for consultations. Jane acted as nurse and chemist. Ada looked round at the leather couch, the table with its metal tray of gruesome-looking tools, more like torture instruments from the Tower than modern medical equipment. Ada had not seen this surgery before and she admired its orderliness, from its anatomical wall charts, its rows of glass bottles, to its state-of-the-art microscope.

'The microscope's made in York,' Jane told her, washing her hands with coal tar soap at a pot sink in the corner. 'I use it a lot for my research. Now I have done some reading around the effects of a traumatic experience.'

'Jane, that must wait. I came to ask you if you had discovered anything in the Refuge records. You mentioned you would check the reports and look at the discipline records for me. You thought Reverend Lindley might have chance to speak alone to the girls about their behaviour?'

'First let's have that New Year drink we promised ourselves while we talk.'

Ada followed her friend into the study across the hallway.

'This doesn't seem the most fitting time for a celebration, but here's to a better year to come,' said Jane pouring sherry into small glasses. She passed one to Ada and they each raised their glasses and took a sip.

'So did you have chance to check the record books at the Refuge?' Ada tried not to sound impatient.

'I asked William if he could bring it back. He's there today with the rest of the men's committee. It's the monthly visit. I'll look at it as soon as he's returned.'

'Thank you very much. William's agreed to help me with some information about an asylum near York. I have the details here. Would you mind giving him this letter?'

'Of course. But Ada I must tell you something,' Jane looked grave. 'I know you have little time, but it is important you know. I am uncertain if, after your injuries in Paris, you are able to carry a child to term.'

'Oh.'

'And I do know your age is against you. Are your bleeds regular?'

Ada was surprised at her friend's directness, but Jane's calm, matter-of-fact manner made this awkward conversation seem easier.

'No. I have none now.' Thankfully, she thought, it was difficult enough doing her job.

Ada looked across and saw that Jane was studying her, waiting for a reaction. In truth she felt numb. She did not know what to say or feel. There was too much going on in her mind. She would have to deal with this issue later.

'I wanted to tell you as soon as possible. We could talk again when you have more time. I will carry on looking into any research. There are books being sent to me.'

'Thank you Jane for your honesty.' Ada stood up and turned to leave. 'Oh I think I've left my bag in the surgery.'

'I'll get it for you,' said Jane turning to leave the room, catching an expression on Ada's face. Perhaps it was a flicker of sorrow. 'Are you alright?'

'Yes. I knew it really. It's not a surprise. I'm fine.'

Jane smiled kindly. 'I won't be long.'

Out of habit her eyes roamed along the shelves as she waited; all the latest medical volumes, *Gray's Anatomy*, Orfila's massively thick treatise on poisons, Darwin's *On the Origin of Species*. Nothing like her bookshelves which were rammed with ghostly mysteries, detective stories and romances. A wooden-framed photograph hung on the wall caught her attention. She couldn't stop herself casting a professional eye over the photographer's technique and composition. It was rather traditional in style, she observed. Five blank-faced young women in a row, Jane and her brother at each end. It must have been taken while they were In London. Her eyes moved over the black and white image, something fleeting registered, but it went quickly and was gone.

'I have your bag,' called Jane from the doorway. Ada rose, embraced her friend and stepped outside into the snow. She turned back and smiled.

'Thank you, Jane, for everything.'

Ada reached home some minutes later and went straight up to her room. Breathing hard, she leaned back against the closed door. Wrapping both arms over her stomach, she doubled over and slid to the floor. She was not surprised by what Jane had told her. She had instinctively known the damage that had been done the night of the attack. She closed her eyes and wept.

CHAPTER THIRTY-NINE

◊

The Seine Valley, France 1861

The September day was still early, not yet noon, but it was already warm in the pale-yellow field. A light breeze rustled the upright ears of corn, ripening under a vast clear blue sky. Ada stood at the edge waiting.

She watched Straker order the Normandy police to force back the oncoming village crowd. His colleagues, linking arms, flanked a large gaping hole in the ground. A human chain, cordoning the evidence. He looked across at her and nodded. It was time.

Ada walked the short distance. The scene of nightmares offered itself up to her. She forced her chest to breathe, short and shallow. Looking looked down into the open grave, she saw five children, infant bodies entwined on the freshly dug soil, the eldest no more than ten or so. The children had not been long in the grave, perhaps a few hours. They looked as if they were asleep.

For what seemed like ages, no one moved. Not the black-coated detectives in a line, the policemen behind her or the weeping villagers beyond them. They watched her reaction.

Ada stood quietly for a moment, head bowed, regaining control over her thoughts of the horrific acts that had been perpetrated. The smell came to her then, an earthy, iron stench of blood that she could almost taste. She raised her head. Straker who had been watching, waiting, came forward, carrying her equipment.

Ada prepared her camera and methodically began to photo-graph the bodies. She needed every angle. She must record the crime scene. The lengthy process, the time she took, riled the onlookers. She could hear shouts of 'sin' and 'blasphemy'. New sciences clashed with old religious beliefs that morning.

The power of Ada's photography was sensational. Her pic-tures exploded in Paris and created a wave of terrified excite-ment. Five unknown children stared out at the crowds from billboards and posters. Their deaths became real, immediate. Witnesses came forward. Their tip-offs created a trail and she followed it with her camera.

Until she got too close.

The most dangerous man in France came looking for Ada Fawkes.

Ada wiped her eyes, pulling herself to her feet and stood before her bedroom mirror. She looked at her reflection. She needed to speak out loud, as if freeing the words into the air could complete the circle of her grief, and bring some peace of mind.

'A movement in the air roused me from my work. I turned. In the doorway a man was watching me. Shadows fell across his face so I could not make out his features.

'He moved towards me. Then I recognised him. And the sight of his face struck at the pit of my stomach. He was hand-some but his dark eyes were the coldest I have ever seen. Maybe he was older than me, maybe younger, it was hard to tell for he wore clothes that belonged to another era. White cuffs at his wrists, an embroidered jacket and long dark hair tied back with ribbon.

'He reached my side and smiled down at me, such a cruel smile. I saw then the long knife he held for it caught the lamplight and glinted. He came closer so I could feel his warm breath on my skin and smell his musky perfume. Before I knew what was happening, he lifted the blade high. I shoved with all my strength at the table between us but I stumbled and he pinned my arms back to a wall. His body was swiftly upon me. I struggled, beating my hands on his chest. He could have killed me in that moment but he did not. I instinctively sensed his need for subjugation. The act of bringing me to submission must come first.

'I would die before I let that happen. "Who are you? What do you want of me?"

"I call myself Raguel and you have something you should not. Give it to me."

'I knew what that was then. I had captured his image with my camera at a crime scene, standing in a small crowd, where he must have returned to gloat. The man was so distinctive, it was only a matter of time before my photograph gave him away. He needed to destroy the evidence.

'I refused.

'I have never forgotten his words, "So be it. You have my face and so I will take yours."

'Then he dropped his hold of me and turned away. I was confused, watching him finger my row of chemical bottles, until he lifted out an amber phial. I could see the skull and cross bones on its label. Potassium cyanide. My head cleared then, suddenly and horribly aware of what he intended. As he pulled out the stopper, I turned to run. He moved swiftly to block my path and with his full force, pushed me backwards. I can remember to this day the amusement on his face as he slowly tipped the open bottle. I held up my arms to protect my eyes. There was a second as I felt its wetness soak my skin and then excruciating pain, scorching every nerve. It was like liquid fire dripping, burning through my fingers onto my collarbone and shoulder. My flesh puckered, bubbled and the agony went on and on until there was blissful nothing.

'The pain came back with a vengeance. I became aware of being dragged, half-carried. Someone was ripping my dress, holding me under a pump, drenching me in icy water until I thought I would drown.

Straker.'

Ada could bear no more of her thoughts and turned away from the mirror. One day, she vowed, one day she would bring Raguel to account for the murder of her unborn baby.

Chapter Forty

◊

Straker stared at crushed glass on the floor of Ada's studio. The negatives of the killer's footprints were smashed and broken. The evidence destroyed.

Glinting shards of collodion plates on the floor, ground into bits. Straker's boots crunched on them as he moved.

He turned to look at Ada. To him she looked even more vulnerable than yesterday. He brushed those thoughts away.

'Tell me what happened,' he demanded.

'Thomas heard a noise early this morning. He looked out of the window into the garden. There was a shadow by the studio door. He ran out. Whoever it was climbed over the garden wall. He saw a dark outline and it was gone. He'd jemmied the studio door open and did this . . .'

'Are the photographs of the footprint safe?' Straker asked.

'Yes, thank God.'

'You're sure?'

'Yes,' said Ada. 'They are in the house, still in my bag. I hadn't taken them out after our meeting with the magistrates.'

'That's some good news at least. We've rattled someone. Someone's scared of what we have. Seven people saw your photographs at our meeting yesterday; Brass, Nutt, the four other magistrates and Hugh Blake. Then I held a briefing at the station so every police officer knows as well.'

'Anyone could have talked,' said Ada.

Straker looked at her pale face. He thought of Paris. He desperately wanted to take her somewhere he could look after her, watch over her, keep her safe for ever. He bit his tongue.

'Ada, until I know what is going on, please do not go anywhere on your own. Can you stay here today?'

'I'm sorry,' she said. 'I must work. I have much to do in my studio. I need to go to Coney Street. I still have a living to earn. I cannot neglect that.'

'Well, I will walk with you.'

'You have so much to do. I haven't got my things together yet. I'm not ready. Besides I am hardly in danger during daylight in a busy city.'

Straker stopped abruptly on the garden path and spun round, glaring at her. 'Are you deliberately being stupid? Last night he came for the evidence. Another time, well easy enough to get rid of the photographer too. Experience must tell you that.'

'I don't need chaperoning by a man.'

'Damn you then. I don't have time to argue.'

She watched him stride away.

It was Thomas who was in her ear now.

'Would you please just admit you need help. I'm not saying that because this investigation is running you ragged, but because you need an assistant so you can concentrate on making this studio profitable. We have to think beyond this case. We have to think of the future.'

It was true. It was impossible to do a photoshoot and at the same time be downstairs dealing with people calling in to make appointments or purchase photographs. She had come to the same conclusion. She badly needed time to prepare for her exhibition in the spring.

Thomas perched on the window ledge watching her work. 'That young man at the lecture you gave last week, you said he was interested in art and photography?'

'Yes, but his father wants him to settle down and become a banker. There was something about him, reminded me of a few young men I've met who were definitely not the marrying types. He was rather nice, but troubled. Benjamin Barclay.'

She was almost certain he was from a Quaker family and she was unsure whether he could accept employment in a profession like hers. 'Do you think his religion would allow it?'

'No harm in asking is there? No one's going to be offended by being asked. I thought he looked the part for working here.'

Ada laughed. 'You mean he actually cared about his clothes and hair?'

'I just meant he might be the right one for you, artistic like. I'll find him and ask him to call by. Anyway, how are you getting on? I came to see if there was anything you want doing.'

'There's a bundle of photographs I need to get to the picture framers if you don't mind.'

Thomas smiled, as he stood up. 'Of course and I'll be back to walk you home this evening.' He saw her look. 'I'm not taking any chances Ada. And lock up after me.'

Ada was roused from her work by a loud knocking. She opened the door a little and with a blast of cold air Straker strode in. He did not bother with any pleasantries.

'A woman claims she was attacked by the Butcher of York, last night.'

Ada stared at him. 'Who, where, is she alright?'

'She's alive, that's all I know. Rufus Valentine has just tipped me off. She lives in a yard near the Refuge. Whoever she is she might have told the police before she went to the newspaper.'

Ada turned. 'I'll get my camera.'

'No.'

She looked back at him in astonishment. He was doing it again, telling her what to do. 'Why on earth not?'

'I'm told she lives in the worst place in York. If this story is true, I'll bring her here. I would like to show her some of our evidence, if I may take the photographs.'

'Where does she live?'

'A yard called Hag Worm's Nest.'

Inwardly Ada recoiled. Hag Worm's Nest was the most filthy, diseased place in the city. It was notorious for being the yard where cholera had incubated before devastating the city. She was a young girl then but she remembered it clearly, every tenant on the family estate had been forbidden to enter York's walls that year, on pain of dismissal. Today Hag Worm's Nest was still home to the unwanted, the sickest, the poorest; the last stop before the workhouse.

Ada took her bag, put it on the desk and opened it. Looking through, she pulled out a handful of portfolios and handed one over.

'Thank you.' He left without another word.

She was replacing the photographs when she saw her pictures of the cross necklaces. They should have been in the folder she had given him. He would need them.

She thought to catch him up and left the studio, pulling her coat on as she went. Out in the street, there was no sign of him. She hailed a cab.

Minutes later she saw his distinctive figure striding past Emperor's Wharf. She shouted up to the driver and he reined in his horse. Snowflakes whipped into her face as she stepped down and called out to him.

Straker spun round angrily. 'What the devil are you doing here?' His rage was like a force coming towards her. 'Why are you here?'

'I, I have the photographs of the necklaces. I hadn't put them in the folder I gave you.'

'You can't be here. It's too dangerous.'

'I can help you. We have so little time.'

'I know that so let me get on.'

'But she may be scared of talking to you.'

'You do understand how dangerous this is now. I don't want you here. If you want to relive what happened in Paris fine, but not on my watch.'

'But a woman like her might speak more easily to me than you. You might need me.'

'When Valentine tipped me off about this, he told me this was a no-go area. He said the brothel keepers pay protection money to keep out snoopers and that's why those two thugs set upon me last week. They were hired muscle guarding some-one's business interests. They'll not be too happy if they find out I'm asking questions again. I can just about take care of myself with my arm as it is, but not you as well.'

He looked up and down Skeldergate. 'Damn. There's never a cab when you need one.'

Straker assessed his options and made a quick decision. He gripped her arm. 'There's no choice now. Come on. Pull your scarf up around your face, don't say a word, keep close to me and keep your head down.'

Closer to the river now, they walked along the dingy street. He glanced down a narrow alley by the side of an old brick warehouse. It led to a plot of open ground and he could see the masts of sailing boats in the gloom beyond. They heard the sound of heavy footsteps, laughing, jeering male voices behind them. Straker looked over his shoulder and recognised their battered faces. They were the two men who had been talking to the mayor's secretary Hugh Blake on New Year's Day. He was certain now they were the thugs who had stabbed him. They mustn't be seen here.

There was nowhere to go but down the alley.

'Come on,' he whispered. He rattled a low wooden door into the derelict building. It was locked.

Straker acted swifly. He took Ada by her shoulders and pushed her roughly against the wall so the uneven brick jabbed hard into her spine. She cried out. He put his gloved hand over her mouth

'Keep quiet. Look at me.' His face came closer to hers.

Straker saw the surprise in Ada's eyes, but there was no time for explanations.

He moved his hand, slipping it around the back of her neck, pulling her head nearer. He pressed his mouth down on hers. He moved his mouth to her ear. 'Act like you're enjoying it, for God's sake,' he whispered, one hand pushing into her cloak, the other yanking her ribbons, tugging her hat until long tresses of foxy hair fell onto her shoulders. He pulled her waist roughly, dragging her into his hard lean body, enclosing her in a tight embrace. He crushed his mouth over hers again, hiding their faces.

'Give her one from me!' Lewd comments came from the passing men.

CLARE GRANT

Straker broke away, not looking round and said, 'Got lucky lads. Clear off, let me get on with it.'

There was coarse laughing as they walked on by.

Warm breath on her neck, soft dark hair brushed her cheek, he kissed her throat. She felt her skin tingle as her body was forced backwards by his chest pressing into hers. Her bones seemed to liquefy and with a queer limpness she clung to his shoulders to keep herself upright.

Then she kissed him back, harder.

'She's well up for it,' called one of the men as their footsteps tramped on along the street. The sounds receded.

The detective abruptly dropped his hands from her waist and pulled away. 'I am sorry for that.'

Her breathing was ragged. She struggled to straighten herself, brushing away her hair, hiding the colour spreading across her cheeks.

'It was all I could think of in the circumstances.' His voice was courteous but chilly. 'It was in the line of duty. I apologise.'

Ada, still breathing hard, was unsure if his coldness was worse than what he had done.

Later that evening as they ate a supper around the kitchen table, Ada told Thomas and Camille about finding Maria Bede in Hag Worm's Nest.

'She looked so old but she was probably younger than me. She was desperate, starving. She thought if she pretended the Butcher had attacked her, she would get money from the newspaper for the story. I think she wanted some attention, someone to talk to. She was lonely, no family left in the world.'

'Le pauvre femme.' Camille shook her head.

'So she's not part of this case?' Thomas asked.

'No. She made it all up. We gave her some money for a meal and that's all we could do. She'll most likely end up in the work-house.'

Ada sighed. 'There's too many like Maria, men, women and children living brutal lives. So many dying of poverty and dis-ease and those in power just ignore their desperation. I want to do something about it.'

Thomas looked at her. 'Surely, and I am simply pointing this out, you have enough to do already?'

'Yes, I do but when this is over – and I have been think-ing a good deal about this – I shall reveal how York really is through my photographs. Not the historic, genteel York that tourists love. The destitute, broken York no one wants to see. I will show the degradation of life here. Vermin-infested houses, starving children in rags, the destitute Irish migrants living by open cess pits, women forced into prostitution to feed their fam-ilies. My photographs will shock. They might even shame York Corporation enough to act.'

The other two were silent for a moment.

'I know. I know.' The words caught in Ada's throat. 'Damn it, we have a killer to catch first.'

Ada awoke from the same bad dreams, long before the grey light of dawn shone through her curtains. She turned over and stared at the ceiling. Now she was awake she could not stop her thoughts roaming back over her day. They all led back to one moment – that kiss. She burned with the memory. Why did she never learn? Why could she not become a logical person, not at the mercy of emotion. She turned her face and let the tears soak into the pillow until, exhausted, she fell asleep.

WEEK FOUR

2 – 6 JANUARY 1863

*'Still photographs are the most
powerful weapons in the world.'*
- Eddie Adams

Chapter Forty-One

◊

Saturday morning, Chapter House Street

The aroma of coffee was pleasantly filling the room. Ada was drinking her third cup, absorbed in reading the morning's newspaper and enjoying the warmth of the blazing drawing room fire. The sound of knocking disturbed the quiet, followed by a man's voice in the hallway.

'Just go in,' she heard Camille say. Doctor Auden came into the room breezily. His eyes were bright, his cheeks flushed and he smelled of the cold outdoor air.

'Good morning Ada. Jane gave me your note and I thought it best I came as soon as I could. I know you must have grave reasons for this concern about your friend's daughter Lucy.'

Ada smiled at him with gratitude. Here was one problem that was closer to a solution. 'I really appreciate your coming. Please have a chair.'

He sat close to the fire, warming his hands and listened without interrupting as Ada laid out for him Lucy's background, her concerns about Alec Lovelace and the warning, written on the sugar wrapper, by Eliza.

When she had finished, he said, 'In honesty I have heard nothing bad about Acomb House Asylum. However a surprise visit may be the best way, just to be sure. Why don't we travel over now?'

He explained his horse and dog cart, which he stabled at Marygate ready to use for visiting patients, was already outside. His practical manner was so calming, Ada couldn't help but think how much easier her life might be if she could grow to enjoy his company further.

'And don't worry Ada, asylums have changed now. We've come a long way since the lunacy scandals of four years ago. Those dreadful stories of perfectly sane people locked up by unscrupulous relatives and dare I say it, mercenary doctors, are from days of old now.'

'I'm glad to hear it,' said Ada.

'Yes, I'll make sure I bring you back,' William joked.

***

She had expected a building of gloomy appearance, barred windows and locked gates, and instead found Acomb House Retreat which was a pleasant-looking red brick house with huge windows and picturesque gardens.

It was in a hamlet once surrounded by vast oaks, so old it was mentioned in the *Domesday Book*. When the country gentleman who'd lived there died, the place had passed to Walter Leach a medical superintendent, who ran the establishment with his wife. Ada had learned this from the doctor on the three-mile ride from York to the asylum's wrought-iron gates. It was a sunny morning and despite everything, she had enjoyed the journey into the countryside and breathing in the crisp, winter air.

They left the pony and trap with a boy at the stable block and following his directions, walked round to the front door.

'Honestly, I'm expecting everything to be well with Lucy, Miss Fawkes, this is York 1863, not a sensation novel by Wilkie Collins.' William rapped on the door.

Nonetheless Leach, the asylum keeper, could not hide a look of shock when Dr Auden told him their business. He recovered himself, smoothed his grizzled hair and clasped his stubby hands together piously. 'I would sincerely like to help. However I cannot allow you to see Mrs Lovelace; the only visitors permitted are those who have consigned the patient to the asylum or the local inspecting magistrates.'

He shrugged with the whole of his small, flabby body. They had no choice but to leave.

'If we wait to come back with official permission, we'll not get to the truth,' Ada whispered as they walked away. 'If there is anything amiss, it will be covered up. Leach will go straight to Lucy's husband.'

'Rest assured Miss Fawkes. I'll not let this pass. This is very irregular. I'll send a note to the magistrates straightaway requesting permission to see her. They'll listen to me. I can sort this quickly.'

'I sense there's no time for that. I feel there's something wrong with all of this.'

She looked back at the house.

'Drive away from here, stop round the corner of the village green and I will skirt back and go to the servant's door. Wait for me. I'll do this on my own, you can't be seen to be breaking any ethical codes. I don't have such a reputation.'

William looked at her sharply. 'You are quite a woman Miss Fawkes, but then you always were. Jane used to describe you as fearless. I see it's true. I doubt I am the man to persuade you not to do this.'

'Good. I'll take a basket, I saw one in the stables then I can pretend I'm delivering something and lost my way. I'm wearing my plain work dress anyway.'

Minutes later Ada had slipped through the backdoor of the house. Inside all was quiet, only her beating heart sounded loud to her ears in the small hallway. She looked round, but could see no sign of where to go. The corridor ahead led to a closed door. She chose to make her way up the back staircase, winding stone steps leading high up into the house. Rather out of breath, Ada reached the second floor which opened into a gloomy corridor and more closed doors. She wondered who was behind them. Slowly she walked along. The windows were draped with muslin cloth, allowing in a little light but obscuring any glimpses from the outside world. She heard a key turning, a door opened and a white-capped maid backed out of a doorway into the corridor, struggling with a trailing bundle of dirty sheets in her arms. Experience had taught Ada that she could get away with much, if she simply brazened it out.

'Oh, miss could you help me. I'm lost. I've been sent from Mr Lovelace's home with some titbits for his wife Mrs Lucy Lovelace. I was her nurse there. I was directed up here and now I'm lost. Which room is she in please?'

The harassed maid looked at her with a startled expression. 'Oh you surprised me. The patients don't usually have visitors.'

'Mr Lovelace sent a note.' Sometimes she surprised herself with how easy dissembling came to her. 'After they read it, they sent me up here. Mr Lovelace was most particular that I should see how she is. He so misses her. He longs to have her home. Between you and me, he chases any glimmer of hope. Poor man.'

'Well, if you're sure miss. She's up at t'other end. That last door.' She turned away gladly and headed towards the back-stairs, trying to keep ahold of all the cumbersome linen.

Ada waited until she heard heavy feet descend the stone stairs before she made her way to the door, surprised, when it slowly pushed open.

She was cowering in the corner. The young woman, a white gown pulled over her bare feet and tangles in her dirty blonde hair, was completely still. Hands clutched to her chest, legs drawn close to her thin body, she looked at Ada with vacant eyes.

'Oh Lucy . . .' Ada ran out of words. She crossed the room, crouched down and put both arms around her. 'I'll be back Lucy. I will come and get you. I promise.'

She stood up and went to confront Leach.

He found her first. Walter Leach was already striding along the corridor, his face contorted with anger, his knuckles clenched white.

'What are you doing up here? Who are you? You have no business trespassing. Get out now.' Spittle sprayed from his mouth.

Ada stood still, keeping her gaze fastened on him. 'I am Ada Fawkes and I have been sent by Lucy's mother. What have you done to her? Why is she here, half-dressed, in this freezing room?'

'That young woman is bad and mad. She's here for her own good.' He breathed into her face so she could smell his break-fast. 'She's troublesome and disruptive.'

'And you, sir, are a cold, unfeeling barbarous monster.'

'You will find no complaints against me, madam. The com-missioners in Lunacy records will not show any history of mismanagement or cruelty. This is the accepted standard of treatment; a few days of isolation with cold showers and bread and water. It is all above board, I will record this in my casebook notes as part of her treatment. With asylum care, and the gentle prayers of our chaplain, she could fully recover her wits in six to eighteen months.'

'She's terrified, cold and clearly not been near any clean water for days. That young woman is skin and bone.'

'It's not my fault if she refuses to eat.' He almost spat out the words.

'Why doesn't her mother know where she is?'

'She is her husband's concern now. She belongs to him. He can do what he wants. And he wants her in here. This is all entirely legal. I suggest you leave now or I will send for the police.'

***

'I hope I haven't compromised you or caused any trouble,' Ada said after she had described to Dr Auden what she had seen.

'I wouldn't care if you had.' He flicked the reins of his horse. 'Let's return to York. I need to sort this with the magistrates as soon as possible. I need the signature of another doctor to get her released. My colleague Dr Scull will do that for me. We can have her moved to our hospital straightaway where she can be looked after properly until her mother can make arrangements.'

'Thank you William.' Ada felt hope replace her anger. Thank God she had some positive news for Isabella, at least she would be able to tell her Lucy was safe.

'You are welcome and I get the pleasure of helping you again.' William glanced sideways at her.

'I really appreciate it.'

'So how are your investigations faring? Your photographs must be so useful to Detective Inspector Straker.'

She found herself talking. William was easy to open up to. He seemed like the sort of man who would always help if he could.

He listened, keeping his eyes on the road, his capable hands gently urging on his mare. The cart wheels slid smoothly over the compacted snow as they talked. She told him about the studio break-in, the destruction of evidence and Thomas nearly catching the intruder.

He turned. 'Did Thomas see his face?'

'No, it was too dark, there was little moonlight.' Ada shivered and William leaned close to tuck the woollen travel rug tighter around her.

***

Later after a warming bowl of vegetable broth, Ada went down to her garden studio. She wanted to examine the photographs again, but it also got her out of the house.

The kitchen was enveloped in smells and noise. Camille was making preparations for salting hams and bacon. The blonde sisters Martha and Grace were helping, or more like arguing, from what Ada could hear. She knew that secretly Camille, who had only one son Pierre, loved the commotion and companionship of the girls.

Ada gathered all the photographs from her bag – which she now always kept in the house – and laid them out in rows on her long table.

And then she looked.

Really looked.

Good God, she must have been blind.

Lucy had been wearing a simple, indistinct asylum gown. In her photographs Amy and Rose seemed to be wearing identical ones. Plain white institutional gowns, covering their bodies like shrouds.

Chapter Forty-Two

◊

The low-lying clouds threatened even more snowfall though Straker barely noticed as he walked from the police station. The jostle and noise of Saturday's market went unmarked also as his mind recalled in detail today's edition of *The Herald*. True to his word, Valentine had published an account of the evidence casting doubt on Tim Trent's guilt. And why wouldn't he? The story was sensational.

'NOT GUILTY.'

'Butcher Suspect Is Innocent. I have proof,' says detective.

Saturday's *Herald* was flying off the newsstands like fresh muffins from the street hawkers' baskets.

Swirling icy flakes caught in his eyes, making them water, as he rounded the corner of St Leonard's Place. Does it ever stop snowing here? he wondered as he knocked hard on Chief Constable Nutt's door.

Nutt, reading *The Herald* avidly as Straker strode into his study, looked startled. He quickly put it to one side. 'What do you want?'

'I saw the two men who attacked me again yesterday. They were roaming about Skeldergate. I have also seen them talking to Hugh Blake. I've been warned off the brothels of York several times now. It makes me wonder who owns these houses in Stonebow Lane, Hag Worm's Nest and Grape Lane?'

Straker looked deliberately through the open door at the huge vestibule, the wide carpeted staircase, the glittering crystal chandelier. He had come to his own conclusions about who was running the brothels in York. 'You see I think those men who attacked me have nothing to do with the murders. They are hired thugs. They collect rents, extort protection money, make sure people keep their mouths shut.'

'I don't know what you are implying Straker, but I don't like it. We police stick together up here. We value loyalty.' Nutt's forehead glistened moistly. 'As it happens, my wife inherited a bit of property, so that's mine now and I let it to tenants. I don't know who they are. I am too occupied with police business to be involved so I leave everything to an agent.'

'And who would that be, Hugh Blake?'

The venomous look on Nutt's face told him his guess was correct.

'You see, I think if your wife inherited property so did her sister Mrs Lord Mayor. I think you and your brother-in-law rent it out and make a nice profit out of the brothel business. And there's a nice little cut for a few others, Sergeant Stone maybe . . . to turn a blind eye.'

'Now look here . . .' Chief Constable Nutt stopped. Mrs Nutt drifted into view down the stairs and stumbled down the bottom step. She didn't look well, her skin had broken into hives and her glazed eyes were failing to focus. She drifted across to the doorway and clutched the frame. Her voice was thin and weak. 'Bobby I need Dr Scull.' She stumbled off again.

They exchanged looks. Straker said nothing.

After a moment Nutt snapped. 'Opium is not against the law Straker.'

'No it isn't and indeed I am sorry for your wife,' Straker agreed. 'But living off immoral earnings is something else and worst of all chief constable is that you've been wasting my time, letting me think this neat little racket might be part of the murder investigation. That is unforgiveable.'

'What are you going to do about it Straker? This is my city,' Nutt blustered.

'I'm not interested in men's petty power games. Fine, it's your city, your mess and one day you will answer for it. I only want one thing from you. I want police officers at Chapter House Street. I want a watch on Miss Fawkes's house day and night. The killer has been in her studio, he's destroyed evidence. I believe she's in danger.'

'No chance, Mr Detective. My officers are too busy. It's market day here, if you hadn't noticed. The lads are needed out there, on the streets, locking up the country yokels out on the lash.'

'I'm not asking. Do it.' Straker rose and his broad figure seemed to take up every part of the room. 'And do it now!'

***

Back inside the police station, the working day had its usual air of apathy. Stone was supping a mug of tea at the front desk, reading a penny dreadful as Straker walked past him towards the office. The detective had a thought as he reached the door and turned.

'Stone. Bring me all the record and log books. I want to go over everything again.'

'Can't someone else do that?' Stone picked up a biscuit from a pile on a tin plate.

'Gage and Bevers are on protection duty from now on.'

Stone looked up, astonishment on his face. 'What? Those two? Protection?'

Straked nodded grimly. 'Yes as from now.'

Stone snorted.

The thought didn't fill Straker with confidence either.

***

In many ways Gage and Bevers made a good team. Friends since boyhood they had joined the York City Police together three and a half years ago. They were opposites, Gage, with hands like spades and legs like tree-trunks waded in with gusto to break up street brawls and best of all, cat fights. Bevers had a talent for ideas, analysis and thorough record keeping.

They complimented each other. Gage made the arrests, Bevers kept the tally.

That cold January evening on watch at Chapter House Street, they agreed how to work it, to make the best of things. One walked up and down the street, while the other had a pint in the Cross Keys at the end of College Street or, for a change, as the hours went by, the Royal Oak up the road towards Monk Bar.

So when hammering disturbed the household, neither of the policemen were watching Ada's front door. Bevers had half a pint of ale before him in a warm cosy taproom. Gage, many pints inside him was urinating against the side of the Minster.

Gage buttoned his flies and sauntered over to investigate. He didn't know what to make of the weeping blonde girl and a younger boy standing on the step at the open door.

'Martha! What is it?' Camille stepped forward to put her arm around her shoulders.

'It's our Grace.'

Gage loomed up, his enormous shoulders almost blocking the lamp light. 'Now then, what's going on 'ere?'

Martha glanced at him and clutched Camille's arm. 'Grace hasn't come back home. Ma's worried sick. Have you seen her?'

Camille shook her head. 'No I haven't. Martha, what has happened?'

'She's gone with 'im and it's my fault.'

CHAPTER FORTY-THREE

◊

They searched through the small hours of the night. Straker hauled everyone out; policemen, neighbours, friends. They combed frozen streets, alleys and doorways. Blurred figures in the snowy haze scoured the city's nooks and crannies. They roused sleepy night watchmen and cursing vagrants, but by early Sunday morning the hunt seemed hopeless.

As dark turned to grey morning light, the searchers warmed their frozen hands with coffee, hot chocolate and strong tea in Ada's kitchen. Camille kept pace with the demand, stoking the range to drive the heat as she boiled kettles of water and pans of milk.

Only an hour or so later, Ada and Straker were back outside, boots sinking deep in the soft layers of overnight snow. Ada struggled to keep pace with Straker's long legs, breathing hard, but she would not ask him to slow down. They remained silent, both lost in dark thoughts until they reached a modest red brick two-story house on St Andrewgate, close to the old church of the same name.

'This is it.' She took a deep breath and banged the black wrought iron door knocker, wishing this wasn't happening.

'Yes, can I help?' An elderly bespectacled woman squinted and held the door firmly half open. Straker introduced them.

She blinked. 'A real detective, like in the penny pamphlets?'
He nodded.

'I'm the neighbour. They're in the parlour,' she stood back gawping.

They followed her into an over-warm, small front room. Christmas cards hung from string over the wood-grained mantlepiece. Around the edge on varying sized chairs, were ladies holding tea cups. One of them, an exhausted-looking woman in black, raised red-rimmed eyes hopefully as they walked in.

Ada crossed the room and knelt down beside her. 'Mrs Croft, I am so sorry. There's no news.'

Grace's mother seemed to crumple back in the chair.

'May we talk together, ask some questions?' Ada noticed the neighbours shift in their seats, as though to hear better.

'I don't know what I can tell you,' Mrs Croft dabbed her eyes with a large handkerchief. 'We were home and I went to bed about nine o'clock. It's so busy in the haberdashers at Christmas. I didn't know Grace had gone out until Martha woke me. I sent her and her brother to you for help. I didn't know who else to ask.'

'You did the right thing. Mrs Croft, where is Martha now? We must talk to her again.'

'Upstairs, she won't come down.'

'May we see her?'

'Go on up then Miss Fawkes, it's the first on the left.'

They climbed the stairs and knocked on the bedroom door. 'Martha, it's me Ada. Please can I come in?'

There was a faint noise which Ada decided to take as permission. She opened the door and saw a blonde head face down on a pillow. Martha turned over, her lashes and cheeks wet with tears.

'Martha, I'm here with Detective Inspector Straker, you met him at my party on Christmas Eve. He wants to ask you some questions.'

Martha opened her eyes wide and shook her head.

'No. I dursn't talk to no detective miss.' Ada nodded, it wasn't a surprise to her that an awkward fifteen-year-old girl should be too shy to talk to Straker.

'Well what if I ask you a few questions instead. How does that sound? Just you and me.'

'And he'll go?'

'Yes, if I ask him to.'

I'll speak to you then.' Martha's voice quivered. Ada looked over her shoulder at Straker to make sure he was leaving. She sat on the bed and touched Martha's hand.

'Tell me what happened.'

'It's all my fault.'

'Why Martha?'

'I can't tell you Miss Fawkes. It's a secret.'

She buried her face in the pillow again.

'Are you scared of something Martha? I can help. Martha please. Tell me what you know, it might help us find Grace. She may be in danger.'

The girl's body shuddered.

'I told her not to . . .' Martha whispered into the pillow. 'It all happened so fast.'

'Go on . . .'

'He promised to bring her a silver necklace. Grace told me he was coming last night to give it to her. She made me swear not to tell anyone. I didn't think she should meet him late, on her own and I told her so, but she said he was coming to the gate of our backyard, that was all. He would meet her there at ten o'clock. She was desperate to see him.'

Ada could imagine the excitement, the heart-quickening anticipation of a romantic tryst, an exchange of gifts, maybe a kiss. The thrill of such a secret when you are a young woman.

'I should have stopped her. I should have told our mother, but Grace was so excited she made me swear on our Father's memory not to tell a soul.'

'It's not your fault Martha. But you must tell me everything now. Your father, your mother, Grace would want you to talk, to tell me the truth. There's nothing to worry about in breaking this promise.'

Martha turned on her side to face the wall.

'Do you know who this man is?'

'He came to our shop.'

'Did you see him?'

'Never. I only know what Grace told me. She couldn't stop talking about him.'

'When was this?'

'Not long since, maybe ten or eleven days ago. Around Christmas.'

'What did she tell you?'

'That night when we were talking in our room, Grace was giddy with the handsome gentleman who had come into the shop that afternoon. She couldn't stop talking about him, said he looked like a gentleman from one of our magazines.'

'Go on Martha. This is so important.'

'Well there was a bit of a queue and when it was his turn, he asked her if she minded that she had to work so hard and she said normally she wasn't on her own, but our mother and I had deliveries. He talked about the shop and asked if anyone else worked there. She said he asked her lots of questions.'

'What did he buy?'

'Handkerchiefs. He said he was going to come in again.'

'And did he?'

'Aye, the next day, when Grace was there alone.'

'What was he like, did she say?'

'A gentleman. Very polite and nice-mannered. He wanted her advice about a birthday gift for his mother.'

'Did he give his name?'

'Of course.'

'What?'

'Henry Temple.'

Ada sighed. The poor sisters had not recognised the real name of the Prime Minister Viscount Palmerston. 'Go on Martha.'

'He came in again, the day after and the next. He asked if he could meet her and they walked out together on her afternoon off. He wanted it to be their secret, he said, while they got to know each other.'

Martha sat up, untidy blonde hair spilling down her shoulders. She pushed it out of her face.

'He gave her a letter too. I never saw it, but I know the hiding place. She thought I didn't, but I did.'

Martha swung her legs over the edge of the bed and walked over to the small painted wardrobe in the corner. She reached up to a shelf for a hat box and lifted off the lid. Inside was a pretty straw bonnet with blue ribbons and tucked carefully under the band was a folded up note.

Ada took it and flattening out the paper read; *'My dear, Meet me by the gate. Ten o'clock tonight, Ever your affectionate friend, H.'*

How easy to bewitch an impressionable young lady, she thought. What sixteen-year-old would not be smitten by a charming man acting as if he had stepped out from the pages of the weekly magazine romances?

'Does it help Miss Fawkes?'

'It could Martha. May I take it?'

She looked baffled. 'What good will it do?'

'I can photograph this note so we have a copy. We can keep the real one safe as evidence but we can show people the photograph of his hand-writing. Someone might recognise it.'

'Oh, I see. You're like a detective Miss Fawkes. But women can't do that, can they?'

'Well, the police don't seem to be able to do it without us. Martha, do you know how your sister came by this note?'

'A boy delivered it to her in the shop about two days ago. He said the gentleman was most particular that he had to give it to the very pretty blonde young lady. She was bursting to tell me. Then she hid it so mother would not find it.'

'And what happened last night?'

'Grace was in a good mood all day. We helped Madame Defoe make her hams and some sausage-things. We got home and made tea. Afterwards we played cards by the fire while we had our cocoa. Then mother said it was getting late so we lit our lamps to take up. Grace was beside herself, doing her hair several times, changing her dress. When she finally heard our mother go into her room, she crept downstairs. She promised she wouldn't be long. She was just going to go into the back-yard, to the gate you see, no further.'

Martha stood up and went to the window, she looked down, as though it might all be a terrible mistake and she would see her sister there. Ada stayed silent.

'I lay on the bed to wait for her. I knew she would want to tell me everything. I didn't think she would be long. I closed my eyes and I, I drifted off. I was so tired and the bed was warm.'

She turned round and Ada saw the anguish in her ashen face.

'It's my fault you see. If I hadn't fallen asleep, I would have gone out to look for her. I would have told our mother. But I didn't realise until a few hours later that she hadn't come back in.'

Ada crossed the room and took Martha in her arms. The girl collapsed weeping against her shoulder.

'One more question, that's all. You've been very brave. Do you or Grace know anything of Bishophill Refuge?'

'No. It's a home for fallen women isn't it? Why, why would she have anything to do with that place?'

'I don't know if she has. It's just something we are looking at.'

Ada could feel tears, wet on her neck and held the girl tighter. 'Martha. I am going to find her. I swear I will bring her home.'

***

When they sat together later in the morning over a hot coffee pot, alone in the kitchen at Chapter House Street, Ada told the whole story to Straker.

She shook her head helplessly. 'We don't know it's him. It might be that Grace has simply eloped.'

418

'I wish that were true as much as you, but we both know it is not. A silver cross? A false name? No. I know this is him. I feel it, call it instinct, whatever.'

'Well then the pattern has changed. Grace has nothing to do with the Refuge. She's not an orphan, she has a family, people who care for her, loved ones who will come looking for her.' Ada rubbed her forehead. 'But why her? And why take this risk by changing his method?'

'What do the victims from the Refuge have in common with Grace? You're a woman Ada, how does he snare them?'

She thought a minute. 'Oh of course it's obvious really. Love. It's as simple as that. That's the link between Grace and the other girls.'

'I'm listening.' Straker poured her more coffee.

'Grace believed he was her suitor, that he cared for her and would take her away from her ordinary life. Young women yearn for kindness, and affection. It is irrelevant whether they are raised in the streets or a palace. It is the oldest of all needs, like food, warmth and shelter. That is how he catches them.'

She rose and paced the kitchen floor as she thought out loud. 'But why Grace?'

Straker looked at her sharply, a light in his eyes. 'He's taunting us. Baiting us. I think he knows of Grace's connection to you. Think. Who would be aware that Grace is known to you and that you are fond of her?'

'Lots of people know. Our neighbours, friends who come to this house.'

'Too many. So why then? Put yourself in his mind.'

Ada stood and walked to the window, thinking out loud. 'You practice with the girls no one notices, the ones you easily pick up, the street walkers. You get away with it. The hunger grows. Everyone is speaking of you. But you want more, no one knows how clever you really are, so you raise the stakes again. You know everyone will pay even more attention if you kill a respectable girl, the public outrage will be greater if you target an 'innocent' girl. And you show your superiority, your contempt for the law by catching a girl for whom we have affection.'

Straker put down his cup and looked at her thoughtfully. 'One name is on my mind. Dr Scull. He regularly visits the Refuge, Emily Eden worked at the hospital laundry. He has many rooms at the asylum.'

'The asylum! The gown! Oh God, I haven't even told you yet.' She gripped the back of a chair. Ada took a deep breath and revealed the whole story about Isabella Fox and Lucy, not meeting his eyes. He listened and watched her, his face growing grimmer. When she explained, though not the whole truth, how she had come to meet Isabella at the sanatorium in Malvern, he stared at her, in shock.

His voice dropped low as if to control a deep anger. 'Why? Why didn't you tell me you needed help. How could you not tell me you needed treatment at such a clinic? I would . . .'

Straker gathered himself. That was the past, this was now. It would have to wait.

'You should have told me about Lucy.'

'I didn't because you would have tried to stop me.'

'And Lucy's white gown is definitely the same as the ones Rose and Amy were wearing? And the other young women Emily and Annie, well we saw for ourselves that they were buried in white dresses of some kind.'

'Yes.'

'If they are standard issue gowns for medical institutions, there may be a thread drawing us closer towards Dr Scull at York Lunatic Asylum.'

Ada shook her head.

'I am still not so sure. Grace told her sister her friend was handsome. You have to think that this is a sixteen-year-old girl's impression. Remember he must be personable enough to appeal to a young woman. I cannot see Dr Scull being so to Grace. He is too old.'

'He's barely even fifty, he's not that old.'

She shrugged. 'Exactly. Through the eyes of a young woman, he's ancient. But Reverend Turner, he's the sensitive sort of man a young woman may feel they could trust. There is opportunity through the Bible classes and what's more Alice Trent told us during her stay there that the girls squabbled over his affections. He's late-twenties and pleasant looking.'

'Mmm maybe you have something there.' Straker leaned back in the chair. 'He's chaplain at York Lunatic Asylum. He would have access to the gowns. But why would he want them?'

'If he kept these women somewhere, he might have wanted night gowns for them. It would look strange if an unmarried vicar went into a shop and asked to buy five night-dresses so he took them. We have wondered before if the killer may show consideration towards the young women because he places their bodies so carefully in death. Maybe he provides night attire for their comfort wherever he is keeping them.'

Straker rubbed his jaw. 'Turner knew all the Refuge victims. But where would Grace have met him?'

Ada thought a moment. 'Oh God, at my Christmas Eve party! Grace was serving the food and drinks. She was talking to everyone.'

He pushed his chair back and stood. 'I'm going to see him now. If the pattern is the same there are only a few days to find Grace before she dies.'

'But a clergyman, a murderer?'

Straker picked up his overcoat. 'There's no more time to think it over. We can't put anyone above suspicion. It's been a long night. You rest. You don't need to come.'

She looked at him coolly. 'Fate has thrown us together for one last investigation so let us finish it together. And this is the only lead we have.'

***

Outside the sun had long given up on the dreary winter Sunday and disappeared behind heavy cloud. In the streets and snickets more flurries of snow made the last few stragglers huddle into their coats and hurry home to find a warm fireplace.

Stamping icy clods from their boots, Ada and Straker passed through the centuries-old porch of St Martin-Cum-Gregory and entered the medieval nave. At first glance the church seemed empty but ahead on the altar, the white candles of the advent wreath were still alight after morning worship, flickering in a draught.

Behind them, they heard the sound of irregular footsteps on stone. They turned and saw an open door into a vestry and, with his arms full of small, black-bound volumes, a wispy-haired man limping along the north aisle. 'Good day, may I help you? Are you here to visit our church?'

Straker shook his head. 'We are looking for Reverend Turner.'

'Let me just put down these hymn books first, they're heavy. I am preparing for this evening's service.' He laid them down on a wooden pew.

'There, that's better. The reverend's away back to the vicarage. He'll be having his lunch. He won't want to be disturbed at home. He likes to eat on his own.'

'Where's the vicarage?'

'He won't like it.'

Straker raised his eyebrows and waited.

'Take that path to the side of the porch door and follow it to the gate in the wall. His house is beyond there.'

Out in the graveyard, Ada and Straker exchanged looks. Were they about to confront the killer?

***

'The Reverend is eating lunch. You can't disturb him.' The housekeeper, who looked far too young for such a position, held her own, politely determined in her refusal to let them pass over the threshold.

Straker's patience was wearing thin. 'A young woman is missing. We are extremely concerned for her safety. We need to talk to Reverend Turner.'

Her long-lashed eyes widened, her expression changed as though her strictness was all a show. 'Oh, that's dreadful. I will see if he can talk to you. Come in.'

They brushed the snow from their coats and stamped their feet before they stepped inside. The house smelled of roasting meat.

She showed them where to hang coats and hats and took them through into a panelled dining room where a fire blazed in the hearth. Jacob Turner rose from a carved wooden chair at the end of a table as they entered. Ada noticed there were two places set.

'D . . . D . . . Detective Inspector Straker and Miss Fawkes. This is a surprise. Please sit down.'

Ada kept her gaze fastened on him as he gestured to them to join him. Turner's white shirt sleeves were rolled up and he had removed his collar though his black cleric's waistcoat was neatly buttoned. Ada tried to appraise him with different eyes, the eyes of an impressionable young woman who believed a man could solve all her troubles. Ada would have to use her imagination.

Yes, he was pleasant-looking, rather shy, his complexion well-scrubbed and he was charmingly self-effacing. His slight stutter, his soft West Country accent was a voice that encouraged confidences and confessions.

'I was just about to have my lunch please do join me?' Turner glanced across at the young woman framed in the doorway. Ada caught the look between them, a raise of a curved eyebrow, a glance at the second place setting, an unspoken question in the blue eyes. She also noticed that the cut of her dove grey dress, though plain enough, could not hide a comely figure.

'No thank you. A cup of tea would be very nice though,' Straker smiled at her as she turned and left.

Reverend Turner sat down again. 'How may I help?'

'We have some questions about a missing girl.'

'How does that concern me? Do I know her?'

'Yes, we believe so. It is Grace Croft. You remember her? A young, blonde woman, less than twenty, she was serving drinks with her sister on Christmas Eve at Miss Fawkes's party.'

'I'm not sure. I wasn't there for long.' He shrugged casually, but his hands gripped the arms of his chair.

Straker nodded at Ada who handed Turner a photograph of Amy. The vicar took it and stared, his mouth slightly open. Turner held the image closer, turning it this way and that and finally let out a low whistle.

Straker watching him closely allowed a moment to pass as Turner absorbed the shock of the picture. 'Have you seen such a gown before?'

'I am unmarried sir. In general I have no familiarity with women's items. Though I visit the sick in hospital and it may be they are dressed in this sort of plain attire. But what's this to do with a missing girl?'

Straker ignored his question. 'We just need to talk to you. I am sure you don't have a problem with that.'

'Of course. I'll do my best to answer.'

'Have you seen this before?' Ada passed Turner another photograph.

'Yes, yes I have, it's a common enough necklace. I'm chaplain for the Refuge, as you know. I take their Bible classes and our committee ladies buy these crosses for our girls. They are little gifts, a reminder for those who leave the Refuge to begin a new life of service, to be grateful to God.'

'Have you ever bought one?'

'No, it's the committee who purchases them. The ladies then have a little presentation.' Turner's voice was dismissive, but his knuckles whitened.

Straker leaned forward, keeping his gaze locked on Turner's face, and spoke slowly. 'The young women who died, Annie, Emily, Rose and Amy lived at the Refuge. We know you take it upon yourself to save so-called fallen girls and place them at this York Penitentiary. We talked to Alice Trent and she told us you arranged for her to be taken to the Refuge. She also told us the young ladies there vie for your attention, to the point they squabble over you, Reverend Turner.'

'Those poor girls. God rest their souls. But how can there be a connection with their deaths and the missing girl? The murderer is in jail and has confessed, has he not? Young Tim Trent. A simple lad but I suppose you just don't know what's going on in a mind like his. Only God sees all. Oh, but of course, I read the article in *The Herald* yesterday. You think he's innocent detective? So you think the killer is still at large?'

Straker pressed on. 'You regularly visit the brothels in Stonebow Lane. You have a calling for visiting such places Reverend Turner?'

The door opened with a clatter of tea cups in saucers.

'Ah. Thank you Rebecca.' The housekeeper set them on the table and left.

'She does well. She came with me when I moved here from Bristol.'

'There's just two of you here?' asked Ada.

Turner's face reddened slightly. He cleared his throat. 'Yes, I have simple needs. I am a single gentleman. I only need one servant.'

He stood, picked up the teapot and poured out two cups of tea and passed them across. 'Help yourself to milk and sug . . .'

Straker's voice cut through. 'Will you answer the question please Reverend?'

'Of course detective. It's true I make visits to fallen women, but it's not what you might think. And it's nothing to do with these terrible murders. I do God's work here in York. I enter into conversations with street-walkers to reclaim them. But more harm than good comes from talking in the public thoroughfares, especially after dusk, so I visit them at houses of ill repute. You see the main reason women take to the street is drink. They form a habit of intemperance and subsequently resort to prostitution in order to procure the means of satiating their desires for stimulating liquors.'

Ada couldn't stop herself. 'Nothing to do with poverty, or starvation then?'

The clergyman turned to the detective. 'You know how it is? You are a man, you've seen what the female sex are like after too much alcohol. I know how this must seem, but I'm only interested in the salvation and redemption of these poor heathen women. You see I am trying to right a great wrong.'

Turner paused.

'Go on,' Straker urged.

'The church in York has old links with houses of ill repute, it goes way back, centuries, and indeed the church still owns some of the brothel leases and sub-lets these properties. These properties are not recorded as houses of ill fame and their occupants are never brought before magistrates, so it continues to this day. I do what I can to atone. I answer to God to save these souls. I persuade the girls to seek salvation at the Refuge, away from the pits of harlotry. It is possible for fallen women to redeem themselves. I am aware that what I am doing may create an impression that might lead you to conclusions. I dread how this will seem. I hope . . .'

Straker cut him short. 'And Alice Trent. What do you know of her? She came to the Refuge because of you?'

'Yes, but I could not save her. She is not one of my successes. Her brother Tim, I was able to help him get employment in Marygate. He's good with horses, but not all there. A mental disorder.'

'So it would be easy enough for someone to coerce him into a confession. Suggest he is somehow complicit, so much so that he starts to believe he is guilty? Reverend may I see the parish entries?'

Turner looked at him in surprise. 'The register is in my study.'

The Reverend showed them through. Every wall was lined with shelves. Books and ledgers displayed in order of height gave an impression of a serious, fastidious young man. At his large desk, by the window, he laid hands on a large, leather-bound parish register. Turning it round, he opened the pages and pushed it towards them. They looked down the neat columns of births and deaths.

'Is this your writing Reverend?' Straker's eyes were like hard pewter.

'Yes.'

Ada placed another photograph by the black-ink writing. She heard Straker make a hissing sound through his teeth and he was shaking his head. She looked down. Turner's hand did not match the writing on Grace's secret note. She felt his disappointment, as palpable as an icy blast of swirling snow.

Straker turned to Turner, who flinched slightly at his look. 'May we see your boot soles Reverend Turner?'

'Why on earth? What is this?'

'Do it now, or I will ask you to accompany me to the station.'

Reverend Turner sat down on a high-backed chair. 'This is most unusual.'

Straker compared Ada's photograph of the footprint in the snow they had found by Amy's body. Their measure confirmed the Reverend's feet were a different size.

Back outside on Micklegate, there was no sign of a cab. They started walking at a fast pace and it was only when they were well away from the vicarage, that Straker noticed Ada was struggling to keep up. He stopped. They stood for a moment looking over the wall of Ouse Bridge down onto the river below. The murky slate-grey of the water matched their despondent mood.

Straker groaned and briefly rubbed his face. 'Damn I thought we had him. It all seemed to fit but the evidence does not bear out our theory. He's hiding something though don't you think?'

Ada nodded. 'Yes, the pretty, young housekeeper. She is a little more to him than he would like people to know? Did you notice the Sunday lunch table set cosily for two. I wonder if she was one of the women he saved from the halls of hell.'

'Not as sanctimonious as he makes out then but if he is our killer his acting skills are impeccable. I fear we are no nearer finding Grace or the killer.'

The wind was whipping down the river. Ada shivered, rubbing her gloved hands together, Straker looked down at her.

'Come on let's keep moving. I think I will call on Edward Atkinson. I want to know where he went on Christmas night. Will you come?'

But Ada would not. She had felt a niggle at the back of her mind that something was eluding her. The feeling had grown stronger. She made up her mind. 'No, I must go home. I need to examine the photographs again.'

'But we've looked and looked. There's nothing more they can tell us.'

'I don't know what it is. There's something. I need to see them. I must look at them again. I have to go back.'

CHAPTER FORTY-FOUR

◊

I t was a long time coming to her.

Ada looked at the photographs over and over. She rear-ranged them in lines and reordered them in rows. She stared until her eyes watered, but she saw nothing, only the shadows of the dead.

She stood up, paced the studio floor. She stopped and came back to the table. She picked up a photograph and held it up to the light, turning it upside down and round.

Time has been severed at this moment. Everything that has gone before is contained here. What am I not seeing? she asked herself.

Ada was home alone. It was some hours since Thomas had left. He could ride like the wind, but it was more than three hours or so hard journey north into Ryedale to reach Mrs Berriman the jeweller's wife to probe her memory of the five necklaces. Camille was still out searching up and down streets with the Crofts' neighbours and friends asking everyone they met if they had seen Grace.

Ada picked up a photograph of the engraved silver cross and scrutinised it through her magnifying glass. She considered the evidence in front of her; the precise slicing out of the stomachs, the missing days inbetween the young women's disappearances and their bodies laid out in public, the white gowns. Did the answer lie at York Lunatic Asylum? It would be easy to hide someone there. Was she wrong about Dr Scull after all?

She made a decision. She gathered her photographs and put them into her leather bag. Straker would most likely still be talking to Edward Atkinson who had some explaining to do about his absence from home on Christmas night. She had left him some hours ago. He had nagged at her. 'Stay at home until I come. Lock the doors. Don't go out alone in the dark.'

She didn't listen to him. She made up her own mind.

The moon was high in the night sky as she left the empty house in Chapter House Street. The cold was biting, but she barely noticed as she walked.

***

In the yard, the beat of horse's hoofs muffled by snow, came to a stop. The horseman drew rein and turned into Chapter House Street. He leant forward in his saddle and knocked on the first door with his riding crop. No one answered. He wheeled his horse round and rode away.

CHAPTER FORTY-FIVE

◊

It was late by the time Straker reached Silver Street.

'Any update on the search?' Straker asked Bevers as he passed the front desk.

'No sir. The neighbours are still out looking. Gage is with them.'

'Thank you Bevers.' Straker hadn't expected any better news.

'Do you think Grace is still alive?'

'Let's hope so.'

In his office Straker lit a cigarette and looked at the old map of York tacked on the wall. Instead of focusing his mind, the rhythm of inhaling and exhaling as he examined the black lines of the streets, caused it to drift. His gaze turned to an inward place.

Have I lost my touch? Am I too old for this? Damn it, I'm letting everyone down, he thought.

He looked around the empty room, at the carriage clock ticking on the mantelpiece. There was so little time left. In less than 48 hours Tim Trent would hang. Hours, he only had hours to save an innocent man, to catch a killer, to keep his job.

Maybe Thomas would return before morning, with a name, a vital link – and all the pieces would fall into place but he had to do something now. He must find Atkinson. He had called round once already but the blasted man was missing from home.

'Another emergency at one of his properties,' Mrs Atkinson had explained wearily, holding her vast stomach.

He had just thrown his cigarette stub into the fire, when Bevers tapped on his door and stuck his head round the gap.

'Yes, what is it?' Straker was impatient to leave, but Bevers wasn't a bad lad. Besides, Straker saw there was an alertness about his face.

'Is there something you want to tell me?' Straker spoke kindly.

'I don't know if it's anything . . .'

Straker realised the young officer was uncomfortable, embarrassed about making a fool of himself and he turned back to the fire. From experience he knew people often found it easier to talk without making eye contact. To give him this opportunity, Straker picked up the poker and jabbed the coals.

'Well you might as well tell me anyway. You never know,' he said casually, his back to the room.

'I'm sorry sir, I know I shouldn't have been there . . .'

'Go on Bevers. Tell me what you saw. No harm in that.' Straker slowly replaced the poker on its iron stand.

'You see I was coming out of the Royal Oak, last night, you know when we were watching over Miss Fawkes's house. We took it in turns you see, Gage and me and it was cold and . . .'

Straker turned. 'It's fine lad. Tell me everything. And fast.'

By the time Bevers had finished Straker was running out into the dark street, his heart thumping hard in his chest.

Because he knew.

CHAPTER FORTY-SIX

◊

A da Fawkes found herself growing restless, as she stared into the orange coal embers. She had waited for half an hour already but she did not know what else to do and the housemaid had assured her Dr Auden was on his way home.

She had accepted a cup of cocoa and was sipping the warm chocolate, her hands wrapped around the white china listening to the minutes tick by on the brass mantle clock. Her mind churned over. She had a nagging sense that the responsibility for the tragedy unfolding lay with her alone. Her dull wit could not work out this killer's deadly game.

She placed her cup on the table next to her and rose from the chair. She began to pace the length of the floor, wrestling with her thoughts, trying to put them in logical order. She had worked with some of Europe's finest minds in forensic investigation. She was an expert in the science and art of photography. Why could she not figure this out?

From the moment she had been drawn into this horrifying case, she knew she was taking her biggest risk so far. She had changed. Once she had felt strong and confident. She had no doubts she could do her job well. Too much had happened to her since. Her mind felt damaged, it was full of fear and uncertainty. She had lost confidence and it was leading to mistakes.

435

Straker did not know her troubles when he had asked for her help because she had hidden her secret from him. She should have told him. But it was too late, it had gone too far and she feared it would end in the worst way. But whatever the outcome she knew she must risk all to catch this killer.

So this line of enquiry was surely worth a chance? Talking over the case with a medical brain, someone experienced in forensic medicine, who had studied the insane, might spark connections in her mind. Ada thought of William Auden's dedication, his razor-sharp intellect, his compassion. In her head she had a list of questions about the post-mortems, the causes of death, the science behind the mind of a killer. She hoped he could help her. William had talked to her of his disappointment when the new science of forensics had been discredited after the disastrous court cases a few years ago. This case could be a way back for him. Perhaps together they could delve into the heart and mind of this madman and come up with a profile of the type of man this killer must be.

And who knew when this was all over, he might prove to be the friend she would no doubt need. She thought of that conversation at Jane's birthday party, when he spoke of his commitment to help the poor and destitute. Perhaps they might work together one day.

The room held something of him, even though he was absent and to occupy herself she looked around. It was as pleasingly calm and ordered as she remembered from her last visit. A striking oil painting caught her eye. She thought it was by Etty a well-known local artist. So William was an art lover too, she was pleased to think so. Perhaps they would turn out to have much in common. It might help her move on. Her gaze roamed on to a smaller framed photograph beside the picture. It was the one she had noticed last time she was in this room, a line of five young women, Dr Auden and Jane at either end.

There was something haunting about the girls' unsmiling faces, dark staring eyes, features bleached out by the photographer's lighting. The image lingered in her thoughts after she had wandered away, so that she returned to it – and looked again.

She felt the hairs on the back of her neck prickle.

It's nothing, she said to herself but still she picked up a magnifying glass from the desk. She returned to the photograph and looked again through the lens. The enlarged image came into sharper focus so she could see the texture of the hair tied in ribbons, the lace detail on their best frocks. She looked again to be certain, her eyes widening – yes there they were, shining, catching the light, hung around each of those young necks, five engraved silver crosses.

She felt stunned with her own stupidity.

Why hadn't she seen it before?

William's face stared out from the frame. He seemed to be mocking her.

Why hadn't she made the connection? She had asked the question herself; what man might easily gain the trust of an impressionable young woman? With whom might a young woman craving romance fall in love? A doctor; a caring, kind, handsome one.

Dr William Auden.

She must get out of the house.

Fear caused Ada's heart to beat so fast she found it hard to breathe. Somehow she was at the door, her hand turning the knob when she heard the front door slam. The sound of a man's tred echoed on the hallway tiles. She looked to the window shutters secured tightly for the night. There was no way out of the room.

Swiftly she returned to the chair by the fire, straightening her skirts and her hair, trying to fix an expression of composure so that he could not read her face. He does not know I have seen the truth, he must not find out, she repeated in her head.

Ada waited, fidgeting, adjusting her pose. He was so long, that it tested every one of her nerves. She must be still. She must behave like nothing had happened. Grace's life – her own – might depend on it.

She felt her throat constrict, she swallowed.

She turned her head to listen for his steps and saw the handle turn. He stood in the doorway. Startled she began to make up a reason for her presence.

'Forgive my calling, I was passing the road end, I was impatient for news of my friend.'

'There is nothing to forgive,' Dr Auden said smiling. 'I understand your keenness to know how our enquiries about the asylum fare. Let us have some refreshment while we converse.'

He crossed to his desk and picked up a handbell. 'It's so cold out there. I am frozen after my calls. A hot drink would be welcome. Oh goodness, I forgot there's no one here. The household has the evening off. Cook will have left a cold supper on a tray.'

He set the bell back down. 'Perhaps a sherry then?'

At a small corner table, he selected a half-full decanter. 'Miss Fawkes?'

She shook her head, trying to smile naturally at him. To her horror, out of the corner of her eye, she saw that the photograph was askew.

With a slender-stemmed glass of sherry in his hand, William sat down in the chair opposite, his back to the lamplight. His face fell into shadow so she could not read his expression.

'I was going to call but here you are so you have saved me the trouble. And for that I thank you. God knows there is enough to keep me busy. My work at the hospital is endless.'

'I am sure it is.' Ada tried not to look at the photograph. Could she straighten it without him seeing?

'So I have been in touch with the commissioners in Lunacy and I am sure we will be able to get this sorted very quickly and get Lucy released. But technically she must be returned to her husband.'

'Thank you William. Once we know the outcome of your request, I will send word to her mother and make a plan. I appreciate your help.' Ada made a play of looking at the clock on the mantelpiece while standing up. The doctor rose to his feet and stood with his back to the door.

'I am sorry to have missed Jane. Is she back soon?' Ada was acutely aware of the silence in the rest of the house.

'I'm not sure. She went to take some medicine to one of my patients. She may well be there a while. You know how dedicated she is.' His mouth smiled but Ada saw that no warmth reached his eyes. She picked up her cloak aware that he had not moved and walked towards the door.

'Be sure to give my best wishes to Jane.'

She looked up into his face.

He was staring over her shoulder at the crooked photograph.

'Well, I must be going. I'm expected home, they are waiting to have supper with me. Good evening William.' Ada forced a smile.

He did not answer her and he did not move. She sensed an iciness in the air that had not been there before. She glanced at his face again and the blue eyes that looked back at her were like flint.

'Excuse me a minute.' He stepped forward. He went around her and straightened the photograph. 'That's better. I cannot bear things out of order. Do you feel the same Ada?'

'That depends but it pleases me too to see beautifully-arranged art or flowers.' She forced herself to speak normally though to her ears she sounded false.

'I admire you Ada. You embrace the new sciences, yet observe them through the eyes of an artist. You are of your time and beyond. You have an enquiring, modern mind, looking to the future, and I know, like me, you are prepared to make sacrifices for the greater good. We have much in common. You understand my curiosity, my work, my passion for change and improvement. I have always enjoyed our conversations very much. But we can talk more later. I must go and prepare.'

He walked to the door. He smiled at her and briefly looked like the man she had trusted.

'If you would be kind enough to wait here, I will not be long.'

He paused.

'Please don't scream Miss Fawkes or try anything unpleasant. I have a sick patient here and she needs complete peace and quiet. There is no one to hear you in any case. Now please excuse me. I must prepare the operating table.'

The doctor shut the door behind him and she heard the key turn in the lock.

His footsteps faded into the house. Swiftly Ada crossed to the window and unfastened the wooden shutters. She tried to push the lower sash upwards. It wouldn't move. Two large iron nails had been driven deep into the wood panelling, securing the window shut.

Ada snatched up the poker from the fireside and turned to the glass panes.

Too late. The door opened again. She gripped the metal rod in both hands.

Auden came towards her, smiling, watching her closely. She backed up to the window and he moved closer to trap her against the glass. She raised the poker and brought it down hard but he was too quick. He caught her upper arm, breaking the force of her blow as the poker made contact with the side of his face. A thin welt reddened over his cheekbone.

'Your anger stirs me, Ada Fawkes.'

He looked down into her eyes, gripping her arm harder still, his mouth close to her cheek. 'We could have been magnificent together, you and I. Companions in mind and body, such a meeting of equals.'

He twisted her arm behind her until she gasped with pain and dropped the poker.

'I don't want to hurt you like this.'

If she behaved meekly she calculated, she might stay alive long enough to work out how to escape. 'I know you don't William. I'm sure this is all a misunderstanding.'

'Come with me. I want you to know it all before the end. Let me show you everything. You will understand me then.'

He turned to the door and held it open for her. She passed into the hallway.

'This way.' He led her down a passageway and stopped before a locked door. He turned the large iron key and pushed it open. Her eyes made out a steep staircase descending into darkness.

'Go down. I will join you in a few moments.'

The door closed behind her. It felt colder and damper as she slowly took the steps one by one, touching her hand to the cold stone wall to steady herself. There was a faint glow of a lantern somewhere below. The staircase turned and she stepped down the last few treads.

At the bottom, in a large windowless room with lime washed walls, there was a bed. Outstretched on the bed was a woman whose face she could not see in the gloom. Her body was still. Her feet were bound with manacles that had been chained to the metal frame of the bed and prevented her from escaping. Ada struggled to draw in breath. Her heart beat too fast in her chest. Thoughts of the horrendous acts which might have been perpetrated here filled her head. Ada's courage almost failed her, though she forced herself to approach the body. The features became clear as did her long hair – as blonde as pale corn.

'Grace?'

Ada laid her hand on the covering and felt the warmth from the young woman's motionless body. She was alive at least.

Ada took a deep breath and looked further. On the other side of the room was an identical bed, empty, neatly made up with a pillow, sheets and a dark wool blanket. Manacles dangled from the bed head. A white gown was laid out upon the covering. Her eyes now accustomed to the dark saw a table towards the end of the room. Beside it was a smaller table covered with a linen cloth and tools; knives, scalpels, forceps, scissors, tubes laid out neatly in a line. This was a surgeon's operating table.

Ada's shock made her limbs weaken. She grabbed the metal frame of Grace's bed, leaning over to get more breath into her tight chest. Her lungs felt like they had no air. An acrid stench caught her nostrils and looking down she saw a pail of vomit on the stone floor beside the bed. She looked back at Grace. The girl had moved, shifting her covers. Now Ada saw she was wearing a plain simple pale gown just like the one worn by all the girls in death. Annie, Emily, Rose, Amy.

Ada straightened herself and breathed in. Her head was spinning. She gripped the bed. Her movement jolted the frame. Grace moaned and opened her eyes. Her pupils were dilated. Her breathing became more rapid. Spittle ran down her chin. Grace's body suddenly convulsed. Her limbs were rigid. Her mouth opened in a silent scream. And then Ada saw that her tongue was raw and swollen. Grace's shoulders heaved. She retched. Ada took her shoulders and held her over the pail. A trickle of black bile came up, her stomach was voided. Grace collapsed back on the bed, her breath shallow, but calmer. Her eyes fluttered shut.

'Grace.' She did not know if she could hear her. 'Grace, stay with me. I am here. I will help you.'

She took up the lantern to look more closely round the room. Perhaps she could use something to force the door, or unpick the lock. She stopped before a glass-fronted cabinet at the end of the room and looked inside. The fluted actinic green jars told her what was happening to Grace. Red labels revealed the poisons within; aconite, digitalis, henbane, strychnine. She reached for a round glass bottle. Half-full. She pulled out the stopper and she smelt the bitterness of the liquid. She closed her eyes and imagined its wetness trickling down a tube, a tongue, a throat, and the poison making its way into the stomach, burning.

When she heard a key turning in a lock, she almost dropped the bottle. Footsteps began to descend. She stayed motionless, watching with every sense alert. He slowly approached. He looked different now his eyes were emotionless and his cold gaze travelled from her to the bottle of poison in her hand.

'Miss Fawkes. I see you are making yourself acquainted with my little hospital. I am pleased to finally show you the medical research I am conducting.'

Ada gripped the bottle and threw the liquid towards his face. Auden side-stepped. She lobbed the whole bottle, mostly empty. It glanced off his shoulder and hit the floor; glass smashing on stone, poison seeping harmlessly into the cracks between the flags.

'You are making a habit of this Miss Fawkes.'

He grabbed her wrist tight and pulled her towards him. He twisted her arm up behind her back until she gasped with pain and swiftly thrust her down onto the empty bed. She struggled, trying to throw him off, and he lost his balance and awkwardly fell on top of her, trapping her body. Their eyes met briefly. She tried to escape. He put his hand on her face and pushed her back. Wrenching her arms above her head and pinning them down, he knelt over her body. He was so close to her, she was breathing in his breath; the warmth, the traces of sherry, she could feel his thighs pressing down on hers. He encircled each wrist in turn and forced them into the metal cuffs, clamping

444

them shut. He looked down at her, his breathing quickening. He moved as if to kiss her. She turned her head to the side.

A groan from the other bed checked him. He pulled away and stood up, smoothing down his hair. The doctor went across to Grace's bed and stroked her forehead. He looked down at her.

'It will soon be over my dear,' he said softly.

He crossed to the cabinet and looked round at Ada.

'You will find this interesting Miss Fawkes.' He selected a poison bottle and picked up a tube from the table.

'Don't!' Ada cried out. 'Let her go!'

He shook his head. 'This is science. I'm making advances in our knowledge of poisons. I will save lives.'

'You're a murderer.'

He shrugged. 'I'm sorry you see it that way. Miss Fawkes you should try and understand the work I do here.'

'I could never understand wilful murder.'

'At one time I thought, I hoped, you had the vision, the imagination, the desire to see how far science can take us. I believed we wanted the same future. But, alas, you are as dull and weak as everyone else.'

'Tell me then, explain everything to me, make me see,' urged Ada, hoping she could stall for time.

He came to the end of her bed. 'These girls are scientific experiments, the sacrifice of a few unwanted young women for the good of the rest of humanity. Do you know how many people die from poisoning every year? Hundreds: innocent men, women and children. Yet we have no chemical tests to prove these killings. Science is still lagging behind. We can prove death by arsenic but the other toxins? No. Anyone can get away with murder if they use the right poison. I am about to change all that. I am developing a test for vegetable poisons. People have killed using the ordinary plants we grow in our gardens. Digitalis, aconite, belladonna, hemlock, henbane, ricin, strychnine. Do you remember the Rugeley Poisoner Dr William Palmer? He nearly got away with those strychnine murders. But that is soon to end. I am on the cusp of a breakthrough. I will bring science into the 19th century. My experiments with Grace will give me the final results I need. I will be able to prove poisoning to the stupidest of juries. I will bring killers to justice. I will be redeemed. When I win the Orfila Prize and I surely must, my name will be lauded throughout the world. I thought you were clever Ada. But you do not see my vision.'

He gazed down at her, a brief sadness in his eyes and then it was gone. His expression changed, she saw it harden. He was lost.

There was no other way now.

'Leave Grace be. Let me take her place in your tests.'

'As you wish, Miss Fawkes.'

He turned away from her. He unlocked a drawer of the medicine cabinet and took out a mahogany box. He turned a small brass key in the lock and lifted the lid. He inspected his gleaming surgical tools: a bone saw, two scalpels with ebony handles, rib forceps, a mallet. He selected a small knife, ran a fingertip along the sharpened blade and then placed it in a pewter bowl on the table. Ada prayed silently, quelling a scream she felt bubbling up inside her.

The doctor continued his preparations, soaping his hands at a small pot sink in the corner. She lay helpless, sweating, dull with fear. He glanced at her to check she was watching him.

'You will be interested in this part Miss Fawkes.' He reached inside the glass cabinet. 'This is digitalis, grown from foxgloves in our own garden. It's a very popular poison. In large doses it stops the heart. And yet it's undetectable in all chemical tests, at least until now.'

The terrors of the past burst into the present. Her lungs withheld her breath. Ada's mind was in Paris, images flashed, engulfed her, enclosed her and she saw another room, another man, another liquid. The burning, the smell, the pain were as if she was there again. Her skin felt the memories and the veins of white puckered scars tightened and itched.

Auden watching Ada struggle saw her bare shoulders where her dress had pulled away. 'Have your scars healed well?'

'Yes.'

'I look forward to examining them closer.'

His words hung in the air. Dear God, he meant on that table, an autopsy. Her naked body slit open for his peering, his prodding. Her skin and muscle peeled apart. But first she had to die. Ada watched him pour liquid into a medicine vial. This he picked up and held it out as he came towards her.

'It's time.'

'No.'

'You must drink Miss Fawkes.'

His grip around her jaw was like a vice. She tried to twist her head and clamp her mouth shut. He squeezed her cheeks so he could force the glass past her closed lips. She struggled, straining her head.

They both heard it; the door at the top of the stairs opening. The doctor paused, startled, then redoubled his efforts to force down the poison. She pressed her lips tighter until they blanched white. A voice called down. Ada tugged at the mana-cles. Footsteps descended quickly.

Jane stood in the room, her body rigid in shock.

'William! What in God's name?'

He leapt back.

'Give me that. You must stop.' She stepped forward and took the poison out of her brother's unresisting hand. For a second, time seemed not to move, as they looked at each other. Then something broke. A sudden movement and the doctor bolted for the stairs. He was gone.

'Oh Jane.' Relief flooded Ada's shaking body.

'Don't speak for now Ada. Everything will be fine.' Jane moved swiftly to unlock the manacles. 'Let's get you out of here, we can go upstairs and talk properly.'

Ada's arms hurt where the irons had dug into her wrists and she rubbed them as she rose unsteadily to her feet. She went to Grace. She was still unconscious. 'We must do some-thing for her. I think she's dying.'

Jane came to the bedside and gently prised open Grace's closed eyelids. She listened to the ragged breath and felt her pulse.

'It's faint, but steady. She will recover Ada.' Jane stroked Grace's blonde hair. 'Let us leave her sleeping here. We'll go upstairs and summon help.'

'What if he comes back?'

'I know he will not.'

'Oh Jane, I can't believe it.'

'I have some explaining to do, but you are safe now.'

Chapter Forty-Seven

◊

When they reached the hallway they saw the front door ajar. A lamp on a side table threw light onto the snow-covered path and the open front gate.

'He's gone Ada. He's left the house.' She heard Jane speak softly. 'Come Ada into the warmth, you have had a terrible shock.'

She felt Jane's arm comforting around her shoulders and allowed herself to be led into the front room, to a chair by the fire. Although the coals glowed with heat, Ada believed she could never be warm again.

'My dear. I am going to get you a hot drink. You look frozen.' Jane left the room.

Ada breathed in deeply, her head spinning. She could not believe what she had just seen. A man she had trusted, admired and even wondered if she could have grown to have feelings for, was a murdering madman.

She shuddered looking around at the orderly, calm room with its semblance of normality while below was a chamber of horrors? How could such she have been so naive and gullible?

And where was Straker when she needed him?

Anger stirred her. She must get word to him. She got to her feet and was almost at the door when Jane came in carrying a tray.

'Here my dear, I have made some cocoa for us both.' She saw Ada. 'What are you doing? You must rest. You've had a terrible shock.'

'Jane, I must go. I must warn Straker.'

'Don't worry. I have already sent a message. The police will arrive at any moment. Come, drink your cocoa whilst it's warm.'

Ada sat down again. She regained her thoughts then she looked her friend in the eye and asked what she must.

'Did you know?'

Ada saw Jane's hands clench tightly together.

'Are you afraid of him Jane? Has he forced you to this? Tell me what's going on.'

'William is searching for knowledge,' she said finally.

'What do you mean . . . Jane tell me?' There was something unfamiliar in her friend's eyes, it puzzled her.

Jane shook her head and stood up. 'Nothing is what it seems. You must rest here. I want to check the doors are locked. I want us to be safe.'

'You think he's coming back. Don't you? You think we are still in danger?'

'Don't worry. The police won't be long, I'm sure.' Jane gave her a ghost of a smile and left the room.

Ada took a small sip of the bitter, dark chocolate. She could feel it warming her.

Thank God, this nightmare was nearly over.

***

Ada started at the creak of the door, a rustle of skirts, a movement in the gloom.

'Jane?' Every nerve in her body was on edge. She realised she had briefly fallen asleep. She looked up and caught her friend's face as she moved into the lamplight. Something about her countenance had changed. She had never seen Jane like this before – her friend's eyes and, mouth, familiar but distorted somehow. There was a coldness in her expression. A chill ran through Ada's blood. For Ada knew then.

'They're not coming are they?'

'No one is coming Ada.'

'Jane, what is going on?'

Ada gripped the sides of her chair, tried to rise to her feet, but her legs buckled, her head spun. She fell back helplessly. It was as if her whole body was liquid. She stared at Jane in bafflement.

'Your cocoa Ada. Did you notice the bitterness? You will not leave here.'

'What have you done to me?'

'I can't let you go Ada. I'm afraid you know too much.'

'Jane?'

'You weren't supposed to find out Ada, no one was. A few more months and this would have been over. We would have claimed the prize. A few lives lost but the gain so great. I didn't want to drag you into this, but William lost his head when you came here tonight. He knew you had seen the truth.'

Ada felt so sleepy. She forced herself to concentrate. 'What have you given me Jane?'

'I'm sorry Ada. It's a sleeping draught.'

'Tell me why at least. Explain. You owe me that?'

'It's true, we have known each other so long, shared so much, two clever women trying to make their way in a man's world.'

Her voice so low and soft. 'You should have seen them Ada. They sat in lectures, rows of entitled, privileged oafs, sneering at my sex. They mocked me, told me women would never be doctors. I worked so hard to prove myself and when I outshone them on the hospital wards, they still objected to my presence. My humiliation was only matched by that which was heaped upon my brother after his forensic science had been discredited. We needed to prove ourselves. Show everyone we were the best.'

Through heavy drooping eyelids Ada stared at her friend.

Jane went on as though she needed to tell someone how she had started. 'You of all people must understand. William was so much smarter than them all; the police, the juries, the judges, but he was broken by their ridicule. The press, the public dismissing forensic science, belittling his work. They didn't understand. It was all in its infancy, it was about trial and error, keeping going. But he lost his position. Then the Orfila Prize was announced. Winning was a chance to prove ourselves. William would regain his reputation, I would prove that a woman was capable of scientific brilliance. It would allow me to become a doctor. We decided to solve the biggest medical challenge of our age. Do what no one else has been able to do. We would invent an infallible test for poisons made from plants. We would save lives, bring killers to justice.'

She said to Ada, almost pleadingly. 'You have to believe me, I didn't mean for it to go this far.'

Ada didn't answer. Her thoughts were drifting, retreating into her skull, to the edges of her mind. She must concentrate.

'I understand your dreams, how you must have felt Jane, but why did these young women have to die?'

'We started in London experimenting on stray dogs, giving them vegetable poisons, working on tests and trying to save them. We grew the plants in our garden and our glasshouse. We tasked ourselves with repeating our experiments on humans. William said we must be certain. Penniless, young women were the easiest to bring to our house; no one noticed or cared. Their joy at the simple gift of a silver cross! I think it helped, that they felt under God's protection. I like to think they were cared for, loved even. When we moved back here to York, we had this house, a garden and a vast cellar. We carried on.'

'But those poor girls. What you did to them.'

'I am not a monster Ada. You know that. Our patients were grateful to be needed. I hope with all my heart they found some comfort from feeling that. They were part of a scientific experiment and we so nearly had the breakthrough.'

Ada struggled to sit up, heaviness in every limb pressing her back.

Jane shook her head sadly. 'William changed after the first death. It dawned on me that he was enjoying this. I knew that he was going too far, risking too much. He took pleasure in outwitting his fellow physicians. That's why he cut out their stomachs so no doctor, in post-mortem, could find evidence of poison and work out the truth. It became a game for him, mocking them, getting one over. We had to get rid of the bodies of course. At first William used our rowing boat, it's at the moorings at the end of Marygate, and at night he rowed downstream and left them on the river bank. Far away from here.'

Jane sat quietly for a moment before she resumed. 'A desire for notoriety festered in him. When a newspaper labelled him the Butcher, it fed his urges. His confidence grew with his appetite for killing. I knew then he would not, could not stop. He revelled in outwitting everyone: the constabulary, you, the London detective. He was obsessed with your floundering investigations. He felt invincible. He wanted to test you, set his powers against yours. He saw Grace at your party on Christmas Eve. He decided to take her, right under your noses. I had realised that night and warned him not to be so blatant. He was pushing the game to its limits. I did not know where the end would come.'

Her confession made their madness sound like scientific reasoning. Did Jane really believe this rationale? Ada wondered. She might have been delivering a lecture to medical students.

Jane's eyes shifted and she looked across at her. 'Ada, I never wanted this. You must believe me.'

No. That was not true. Jane wanted the prize. She had helped procure these girls. This woman had murdered. Ada tried to rouse herself but the room was receding.

'You are tired Ada, do not fight it. Give in to it,' said a gentle voice from afar.

Ada dug her nails into her scarred hands until she could feel pain jerking her awake. 'Tell me about Tim Trent, he worked here didn't he?'

'Yes, poor simple Tim, he was given a job in our stable. One night he was sleeping in the straw. He had nowhere else to go. He saw William come home with Amy Ward after the Horse Fair. When her body was found on Boxing Day he tried to say something to us. You know of his mental disorder. He was like a bewildered child. It was easy enough to twist and coerce him believing he was accountable. And he really did believe he was responsible. William even took him to the police station and left him there. He made a false confession. Police were very happy to believe that. I doubt they looked into his explanation too closely.'

'You would have let him hang?'

'We had to do something. We turned our bad luck into an opportunity. He became our scapegoat. You see with the Butcher executed, we could quietly finish our work. It was only days away from completion. We would have won the prize. And no one would ever have known how. But you saw the truth through your lens. I should have known it would be you. I regret the world must lose us both. Are you ready? It is time and I am finished here.'

Jane stood before the fire. 'Is there anything you do not understand or would like to ask me, before . . .'

Ada shuddered.

'Don't be frightened. It will be painless, I promise. I am your friend, am I not?'

Helpless, unable to move Ada watched Jane come to her. She felt soft hair brush against her cheek, a firm hand clamp over her nose and mouth. 'Rest now. You have suffered much. Your work is done.'

Ada's eyes closed.

***

She heard the crunch of splintering wood. She heard someone shouting her name. Blood pounded in her head, her body struggled for air. She heard her own deep breaths as her lungs filled.

She opened her eyes.

Straker was bending over her, his face fierce and terrible.

And then darkness, again.

CHAPTER FORTY-EIGHT

◊

A figure was snaking its way through the museum gardens towards the water. Straker standing on the icy river bank sensed it approaching, as though he felt the very shadows creeping. Then, there he saw it, a flash of blond moving between the trees.

Straker ran along the path towards the pier at the end of Marygate, where the street's residents moored their rowing boats, hoping to head him off. Bevers was hurling himself down the street, almost tripping over his skinny legs. Dr Auden reached the river, his eyes darting from side to side, weighing up his options. No time now to untie a mooring. He ran to the left.

'Gage. He's heading your way!' Straker shouted the warning.

A man-mountain materialised from the dark street-end. Police Constable Gage stood astride the path like a Greek Titan.

'Come on then tha bugger. Art-ta fit?'

Auden was trapped. He turned towards Straker moving towards him. For a long moment they looked at each other. Then Straker saw a brief look of triumph flicker over the doctor's face. Auden lunged forward and noiselessly, in the blink of his eye, slipped into the fast current of the deep, cold river.

The three policemen ran towards the water's edge.

Straker threw himself to the ground and leaned over the bank, frantically looking for where Auden had gone into the water. The tails of a black frock coat floated upwards. He plunged his arms into the water and grabbed at the material. He caught an arm and held on to it with all his strength. For a moment, there was resistance, too much weight and he felt himself sliding into the deadly water of the Ouse.

A pair of enormous hands gripped Straker's legs. Gage had hold of his calves. Bevers was there now and together, the officers hauled Auden from the brink of escape.

The four of them collapsed on the riverside into a sodden, watery pile of limbs.

They had him.

Panting with exertion, the policemen hauled themselves to their feet. Auden was still on his knees when Gage raised his fist. Straker gripped his wrist. 'Just cuff him Gage. We'll do this properly, by the book.'

Straker watched the officers lead Auden away, flanking their prisoner in a tight squeeze, as they escorted him to the city lock-up. For a moment Straker felt the raw and sublime emotion of profound relief.

It was a brief moment. He turned from the river and walked swiftly towards the Audens' home.

He did not know if Ada Fawkes was alive.

***

'That was bloody stupid . . .' In the carriage Straker turned to her, fury in his face.

Ada looked out at the falling snow. 'I know.'

'What the hell were you thinking? Not telling anyone where you were going, I mean of all the foolish things,' snapped Straker. He felt like he had been taken apart and put back together again. He had almost lost her.

'To be fair, I didn't expect my oldest friend and her brother to turn out to be murderers.'

Straker felt her body shaking, heard her teeth chattering as the shock took hold.

'Damn it,' Straker said more gently. 'I'm sorry.'

'It's fine. How did you . . .'

'What, work out that the handsome, obliging doctor was a madman and your dear friend his sister a calculating murderess? Good old-fashioned instinct in the end. Bevers was coming out of the Royal Oak on Goodramgate, the night Grace disappeared. He was supposed to be keeping a watch on your house. It was shortly after ten o'clock and he was on his way back to relieve Gage as they had agreed. Bevers saw Auden riding towards Monk Bar. He had someone with him, on his horse, a young woman. When Bevers told me later, the pieces fell into place; the timing, the good-looking doctor riding away with a woman, in a street very close to where Grace lives. I knew it was him then, the man that any girl would admire and trust. I came over to warn you. But you had gone. And I had no idea where.'

He bowed his head. It had been a heart-thudding and lonely moment. And he had never run so fast.

'I still can't believe it. And Jane she's really dead?' Ada asked.

What Straker found at the house he would keep to himself. Jane had fled down into the bowels of the cellar. He had followed her and he would never forget what he saw. He had reached Jane too late, as she lay dying at her own hand, poison burning her from inside out.

'Yes. Jane made a choice, a trial may have been worse for her.'

'I thought she was my friend.'

He shook his head. 'I know it's hard to gather your thoughts around this. We have always tried to understand the crimes that come under our scrutiny, but this, this is like nothing we have come across before. I think Jane and William Auden murdered out of arrogance, a sense of power, belief in their right to decide life or death. Ada, I really believe they cared for you, but something less human, a compulsion gripped them.'

Ada, still half-drugged, struggled to follow his words, the gentle rocking of the carriage was making her sleepy, her head lolled forwards. He put one arm around her and gently pulled her to him, pressing her shivering body into his warmth. She laid her head on his shoulder and breathed in the smell of tobacco and cologne.

He felt wetness on his neck.

'It's the shock.' His voice was hoarse.

She could not stop her tears. 'I can never do this again.'

He felt her soft cheek against his own as he whispered into her ear. 'It's over. It's finished.'

She vaguely remembered him carrying her, laying her on her bed. Did she speak? Did she say: 'Don't leave me?' Had he bent down and kissed her? She couldn't be sure, and fell into a deep sleep.

***

Ada did not know if she felt so weary because of the sleeping draught or the shock of last night; she forced herself to move. She must gather her photographs. Straker would need them today. Her evidence would be essential, but some things were better left unremembered. If only she could forget. At least Grace was safe now, being cared for by her family. And Thomas was back home in one piece. He had told them earlier that morning about his night ride, laying out for them the sight of the sleeping farmhouse, the kerfuffle of waking up the household, the excitement of the jeweller's wife. It didn't matter now that she hadn't been able to remember much other than it was a woman in a black dress who had bought the necklaces. They knew now that had been Jane.

Ada's legs suddenly felt weak. Dizzily, she grasped for the edge of the table.

Images came fresh to her. She saw herself drinking cocoa by the Auden's fire, William luring lonely young women with promises and pretty silver crosses. Jane distilling poisons from plants in her garden borders. Friends she had held dear. Of course she trusted them. A doctor and his sister? Offering her confidences to Jane, her deepest secrets. She saw handsome William, remembered his charming manner. For a short while she had thought . . . how could she be so stupid?

'Ada!'

The locked door of the garden studio rattled. 'Ada!'

She remembered Christmas Eve, the night of her party, watching William smiling at Grace, saying something that made her giggle as she passed by with a plate of food. I saw him choose his next victim. I saw him select Grace, she thought.

The look between sister and brother that was Jane, she was trying to warn him to leave Grace alone.

She closed her eyes. The gown, well she had made that connection. How could she not have thought that through? Standard asylum issue, easily obtained by any doctor.

And the evidence she had stupidly revealed to Jane – the photograph of the footprints in the snow? Dear God . . . The studio break-in, the broken glass negatives that must have been William trying to destroy that evidence against him.

She thought of Jane's birthday supper, drinking champagne, all the while, in the cellar below . . . she shuddered.

'Open the door. Just open the bloody door.'

She turned the key.

Thomas, still in his greatcoat from his overnight ride home, barged in and took her into his arms. 'There, there love. I've got you.'

He held her tight as she sobbed. 'It's not your fault. You saved Grace. Your photographs will convict Auden of the murders. He won't get away with it, because of you. Do you hear me Ada?'

Ada nodded, glancing at the photographs: Annie Wren, Emily Eden, Rose Fisher, Amy Ward. Evidence that would damn a killer.

'That's my girl. Come back in.'

Thomas steered her into the warmth of the kitchen. Ada took a stool close to the range and the hot coffee offered to her. She took a sip, then stopped. She had nearly forgotten. Isabella Fox was due at York Station this evening. Her daughter Lucy was still in the asylum and the man who was going to free her was locked up in the Castle for murder. She was on her feet looking round for her work bag.

Her mind was racing ahead when Camille said something.

'Sorry what did you say?'

'A message arrived while you were out in the studio. It's on the dresser.'

Ada grabbed the sealed envelope, opened it, and swiftly read the familiar looping handwriting. 'It's from Straker. Scotland Yard has ordered him back to London.'

'When?'

'Tonight.' Her chest clenched. 'He's coming here. I cannot stay. I have to get Lucy out of that asylum.'

'Ada. You should see him. He saved your life.'

'I have to go. I must free Lucy or I think she will die.'

Outside the front door, a black horse was jerking its head impatiently, snorting trails of mist into the cold air. Thomas leaned over the side of the open carriage, held out his hand and hauled Ada up beside him.

'We need to go to *The Herald*. I must see Rufus Valentine.'

***

It was after half past five when Ada finally reached York Station. She looked up and down platform two and across to the main entrance.

Could Valentine be trusted? Would he honour their deal?

Ada thought how Valentine had listened to her proposal, his sharp mind quickly grasping the threads of her tale. She knew every word she told thrilled the newsman in him; her story was headline grabbing; royalty, a pretty young woman locked in an asylum, a cruel husband Alec Lovelace, the most black-hearted cad imaginable.

Readers would love being outraged at how Lovelace had plotted to get rid of his wife for financial gain, that he had cold-heartedly wooed the daughter of Queen Victoria's lady-in-waiting. There would be no saving Lovelace's reputation. He would be as infamous as the author Lord Lytton whose imprisonment of his sane wife for lunacy had caused a national uproar. The story was so irresistible that the deal Ada offered him for not publishing had to be just as sensational.

Valentine had bargained hard.

They had come to a deal. In return for his help, Ada would give him an exclusive interview with her. 'The workings of the mind of a lady forensic photographer'. Gold dust.

And dinner – at a place of his choosing.

Of course Ada had not been there when Rufus Valentine had knocked on the door of Lovelace's grand house on The Mount and winked at the young maid who let him into the entrance hall.

'Miss Fawkes says to tell you Mrs Lovelace is safe and she is going to help you get away from here,' he had whispered as he followed her to the double doors of the parlour.

There he had outlined two options to Lucy's husband and his mother. Stunned, mouth agape, Lovelace had protested.

'Let me explain again. This is how it goes.' Valentine had smoothed his elegant jacket sleeves. 'I've seen the asylum report on your wife. Bodily torture, beatings, bad enough, but what will really perplex and horrify our readers is this; the notorious state of Mrs Lovelace's undress. Did the daughter of our dear Queen's favourite lady-in-waiting tear her cotton chemise after she was taken away or was she dragged naked from bed and manhandled into the Acomb House carriage?

'There is not just the matter of this young lady's liberty, but her very right to avoid indecent and improper circumstances. Her nudity will be given the same weight in the public mind as the beatings, the starvation and the cold showers. My readers, those of *The Times*, *The Telegraph* and so on, will consider all your actions in their judgement of you. You get the point, I'm sure. Oh I have a photograph of Lucy too. *The Illustrated London News* will love that.

'So Lovelace I suggest we take a trip together, now, to Acomb House Asylum.'

***

It was nearly six o'clock now.

Ada still wasn't sure their plan had worked when Valentine's unsmiling face appeared above the heads of the waiting passengers. Then, at his side, clutching his arm, wrapped in an overlarge grey cloak, she saw Lucy.

Right on time the London-bound train rumbled into the station on its long journey down from Scotland, steam flowing in trails from the chimney, brakes hissing and grinding, the smell of burning coal filling the station.

'York, this is York,' bellowed the guard.

A passenger stepped down from a first-class compartment, looking anxious. As the steam and smoke cleared Ada saw her and hurried forward, waving.

'Ada, thank God.' Isabella came a few steps to meet her and they hugged. 'Please, tell me . . . is she . . .'

Ada turned and Isabella's eyes followed her gaze.

'Lucy. Oh Lucy.' She ran forward to take her daughter in her arms.

'Stand clear of the doors.' A whistle sounded.

'Quickly.' Valentine stepped into the compartment with Lucy's portmanteau bag, hauling it easily into the overhead rack. He helped up Isabella, Lucy and then jumped onto the platform, slamming the door. Isabella opened the window.

'I'll write and explain,' Ada walked alongside as the train rolled onwards.

Isabella leaned further out as it began to gather speed. 'Thank you, Ada. I will never forget this. If I can do anything in return, ever, I will.'

Ada turned round to thank Valentine.

'Not at all, Miss Fawkes. I will look forward to our dinner.'

He smiled wickedly and was gone.

Chapter Forty-Nine

◊

Straker had spent much of the day dashing from one place to the other, meeting with many black-suited officials. There were many loose threads to tie up. He had sat with Grace, holding her hand, as he listened to her harrowing account. He had negotiated Tim Trent's freedom with Chief Constable Nutt and the city magistrates. Much time had been needed to establish that all the photographic evidence against Dr Auden was properly understood. 'But he's such a decent chap,' said one of the judiciary indignantly. 'I had him marked as one of us, a future member of the Antediluvian Order of Buffaloes.'

Straker did not feel euphoria and triumph, he felt empty and weary. Doubt plagued him. He should have done better. He should have saved Amy Ward.

Earlier in a small, damp prison cell he had looked into the eyes of a killer searching for answers. There were none. Auden refused to speak.

Straker started to pack his valise. He would leave all the glory to Nutt. He didn't want any of that. Let the police chief take the credit for catching the killers. George Brass was like a pig in muck with all the publicity and a trial to come. Tomorrow Brass's Twelfth Night Ball, as eagerly anticipated as a Royal wedding, would go ahead and his latest money-making scheme Lendal Bridge would open. Tourists who had paid to travel on his railways, would pay again to cross the bridge into the city.

No one here, apart from the poor, wants change, he thought. Brass will get richer, Nutt's wife will get another opium supplier, and Nutt? Well he will carry on abusing his position, riding on the coat tails of his powerful brother-in-law.

Straker threw his shaving kit into his bag and shut the clasps. He was sick of York and sick of the hypocrisy. Behind all this mess; police corruption aided by the complicity of the tight-fisted corporation.

There was only one matter outstanding now.

Ada. I must not see her again. Nothing has changed. We are not free, he told himself.

There was still time before the train. A last walk round York to stretch his legs, get some fresh air, it would set him up for the long journey south.

Straker walked into the cold. He could not believe he must lose her again.

***

In the foyer of Harker's Hotel, logs blazed in the fireplace while white-gloved waiters carrying silver trays were bustled around the room bringing champagne and whisky to tables of black-tied men and women in glittering jewels. The atmosphere was lively and the conversation humming. The guests here for tomorrow's Twelfth Night Ball were settling in.

Ada walked straight up to the man at the reception desk. She stopped listening to his words once she had absorbed the answer to her question. Straker had gone. She turned and left. Now she began to walk across the square, hardly knowing what to do, where to go next. She wanted, needed to tell Straker everything.

She reasoned with herself. On balance perhaps it was better that he did not know the whole truth. It would not change anything. They could not be together. Yes, she would go home, but feeling so wretched she decided to walk a longer way. She set off along Davygate. The city streets were quietening down, market traders, delivery carts, hansom cabs finishing up for the day. The air was biting and she pulled her scarf tighter. Most likely it was the cold, but she changed her mind and turned around. Retracing her steps, she walked the quicker way along Stonegate instead. There was no hope of seeing him now, she might as well not add hypothermia to a broken heart.

The Minster loomed into view at the top of Narrowgate. She found herself uneasy as she walked around the dark stone walls. She didn't know why, the streets were safer now, the killer was caught. Then, ahead of her, she saw a dark shadow move. Her stomach twisted.

A figure stepped out from the darkness into the light of the street lamp – a broad man in a long greatcoat.

Straker.

She slowed her step, even as her heart thudded faster.

'Miss Fawkes. We need to talk.'

'Detective Inspector Straker.' Couldn't she think of anything better to say? He came closer. 'We need to talk. I will walk with you.'

He came nearer still. 'Ada?'

Her head dropped, hiding her face and she fell into step beside him towards her home.

'I'm returning to London tonight,' Straker said.

'I know. I thought you had already gone.'

'I have an hour still. I tried but I could not leave without seeing you. I went to your house.'

She looked up at him. 'I went to your hotel. I came to find you.'

'Why?'

'To say goodbye.'

He seized her arm, drawing her to a stop.

She held her breath.

Straker's voice had an edge. 'I think you have more to say than goodbye?'

She shook her head.

He let go of her. 'I know you are keeping something from me. Something happened in Paris. I think I have a right to know.'

'You do know what happened.'

'No. There's more, I feel it. What is it? Tell me, Ada. Was it my fault? Is it because of Clara? You know she cannot love me in that way. We still live separate lives.'

Now she was angry. 'Don't be so bloody stupid Straker. I don't care about that. I don't need to be married for God's sake.'

'What then? You did not explain. You broke my heart when you left. If I am honest you wounded my pride too. But that is no matter now. I was a fool.' He gripped her shoulders harder. 'I should have fought harder for us.'

'It's too late now, we are done.'

Maybe there was something unconvincing in the way she spoke for he reached out and touched her cheek. 'No.' He shook his head gently. Their eyes met, neither could look away. Swiftly he gathered her around the waist and pulled her to him.

'We are not done. Let's go back to Paris. My feelings are the same. Say that's true for you too?'

He took her face in his hands and tilted it to his.

'Say it.'

She could not speak.

'Say it. Say it, damn it. If you love me still I can bear the rest of it. I can bear anything.'

'I thought . . .' She hesitated.

'What?'

'That you would not want me because I am scarred, damaged by the acid. I thought you would only stay with me out of pity.'

'I am not that man Ada. When you fled from Rue du Bac, I looked for you all over Paris. No one knew – or would say – where you had gone. By the time you sent word and told me not to seek you out, I accepted your decision. I convinced myself you no longer loved me, a married man and one far older and uglier than you at that. I should have followed you, begged you. I thought I was doing the right thing, setting you free to start afresh.'

He gripped her tighter and buried his face in her neck. He murmured his love, his sorrow. Long moments passed as he held her close.

Finally he said, 'Ada, my darling. Let's start again. We can go back to Paris.'

'No,' she whispered, though her insides felt like they were melting with the intensity of her love. 'I have to stay here.'

'Ada I cannot bear to lose you again. I can take care of you.'

God, she loved him but not enough to give up her life; she had another purpose, another calling.

She pulled away from his arms. 'You know as well as I do that as a woman, I cannot have both you and my work in this world. I cannot openly love a married man. We would have to hide somewhere, in another country, but I have my work here. I must be free to carry it out. I need to open people's eyes: make them see the suffering, the injustice, the cruelty in our society. I'm not free to go where I want. I must stay here, in York.'

Straker dropped his arms and stepped back. 'I understand. I will not trouble you again. Just know if you need me I am here. I too have my work, there's little else in my life these days.'

He looked down upon the face he knew so well and gently pushed a strand of red-gold hair from her cheek. 'Maybe one day we can be together. Whatever happens to us in this life I hope you will be happy.'

'Don't say anymore.'

He bent his head towards her lips.

'Detective Inspector Straker. At last,' a loud voice called out.

Gage and Bevers were coming towards them from round the corner. Bevers shouted again. 'We've been looking for you everywhere sir. We are to escort you to the ferry. Chief Constable Nutt said we must make sure you leave York, but less politely.'

Straker sighed.

***

It was a departure as fitting as his arrival, he thought grimly. A damp chill from the river seeped through his heavy greatcoat and the ink-black water slapped against the wooden boat as the oars dipped in and out. In the dark sky, above York a sliver of crescent moon shone brightly in a clear, cloudless night.

'See that t'bridge, up there, opens tomorrow,' said John Goodricke. 'By gaw, forty-five years, gone like a flash. I've seen some sights an' all. Aye, ah've done ma time.'

He was the ferryman's last fare.

Straker looked ahead, his face fixed on the approaching bank, the old steps up to the station and the night train to London. He did not look back.

She would not change her mind.

He touched his breast pocket and smiled to himself. Safe within, close to his heart, a precious photograph.

His love.

***

Across the city, Ada looked in the mirror. This pain would go, she told herself, this ache might stop one day.

She walked downstairs into the warm kitchen, bright with candles. The table set for a late supper; silver cutlery on a white cloth, a vase of winter roses picked earlier from the garden and three sparkling long-stemmed glasses. Camille, a bottle in her hand, was coming in from the scullery. She stopped when she saw Ada. Thomas glanced up from sharpening the carving knife which he was preparing to slice the meat.

They looked at her expectantly.

'He's gone.'

They said nothing and for that she was grateful. Camille Defoe and Thomas Bell were very different, but both could hear momentous news without overreacting.

Thomas walked over, took her arm, sat her down and poured her a glass of champagne.

'It's roast loin of pork, with lots of crackling and braised red cabbage for supper,' Camille said.

'Thank you both.' She managed a smile.

'By the way I found Benjamin Barclay,' said Thomas. 'He's coming to see you about a job next week. That will be a big help in the studio. You are going to be very busy in the coming days and weeks.'

'Speaking of the future,' Ada explained her plan to help Eliza, still living at the mercy of Alec Lovelace. She had not forgotten the expression on his arrogant face as he anticipated disciplining his young servant.

'Eliza looked scared of him. I want to get her out of there. I thought perhaps she might come to us. She has no home I believe.'

The two others around the table murmured their approval. They saw that Ada's strained demeanour was softening, that she was beginning to relax with the warmth and the wine.

'Feeling better?' asked Thomas.

Ada looked at him. Yes, maybe she was. She was older and sadder, but something else too, she felt an energy, she felt ready to move on and out of the shadows of the past.

'I will never forget. I am changed by grief and loss but I feel I have myself back.'

Thomas picked up his drink and raised the glass to her and Camille.

'Here's to us all then and a fresh start in York and here's hoping that snow shifts itself soon.'

'I think winter really will pass quickly, we have so much to do,' said Ada.

They were silent then for there were still many days ahead before the spring.

FIFTY

◊

The Condemned Cell, York Castle, Twelfth Night, 1863

He hadn't wanted them to die – not at first anyway. And he wasn't disheartened by the fact they had not perfected the science. The important thing was he had known they were on the right path. Deserving of a place in medical history.

The Butcher of York? He had laughed when the journalists called him that. Idiots. He wasn't carving up pigs in the Shambles. He was a doctor. He had cared for the young women. He was kind to them. Their sacrifice was for the greater scientific good.

How he had outwitted everyone, removing the stomachs, all proof of poisoning gone. It gave him time to experiment and with each girl they had come closer to success.

And he liked it; slicing them, leaving his mark, his stamp on their bodies, it was a sign that they were his. He liked that as much as anything.

Placing the whores so publicly, right under everyone's noses, had made him laugh. He was clever. Maybe too clever, Jane had warned him of it. Jane. His hands twisted around a thin silver chain, a small engraved cross. Never mind, once he got out of here he could start again. There would never be a shortage of supply. There would always be more invisible women.

And no one ever cared about them.

Did they?

Author's Note

◊

A da Fawkes, my fictional photographer of the dead, came into being because women really have been solving crimes for centuries with only the scantest acknowledgement of their skills. Historically they have been secret sleuths working alongside male law enforcers to solve the most puzzling cases, yet it wasn't until 1919 that British law finally allowed women to become official police officers.

Evidence suggests women were as brave and as resourceful in their pursuit of criminals as any man. Their sex also gave them advantages. These shadowy female investigators stepped in when it was thought to be inappropriate or impossible for men to investigate. The range of their 'hidden' work was as wide as any male detective; questioning, observing, listening, shadowing and examining female and child victims. It was rarely recorded, but here and there are accounts of murder investigations such as those of the infamous Road House Murder of 1860 and histories of local police forces reveal the real role of women in crime fighting.

I was fascinated to come across such women during a research project and the idea for *Winter of Shadows* began to form. I wanted to write my own fictional series inspired by these unacknowledged detectives. I imagined an independent Victorian woman struggling to navigate a world where options were limited, but who had such a gift for crime solving that she could not be ignored by the likes of Scotland Yard. I wondered what it might have been like to be part of a criminal investigation, but without official recognition – or a pay packet.

The flash bulb moment that gave birth to my heroine Ada Fawkes as a crime scene photographer came to me while I was staying in one of my favourite places in the world, the North Yorkshire Moors. My holiday reading was *Bleak House*, Charles Dickens's murder mystery. I was enjoying the investigations of one of the earliest detectives in English fiction, Inspector Bucket. And of course, the case is finally cracked because of a woman's sleuthing skills, the inspector's wife Mrs Bucket. But I wanted my female character to be independent and self-reliant, to have talents that were so crucial to a criminal investigation that she had to be acknowledged in her own right.

That same week I visited the fascinating Ryedale Folk Museum, a collection of heritage buildings set in a particularly beautiful corner of North Yorkshire. I walked into an original photographic studio. I looked at the painted backdrop, the old wooden box camera on its tripod, the evocative black and white photos and I knew in that instant Ada Fawkes was a crime scene photographer. The fictional events that befall her were inspired by the ground-breaking role of photography in solving and proving real criminal cases.

Anyone who knows York will not be surprised that I set the book in this beautiful atmospheric place. I grew up near York so I have visited and loved the city for as long as I can remember. But York has another side. The events of this book while fictional acknowledge the dark underbelly of York at that time.

My starting point in reading was Frances Finnegan's *Poverty and Prostitution. A study of prostitutes in York*. Its heart-breaking accounts and photographs reveal the levels of poverty and desperation experienced by many. I drew on this heavily for my scenes from the Refuge. Here girls were put to work in the laundry doing hard physical labour – scrubbing clean the clothes and metaphorically their sins. It was every bit as harsh in real life as my fictional version of the Refuge.

While Ada is a character of my imagination, her experiences as a Victorian woman are very broadly based on true stories. The life of the famous nineteenth century photographer, Julia Margaret Cameron provided valuable insight. Cameron outraged Victorian society with her experimental portraits, which were perceived to push the boundaries of womanhood and photography. There were many fascinating details in Cameron's life – such as her permanently chemical-stained hands – which I drew on to give authenticity to Ada's experiences.

It was also a fact some women in the nineteenth century left their homes in Britain and America, moving to Europe, to be able to make free choices around sexuality, gender and career. The mid-Victorian feminist Frances Power Cobbe rejected the idea of being a single woman dependent on her brother's family and took off to Italy. There, Cobbe met like-minded women including the American artists, sculptor Harriet Hosmer and actress Charlotte Cushman. Ada's own choice to live in Paris intertwines their realities with fiction.

Researching this book and reading of the histories of Victorian women; the tragic lives of prostitutes in York, the treatment of female victims of crimes, the struggle to raise children in poverty has been both absorbing and moving. The past and present echo each other, so much has changed and yet so much stays the same. The challenges are still there and thankfully there will always be brave and resourceful females like Ada Fawkes and her real-life contemporaries pushing the boundaries for women.

Clare Grant, 2024

The following books were of assistance to me in writing *Winter of Shadows*:

Beaumont, Robert, *The Railway King A Biography of George Hudson Railway Pioneer and Fraudster* (London, Review, 2002)

Caine, Barbara, *Victorian Feminists* (Oxford, Oxford University Press, 1992)

Carlyle, Jane Welsh, *Jane Welsh Carlyle Letters* (London, Grey Arrow, 1959)

Christiansen, Rupert, *Tales Of The New Babylon Paris in the mid-19th century* (London, Minerva, 1995)

Dell, Simon, *The Victorian Policeman* (Oxford, Shire Publications Ltd, 2004)

Finnegan, Frances, *Poverty and Prostitution A study of prostitutes in York* (Cambridge, Cambridge University Press, 1979)

Flanders, Judith, *The Invention of Murder How the Victorians Revelled in Death and Detection and Created Modern Crime* (London, HarperPress, 2011)

Goodman, Ruth, *How To Be A Victorian* (London, Penguin, 2014)

Hanmer Jalna, Radford, Jill & Stanko Elizabeth A. Ed. *Women, Policing, And Male Violence: International Perspectives* (London and New York, Routledge, 1989)

Higgs, Michelle, *A Visitor's Guide to Victorian England* (Barnsley, Pen & Sword History, 2014)

479

Lock, Joan, *Dreadful Deeds And Awful Murders Scotland Yard's First Detectives 1829 – 1878* (Taunton, Barn Owl Books, 1990)

Jackson, Lee, *Dirty Old London The Victorian Fight Against Filth* (Newhaven and London, Yale University Press, 2015)

McDermid, Val, *Forensics The Anatomy Of Crime* (London, Profile Books, Wellcome Collection, 2015)

Melville, Joy, *Julia Margaret Cameron*

Moss, Alan & Skinner, Keith, *The Victorian Detective* (Oxford, Shire Publications Ltd, 2013)

Ramsland, Katherine, *Beating The Devil's Game A History of Forensic Science and Criminal Investigation* (New York, Berkley Books, 2007)

Sims, Michael, Ed. *The Penguin Book of Victorian Women in Crime* (London, Penguin, 2011)

Stratmann, Linda, *The Secret Poisoner. A Century of Murder* (Newhaven and London, Yale University Press, 2016)

Swift, Roger, *Police Reform in Early Victorian York, 1835-1856* (York, Borthwick Papers, 1988)

Wichard, Robin and Carol, *Victorian Cartes-de-Visite* (Princes Risborough, Shire Publications Ltd, 1999)

Wilson, Colin, *Written in Blood A History of Forensic Detection* (Wellingborough, Equation, 1989)

Wilson, David, *A History of British Serial Killing* (London, Sphere, 2009)

Wise, Sarah, *Inconvenient People Lunacy, Liberty and the Mad-doctors in Victorian England* (London, Vintage, 2012)

Mayhew, Henry, *London Labour And The London Poor* (London, Penguin, 1985)

ACKNOWLEDGEMENTS

◊

My grateful thanks to Todd Swift, Amira Ghanim and everyone at my publisher, Black Spring Press Crime, for their belief and support.

I would also like to properly thank Luca Veste for his crime-editing skills, his page-turning books (especially my autographed one) and for making me laugh out loud with his podcast Two Crime Writers and a Microphone. It has been a pleasure to have your guidance and help.

I am truly grateful to Helen Sutherland and Tabitha Bell for honest feedback and unwavering support for this book.

The following people have my gratitude for their kindness, friendship and encouragement: Karen Power, Isabel Wilson, Suzy Walker, Karen Leadbitter, Nicola Taylor and Judith O'Reilly.

My appreciation to Martin Fletcher whose insight and patience pushed me to make my book better. And my warmest thanks also to Fiona Mitchell for her generous advice.

To the friends I am lucky enough to walk and talk with by the beautiful North Sea, thank you for the fun and joy.

And my love, as always, to my wonderful family.

ACKNOWLEDGEMENTS